The Cougar

Book

Edited by Jolie du Pré

ISBN: 978-1905091-56-0
Paperback version
Published by Logical-Lust Publications © 2010

Cover image by Helen E. H. Madden, pixelarcana.com
© Logical-Lust Publications 2010
Additional editing by Zetta Brown

The Cougar Book is a collection of works of fiction. The names, characters, and incidents are entirely the work of the author's imagination. Any resemblance to actual persons, living or dead, or events, is entirely coincidental.

"It's cool to date an older woman today."

-- Valerie Gibson

Introduction

Cougars and sex. It's as perfect and natural a combination as, say, coffee and cream and just as delicious.

People may ask (and they do) what it is that makes cougars so attractive to younger men and, apart from the long list that includes independence, sophistication, intelligence, experience of life and being a free spirit, one of the most exciting and attractive assets, not only to younger men but all men, is that cougars love sex.

Perhaps most important, they're skilled—and creative—in the sexual arts . . .

They love to make love and enjoy it for what it is—a joyful, satisfying, energizing, and life-enhancing activity that keeps you youthful and vital. What's more, it's fun!

It's a rare and precious attribute for any woman, but when it comes with enthusiasm and few strings attached? Priceless!

No wonder the cougar trend, which I set in motion at the beginning of the millennium, is now being spearheaded, so to speak, by the younger men who are in hot pursuit of sexy cougars all over the world.

And the women who embrace "cougardom" openly without fear or reservation, are, in fact, pioneering a new social phenomenon—prime women not only acknowledging their continuing sensuality and sexuality, but embracing it wholeheartedly.

It may have taken centuries, but their time has certainly come!

VALERIE GIBSON
Relationships expert, writer, television host and author of
Cougar: A Guide for Older Women Dating Younger Men
www.valeriegibson.com

Contents

Boston. Breasts. Bohemian.

Jeremy Edwards

I was an aesthete, not a power seeker. Why did so many people rush to assume that a successful female entrepreneur was in it for the power? Sure, I didn't want to be held back . . . but I hungered to express my talents and make a more beautiful world, not to warm a throne with my ass and give orders.

Likewise with my young men—my bohemians. People saw a polished, well-turned-out businesswoman in her forties with sweet, shaggy boys hardly out of college, and they assumed it was a power thing, or a status thing. Hell, no. It was an aesthetic thing with me. They were just so pretty—not only their baby-faced faces and their silly hair, but also their personalities, all wrapped up in the awkwardness of make-believe sophistication, or brightly bare in their un-self-conscious charisma.

I was never taken with the ambitious ones. Even if they were nice . . . even if I judged that their interest in bedding me had nothing to do with their career aspirations . . . I simply didn't respond to their suits, their calculating punctuality, and their disconcertingly smooth adaptation to the yuppie milieu of 1980s Back Bay Boston. Damn it, a twenty-two-year-old—male or female—should not look totally natural with a briefcase, I thought.

No, I liked the guys with the ratty knapsacks. The guys who weren't sure when or when not to drink at lunchtime; who didn't see that as cool as their thrift-store vintage jackets looked on the hanger, they didn't fit right; who still believed, thank goodness, that it was their art or writing or music that mattered, and not getting to the "day job" five minutes early—and who would say so out loud in their cubicles, being too naïve to realize I listened from my open-door office around the corner. They figured I disapproved of their chronic tardiness and forgave them; but in reality I loved them for it. It made

9

me want to fuck them. It aroused what had never died in me, no matter how many meetings I had to take with marketing people and accountants and lawyers: my passion for beauty. And my passion for young men who really, really cared about something—who weren't, for instance, too occupied or tired or lazy to go see some incredibly important underground band I'd never heard of on a Wednesday night, even if it meant they had to walk home afterward and get shortchanged on sleep. I had no intention of listening to the latest "amazing" album, but I wanted to know my bohemians bought it the day it came out.

And I would have set my alarm and driven to Kenmore Square to pick any one of these boys up after a concert, at 2 a.m. on any Wednesday he liked. But then, I suppose, he would have been even more shortchanged on sleep.

For the ones who wanted me as much as I wanted them, I tried to project what they desired in me. Self-assurance. Stability. Poise. Savoir-faire. I tried to give them the complete grown-up woman—a soft, fleshy rock of adulthood, sculpted into a svelte hourglass.

It's odd to recall that Ned did not seem especially pretty to me that first morning when he showed up for work at my art-book publishing house. He'd been hired by my editor as one of the three all-purpose proofreaders/rights researchers/caption writers he always kept on hand—our version of an entry-level position. I was comfortable letting Bill do his own hiring, so I never met his assistants until they were already on the payroll.

Shaggy was great, but Ned's straw-blond hair verged on unkempt. And since his eyes refused to meet mine while I was doling out his paperwork, and his head refused to orient itself away from the sight line to his shoes after I'd collected the completed forms, the hair was practically all I got—that, and a thin, cute ass in nondescript jeans, as observed when I followed him out of my office.

The first thing Ned did when he'd been assigned a cubicle was put a cartoon up on the wall. I winced—tape marks!—but when I read it over his shoulder and he volunteered that he'd created it himself, I got a squishy sensation in my belly. The cartoon showed a woman declining, as I inferred from the bubbles, champagne (served in what Ned presumably didn't realize was the wrong kind of glass), and saying to her male companion, "Yes, Frank, I *know* that was a good year. It's just that I'm not ready to relive it yet." Frank. If I'd encountered this in the *New Yorker,* I might not even have lingered to bemoan their sagging standards. But standing almost on top of the boy who'd taken the trouble to draw this slim idea—smelling the youthful, citrusy essence of this kid who'd risked ruining a cubicle wall his first day on the job in order to display his work—all I could feel was admiration. Admiration and a warm tingling between my legs. Suddenly, I was very interested in Ned.

"Sorry about the breasts," he said nervously, stepping to the side so he could face me. I took a peek at the cartoon lady's cleavage, which I hadn't noticed before. "I didn't mean to draw them so large. I don't want people to decide I'm one of those guys who thinks a woman amounts to a set of breasts."

I felt a flush in my own, relatively generous, chest. "It's okay, Ned. Hey, women have breasts. And breasts are nice, right?" I laughed, more self-consciously than I was used to in my workplace. In my time, a parade of seasoned men, my peers, had tried to flirt and banter and grope me into losing my cool at the office—had tried to make the always-in-control goddess blush or stammer or run off to change her panties. They had all failed. But poor Ned was nearly succeeding, without even intending to. The sincere way he both cared and didn't care about the size of his cartoon character's bust seemed to tug at my nipples and tickle my clit.

"Some of us have larger ones than others," I continued, masking my flutteriness with a reassuring, didactically matriarchal tone, and trusting that my injection of self-referential language wouldn't completely give away my agenda—yet. "You happened to draw one such woman."

He gave me a sensitive, tentative-looking smile, and that's when I understood that his face was capable of more complexity than silently framing the question, "What time is lunch?" I was about to ask him—I don't know—about his life, what he'd liked best in college, about his family . . . but he spoke again before the words formed.

"What time is lunch?"

In fact, it was my policy to take a new hire out to lunch on his or her first day—just the two of us. These kids worked closely with Bill day in and day out, with a healthy share of collegial staff lunches sprinkled over their tenure; but I wasn't involved in any of that. I welcomed them in and had little directly to do with them thereafter—unless I chose to offer extracurricular attention, and they chose to accept it.

Spending an hour alone in a quasi-social situation with a publishing-world rookie could be anything from a cougar's wet dream to a nightmare of stifling silences. But whether it proved, from case to case, to be drudgery or delight, it was a non-negotiable duty that I'd long ago assigned myself.

This morning, I was so eager for "lunch" that I couldn't focus on the contracts I was supposed to be reviewing. Fifteen minutes before I was due to meet Ned in the foyer, I finally stopped trying to concentrate. I gave myself a booster shot of perfume in front of the mirror in my private bathroom, and I went to bother Bill with interoffice chitchat, merely as a diversion.

It had long been my philosophy that if I was going to come on to an employee, I should do it at the outset. Things are less complicated when your young man hasn't yet breathed much of the company air—when you're still more an intriguing older woman than a familiar edifice looming on the skyline, engraved with the gray legend *BOSS*.

I knew how to broach the matter, having done it many times—sometimes in this very restaurant. Step One—ascertaining that he was single in the real-world sense, and not only in the IRS-form sense, had been taken even before the server brought our water.

I let the conversation wander naturally as we awaited our meals. Once they'd arrived and we'd begun eating, I proceeded.

"I'm so glad to have a chance to get to know you a little, Ned, before you get immersed in the hectic routine with Bill and the gang."

"Uh," said Ned, nodding graciously.

"I'm usually in a whirlwind of my own. You'll be happy to learn that you won't see a lot of me after today."

I gave him my seductive stage-chuckle. Then I gave him my standard three-beat pause, before continuing.

"Unless we get together *outside* the office, of course."

No pause this time—momentum was key here. "This has nothing to do with your job, and there's no wrong answer . . . but I was wondering if you might like to join me at my place for dinner some night soon. I've been in the mood to cook lately." I winked. Subtlety was not the way to go with these boys. It was important to be unambiguously bold, and to refuse to be daunted by the possibility of a brush-off.

He stared at me as if sizing me up for the first time. "Ms. Bruxelle, you're my employer," he said slowly. I'd certainly heard that before, at this stage of the proceedings—though it wasn't articulated as often as you might think. One had a tendency to catch on that at Bruxelle Art Books, we didn't stand on ceremony.

"So what?" I said, calling into service my most laissez-faire body language—the devil-may-care cock of the head, the flirtatious, mock-dismissive wave of the hand. "I've frequently—mm . . . *socialized*—with my employees."

He ate a bit of his omelet. "I don't know whether that should make me more or less concerned."

He wasn't attempting to be witty—he meant it. Damn, I adored men who didn't always know what to think right away. They let you breathe.

It was part of my ethos to be assertive, but never aggressive. "Anyway—for what it's worth—I'm not really your boss. Bill is really your boss." I tossed this dubious technicality his way as a peripheral remark, and then changed the subject temporarily to take the pressure off. "How's your omelet?" Fuck, I was wet. The kid wasn't doing anything, but that in itself was doing *everything* to my insides.

It was funny to think that in Ned's eyes, I probably appeared cool as a cucumber—as I intended to. He probably assumed I could do this in my sleep. After all, why would it ever occur to him that a self-actualized, experienced woman at the top of her erotic game got butterflies—that she sometimes had an impulse to run to her room and hide her head beneath pillows, crying with embarrassment even while furiously masturbating off her screaming sexual tension? I never ran, but that didn't mean I never thought about it.

Ned kept eating. He began to speak—and then hesitated—wiping his mouth with the napkin an extra, unnecessary, time before breaking the silence. "I don't know, Ms. Bruxelle." It was obvious he wasn't addressing the "how are your eggs?" issue.

"Claudia." That part wasn't seduction—*nobody* called me Ms. Bruxelle, except people trying to sell us advertising.

"I guess it's not the boss thing." He looked at me with uncompromising innocence, his gaze steady and clear. "But . . . seriously? You want me to . . . y'know, come over to your house?"

"I wouldn't have invited you if I didn't."

"Yeah," he admitted. "Can I think it over?"

Of course he could. And that night, while Ned presumably thought it over, "Ms. Bruxelle" gave herself seven fantastic orgasms, riding a vibrator and visualizing the face of this man who was too casual to have recited the "it's not that I don't find you attractive" speech.

But something told me that it really *wasn't* that he didn't find me attractive—that despite the layers of surprise and wariness, Ned had been looking at me with a three-dimensional appetite idling portentously in the background. That steady gaze. It bore into me, in absentia, in my bedroom, as my cunt danced contractions over hot sheets and I banged my ankles together, whimpering my lust.

The company's tenth-anniversary party happened to be scheduled for the weekend right after Ned started. And when I brought this up the day following our lunch, I was afraid he might inform me that he already had plans. But one of the things I treasured about my bohemians was that they almost never had firm plans for anything. As was typical of these boys, Ned had "a few" parties he was thinking of attending that Saturday, but nothing definite on his agenda.

"Well," I assured him, successfully keeping the college-girl longing out of my voice, "you're not obligated to attend. But I'll be delighted if you can." After throwing the singular pronoun his way—*I* rather than *we*—I allowed my eyes to flash him for an instant. *Don't forget: Sex here, my bohemian boy—if you want it.*

As I skated back into my office, I wondered if he had been as wakeful and auto-erotically engaged as I had the night before. Had he dreamed cartoonishly of my breasts? In any event, I'd been with enough young artists to accept that "Maybe I'll be there" was the closest I was going to get to an R.S.V.P., and I forced myself to assume optimistically that Ned would be at my disposal on Saturday evening—and perhaps, if I was lucky, on Saturday night.

A party like this was a whopping expenditure. But in the circles I traveled, we understood that additional business would result from the friendly bookstore-chain buyers we plied with friendly drinks, as well as the difficult-to-court customers who couldn't resist a free, classy affair and who were bound to find things they liked once our catalogs were shoved under their noses.

As the charismatic, impassioned, but business-shrewd CEO, I was center stage most of the evening. Ned had arrived soon after the affair had begun—looking even more rumpled in his "nice" clothes than his clumsy-vintage duds—but it was hours before I was able to break away from the latest round of schmoozing, grab a plate of food, and casually float him toward the back rooms in the "rent for your function" Victorian we'd taken over for our celebration. I was, ostensibly, giving him a tour.

We nearly walked in on Bill and his fiancée. I halted myself—and Ned—in the doorway of the sprawling back parlor, just in time to keep them from realizing they'd been interrupted.

Only they hadn't, in fact, been interrupted—because, deep in the parlor and oblivious to our presence, they proceeded with their business. Good old Bill had Felicia's long, elegant skirt up at the back, and he was lazily fondling her mauve panties, just massaging her ass in there . . . showing her how private he wished to be with her, how intimate, despite the call of the festivities. Felicia, serene and content, was holding her drink right below her lips, and mouthing involuntary kisses toward a mirror. And, involuntarily, I felt my lips yearning to imitate those quiet kisses, and my ass yearning for a roaming hand.

"Shouldn't we go?" whispered Ned. His breath tickled my earlobe.

I turned to look at him, my breasts still pressing against the heavy Victorian doorjamb. I took hold of his arm—firmly and purposefully. "Yes," I whispered back. "Yes, we should."

He studied my face, and then he broke into a sly grin. He looked down to my hand, where it rested on his forearm, and he removed my fingers from his person. But instead of letting my fingers drop, he guided them to my chest, where he boldly squeezed my right breast, using my own grip as his proxy.

His face glowed with unrefined want.

Of course, I couldn't take Ned home until the guests had finished depleting the canapés and Cabernet. Fortunately, the catering firm that had rented us the space and their services were responsible for cleanup, and Bill and I had no obligation to hang around washing dishes or vacuuming up crumbs. I said a quick goodnight to Bill and Felicia—getting a frisson as my mind leaped back to what I'd observed earlier—and I left the building with Ned.

"Did you take the 'T' to get here?" I asked him after we'd driven a few blocks. I was surmising that he didn't have a car, and that the subway would have been the logical option.

"Yeah."

"I guess you'd be at a party with your friends tonight, if you weren't with me."

He shrugged. "Some weekends I just stay home and draw."

At my condo, my libido found a comfortable plateau. I'd figured out by this point that he wasn't an animated talker. But I didn't want to jump on him, first thing in the door—well, I did, but I knew it would be more civilized to pace myself. So I enjoyed simply sharing my space with him for a while, having a drink and taking him on his terms—letting him set the tone of what passed for a conversation. He complimented me on the wine I'd served him and catalogued his favorite dollar-fifty beer bars.

He was poking around my living room when I returned from the kitchen with our second round of drinks. I joined him in front of the bookshelf, where he had just stopped to admire a photo of me at about twenty-five, shaking my ass in a fringed miniskirt and go-go boots at a discotheque.

"You must have had some wild times in the '60s," he said—name-checking the legendary decade with the reverence my generation saved for the names of movie stars and European cities.

I smiled knowingly, and the comment that came out of my mouth surprised me. "Yes, that was a good era. But I'm not ready to relive it yet."

It was as if my discovery of the lingering profundity in his one-panel rattled him, and all he could think to do was grab me by the waist and kiss me, hard. It was as good a trigger as any.

When his lips released me, I took a moment to set my drink down—feeling my juices flowing, my every atom ready. The next deep kiss would be served by the hostess, I decided.

But Ned had something more to say. "When I got to the party, I was thinking I was going to turn you down."

"What?" This caught me unawares: I thought I could read a situation. And he'd picked a hell of a time to tell me this. Still, I was intrigued. "Why didn't you?"

"Your face. When you saw Bill and what's-her-name."

"Felicia." The word rushed out of my mouth.

"There was something in your expression that made me think I might regret it if I didn't"—he scanned the room—"do this."

"I see," I said hoarsely.

"Yeah, you looked sort of naked, for a second. It was great."

I would reflect on this later—how Ned had wanted me to be raw and churned up, not calm and in control. Other boys hadn't felt that way. Or, if they had, they hadn't told me.

But right now, I couldn't take any more time to think. "*This* is what I look like when I'm naked."

I'd dressed intelligently, and almost everything came off in one piece. My slip clung cooperatively to the inside of my floral dress—so that with one sibilant *swoosh,* I was left in only my bra and my jewelry. I had not worn panties.

As I unclasped the bra, Ned started laughing benignly.

I laughed with him. "What?"

"I was remembering that discussion we had about breasts. You know, the cartoon. And now you're . . ." His laughter trickled off. "They're so gorgeous, Claudia."

He stood there worshipping me with his eyes—and with the hard-on that strained against his ill-fitting dressy trousers.

"I need you to touch me, Ned."

The hand on my ass cheek was the warmest thing I could ever recall having in my living room. I hadn't realized quite how hungry I'd been for contact with male flesh.

I luxuriated in his palm, feeling the honey seeping down toward the mouth of my pussy. It felt too good, too fast, for me to be surprised that he'd gone for my ass first, rather than my breasts. I only thought of that afterward, conjecturing that Bill and Felicia had inspired him.

And, man, that boy knew how to caress a woman's ass. The alternating circles, back and forth from cheek to cheek. The vigorous squeezes and delicate pinches. The thin finger dragging itself down the crack, like a languid exclamation point streaked onto a foggy car window. The no-sting slap of approval, gentle but lewd as hell.

I wondered if he was going to stay back there all night—and, frankly, I wouldn't have cared if he had. But his hands finally traveled to my belly, grazing my bush, and his cock—still in his pants, but hard as fuck—nudged the pleasure-tingling bottom that his hands had just abandoned. I squirmed into him like the horny, in-her-prime sensualist I was, while my nipples buzzed like dried chili peppers. Then I turned around in his grasp. "You should get undressed."

"I want to make you come."

Again I laughed. "You will. Trust me. But I want to see you. I want to see that handsome cock of yours. Okay?" I kissed him.

He shrugged diffidently, but I sensed he was gratified.

He was hairier than I'd expected, but the blond, translucent fur that ran down his chest was soft and smooth, almost unreal. His beautifully-proportioned cock felt smooth, too, in my hand—but definitely not soft, and certainly not unreal.

He let me stroke him for a short while, and then he dropped to his knees. He began kissing his way wetly up my thighs—he seemed increasingly passionate, now that we'd moved beyond the barriers of age and etiquette and uncertainty and clothing.

"You smell terrific." His face was millimeters from my pussy. "I mean, I liked your perfume, but down here—oh, wow."

I just stood there, clasping his head between my thighs, while he ate me out. I felt like a fine meal, like a treasure, as he sucked and kissed and licked from out to in and back, drawing silken pulses of ecstasy from my depths.

My ass was still sizzling from his lavish attentions, and my breasts melted in my own hands—because my nipples had needed to be engaged by whoever was available, and my fingers, seething with pre-orgasmic tension, had needed something to do.

His appetite seemed only to grow as he feasted. By the time my clit telegraphed a string of climaxes onto his tongue and my juice ran wild over his lip, the room was alive with his desire.

When he emerged from my sanctum, I stepped away, turned, and bent over the back of an armchair—trusting that he would take the hint and assume his . . . entry-level position.

He took the hint.

Now, at last, as he fucked me powerfully from behind, Ned redeemed the voucher I'd implicitly offered him back in his cubicle— the invitation to celebrate my ample breasts. Though his thrusting honored a steady, linear rhythm—deliciously serviceable, given that we were a good fit—his fingers fluttered capriciously, titillating and molding me, imparting a constantly blossoming bouquet of tactile surprises. While his cock made me moan, his hands made me giggle; and, helpless in pleasure, I lost it, barely needing the feminine forefinger on my clit to fly into a heaving orgasm, as Ned pumped his condom full of raw enthusiasm.

Later, he asked me to drive him home, rather than choosing to stay over. Yet in the same breath, he asked if he could come back the next night.

Of course he could.

Ned moved on to New York after a year, and I moved on to the next bohemian. We'd never felt remotely "permanent"—but I remember Ned more distinctly than most of them.

And not just because I get a hand-drawn, one-of-a-kind birthday card every year, featuring a cartoon woman with nice boobs.

What Pretty Girls Do

Rachel Kramer Bussel

Sheena looked in the mirror, peering at the fine lines that had crept into her skin over the years, and in the last month or two, it seemed, suddenly take up permanent residence. She smoothed her cheeks, the ones that used to glow, smooth and sparkling as peaches. She used to thrill to the compliments that were passed her way, gracing every such stranger with a smile that would make his day, perhaps even his week. Being a model, she'd gotten used to the looks, the covert glances, the whispers, and the constant, eternal adoration. She'd worshipped herself, too, always had, ever since she was a little girl, twirling by every mirror she passed, learning early on to toss her hair back and bat her eyelashes at every man or woman she came across. Those skills had come in handy, and she'd certainly bedded some of the best. But she'd never expected to be washed up at forty. She'd had surgery to make sure of that. Sheena had never even really thought about what life might be like once she stopped being perfect.

The thing of it was that it was only up close that one would notice any crack in her armor, any slight imperfection to mar her otherwise magnificent body. She'd made sure of that, visiting the gym so regularly she didn't even need to flash her card, simply gave a divine nod before heading off into the back to sweat and sweat and dream about being able to lie back and have handsome waiters bring her elegant drinks while she floated in the pool. If she even had a pool. She'd been reduced to living in a small cottage, just far enough away from the major Hollywood players, the ones who'd undoubtedly made it, no questions asked, to make visiting her not-so-desirable. And today was her birthday. Her fortieth—although officially, on the record and in the press, she was only thirty-five—and intended to remain so for some time. She'd been lying about her age for so long that even she had to double check, and realizing that the big four-oh was approaching had shocked her to her core. She remembered starting out; a bright, young, eager wisp of a girl, and that was often how she still felt.

It had come as a rude awakening, this impending day. For Sheena, a birthday had become not something to celebrate, but to hide, tucked far away like some naughty little secret. Birthdays were a sign, an omen, a portent that the apocalypse was near, and she was not looking forward to this one. She continued to peer deeply into the mirror, hoping to find some secrets or universal truths hidden within her pores, or at least some hidden hairs she'd missed as she tweezed and tweezed and tweaked and tweaked. She couldn't remember a time when she hadn't spent hours in front of the mirror, grooming herself into the perfect specimen. She sat back, placing the highly coveted, expensive tweezers down on the sink's edge, and tried to think back.

She mentally scrolled through all the magazine covers, the way she'd tossed her hair back and laughed the uproarious laugh of the young and beautiful, the ones who have nothing to lose. Little did she know that her youth and beauty were exactly what she had to lose. But still, the longer she stared, the longer she was transfixed, as she'd always been, by her image, because despite all the accolades, the awards, and boyfriends, and trips to Milan, the hundreds of thousands of dollars her body had earned her over the years, sometimes she didn't see what all the fuss was about. She never had. She put down the tweezers and took a step back, surveying her naked body. Her hands skimmed down over her still-ripe breasts, heavier and lower now than at her prime, but still responsive. As she squeezed the bright pink buds, they sprang to life, and she held her hands underneath them, an offering to some unknown god, begging to be claimed once more.

She let her hands drop lower, cradling the belly that twenty years ago would have had her sobbing in horror with its rounded softness, its jelly folds, which made her think of comfort foods like rolls and potatoes. She was a lumpy mess, and yet as her hands lingered on the gently rounded stomach, she held them there, in front, the way pregnant women do. Sheena wondered what that would have been like, to have this mass of jiggling flab turned into smooth, hard, baby rock, to feel its strength and solidity even as she nurtured a child inside her. She'd almost done it, once, had been ready to devote herself to someone else, and then her chance had ended, just as quickly as she'd started planning for it. She moved lower still, peeling apart the lips that she hardly dared look at.

Who wants to see this? she thought. She never had, and always marveled at lovers who took delight in spending hours down there, playing and tasting, sucking and biting.

She thought back to Don, the one who had given her her first orgasm those many years ago, the way his fingers would splay her open and his eyes would light up like he'd just seen the crown jewels. How she'd thrilled at that look, and thrilled even more when his big, rough, man's tongue had dove between her lips, getting all the way inside, messy and sloppy, taking her as far away from the world of high glamour as could be, into one filled only with pleasure and moans, aches and needs, wants and fulfillment. He never wanted to stop either, and would only do so at her absolute insistence when she was wrung dry, left panting and gasping for breath, utterly stunned, turned inside out. Thinking about Don had made her wet, and she slipped two fingers inside herself, leaning against the sink for balance as she tried what she'd given up during her teenage years. Now she regressed, back even before Don, to that first time she'd played with herself. She'd known so little and she had no clue about what she was after as her young fingers had squeezed and pinched the little nub of hardness at the part of her legs. She'd been scared though, and when she got too close, she backed off.

Not this time. This time she kept going, pushing past all of those memories as she stroked both her clit and her cunt, the fingers of each hand working double, and then triple time to give her what she now realized was rightfully hers. *I want my goddamn birthday orgasm*, she thought, and she pictured herself in a room with everyone she'd ever loved. Not every lover, because that was far different, but everyone she'd ever loved, even the ones she never told, the ones her heart secretly pounded for behind her full-lashed lids. She worked herself into a frenzy, rocking against her own fingers and losing herself in her ecstasy, finally coming in a shuddering heap, tears dripping down her face as she struggled for breath. She looked back into the mirror, and even with the tears, she looked ten years younger. *Big four-oh, my ass*, she thought, and went to dress for her friends.

In hardly any time at all, the party had started, the room filling with people half her age and the occasional old friend, and she could almost convince herself it was just like old times, where the nights had been forever young and nothing had fazed her. She'd let Aaron, her assistant, organize the night, not wanting to be bothered with worrying over who'd RSVPd or hadn't, what to serve or how to act. She wasn't exactly welcoming forty with open arms, but he'd insisted that she find some way to make the occasion festive, and was always on the lookout for any way to get her in the news, even though she didn't particularly care about making the gossip pages any longer. She'd seen and done it all, and had never really mellowed out, but those around her had, so by attrition she'd been forced to slow down. She didn't go out every night, and didn't carry only the tiniest of purses when she did, blowing a kiss to her doorman and telling him not to wait up. Now she carried an enormous weight of a bag, one that said, if anything, that she needed reinforcement.

As the party swirled around Sheena, she felt increasingly removed, as if watching it from afar, all the glittering, twinkling, bejeweled people, their laughter swirling through the air as they munched on mini quiches and drank champagne. Most of them barely knew whose party this was, only that it was their first stop of the night, as instructed by their managers. Necks craned continually, wide eyes hoping to see the next big thing, or yesterday's It- girl, or anyone who'd provide a smidgen of gossip to brighten up their already-charmed lives. Sheena had somehow wandered back to the deluxe bathroom, needing a break, and since she'd quit smoking, this was her private refuge. She stared until she couldn't stand it anymore, and then she closed her eyes and tried to hold back the tears, tried to practice what her yoga teacher and therapist had said about visualization.

She thought about lovers past, about how they'd worshipped every inch of her body, making her feel like the princess she'd longed to be ever since she was a child. If she were honest with herself, which only happened about once a year, so she figured she was due, she wanted that again. All that self-help mumbo-jumbo about independence and self-sufficiency sounded good for those "Where are they now?" shows she kept being asked to do, those programs that implied, if not stated outright, that her life as she knew it was now over.

And then somehow, mid-thought—there was Braden, all of twenty-two-years-old old Braden, who could have pretty much any girl he wanted, her employee—oh so wrong for her, yet just right. He came up behind her, his strong hands reaching to claim her, to rub her neck, which all of a sudden she noticed was throbbing. She'd jokingly called his job a "right-hand man," because it was more than just being an assistant, but just then, he was making it clear that it was also a two-handed job. The pressure eased from her shoulders, flowed into him, and Sheena felt him literally pull all her worries away from her.

She hadn't seen him come in, hadn't heard the door open, but she was more than grateful for his presence, as if she had somehow conjured him with her thoughts. She leaned back against him, her knight in shining armor, even though his armor consisted of artfully torn jeans, a heavy metal t-shirt, and a chin full of stubble. He was hot, but not the rescuing type, exactly. But what he lacked in wealth, he made up for in other ways. She'd thought about him touching her before, but Sheena never could've made the first move. At forty, she'd have looked too desperate, not to mention opening herself up to lawsuits.

Yet here he was, touching her in a way that was not at all professional. Touching her in a way that made her feel beautiful, from the inside out. The irony of it all did not escape her. She had dated some of the most famous and fabulous men in the world in her youth, when her picture had been plastered all over so many magazines that she'd had to hire a publicist to try to stop the swell of press swarming over her to give her a little breathing room. They'd had fun, but she'd often woken up in the middle of the night, head aching, wondering what would happen to those men once she was no longer gracing their local magazine racks. Sheena had ignored those dark thoughts, though, because to ask where the men would be would beg the question as to where she should be. She hadn't wanted to think of herself playing the mom in commercials for dishwashing soap, watching as this year's It-girl looked at her like she was nothing, over the hill.

Now she could only laugh at the excesses of youth. It was all a con game she'd become an expert at. Flash a toothy, white smile, get paid thousands, and she'd literally laughed all the way to the bank, tears coming to her eyes at times when she peered at a statement full of numbers so big they boggled her mind.

Most of all, she hadn't wanted to let go of the men's glances, the adoration, the attention. She looked good, sure, but not like she had.

"Stop thinking," Braden said, and brought her lips to his. "And get ready, because I need you to keep up with me. I can go a long time."

She giggled, a girlish sound that got trapped in her throat when he placed his lips atop hers, sucking the air right out of her. Her laugh became a gasp as Braden grabbed her ass. Frankly, she would've thought him incapable of such aggression earlier. He was a man, but seemingly a docile one, but maybe that's just what she paid him for. Off the clock, he was tough, powerful, and knew what he wanted.

Even as she struggled, Sheena knew she'd finally found a man who could keep up with her, who could make her feel not only gorgeous, but who could challenge her too. She needed someone to push her—and push her buttons. Just when she was ready to dig her perfectly manicured red nails into his skin, he broke their kiss and went back to massaging her, this time peeling off her blouse.

"Relax," Braden murmured as his tongue gently licked her shoulder. Maybe she imagined the word, since she was so focused on doing just that. Relaxing wasn't that easy for her, especially these days, but he got her there with those hands, those powerful, manly hands that somehow made him seem older, wiser than his years. They dug deep into her shoulder blades, going past relief and into pain, memory. She felt his thumbs digging into her skin, asking her permission, granting her something she hadn't known she'd needed. "Let it out, baby, let it out," he whispered, or maybe she once again imagined it.

Sometimes she didn't know what he was saying exactly, his quietly-accented voice and gentle manner making it hard for her to ask him to repeat himself. Add the immense sexual tension exploding between them and she was a goner. She didn't need to tell him. Braden, with a surety that was either despite or because of his youth, just took over.

He stood behind her, pressing his cock against her ass, and she realized she wanted him more than she ever had, even in her fantasies. Her pussy contracted, tightening, and she felt the emptiness there, felt an ache so strong she had to grit her teeth. If he didn't fuck her here and now, she would die. She looked back in the mirror, at their faces next to one another: his stubbled brow and dark eyes, rough but sexy scowl, and then she closed them as his fingers sought out her hardened nipples, pink and pert and on display in the mirror. He pinched them firmly and twirled them between his fingers. She wanted to scream, but stayed quiet, just aware enough of her guests to stifle herself. Sheena let out a gasp as he shifted his hips just enough to bring his cock closer to her core. "Yes," she heard her voice echo in the room, even though she couldn't consciously remember speaking the word. His hand dropped between her legs, fondling her opening beneath the sleek silk of her pants, surely ruining the fine fabric, but he could have ripped the silk right off her and she wouldn't have minded, as long as it got him inside her. In moments, his pants were on the ground around his ankles, and hers met a similar fate.

She arched her ass, pressing back against him as she urged him inside. He fastened his teeth around her earlobe, somehow knowing this was a particularly sweet spot for her, and then he eased the head of his cock into her. She let out a long breath, one she hadn't realized she'd been holding, as she pushed back, beckoning him inside. He thrust into her, until she claimed all of him, all of that glorious cock she'd dreamt about long after he'd gone. The cock he managed to wield with a combination of authority and questioning, assertiveness and timidity, claiming her even as he let her set their course. He followed her lead, slamming into her hard as she rocked against him, able, as always, to read her mind through her cunt.

His cock seemed to know where to go, where it needed to be. He held still, letting her adjust to his girth, while one hand snaked around and massaged her clit. Slowly at first, long, intense circles that seemed to rocket straight through her. Then he began pinching, strong, short nips that left her clit suffused with heat and made her want more and more. He began thrusting again, and she relaxed against him, letting him take over and give her what she needed like they'd been doing this for years rather than mere minutes. He wrapped his other arm around her waist, pulling her close as his cock and fingers drove her mad, taking her higher and higher until she thought she couldn't go any farther. But she could. He made sure of it, and somehow when he next pushed into her, his cock felt bigger, taking up every spare space inside her until it was all him. She moaned as his tongue invaded her neck, licking the tenderest area along her neck, the one that always made her feel like she was levitating.

This was it, and they both knew it, and he slammed into her over and over, taking both of them somewhere far removed from her tiny hillside bathroom, and into the past, the future, outer space. Taking, taking, and then returning, returning, giving Sheena's body back to her one glorious spasm as a time. As she shook against him, the shudders running from the hairs on her head to the tips of her toes, making everything inside her curl and twist and transform. She felt weightless, soulless, ageless. Looking at herself in the mirror, she thought she could see the years shedding away, returning her not only to a youthful appearance, but to that same anything-goes spirit she'd lost somewhere along the way.

"Happy Birthday, baby," he said as he erupted inside her, bathing her with its warmth. She smiled at him in the mirror. Finally, because of him, it was.

Whisky Spread

Sascha Illyvich

Morganna washed the last glass of the afternoon before casting a longing glance at the door. Her bar was clean, liquor cabinets were stocked full and ready for more patrons to come in and fill the place with lively stories, cigar smoke, and booze until 2 a.m. when the place closed. She set the rag down on the wood bar and sat on a stool beside a rather large collection of whiskeys, bourbons, and cognacs.

All the ashtrays had been wiped out again, the humidor stocked full of premium smokes and a few empty match boxes with the bar's name had been thrown out, replaced by fresh, full boxes for her regulars and the casual stranger who strolled in.

It was Tuesday, meaning her favorite customer would probably wander in around eight or so; thirsty and ready to stare at her breasts while she worked.

Nicholas was an unusual man. For starters, he was young. She guessed he was probably in his early twenties, but that was based on his appearance, not what he chose to drink or where he decided to hang out. The age of her normal clientele averaged mid-fifties unless someone stumbled in, not knowing this was a cigar bar, not a club atmosphere. Nicholas never paid any attention to women closer to his age, either.

Also, he normally ordered a high-end scotch, neat. And he always smoked his own cigars, usually Nicaraguan or Dominican high-end like Padrón or Diamond Crown Maximus. Said he liked the older flavors.

She liked the fact that he liked mature things.

Licking her lips, she walked past the bar to the door and flipped the sign to reflect that they were now open for business until 2 a.m. Making her way towards the humidor, she slid the glass case open, pulled out a vitola and scanned the bar for a cutter. Spotting one by the beer tap, she retrieved it, held the uncut end of the cigar to the guillotine and clipped off a part of the cap. Bringing the cigar to her lips, she pulled out her torch lighter and lit the end of her cigar, puffing until the entire end was on fire. She cut the flame and took another puff, sending a thick cloud of sweet smoke billowing throughout the air to erase the faint yet distinct smell of cleaning products.

She took her time to savor the earthy, coffee flavors of the Honduran made cigar before returning to behind the bar.

A few minutes later, the stereo played old school jazz music and a few older businessmen had come in ordering mixed drinks and smoking. Morganna tended to their needs, keeping a watchful eye on the front door in hopes that Nicholas would show up sooner, rather than later.

After a few more hours had passed, the bar had begun to fill with the after-work crowd. The business set from the financial district in downtown San Francisco came in to smoke, chat and unwind in a smoker-friendly haven. John, the new second shift bartender, handled most of the customers while Morganna slipped off into the office behind the bar to handle paperwork and freshen up.

Shutting the door behind her to drown out the music, Morganna looked into an old mirror that hung on the back of the door. The little makeup she wore emphasized jade green eyes while ruby red lips accentuated her freckled skin. She tugged at her sweater, adjusting it so her ample bosoms showed better. Jeans fit her hips snuggly complete with ankle high boots with pointed toes. Her hair had been held away from her face by a clip in the back that centered a pony tail down the length of her back along with the rest of her mane.

She had no idea why she was going to all the trouble to make sure she looked so good for this one customer. He was probably in a relationship like many men his age.

Chalking her insecurity up to her age, Morganna shrugged her shoulders and reached for the door.

She stepped back into the bar area but took a quick step back out of sight. Nicholas was sitting at a seat by the window, and there was a brunette with him.

Her heart sank.

The brunette leaned forward on her elbows, waving her hand through the thick cloud of smoke coming from Nicholas's cigar.

His hair hung down the length of his back and caught the light off the fixture above so that it reflected a deep blue so dark it looked black. His charcoal gray shirt fit snuggly over broad shoulders and was tucked into navy colored slacks.

Morganna licked her lips; her nerves ready in anticipation of Goddess only knew what. Then she took a glance at the brunette sitting across from him nursing a . . . *cola*?

Was *she* his girlfriend?

Sizing her up, Morganna stepped out from behind the spot she was in. A tall patron caught her attention, waving a credit card.

"Damn it." Impatiently, she waved at him to signal he had her attention. "What can I do for you hon?"

He blushed, ran a hand through his curly, blonde hair and opened his mouth to speak, but no words came out.

She followed the line of his baby blue eyes roaming down her body until they'd met her assets. Or rather, her breasts. "I see. You're new here, aren't you?"

He nodded.

She cleared her throat. "No wonder. You're too obvious. I take it you'd like to close your tab?"

He set his card down and nodded. "Yeah. I'm sorry. It's been a long day and seeing someone as pretty as you made my day."

Morganna forced a smile to her lips and took his card. "Just the two beers, Rob?"

He shrugged. "I just don't have it in me to drink much anymore. I'm getting older. Have to rein it in after a few, ya know?"

An eyebrow rose. Pursing her lips together at the sight of the brunette leaning into Nicholas and brushing a hand across his arm irritated her further. "Just how old are you?"

Rob winked, dropping his tone so that clearly he was flirting. "I could ask you the same thing."

She smirked. "Yeah, but I'd answer honestly."

Frowning, Rob took the slip from her and put his card in his pocket. He offered her a fake smile and slid off his bar stool. "You a regular here, hon?"

He was trying for more charm. Great. "Yeah. I happen to know the owners very well." She winked for emphasis and waved him off while another customer ordered a beer.

Morganna sighed and looked in the direction of where Nicholas and the rather annoying brunette were sitting.

He was gone but she remained.

Something possessive inside her drove her to maneuver past John to get a better look at this annoyance who felt she could capture Nicholas's company.

Grabbing a bottle of eighteen-year–old Glenlivet, she poured a scotch into a rocks glass and made her way to Nicholas's table.

The brunette wore a simple black skirt and a salmon-colored top that came down about half shoulder. Her hair was pulled back tightly, her lips were too thin and her eyes reminded Morganna of the vacuous stares of too many stupid, nonsensical thoughts running around her head just waiting for someone to ask, "What's on your mind?"

Setting the drink down on the table, Morganna picked up Nicholas's empty glass.

The brunette spoke in a high pitch that irritated Morganna further. "Excuse me, we didn't order another round."

Morganna shot a vicious grin at the brunette. Her shoulders stiffened but she forced herself to remain polite. "I know. Nicholas is one of my regulars. This one's on the house."

The brunette waved a hand to cut through the thick smoke from Nicholas's cigar. "Ugh, I hope he's almost done here."

Morganna spied him outside pacing back and forth with one hand up to his ear to cover it from the noise that often occurred around Pine Street.

Reaching for the window, she slid it open. A breeze blew in and sucked some of the smoke away from the stupid bitch. "You his girlfriend?"

Brunette coughed into her hand. "As if. I couldn't date a man like him. He'd have to quit smoking and drinking."

Morganna snorted. *As if.*

Stupid Bitch turned in her seat to face Morganna, giving her a clear view of the woman with too-thin eyebrows and a waifish face. She crossed her arms over her tiny chest in a defensive posture. "My name's Shannon. You are?"

"Morganna. I own this bar and am quite fond of smokers and drinkers, at least those with sophisticated taste."

Shannon spoke dryly. "Pleasure. Hopefully we'll be done soon as we do have personal business to tend to after this is over with." She gestured with a hand.

Blinking in disbelief, Morganna cleared her throat and stuck out her chest. "Tell Nicholas once he gets back in that this one's on the house. He'll know who from." Satisfied, Morganna sauntered back to the bar to assist John with the rest of the night until her shift ended.

Dragging herself out of the bar around 12:30, Morganna took one look up and down Pine Street and decided to head home. She'd already had a few drinks, smoked her share of sticks for the night and had worked her ass off.

The cool breeze that San Francisco was known for whipped around her, blowing her hair back from her face. Deciding to grab a taxi back home, she sighed in exhaustion and made her way down Pine towards Market Street where most of the cabs would still be running this late at night.

Once she'd acquired a cab, she piled into the backseat and gave the cabbie the address to her home. Slumping against the seat, she pondered what Nicholas was doing with such an airhead of a woman. Shannon said they had personal business together, which meant she wanted to fuck Nicholas. But he wasn't the type to go for the rip it and dip it girl.

He liked longevity. Maturity.

And a woman with a figure.

She swallowed hard. What if she'd avoided his flirtations too much back at the bar and he'd decided to move on.

No, she told herself. That wasn't possible. He'd been a regular on Tuesdays for the last three years and hadn't once brought a woman in with him. He'd always come alone.

By 1:30, Morganna had slid into the warmth of her bed, wishing for company. She knew exactly who she wanted and let the thoughts of Nicholas's strong hands gripping her thighs while he drove himself into her settle her into sleep with a renewed determination to go after what she felt belonged to her.

The next day Morganna slid out of bed, padded into the shower and began to wash, taking time to masturbate beneath the showerhead. She liked her curves, didn't mind the extra few pounds and knew she had the attitude to back up her choices in life. Having spent enough years doing the various things she had made her a solid woman any man would be proud to call mate.

But Nicholas was with some airhead last night.

Bartenders often developed relationships with their regulars, but this was beginning to feel strange for Morganna. Perhaps it was the routine of every Tuesday night for the last three years. A girl got used to routine that excited her.

Two hours later, Morganna was exiting the BART train station when she bumped into a very tall man. Her eyes widened when she realized who it was.

Nicholas.

He turned around, a scowl on his face that quickly changed into a smile.

She frowned. Despite her disappointment at seeing him so quickly, her body reacted to his presence. Nipples puckered beneath her velvet top. The material irritated her more. Not wearing panties, the crotch of her jeans rubbed against her pussy when she took a step back.

Dressed as handsomely as ever, his facial hair reflected a five o'clock shadow pattern. The deep blue shirt he wore complimented his eyes and made the tint of blue in his hair stand out. Eyes widening, he extended his arms and opened them to hug her. "Morganna!"

She couldn't resist his embrace.

His arms wrapped around her, pulling her into his body.

The hardness of him against her softness made her wet between her thighs. She gave in and hugged him back.

Pushing her at arms length, he offered a shrug. "I'm sorry about last night."

Her lips pursed together in a thin line. "What do you mean? I have no claim on you."

She covered her mouth at the realization that she'd blurted out something that sounded completely obnoxious.

Tilting his head, Nicholas blinked. "Actually you sort of do. See, last night was the three year anniversary that we met and I wanted to bring you a treat."

Her heart thudded loudly in her chest. "Really?"

He nodded. "Yeah. I figured you might not remember because you see tons of people come through your bar but . . ." His voice trailed off.

She arched an eyebrow. "But what?"

He set his hands in his pockets. "But fucking Shannon. She's been after me for weeks. I tried to brush her off but she was persistent until last night."

"Oh?"

Nicholas nodded slowly. "Turns out, she can't stand the fact that I don't go to church, like fine cigars and scotch and even worse? Apparently I flirt with the older women."

Heart still pounding, her lips curled upwards in a smile. She wasn't going to give into her desires this early, but she was going to have some fun with him.

Running a hand through his thick mane, Nicholas continued, looking downward at the ground before setting his gaze on her lips. "I wanted to spend the night with you and close down the bar. I even planned to take the next day off."

She saw color appear on his cheeks and had to stifle a giggle. "What happened?"

"Shannon drove me back to my place and tried to seduce me. She got sick because I smelled of cigars and whiskey. I had to drive her back to her car. Ended up coming back here only to find you'd left for the night."

Morgan's eyes widened. She hadn't thought he'd come back. He never did. "You always leave just before my shift ends."

He cupped her cheek, his hand warm against her skin. "I hate disturbing you at the bar. I love your company honey but . . . ," his voice trailed off.

She leaned into the palm of his hand. Sensing he was holding back information from her, she decided to press him. "But what? Come on, spill it."

Nicholas dropped his hand. Inhaling a deep breath, he let it out slowly. He muttered the words Morganna barely caught. "The only way . . ."

Her breath caught in her throat.

Grabbing both her shoulders, Nicholas pulled her to his and dropped his lips against hers.

Pressing into him, she tasted the faintness of cognac on his breath along with the velvety steel tongue of his that plowed between her lips.

Her body responded to his kiss, every nerve steadied to alertness. Her hands clutched at his biceps, pulling him deeper into her.

Their tongues wrestled for control of the kiss and even though Morganna was a good six inches shorter than Nicholas, she won out. Molding her body to his, she shifted so her thighs trapped one of his between hers. She wasn't a hussy, but damn did she get what she wanted!

Hands tangled in her mass of hair, pulling her head back to expose her neck.

Kisses trailed down along the line of her jaw, down her neck and back up to meet her mouth. His lips were pliant beneath hers.

She swirled her tongue over his bottom lip before invading his mouth, exploring, touching, caressing his until he'd pulled back and smiled.

Her heart pounded against her chest, and she staggered until he reached out and caught her with a gentle grip.

"Wow." Morganna's pussy clenched in anticipation of more to come, but Nicholas just stood there.

The goofy look on his face didn't disappear but he wiped a hand across his lips. "I'm going to remember that taste forever. I almost need a smoke after that alone." He wriggled an eyebrow.

She smiled, licking her bottom lip. "I have an idea," she reached for him, twirling a fingernail around his chest.

A sparkle appeared in those deep, sea blue eyes. "Yeah?"

"Come by the bar Sunday. We're doing a special scotch tasting and I think I have some stuff you'd be definitely," her voice dropped several notches, "interested in." She patted her stomach for emphasis. Fingers slid into the waistband of her jeans and down lower until she reached her pussy. Dipping her fingers in just slightly, she kept them there a moment, watching him watch her.

His eyes remained fixed to hers though she swore she could see his mouth watering at the prospect of whatever she had to offer.

"You've got it. But wait, isn't the bar normally clos—"

She pulled her fingers out and pressed them against his lips.

He inhaled sharply, letting his tongue dart out over her fingertips just to taste.

The sensation sent her hormones racing. "Yeah, it is. But this is a private tasting. Be there at 2, okay?"

By now he'd drawn more of her fingers into her mouth.

She didn't want to move, other than to go to a private place and continue their game.

His tongue swirled around her fingertips, cleaning her scent from him.

Pulling her fingers out of his mouth, she smiled and pushed past him. "Remember," she ran nails across his flat stomach.

He shivered and cupped her ass with a hand, squeezing her.

She giggled and walked past him, letting the taste of his mouth linger on her lips during the rest of her day.

34

The entire week passed way too slowly for Morgana's taste. She hadn't seen Nicholas since bumping into him on Wednesday and had begun wondering if he would show up today.

Her gut told her that he would.

No man kissed a woman like that without intent to seduce said woman.

She'd chosen to wear white today. Stockings, garters, white form-fitting skirt, and short, boy-cut, crotchless lace panties to complete the look. Oh, and her favorite, white, three-inch boots to give her some added leverage for her Adonis. She chose to leave her red hair down so that it swept over the curve of her ass with each step.

Part of her wanted to stop calling him hers, but the sensible part of her wouldn't let it happen. He was hers, damn it!

Setting up a few rocks glasses with various bottles of whiskey behind them as she would for a professional tasting, Morganna made sure to leave ample room on the bar and push all the ashtrays aside for her big surprise once he came in.

Drawing the shades over the windows, she looked at the clock on the wall. Ten 'til 2.

If she knew him as well as she did, he'd be slightly early.

Her body hummed in anticipation of his arrival. Nervousness wasn't something Morganna normally dealt with but the fact that another five minutes had passed way too slowly and Nicholas hadn't arrived yet bugged her.

She looked down at an empty shot glass. Picking up a bottle from the bin, she poured herself a shot of single malt and knocked it back. Dutch courage for a cougar, she laughed.

The handle at the door jiggled.

Morganna looked up and walked around to the front of the bar. Reaching for the handle, she pulled the door open to see Nicholas standing before her in black jeans and a faded, gray tank top. His suit coat hung over thick shoulders.

She licked her lips. "Come in."

With a smile, he nodded and stepped into the bar. "Wow," he looked around. "It's odd being here when it's quiet."

She chuckled. "Yeah. It's kinda nice sometimes. I can fire up a smoke, sample inventory or just clean extra thoroughly if I want. But you're here for a different reason." She winked.

He didn't miss a beat. Shutting the door behind him, he reached for Morganna with one hand. Catching her by the shoulder, he pulled her forward and wrapped his arms around her.

Crushing her chest against his, she felt the firmness of strong muscles beneath the cotton shirt. Hands cupped her bottom, squeezing her.

She squeaked and stepped back from him with a glint in her eye. Looking up at him, she saw her smoldering desire reflected in his gorgeous eyes.

He started to speak, started to dip his head down to meet her mouth, but stopped short.

Morganna parted her lips.

Nicholas didn't move.

She arched an eyebrow. "Something the matter?"

He shook his head. The look in his eyes definitely spelled out desire. If there was any doubt, the bulge beneath his jeans reaffirmed his arousal.

"Then what, sweetie?" She touched his cheek, running fingers over the smoothness of his face. He'd shaved, making it easier for her fingers to glide over smooth, masculine skin.

Stepping closer, she inhaled. Picking up the rich scent of cigars, light sandalwood and his aroma, the smile on her lips widened. "You're not used to being the seducer, are you hon?"

Nicholas nodded.

She smirked. "I thought so. Come this way and we'll make this easier for both of us." She turned, sliding her hand down his chest until she'd captured his hand.

Pulling him towards the bar, she led him into a seat where the first rocks glass and a bottle of Highland single malt sat. She walked around to the other side of the bar and pulled off the top. "This is a standard, Highland, single malt, similar to the one you normally drink." She poured a one ounce shot into the glass, and then retrieved a glass for herself.

Nicholas picked up the glass and swirled it around. Shoving his nose into the glass, he inhaled a deep whiff of the liquid before bringing the scotch to his lips. Taking a sip, he kept his eyes on Morganna the entire time.

She mimicked his movements and took a sip of the strong scotch, picking up caramel notes along with charred oak before the liquid slid down her throat and confirmed her thoughts. She should know what the drinks in her bar tasted like.

Her eyes roamed up and down the length of Nicholas's body. After the rest of the first shot hit him, he relaxed his shoulders just slightly. Leaning forward, he set the empty glass down on the bar and smiled. "Good stuff."

Morganna moved down the line to the next bottle. Pulling the top off, she poured another shot into another empty glass and slid it forward before pouring a shot of her own.

Nicholas did the same thing, swirling, smelling and sipping the scotch.

By this time, the warmth of the liquid hit Morganna. She wasn't feeling light headed by a long shot, and her inhibitions were never really a problem but the draft from the fans had ceased making her cold once the second shot of Highland single malt hit her.

Licking her lips, Morganna poured another round for them both from the second bottle. "This particular Highland malt could go great with those Hondurans you always smoke. The Patels?"

Raising his glass to Morganna, he nodded. "Good point."

Watching the line of his throat work while he took a large sip excited her. The motion called to her desire to lick a trail down his neck and peel off that tank top to caress his chest with fiery kisses.

Setting the empty glass down, he slid it forward and smiled.

Morgan decided it was a good time to switch to shot glasses for his special treat.

He eyed her with curiosity. "Why the switch in glasses?"

Inhaling a deep breath before letting it out slowly, Morganna's lips curved upwards in a wicked smile. She leaned forward, reaching for Nicholas. Catching him by the collar of his tank top, she tugged him forward. "I have a surprise for you, my favorite scotch drinker."

Nicholas's body became pliant to her pull. He moved forward, planting his lips against hers.

His mouth curved upward against her lips before parting. She slid her tongue inside his mouth, swirling around the contours and his own tongue. The two wrestled for control of the kiss. Morganna inhaled deeply, the taste of scotch on his breath mingling with the heady, after-scent of Nicholas. Pure, masculine. Not in control. Leaning further so that her breasts brushed across the bar, Morganna pulled back and nipped at his lower lip.

Fingers stroked her chin and along the side of her neck before reaching for her hair, capturing tangles between nimble fingers. Another hand pressed against the top of her breast.

Morganna adjusted herself and let his fingers wander down into the neck of her oh-so-tight top. His fingers skittered along her skin lightly.

Her flesh tingled from his slight touch. She purred into another kiss, tasting him with a subtle sweep of her tongue. Her panties were wet now; her nipples had become taut against the fabric of her top.

Pulling back from the kiss, Nicholas's eyes were somewhat glazed over.

Morganna felt a surge of pride at her ability to turn this man on. He may not know how to approach a woman bent on seduction, but he sure as hell knew how to use his mouth. Bending over more, she nipped his bottom lip and grinned into another kiss before stopping to notice her feet were no longer on the floor. Swinging back, she giggled and moved the bottles away from where she planned her next pour.

The smug look on Nicholas's face confirmed what she suspected. He wasn't sure where this was going, but was about to enjoy finding out.

He cocked his head to one side and licked his lips. "What are you doing?"

Morganna squared her shoulders. "Giving you a final taste of the last whiskey. This," she said, picking up a shot glass and showing it to him, "is a special blend of various single malts from different regions of . . ." She pursed her lips together for a moment, and then decided that her body was right. She needed him in her. "Me."

His eyes widened in surprise.

Grabbing the bar for leverage, Morganna hoisted herself up on top of the bar so that she squatted before him. Her skirt bunched up. Standing straight, she hiked up her skirt so that her panties showed.

Nicholas swallowed and kept his gaze on the line of her thighs and where her hands stopped.

Kneeling down again, Morganna placed a hand on the bar and extended both her legs, aware of Nicholas's reaction.

He stepped back to give her room, but kept close enough to touch her.

Her boots clicked on the wooden bar. Setting herself firmly down, she picked up the shot glass and bottle of whiskey. "Do you want a taste?"

Slowly, Nicholas nodded.

Morganna saw flames of desire dance in his deep blue irises. Looking down at his body, she swore the bulge in his pants grew even larger. Hopefully she'd taste that bulge soon.

Pouring almost a full shot into the glass, Morganna scooted forward so her hips were at the edge of the bar, touching the rounded part where patrons rested their tired arms. Leaning back, she brushed Nicholas's arm with one leg.

He stepped into her.

Her voice dropped several notches, sounding very husky. "This particular scotch has to be tasted just right." She winked.

Nicholas swallowed again. The gentle rise and fall of his chest was evidence of his arousal reaching his heart.

Morganna had no doubt that he'd take what she offered. Now was he a competent lover?

With deft fingers, she slid a hand down the front of her body and over her panties. Parting the slit of the fabric revealed smooth, shaved pussy lips swollen in anticipation.

Parting her lips, she smeared wetness around the bottom of the shot glass, careful not to spill any of the alcohol. Lowering her eye lashes, she held the glass in place. "Taste from here."

Stepping forward, Nicholas bent from the waist and braced himself against Morganna's thighs.

His hands were rough, firm. She liked that about him.

He dipped his head down, lapping the tiniest drop from the shot glass before repeating the motion.

Carefully, Morganna slid the shot deeper into her pussy, unable to resist a moan.

Nicholas inhaled. Peering over the rim of the glass, he smiled. "I like the way this particular whiskey smells. It has a very pleasing aroma, smells like woman. And a fine, hand-crafted taste it seems."

Morganna nodded. "It's well cultivated."

"I can tell. What if . . ." His voice trailed off when he dipped his head between her thighs again, giving her a view of his beautiful dark mane spread across his broad shoulders.

"You should—OH!"

He nipped her thigh.

Morganna smirked and narrowed her eyes at him. It seems he was enjoying this tasting. Her body shuddered, pussy tightening around the slick shot glass. It slid out of her.

She sat up to catch it but stopped short.

Nicholas held the half empty glass between his thumb and forefinger. "Dangerous habit you have there, sweetheart." He stood to his full height before Morganna and knocked the shot back. With a sigh, he reached for the bottle. "I had another idea."

An eyebrow rose. "Oh?"

"Yeah." He poured another half shot and set the bottle down on the other side of her thigh. Bending over again, he settled right between her thighs. Pouring the shot over her plump leg, he leaned forward to capture the liquid.

Swirling his tongue around her leg, he tasted, licked and kissed her inner thigh.

Shivers raced up her spine. Morganna had to grip the bar for purchase, lest she fall backwards. Tensing her legs, she watched him pour more liquor down the other leg before mimicking his earlier movements.

His tongue pressed against her skin, circling around in swirls upwards until he reached the fabric of her panties.

He looked up from between her legs with a glint in his eyes. "Are these panties part of the tasting?"

She snickered. "You might say they're a filter for the finer things."

He stepped back and grabbed her thighs. Tugging them together in one swift motion, he spread his fingers over her bared skin. "You know about unfiltered beer?"

She nodded. "Yeah. Some customers have complaints about sediment but not you." She winked.

Nicholas blinked. "You might say I heard some things are better tasted without filters."

Morganna set her hands on both sides of her and looked down her legs at the yummy man in front of her. "What do you intend to do about the filtration here?"

Gliding his hands up the length of her thighs, Nicholas spread his fingers to touch as much of her as he could. "Remove the filter, of course."

Fingers brushed over the tops of her thighs before catching the bottom of her panties.

Morganna lifted herself up, holding her legs in place. Her stomach muscles clenched.

Quickly, Nicholas slid her panties down until they reached the tops of her boots. "I like these." He licked his lips.

Morganna tilted her head to one side and closed her eyes.

Careful not to tear her underwear, Nicholas pulled them off her and over her boots.

She opened her eyes to see him stuffing her panties in his jeans pocket. "What are you doing?"

"Memories. I don't know how often you'll do these kinds of tastings, and I'd like to never forget."

40

Their eyes met. Morganna watched him part her thighs with one hand and grab the scotch bottle with the other.

He popped the cork off and took a large swig before stepping into her body.

Her thighs brushed against strong arms. She couldn't help but giggle.

"What? I take my liquor very seriously." His eyes narrowed into thin slits that spoke more of arousal than annoyance.

Morganna watched him pour more liquor down her bare thighs. The wet, cold alcohol tickled and the scent of charred oak rose over her nostrils, mingling with her own arousal. Her pussy clenched when droplets of scotch landed on her lips. The entire front of her body had grown warm in anticipation of Nicholas's idea of a tasting.

He dipped his head between her thighs, placing his hands on her butt. Yanking her forward, he buried his tongue between her swollen lips.

She cried, clenching the bar railing behind her. A shudder raced through her body.

His tongue felt like velvet steel swirling around her core, soft and hard at the same time.

Nicholas grabbed both her thighs and carefully straightened them out in front of him. Then he pushed them gently back towards her.

She felt her thighs stretching, muscles loosening. Then she felt Nicholas's tongue brush against the back of one leg. The tenderness of his tongue sent another shudder racing up her body and straight to her core.

Nicholas's lips brushed over her other thigh before he captured her skin between his teeth and nipped her. She yelped but held her legs firmly in front of her.

"I'd like nothing more than to taste you again, Miss Morganna. I think I didn't get a good impression of the whiskey."

She nodded. Parting her thighs, she looked down the line of her body at him. He was masculine, muscular and hot. His hair parted on the sides of his face, creating a shadow around his eyes that made him seem darker, more grown up despite his younger age.

"How old are you, Nicholas?"

He lifted his head and narrowed his gaze at her. "Why does it matter?"

"Just curious," she offered a smile.

His tongue licked up her thigh. "I'm old enough."

She shivered. "How old, baby?"

41

Nicholas blew a cool breath over her thighs. He didn't respond other than to run his hands over her thighs.

Anticipation welled in her stomach and her muscles clenched from contact. She stuttered the words. "How old, b-b-baby?"

Nicholas growled. "I'm far from a baby. I'm twenty-seven. Does it matter?"

She started to respond.

Nicholas nipped her leg again.

Morganna stopped and gripped the bar behind her. "No," a breath whooshed out of her lungs so fast from the contact of his teeth scraping against her skin. "It doesn't."

Nicholas groaned, his lips vibrating against her thighs. "Good. Because Goddess knows the only thing that matters is how soon I get to bury my dick inside your hot cunt."

He licked down her legs, over the curve of her ass until his tongue swirled around the center of her heat.

Morganna's breath came in pants with each word she spoke. "I need you inside me, lover."

His tongue stopped lapping at her clit. He withdrew from her and spread her thighs open.

Their eyes met.

Morganna felt the heat from his stare.

He wanted her.

Her breath caught in her throat. She needed him. "You don't care how old I am?"

He made a noise. "I figured you're in your late 30s. I don't care. You're a sexy woman. I've wanted you since the day I met you."

Her grin widened. "I'm almost forty-seven. Now fuck me, Nicholas. Take your cock out of your pants and fuck me."

Nicholas stepped back from her. Unzipping his pants, he shoved them down past his hips, giving her a view of a rather large cock. The head was large, purple, and swollen. Glistening with precum, it looked ready to do exactly what she wanted.

Morganna tilted her hips upward.

"No. You need to come forward." Nicholas didn't bother waiting for her to react. He grabbed her thighs and yanked her towards the edge of the bar.

She squealed and her ass bumped against the rail with a thump.

Nicholas placed his hands on her calves and pressed her legs slowly towards her.

Muscles in her legs stretched slowly, carefully. Nicholas was a patient lover it seemed, taking his time with her body despite the desire she had to practically jump his bones right then. His cock head brushed against her swollen lips. She lifted her hips towards him.

Taking himself in one hand, he rubbed himself up and down her slit.

The ache in her belly pulled her muscles tighter. She lifted her head up to see him press his cock into her. Slowly, carefully, he lifted himself up and pushed himself deep inside. Opening herself up, she reveled in the feel of the connection they'd created. He grabbed her around the waist and ass. Tugging her forward, he pulled her off the bar. She felt her body slide around the railing so that she rested on powerful thighs.

His cock pushed deeper inside her until he was balls deep.

They both groaned in pleasure at the contact. Skin against skin, sweat breaking out on her forehead reminded her that this was real, this was what she wanted.

He'd be hers forever, even if the moment was only in her mind. It'd last forever.

Nicholas gripped her thighs, sliding his hands around to cup her ass. He dug his fingernails into her flesh. She cried out, throwing her head back. An arm slid around her back, pulling her closer to him. He pulled out and rammed himself back in with a grunt.

She moaned. "Finally."

He drew back, gripping his cock with a hand.

Grinning, she looked down her body to watch him tease her. Concentrating on the sensation, she closed her eyes. Spreading her thighs, she opened herself wider for him.

He slid inside her again, slowly. Inch by slow inch, Nicholas impaled Morganna.

Her muscles clenched around his cock, feeling the fullness of him. She inhaled a breath, and exhaled slowly when he pulled away.

Nicholas again slid himself inside, balls deep.

Morganna shuddered at the contact, her pussy clenching around the thick shaft filling her. She gripped him, felt the way he slid out of her, into her.

He slid out, slowly. Oh so slowly while his fingers dug into her thighs. He bent forward, kissing her calves, one at a time; first the left calf and then the right, licking a trail of heat over her skin.

Morganna shuddered again, her stomach muscles clenching and forcing her pussy to contract around his cock.

Nicholas picked up a rhythm that started out slow, building with each thrust into a steady momentum.

She gripped him, held onto the girth that was the twenty-seven-year-old. The thickness that filled her, pulsated throughout her body gave her a new meaning of life that made her feel complete.

Nicholas undulated his hips, brushing his cock against her clit.

A groan escaped Morganna's lips. She clenched her muscles around his swollen prick.

He grunted in response, a low sound that came from deep within. Nicholas rolled his hips upward, brushing his cock upward.

Sensation wracked her body, expanding throughout every limb. Morganna squeezed him tightly with her hips. Her hands slid down her body until she caught her hips. She dug her fingernails into her flesh but the pain was nothing compared to what Nicholas gave her.

Nicholas mimicked her, pressing his fingers into the tender spot where hip and thigh met.

She cried aloud and clenched her muscles around him, shoving him in deeper.

He started with a slow undulation of his hips that held her firmly against the bar and his body.

A hand tugged at strands of hair that fell over her shoulders.

Her breath picked up with his pace.

She ran hands down her breasts, pinching her nipples into very taut peaks. Her body shook from contact.

Slowing his pace, Nicholas shoved his hips upwards, brushing his shaft along her clit.

Letting out a long, slow moan, Morganna clenched her hips around him, scrambling to get him deeper inside her.

Pounding harder, faster, and faster Nicholas held her against his body, his lips finding a spot on her neck.

Those lips bit at her skin, sending shivers racing throughout her body. She pushed against him and let herself fall back on his cock to drive him in harder.

Sensation flooded Morganna's body, the scent of their sex, scotch, and him filling her nose. She rested her head on his shoulder, feeling her stomach tighten in response to the impending orgasm.

Nicholas continued pounding her pussy hard and fast for another moment before stopping altogether.

She cried aloud and glared at him.

He smiled. "I want this to last."

Panting, she had to catch her breath. Her muscles clenched in response. Her voice sounded shaky. "Me too. So come back again in a week. Or take me home. But right now, fuck me!"

The demand in her eyes was reflected in his. Nicholas pulled her closer so that with his next thrust, his balls slapped against her pussy.

The feel of him holding her tightly, lovingly resonated deep within her, and called out to that part of her that needed something.

With one hand settled on her back, the other cupping her ass, he pulled them both away from the bar and began bouncing her against his body.

Before long, they were both sweat-covered, groaning, and panting hard. Her heart raced with each thrust that brought her closer and closer.

After another moment, Morganna closed her eyes and bit into his shoulder, the tightness in her belly that became pleasurable warmth.

Muscles tightened, nerves felt a desirous heat, and the flood gates opened. Digging into him, her head slammed against his shoulder, Morganna called out his name in a glorious wave of orgasm that continued with his every movement.

"That's it baby," he growled and slammed into her. "Ride me!"

Milking him with her pussy, Morganna used her hips to drain him.

A few seconds later, fingers pressed urgently into her skin, tearing at her top. His mouth locked onto hers, tongue thrusting past her lips.

Sucking on his tongue, Morganna felt the hot wash of cum filling her.

Nicholas groaned into the kiss.

Under her weight, she felt his knees grow weak but she didn't want him out of her just yet. His breath came in ragged spurts with each thrust slowing down until he'd stopped and settled her against him.

The two stumbled back to the wall. Leaning against it, Nicholas slid them both down until he saw her straddled across him.

"Wow," she set a hand against his chest. Blinking, she looked into the face of the man sitting before her. "You're not so delicate."

He offered her a wide grin that reached his eyes. "No, but you are a lovely cougar."

She smirked.

Nicholas arched a brow. Stroking her hair with one hand, he tilted his head. "Be mine?"

She licked her lips. "I already am."

Spring Training

Heidi Champa

The signs of spring were everywhere. The campus that had spent the winter slumbering in a blanket of grey skies and mushy snow was now alive again. The smell of the newly-forming flowers filled the warming air. But, I truly knew spring had sprung when I saw the college baseball team taking the field, preparing for their season. The rowdy voices echoed off the brick wall of the building, their laughter and jokes filling the silence of the staid admissions office. At first, I balked at having my window so close to the playing fields. But, now I saw it as one of the few perks of my new job. The college had seen fit to shove me into a crappy, makeshift office with mismatched furniture and a fake wall. My only solace was the window. It let in a lot of sun and gave me an increasingly great view.

Despite the growing stack of papers and backlog of work on my desk, I found myself distracted by the noise and movement going on outside. Although the day started off dank and cloudy, the sun had finally broken through the clouds, causing the temperature to spike. That week, the team started their routine of grooming the infield dirt and preparing the chalk lines for practice. For the last few days, I'd spent countless, valuable minutes with my face near the window, watching boys half my age exercise and do manual labor. I should have been ashamed of myself, especially when I looked down and saw the picture of my children staring back at me. Somehow, I didn't feel bad. My divorce had been finalized for nearly a year. In short, it had been way too long. I deserved a distraction. Hell, I deserved more than that. The fantasy would have to do for now.

I sat up higher in my chair, trying to catch a glimpse of my favorite first-baseman. Finally, he came into view, striding out of the dugout with the casual confidence only a twenty-year-old could possess. He stood a few inches taller than the others, his lanky frame just a bit thinner than the rest. I watched intently as he stooped over his rake, pulling the red dirt back and forth to smooth out the divots the cleats left behind. His laughter rang out through the air, the deep rumble making my ears perk up. I rolled closer to the window, getting a better angle on the situation.

He really was a gorgeous kid. His dark, brown hair was short but messy; his hands seemed so big even at a distance. I swallowed hard at his arms flexing back and forth, while he chatted away to his teammates scattered near him. It was suddenly hot in my office. The air conditioner was anemic at best, but I knew the heat was coming from inside my pants. A slight sheen of sweat was forming on my back, and my cheap blouse stuck between my shoulder blades. I shrugged off my jacket, squirming to get comfortable in my hand-me-down chair. As I straightened myself out, my eyes went back out the window. I was shocked to find my first-baseman staring straight back at me. He had stopped working, his large frame leaning lazily on his rake, his eyes registering my presence. I watched, breathless, as his full lips curled into a smile. His attention was soon stolen, his eyes gone as quickly as they had come. A knock at the door startled me fully back into my day.

"Hey, Sandy, are you ready to go to lunch?"

It was Debra, my co-worker, salad in hand. I sighed, throwing one last glance out the window before I opened my drawer and pulled out a crumpled paper bag. My dreamboat was walking away. Another day to wait before he would return. Thinking about another ham sandwich in the break room, I sighed again. It wasn't the tasty treat I was looking for, but it would have to do.

The next day, I woke to rain pounding on my windows. My mood was immediately depressed. Rain meant no cute shoes, a horrible commute, and no eye candy out my window. The team would be banished into the gym. Rolling over in bed, I closed my eyes and pictured the bright sunshine of a perfect spring day. It didn't work. The skies didn't change. I was resigned to spending my day without my favorite escape. Maybe I could finally get some work done. Lord knows I had fallen hopelessly behind.

The week stayed rainy, and it wasn't until Friday that the baseball team reemerged from their exile. The ground was muddy and soaked with water, but that didn't stop them from standing far apart from each other and throwing baseballs back and forth. My boy, my first-baseman, was a junior. My restlessness during the week had led me to the school's records. I had become curious about him in a

48

strangely overwhelming way. It wasn't an easy task to find my fantasy guy. I had to search out old baseball programs, and once I found his picture, I finally learned his name. Derek Miller. The name felt too plain, too ordinary for him. I stared at his picture for longer than I should have before I got itchy fingers. My need for information grew every day the rain fell. I learned his major, class schedule, and home address. But, it wasn't enough. I found out where he lived on campus, what his grades were, and how many times he'd taken a class pass/fail.

The more I learned, the more I wanted to know. He was smart, active and obviously popular. He had been in the school paper more than most and was nominated for Campus King at the yearly formal dance. He won. I stared at his picture, his arm around a cute blonde, and felt things I had no right to feel. Jealousy and envy. Not of her youth and beauty. I had long come to terms with my body and myself. I was jealous of her position. Jealous of the fact that she got to feel the heft of his arm around her shoulders and spend an evening in his company. She had what I wanted.

I looked out the window, watching the fluid, easy motion of his arm. He barely looked at the ball when he caught it. It was as if he were on autopilot; until the ball thrown by his partner sailed past him, and went careening off the wall of the building where I was sitting. My heart skipped a beat as I watched him running straight towards my window, his legs pumping hard. The ball skipped up against the base of the building. Before I knew it, Derek was standing right in front of my window. He bent down to pick up the ball and stood up, his eyes staring right through the glass at me.

I froze, unable to move an inch in my chair. I expected him to just run off, but he didn't. He just kept staring, his eyes fixed on mine. A deep flush rose up in my face. His smile surprised me, as did his apprising gaze. His hand reached out and touched the window, just for a second. His hand truly was large, his fingertips leaving smudges on the thick glass. It felt like he was touching me, a jolt of electricity shot through me. He turned and ran away, returning to his buddies and their game of catch. Nothing had happened, but it felt as real as anything ever did. Turning away from the window, I tried to calm down. But, my breath was ragged and quick. I could feel a rush of moisture between my legs. My reaction seemed out of proportion, somehow odd. I looked at my clock. It was almost lunch time again. I cast one last glance out the window, before heading to the break room. Somehow a boring sandwich seemed like just what I needed.

The rest of the week went by without incident, my boy too distracted by playing to give me another glance. It didn't stop me from peeking and spending time watching the athletic display of cute young men. I secretly wished for another glance, another flash of a smile through my portal to brighten my day. But, it was all business on the other side of the glass. After all, the season was fast approaching.

I worked late the next week to try and catch up on all the work I'd been shirking. By Friday, I was almost completely caught up, but it was after five when I finally finished the last stack of forms for the next semester. My file cabinet drawer slammed shut, when I heard the glass shatter. The shards were all over the floor, a dirty baseball coming to rest in the corner. Voices and footsteps were in panic outside, but when I went to the window, I didn't see anyone. My feet were on top of pieces of glass large and small. There was a dust pan in the break room, but I just stood stunned, looking around the damage in my office. I'd have to call the maintenance department to board up my window. So much for my decent view.

I tiptoed over the glass. As soon as I put my hand on the doorknob, there was a knock on the other side. I pulled the door open tentatively and saw him standing there. Derek, my dream boy, was standing outside my office, his baseball glove still in his hand. My mouth was open, and my heart was in a skipping panic.

"Hi. I'm sorry about the window. It was totally my fault. The ball just got away from me."

I stood helpless as he stepped past me into my office. Surveying the damage, he stooped to pick up the ball that was in the corner. He tossed it repeatedly into his glove, looking down at me from across the room.

"We were just goofing around. Dave told me not to throw it so hard."

He kept talking, but I was barely listening. It didn't seem real, to have him right in front of me. We had been close that day at the window, but the glass stood between us. I knew I should say something, but words failed me.

"Here. Let me help you clean this up."

He set his baseball glove on my desk and stooped down to pick up glass.

"You don't have to do that."

My voice sounded weird, like it belonged to someone else. He looked up at me, his hand full of sharp pieces of my beloved window. He stood up pausing to deposit the trash into the metal can next to my desk.

"It's the least I can do after being so clumsy."

"That's funny. You don't strike me as the clumsy type."

My boldness had returned after my heart finally got itself under control. I stared into his eyes, which were the palest blue I had ever seen. His smile returned, a sly look in his eyes told me I was on to something.

"Okay. I admit it. It wasn't so much of an accident."

"Then, why did you break my window?"

"I've seen you staring at me, at us, for the last few weeks. After I got a closer look, I knew I needed to meet you. Sandy."

He surprised me when he said my name out loud. He took two steps closer to me, his large hands wringing together in apparent nervousness.

"There are easier ways to meet me. All you had to do was make an appointment."

"It's not an appointment I want."

"What do you want?"

"I'm pretty sure I want the same thing you do. You've been paying pretty close attention to me out that window. Unless you are just a really big baseball fan."

His hand touched my shoulder, the heat of the contact making my mouth fall open. It had more of an effect than it should have. My brain was screaming for me to be reasonable, but my body was ignoring the protest.

"I love baseball."

"Sure you do."

Before I could say another word, his lips fell to mine. His fingers reached up and grabbed the hair at the base of my neck. His arm curled around my back, pulling me into a deep embrace. His mouth was softer than I ever imagined. The eagerness of his youth was evident, a refreshing change from the last indifferent mouth I had kissed. I was more surprised by the hand on my ass, squeezing gently as he pulled me closer still. I could barely breathe when he let go of my mouth, his smile bigger than I had ever seen it before.

"I have to admit when I first saw you watching me, I was a little freaked out."

"So, what changed?"

"When I looked in your window that day, I thought you were one of the most beautiful women I had ever seen."

"Come on. Does that line work on the girls at the bar?"

"No, because it's not a line. It's true. Don't tell me you've never heard that before?"

His mouth on my neck distracted me from answering. I had to admit he was persistent. And, I liked it. I also liked his teeth scraping against my skin, the sucking pull of his mouth no doubt leaving a mark. He pushed me to sit on the edge of my desk, his legs pushing my thighs apart.

"No. I've never heard that before."

"Well, now you have. You are beautiful, Sandy."

Despite my better judgment and my cynicism, I swooned a little at his earnest appreciation. He really was charming.

"Derek, you are too cute."

"I'm more than just a cute kid, you know."

His hands yanked my hips forward on the desk before moving to my belt. For a moment, I panicked, suddenly unsure of what I was doing. His fingered fumbled slightly on the button of my pants, the zipper easing down slowly as he assaulted my mouth with another deep kiss. His long fingers slid into my panties, a moan escaping my lips when I felt his fingers touch my clit. I was wetter than I thought, his skin slipping easily over my swollen pussy lips. He pushed further, a single finger slipping inside me as his tongue moved deeper into my mouth. I gripped his shoulders for dear life, my hips moving without thought. I whimpered when his hands left me, leaning forward to nibble his lips as he dropped to his knees in front of me. Pulling my pants down my legs, I let myself be exposed.

"Come closer. I want to see you."

I couldn't help but moan out loud at his words. No one had ever asked to see me before, and the mere thought of it turned me on. I moved my hips to the edge of the desk, spreading my thighs wide for Derek. I waited for him to touch me, to feel his fingers on my cunt again. But, instead I saw him just staring, his eyes shining as he smiled. Finally, I felt a finger drag over my slit, the pressure barely parting my swollen lips. I propped myself on my elbows to watch his face, to read his expressions as he moved. His thumbs pushed my pussy lips open, revealing my slick hole and hard clit to his hungry gaze. I watched in awe as his face disappeared between my thighs, his tongue meeting my clit for the first time. I sighed as I lay back, letting my head hang over the other side of my desk.

I expected him to be timid or clumsy, but he was neither. His tongue moved over me slowly, but he was confident in all his movements. My eyes shut tight when I felt two fingers slid inside my pussy, the impossibly long digits twisting and thrusting while his tongue tortured me. It was beyond me to be quiet, and my moans filled the small room. Again, his enthusiasm overwhelmed me, his hand gripping my thigh as he moaned with every sweep of his hot tongue. I felt a familiar tremble run through me as I got closer and closer to coming.

He pulled his mouth back, hurrying to shuck his clothes off. I stared up at him, his well-muscled chest and stomach giving me more of a show than I had ever gotten out the window. But, when my eyes dropped to his hard cock, I gasped. He smiled proudly at my reaction; one I was sure he had never gotten tired of. I got off the desk, and stood in front of him, pulling my own shirt and bra off as I went. It was my turn to drop to my knees and place my face right in front of his young, hard cock. I marveled at it, admiring its every detail. The thick drop of liquid at the tip begged to be licked away, and I obliged. His ragged breathing gave away his nerves, despite his calm façade. I let my tongue swirl over the head of his cock. It felt thick and silky soft, his salty-sweet taste filling my mouth. I sucked him gently into my throat, easing down slowly. His hands fisted my hair, his hips pushing forward, trying to urge me on. Trying to keep us both on the edge, I teased him, not giving him too much too soon,

"You're killing me, Sandy."

I just smiled before devouring him fully, my nose touching his flat belly. But, my reward didn't last long. I pulled back, rubbing my lips against his weeping head, avoiding his advances.

"Please, I can't take much more."

"You need to be punished for breaking my window. Or would you rather I report you to the school?"

"No. We can handle this your way."

I went back to what I was doing, but my own desperation was outweighing my need to exact my revenge. After a few more deep thrusts of his cock in my throat, I stood up. His mouth was immediately on mine, kissing me frantically as I felt his erection poke my belly. I yelped as he turned me around, pressing my hands into my desk with his big palms. I got one hand free to fumble through my desk drawer where I found the condoms Debra had stashed there as a joke for my birthday. Handing one back to him, I waited as he tore open the packet with his teeth. His sheathed cock nudged at my dripping, wet pussy, trying to find its way inside. Finally, I reached under my body to guide him with my steady hand.

"Oh, fuck. God, you're hot."

His words pierced me as hard as his cock did, splitting open my desire that had been dormant for too long. His thrusts were erratic, the undisciplined timing of a young, horny man. I didn't care. I knew neither of us would last long. His fingers tripped over my clit, rubbing an unsteady beat while he drove into me. He leaned into my back, his huge body covering me. I put my own hand over his, focusing the pressure on my clit. Rutting back against him, I felt my orgasm ready to explode inside me. Hollering out, I rode the waves of my pleasure, my pussy clamping down on Derek as he continued to pound into me. His own climax soon followed, his teeth sinking into my shoulder as he stuttered out unintelligible words.

He body lay heavy on top of me, our sweat mixing together as we panted in silence. He withdrew from my body, the condom tossed into the trash. I heard him dressing behind me, as I finally regained the ability to move. His shorts slid up his narrow hips, his chest flushed and wet. I couldn't resist reaching out and touching him. He pulled me close, our lips meeting gently.

"You're amazing, Sandy."

"You're not so bad yourself, Derek."

"So, am I off the hook with the window?"

"I don't know. I might need more time to think about it."

"I'm sure if you let me, I can make it up to you."

He nuzzled my neck as I pulled up my pants, my thighs still trembling slightly from my orgasm. Derek really was a good kid; too good to only have once.

"I have no doubt, Derek."

After we dressed, he helped me clean up the rest of the glass. He picked up his baseball glove, but hesitated before he walked out. His face was serious as his grabbed me, kissing me hard.

"What was that for?"

"I don't know. Just because."

God, he was so damn cute. He took the baseball that had cracked my window and handed it to me. I rolled it between my hands, looking up into his sparkling blue eyes. His smile was enough to drive me mad.

"Thanks, Derek. For everything."

"No problem. I guess I'll be seeing you."

"Yeah. You know where to find me."

He walked out, his cleats echoing off the linoleum floor. I picked up the phone and called the maintenance department. I needed my window, after all.

Labeled

Tara S. Nichols

Toni stood outside the front door of the little tattoo parlour just staring at the sign. She'd visited the shop on a whim once before with her friends, intending to break free of the dull, safe life she'd built for herself by acquiring a tattoo, but nothing could have prepared her for the impact the young stud managing the tattoo parlour had on her. A sex god wielding a tattoo needle, Sawyer was a fantasy come true. After just one, brief consultation he'd broken through her polished exterior, seen through the practiced business spiel she reserved for all serving staff, and distracted her with his rugged good looks. With one flash of his radiant smile Toni had become a jabbering fool, blurting and stumbling all over the place, offering up more information than necessary like a sinner in a confessional. He'd never asked why a successful, forty-three-year-old, uptown business woman was in his disreputable shop looking to mar her perfectly preserved body, but she told him anyway, and then promptly ran away.

Now she'd returned, and she wasn't entirely sure she trusted her motives. No matter how much she tried to convince herself, she knew full well she was there to pick up a man rather than a tattoo. It was possible she'd read his body language wrong, or had fallen for the oldest trick in the book, but Sawyer had given her all the right signals that the feeling was mutual. She glanced at the name on the business card she held between her fingers and smiled, suddenly certain her motive's name was Sawyer. Now only the door separated her from going after the man of her dreams, or remaining an unadventurous woman, living a stifled life.

She took a deep breath before entering. A little bell above the door chimed announcing her presence and a deep, male voice from the recesses of the store called out, "I'll be right with you."

Gathering her courage, she inched her way into a claustrophobic's nightmare, a small room crammed full of mismatched furniture and magazines, with dark red walls that seemed to close in from every direction. Somehow, she'd thought she'd be better prepared for the culture shock on her second trip in, but compared to her well-organized life; it was a lot to get used to.

Looking around, she could see through a gap in the heavy velvet curtain that served as a door to the room in the back. A client sat in an old, red, leather and chrome barber chair, with her fingers gripping the armrests. Sawyer stood by the girl, a metal ear-piercing gun in his hand, poised to shoot a tiny rod through the girl's ear lobe.

"You'll feel a slight pinch," he said, followed closely by a mechanical snap. The client stifled a yelp and Toni's stomach lurched. If she went through with the tattoo, she was in for much more pain than that. Another snap came and Toni jumped. A smart person would just leave, but before she could, the girl came out with a shiny new stud in each red ear lobe, followed closely by Sawyer.

Dressed in tight, black jeans and a loose, black T, the young man who'd haunted her dreams every night since she'd hastily departed that first time, stepped out into the main room, and her body immediately responded to him. Her nipples beaded into tight points and a surge of heat rushed to her cheeks. His face brightened upon seeing her, sending her hopes spiralling off in an inconceivable manner before she reasserted herself and remembered why she'd returned. A tattoo. At least that's what she was going to tell him.

Her courage faltered, thinking about it. What did it matter? He couldn't be a day over thirty and certainly not interested in an old gal like her. So why was she worried about the visible grey in her ash-blonde hair and wondering if the silk scarf around her neck made her look dowdy? She told herself he was nothing more than an overgrown punk, with his silver-studded tongue and more holes in his ears than she'd ever had, but she couldn't deny he had sex appeal down pat.

A day's worth of growth darkened his cheeks and she could barely make out his eyes for all his dark hair hanging over them. The lack of product in his shaggy, black hair told her he wasn't vain or put on, yet the tattoos covering his ropey forearms said appearances mattered on a more personal level.

With the red-eared girl rung through and out the door, he turned his full attention on her. She felt the intensity of his gaze all the way down to her toes. Even her panties were damp.

"Has anyone ever told you how much you look like Michelle Pfeiffer?" His question threw her off guard and she scrambled to answer.

"Yes, actually."

He smiled, pleased. "Well then, what can I help you with?"

"A tattoo," she said with a glance to the door. There was still time to excuse herself and far better ways to pick up a man. She didn't have to actually go through with it.

He studied her for a moment. "Oh, yes. The butterfly, right?"

Hearing him say it out loud made her wince. "God, it sounds pathetic."

"What?" He shrugged. "Many people get a butterfly." Then he hesitated, his brow knitted together as he regarded her. "But maybe you're looking for something a little more original? Something that speaks to you on a personal level?"

She took a step back and glanced to the door again. "I don't know." She edged her way toward it, but stopped when he came around the counter to stand next to her. He never took his eyes off of her, and she wondered if he was seeing her as a woman or a blank canvas.

"Can I ask why you want a tattoo in the first place?"

No, she wanted to say, but much as she'd done the time before, she blurted the truth. "It's more the act of getting a tattoo rather than what I get. I'm pushing boundaries, restabilising myself, fulfilling a pointless goal."

"Nothing wrong with that." He grinned and held up his arm for her to see a snake wrapped around from wrist to elbow. "That's when I got this."

She grimaced. Seeing the serpent didn't help.

His laugh surprised her. "I'm not suggesting you get a snake. The point I was trying to make is that a tattoo is forever, or until you laser it off, so you should go for something you really like. You can have whatever you want." He arched his eyebrows and she wondered if he was offering more than just his skills as an artist.

He looked so hopeful she couldn't help but smile.

"How about we address the issue of where you are going to put it then?"

This was something she'd given plenty of thought. "Somewhere discreet. Like on my ankle."

His face fell and she thought he looked disappointed. "Are you sure?"

"No," she admitted. "I'm not sure about any of this. If it weren't for my friends, I'd have happily let this fade into the past and chalk it up to one of my bad ideas."

"Why is it a bad idea again?"

"Look at me." She spread her hands out, offering herself to be judged. "I feel like a joke standing here in your shop." The confession rushed out of her mouth. "I'm out of date, out of touch, and way out of my element. I don't belong here. I don't know the lingo, or what's hip." She waved her hand at her pants as though dismissing them. "I'm wearing navy slacks, for Pete's sake."

"And you use phrases like 'for Pete's sake'." He grinned, but she wasn't in the mood to laugh.

"Who am I kidding, pretending to be cool, and coming in here thinking I'll impress some hot, young stud? This is just a typical midlife crisis. I'm hanging onto the scraps of my youth like a dog to a bone. I'm no better than my friend Mary, who I criticised for wearing glitter toenail polish and pig tails."

He grimaced. "In my opinion, pig tails don't work for anyone, but this hot, young stud thinks you'd look hot with a tattoo."

She stopped her rant, hearing him, and realized what she'd admitted. He wasn't running for the hills.

"Really?" She wanted to be doubly sure.

"I never lie."

"Not even to desperate old ladies in order to make a buck?"

"I don't know." He shrugged. "I've never had one in my shop."

The line sounded so cheesy she had to drop her head so he couldn't see her smirk. "You're one cool cucumber, aren't you?" she said, lifting her eyes to meet his gaze once again.

"Yeah, but I can turn up the heat when I want to as well."

There was no mistaking the sexual innuendo in that comment she decided. He was flirting, and it was contagious.

"Tell you what," he said stepping over to the front door. She watched as he turned the Open sign to read Closed and flipped the small deadbolt, locking it. "I'm going to give you my full attention. No one else comes in to disrupt this process until you're satisfied." He walked past her, around the counter, and pulled the curtain aside, indicating for her to pass through into his work space. "I think we should start with you telling me why you need to re-establish yourself in the first place. You look just fine to me."

She swallowed thickly, staring at the heavy curtain as though it were a portal into another dimension, but after another moment's thought, she nodded and walked through. *Think positive*, she told herself.

"So?" he prompted once the curtain fell back into place.

"My divorce," she simply stated. "When I turned forty, my husband left me for someone younger. It would have been such a cliché, except it was a man. We realised neither of us were getting what we wanted out of the relationship, but at least he had the courage to go for it. I suppose it got me thinking along the same lines."

Telling her young companion about her shame made her feel exposed and even more unappealing, so she was doubly surprised when he came to stand beside her. "I can't imagine leaving anyone so beautiful." His hand rose as though he were about to caress her cheek but he hesitated.

Her mouth opened, about to speak when he spoke first.

"Might I suggest something?"

She nodded, feeling wary.

"Get the tattoo, but keep it personal. Put it somewhere only you will see it."

"Like where? My ass?"

"Or your breast." His hand moved again, this time forward. "Here." She felt the slight pressure as the back of his fingers followed the curve down and around. They rolled over the fabric, and then wrapped around one soft globe.

Stunned, she met his eyes, demanding an explanation, but he neither apologised nor backed down.

The old Toni would have come up with some excuse and fled the scene, but she was determined not to let that happen. *This is the new Toni*, she thought, feeling a burst of courage, a rare, *Oh, screw it*, frame of mind. She pulled on the fabric of her blouse, lifting it, exposing her midriff to the cool air. She didn't stop until she'd uncovered both breasts from her bra, and left the material bunched up under her chin. Sawyer's gaze swept across her chest, and a wicked smile played across his lips. Taking quick, shallow breaths she watched as he reached behind him and retrieved a marker from a nearby shelf. The tip of his tongue swept across his upper lip as he held the marker poised over her flesh. Concentrating only for a second, he brought the marker down and she held her breath against the ticklish sensation.

The outline of a butterfly wing appeared beneath his skilled fingers, and she marvelled at the stark contrast of the black ink against her pale skin. He drew the insect as though it had just landed, her breast an open flower, and her nipple the center. She didn't object when his other hand roamed freely along her body, lightly caressing her other breast, her hip, her thigh. Somehow, even though his focus remained on the illustration, he'd managed to rid her of both bra and blouse in the process, and she marvelled at his abilities. Every once in awhile his groin would bump against her and she could feel his hard shaft beneath his jeans. She grew wetter knowing it was in response to her.

When he finished the drawing, he threw the marker over his shoulder. It clattered to the floor, already forgotten. Before she got a chance to see the design, he brought his mouth down upon her nipple and drew it between his lips. She moaned loudly at the intense pleasure he elicited, and he chuckled. She stiffened, assuming he thought she was amusing, and would have pulled back but he held her in place.

"You must think I'm a sex starved old bat."

He lifted his lips off her nipple long enough to speak. "Not even close." He ran his hands along the waist band of her pants and swiftly unfastened the front. Well aware of his intentions, she knew she should try to stop him. It was absurd. He represented everything she'd denied herself for the sake of social etiquette. Yet she allowed her pants to fall away, and paused to kick them away from her ankles. She must be mad. He was far too young for her. What could she expect from him but a moment of bliss? *A moment of bliss*, she thought. That and the satisfaction that she'd finally done exactly what she wanted, and right now, she wanted Sawyer.

His hands slid under her buttocks and again she didn't resist him. Lifting her, he set her bottom down on the table in the middle of the room. He coaxed her gently until her back touched the table top, and then he stood back to pull his belt buckle open. His jeans were gone in a matter of seconds, followed closely by his T-shirt. His actions were fast, impatient, even demanding, and all for her.

She propped herself up on her arms and openly stared at his naked figure. He was nothing like her ex husband who, until recently, had let his body go, taking his libido with it. The man standing before her was primed like a new engine, his body finely muscled and lean, and his eyes full of fire and mischief. He seemed sure of himself, and even surer of her.

Her gaze wandered lower and her eyes widened at the sight of the tiny, gold hoop poking through the plump tip of his cock. Just looking at him set waves of pleasure rippling through her core. He was wild and daring. She'd never met anyone like him.

"Take your panties off," he commanded, stepping close again. His muscular cock pointed straight to her sex and her stomach filled with butterflies. In a few minutes she was going to feel that hot rod plunging deep inside her.

"Please," he added.

She hooked her thumbs on either side with a shy smile, rewarding him for his manners. As she slid her last remaining item of clothing off, he would see she was dripping wet. The evidence was visible on her panties.

"Beautiful," Sawyer purred, dropping to his knees. His face hovered between her legs. "You're a goddess," he praised.

She felt the nagging doubts return. "This can't be real." She tried to pull away but he drew her back in, and closed his lips down upon her mound.

"It can." His hot breath brushed against her inner thigh. "It is." To prove it, he planted a kiss on her pussy lips. "Ever since you walked in here that first day I've fantasised about doing this very thing, and now that I've got you right where I want you, my nerves are threatening to ruin everything."

Her heart swelled at his confession.

"I didn't dare hope you'd look my way, fearing you'd see me as nothing more than a kid, but here you are, and I'm damn near numb with disbelief."

His tongue swept across her sex, delving into her contours and teasing her swollen clit. She arched her back against his sweet assault, moaning loudly as she'd never done before. He had barely touched her, yet he was awakening long, repressed desires, sparking nerve endings into life, exploring areas her husband had never dared to touch. She writhed as he nipped and caressed her until he had to hold her hips in place to attend to her. Just when she thought she would explode into a million tiny shards of pure bliss, he pulled her forward so her bottom hung off the edge of the table and brought his body down upon her. Instinctively she wrapped her legs about his waist, grinding his cock against her mound.

"Not so fast," he said, reaching to the shelf once again, and her mouth went dry. *What had gone wrong? Why was he stopping?*

A moment of disappointment was erased when she saw that he held a box of condoms, and was even more relieved to see the dust covering the container.

He rolled the latex sheath over his cock with an indulgent smile, and then returned to his position between her legs. The head of his cock nudged her sex lips apart and his smile widened. "So ready," his voice rumbled with pleasure.

He didn't waste any time, thrusting up into her with an impressive force, and she felt her walls expand to grip him. He gave her one more insistent push before lowering himself down to kiss her. Their lips locked with their passion and his tongue probed the depths of her mouth. A foreign object knocked against her teeth as his tongue swirled about. She recognised the stud and fixated on it by drawing the tip of her tongue over and over it. His hips began to rock in a steady, slow rhythm, pulling all the way in and out with strong, slow, deliberate movements. As he did, the stiff metal hoop rubbed against her tight canal in a surprisingly pleasant way, ramping up her libido another notch with each thrust. Her hands gripped his ass, drawing him in and he groaned as his cock hit her end. She felt the entrance of her pussy pulled tight from his girth and sensed his pulse beating there. He paused a moment, his eyes luminous with his pleasure.

The contact was intense and she wondered, now that she'd had a taste, how she would ever go without him again. Just the thought pained her, yet she couldn't imagine he'd be willing to take a relationship with her seriously. If they went out to a restaurant, people would assume he was her son, for Pete's sake. She didn't know if she could bear that, yet she couldn't deny the instant chemistry she sensed with him, nor how good he made her feel.

He thrust into her, drawing her back to the present with a gasp.

"You seem distracted," he said grinning down at her and she blushed.

"How old are you?" She finally asked what was on her mind.

"Twenty-nine calendar years," he said, not breaking tempo and thrusting again. She shut her eyes tight. *Not even Thirty.*

"But that's not how old I usually feel."

She opened her eyes again, curious.

"When you came in the first time, I tried to think of a way to ask you out that didn't make me sound like an awkward teenager. It's not often someone makes me feel young." He paused mid-thrust, making her angle her hips up, trying to get more. He grinned, and teased her entrance a little, and then planted a kiss on her forehead. "I know you think I'm full of shit, but it's the truth. I left home young, intending to make it on my own. I lived as a squatter along

Sombrio Beach, living rough till I got sick of it, sick of the people, and the regular police raids." He took a deep breath. "I came to Vancouver and set up here, but it has its downsides too. The people are the same. I still get raided. Just the view has changed." She smiled at the roll of his eyes. "I've been in this business for six years. That makes me either an old fogey or a legend to most of my clients."

She looked to his weathered skin, the crow's feet around his eyes, and the wisdom resounding within them. She hadn't noticed it before, but he did have the look of someone much older than his years.

He began to rock his hips again, and she sighed with relief.

"You, on the other hand," he continued, and she tried not to make fun of his prologue in the middle of sex, "make me feel like I did when I was eighteen."

She was about to protest, saying that didn't make her feel any better, when he spoke again. "My thoughts weren't so dark back then, and my cock was always hard. Just looking at you, I'm already thinking about the next time I fuck you, and I haven't even come yet."

He thrust into her to accentuate his point.

"Well then, maybe we should remedy that," she said giving him an upward thrust of her own.

His eyes changed from soft to wicked, and he flashed her a lopsided smile. "You first," he said bucking his hips and picking up the pace.

She bore the brunt of his forceful thrusts with an eagerness that had them both smiling. She embraced the onslaught with vigour, relishing in the fact that it was a young man's cock sliding in and out of her body.

With each table-jumping slam of his hips, she drew one second closer to the biggest orgasm she'd ever experienced. When it came, it was all she could do to stay on the table.

He followed soon after, uttering a sound that was a cross between a groan and a growl, and then he sagged on top of her. She wrapped her arms around him, kissing his face, his mouth, his neck. He smelled so good she inhaled deeply, basking in his musky aroma, and marvelled at the beating of his heart so close to her own.

She had a million questions she wanted to ask him, so many doubts and fears still lingered. Only a week ago, the thought of getting a tattoo seemed radical, and she'd ended up fulfilling so much more than some silly goal. She'd never felt such joy, and it threatened to burble up out of her until she laughed out loud.

Sawyer lifted his head to look at her. "What's so funny?" His grey-green eyes searched hers.

Her heart nearly melted, as she recognised the same doubts and fears mixed up in his afterglow, and she came to the conclusion that it was the same for everyone where matters of the heart were concerned. No matter what age she was, starting something new was always messy, tentative, and unknown. She'd never been as bold as she just was, but at least she'd taken a chance, pushed her personal boundaries, and maybe, because of that, she'd found real happiness.

Pleasant images filled her mind, a future with Sawyer that included a lounge chair by the ocean. It felt possible, almost tangible.

"I'm happy," she said, feeling foolish.

Relief flashed across his handsome features, "I'm happy to hear you say that." He kissed her lips. "So, this feels like a rather roundabout way of asking you to dinner tonight."

The familiar doubts flooded back into her mind. "Where would you have in mind?"

He must have read her expression and saw her fears. "I'd love to take you all over town, but let's not overwhelm ourselves with public opinion just yet. How about my place? I cook a mean Mandarin stir-fry." His heated gaze swept across her naked body beneath him. "And maybe afterward we could do this again."

She smiled, and felt her remaining fears slip away. "I'd like nothing better, if you think you can keep up."

His smile widened, delighted by her challenge. "Oh honey, I'm definitely up for it." He moved his hips slightly, and she gasped as he stirred the lasting effects of her orgasm. Never had she thought getting a tattoo would be so pleasurable.

Adrian's Lover

Craig J. Sorensen

Adrian didn't have a Wiki page. No band site, no MySpace, no Facebook. From a web perspective, Adrian was nearly *persona non grata*. I found some references to an album at an old-school, text-based website to something with the simple title, *The Adrian Parker Band*, and a list of song titles. In one blog I found a post: "Do you remember a song by someone named Adrien (sic) Parker that had the words, 'if you can't find enough, stop looking so hard' or something like that? I heard it one night on an FM station when I was a kid. Stuck with me and I heard something made me think of it a couple weeks ago."

No replies.

If I'd had more time, I'd have gone to the library to see if there might be some footnote in some *Rolling Stone* article.

Instead, I rolled into Willie's Bar early to secure a seat near the band.

"Five dollar cover charge, babe."

I folded a ten dollar bill and thrust it forward like a hungry erection.

"Need a beer too?" Talia grinned—she still thought we were *an item*.

"Yeah, I'll take a glass of—oh, shit!" I pulled out my cell and dialed.

She grinned. "I know what you like babe."

I'd been working on getting a date with über-hot Jenn for two months. Seriously, this girl hardly ever accepted dates. When she finally gave in, she'd all but said we'd end up in bed. Why did Adrian Parker pick tonight of all nights?

"I can't make it tonight, but I'll make it up to you, Jenn. My editor really wanted me to do the interview . . . Willie's . . . Yeah, the bar . . .

It's not so bad . . . Some folk singer or something from the Seventies. Hey, why don't you come down and hang out?"

Yeah, right. From a date at the best restaurant in the county to a show at a township dive. Jenn was pissed, but she didn't tell me to fuck off.

Talia's big, brown eyes sparkled as she set the Sam Adams down. She rotated one shoulder to draw my eyes to the wide V in her silky blouse. Who am I to argue? She set the change down in my hand and curled my fingers around it.

I patted her hand. I would still probably be here at closing time. Maybe it wouldn't be a total loss.

Along one wall stood a bass drum, a Black Beauty snare, a ride cymbal, a crash and high hats. A vintage Fender Jazz bass sat to the right of the kit. On the other side of the kit were a TV, yellow Gibson Les Paul Jr., and a Fender tweed amp.

I figured Adrian would be the guitarist, and as luck would have it, the booth beside the guitar rig was open. There was no stage at Willies, just a stretch of floor along the wall in front of an out-of-service fireplace. I would be close enough to reach out and touch Adrian.

I sipped my beer and accepted occasional flirts from Talia until three people walked in and snaked through the tables between the front door and the gear. A relatively tall woman, with full hips, and a sloping, soft, belly crowned by full breasts approached. Her long, curly, jet-black hair with streaks of pewter gray framed her angular face tightly.

A heavy-set man with a long beard that would make the guys from ZZ Top envious sat at the drums. A skinny, wrinkled man with faded tattoos and absolutely no hair—I kid you not, he didn't even have eyebrows—lifted the bass.

The woman began to tune the yellow guitar.

"Adrian?" I leaned forward. She didn't look up. Maybe she needed a hearing aid? For a moment it occurred to me that maybe Baldy or Beardy was Adrian. "Adrian?" I said it louder and scanned all the musicians.

The guitarist lifted one brow and almost looked at me. "Hmm?"

"I'm Brendan Vivaldi, from the Daily Mail. Would you consent to do an interview?"

"Vivaldi?" Her head lifted. A half smile carved one cheek. "Ahm kinda busy, hon." She had a thick southern drawl.

I'd have preferred folk music. I hate country. "Maybe between sets?"

Her eyes were an odd color, something like olive. She looked at a table on the far side of the room. "That's when ah sell mah CDs."

"Talia!" I called out and Talia turned back. "Will you watch Adrian's table over there between the sets?" Talia nodded. I turned back to Adrian. "Girl could sell space heaters to equatorial rain forest aboriginals."

Adrian laughed as she trimmed the G-string tuning knob. "Well, thank ya darlin'. 'Specially for thainkin that's whut ah naid."

"I—um—I mean . . ."

She let me fumble for a time, and then winked. "Relax. Ya got your interview, cutie."

Beardy cross-sticked the time, and she dove into a deeply bluesy song. Tints of rock but on a very strong blues structure. She played finger style, her hands were long, and slim, but with big knuckles. She leaned to her left side as she played, and the strap of her olive, spaghetti-strap top drooped down her shapely upper arm. She sang without a mic, and she belted it out like a soloist in a gospel choir. Her powerful, deep but sharp voice literally took my breath away.

Between songs, she'd return the drooping spaghetti strap to her shoulder, and warmly announce the next song. All were originals. The lyrics, dark but hopeful. They seemed cohesive in an odd, found-object way.

For the end of the first set, she pulled out a powerful, rocking ballad with a lead guitar section that conjured Jimmy Page crossed with Stevie Ray Vaughn. Her shiny bare knee protruded through a hole in her jeans as her right leg bounded in time with Beardy's quarter notes on the hi-hat.

The modest crowd whooped like a mosh pit at a festival.

"Thank ya!"

Adrian's silky palm choked my hand. "I ain't been interviewed in a coon's age, so you'll pardon if I'm a bit rusty?"

"No sweat, Ms. Parker."

"Good God son, just Adrian."

"Sorry, 'Just Adrian.' First question: why here?"

She winked. "This is a nice town. Good people, salt of the earth, you know." She sipped her club soda with a twist of lime and licked her lips. She wiped the dew from her forehead with her long thumb.

The answer seemed odd. I just lowered my brow.

"Hon, when you get thrown, you ain't likely to mount up a thoroughbred. You gotta start someplace. Ponies are horses too."

She wasn't an easy interview. Didn't offer much more than concise answers to the questions interspersed with folksy phrases. She was a very good guitarist, so I pushed a guitarist's often-favorite button: gear. I nodded toward her guitar. "Nice Les Paul Junior. Do you have a preference for P-90 pickups over humbuckers?"

Her face opened into a grin. Jackpot! "Varies from guitar to guitar, but in general P-90's are fat like humbuckers, but more focused and tight like a single coil. I even like that warm hum that everyone tries to 'buck.' But you know what I mean. You know your way around six-strings, don't you?"

"My brothers and sisters were."

"Guitarists?"

"No, six strings."

Adrian belted out an earthy laugh like her singing. "Cute."

"I come from a musical family."

"Like Vivaldi."

"Yeah, something like that." I get that a lot

"And how about you?" She pressed her ribs tight to the table.

"Me what?"

"Are you musical?"

"Who's doing the interviewing here?"

"Seemed like you were losing traction. Just tryin' a-help. I gotta get back up there." She winked and patted my cheek softly.

The last vestiges of motel soap had succumbed to Adrian's sweat by the end of the second set. I'd always liked women neatly perfumed. Still, my cock felt a bit heavy. I figured it was from my lost date with Jenn and my occasional glimpses at Talia's tight body.

Adrian's sudden directness when I brought up her parents surprised me. "Momma died when I was thirteen. Daddy didn't hang around, so my grandma raised me. She was a hard woman, and cold as an Alaska winter, but she did teach me music, an' I had me some talent. When I was sixteen, I just took off. Went on the road."

"Sixteen? That's pretty young."

"Mmm hmm. I didn't want to hang around with grandma, and she didn't put up no fuss 'bout it. I was skinny, and I was pretty, and had a strong voice, and could play the guitar pretty well. I worked a lot of dives that made this place look like that Russian Tea Room thing."

"Are pretty."

"This bar?"

"No, you. You are pretty." I winked and grinned. It was my charm reflex.

She shook her head then shrugged. "Are you trying to seduce me, Mrs. Robinson?"

"Mrs. Robinson?"

"You know, *The Graduate*?"

"What graduate?"

"The movie."

"I have no idea."

She covered her eyes her left palm. "Oh, darlin'." A thick band on her ring finger gleamed.

"Tell me about your husband?"

"My what?"

I pointed at her hand.

"Oh, that. I ain't married. This was my mama's ring. Don't get me wrong. I been married. I been married four times, for them that keep count. I'm good at getting married, not so good at keepin' that way."

"Did the marriages fail from life on the road?"

"No." We stared at each other for a long time. "See, how it works, Brendan, you're the interviewer, I'm the interviewed. You set to askin' the questions, I set to answerin'."

I laughed. "Alright, why did you marry so many times?"

"See how easy it is?" That wink was infectious. "I married a couple good men, and a couple bad. Even in the day of the emancipated woman, I thought I had to marry when the music thing crashed. I kept tryin'! You know, for years I bought guitar after guitar, every tip I squirreled away, even though I only played at home. I'd play 'em in the store and think, 'that's the one.' Never was."

"That one seems like it might be it." I pointed toward her Les Paul Junior. "Is that a custom shop model?"

"Nope. You never answered my question. Do you play?"

"I know every note on the fret board. I know formulas for triads and chords, know the scales, classical music, jazz music, blues."

"So you do play."

"Yes. Badly. To share a family secret, I'm tone deaf."

She looked sad. "For real?"

"I couldn't carry a tune in a bag. But to make for it, I have an appalling sense of time."

She laughed and took a sip of her club soda.

"You said the music thing crashed. Tell me about that."

"No." Her expression was more emphatic than the word.

We stared for a minute. "Okay, so what color are your eyes?"

"You ask some strange questions, Brendan."

I leaned forward and studied her eyes. "So answer the plain ones. You aren't the easiest interview I've ever done."

"Why should I be?" Her breath had a hint of lime and the fruit salad she was slowly eating as we talked. "My eyes are gray, but they kinda reflect what I'm wearing. See?" She pulled a blue silk scarf from her pocket and draped it across her wide cheeks like an Arab woman and leaned forward.

Her eyes indeed looked suddenly bluish. "They're stunning . . . I . . . uh, I mean . . ." I couldn't recall the last time I'd fumbled on my words.

She pulled her long hair back from her shapely ears ornamented with big, gold hoops. She bound her hair in the scarf. "Thank ya, darlin'." My cock began to feel heavy again.

"Tell me about the album."

"My CD? It's not much better'n a homemade thing . . ."

"Actually, I'm asking about the album, *The Adrian Parker Band.*"

"You know 'bout that ol' thing? We sold every copy."

"Wow."

She winked. "Don't be impressed. It was a teeny label. They just made five hundred total. Back then it was Heart, and Fleetwood Mac, and such. I was kind of odd. Southern but not playin' country. They wanted to turn me into a star. Shape my music into 'it' by leaning it toward country rock. Somthin' like The Eagles or the Allmans with a puss."

I nearly spat my beer across the table. She winked.

"So, you wouldn't sell out?"

She leaned back in the booth and laughed hard. Her knee pressed mine. My cock sprang through the leg hole of my bikini briefs. I casually turned it up along my zipper and wiped my pre-come on the hip of my jeans.

"Honey, I sold out like a cheap whore in tore leotards. Then I got me a head so big I couldn't keep it straight up. I pissed off some mighty powerful people and crashed down like that Skylab thing. Pieces of me are still all over Texas." Her face became serious and she tilted her head softly. "Best thing ever happened to me."

"The crash?"

"If I'd made big money, I'd of put it up nose or in my vein or just plain down my gullet. Probably all of 'em and be six feet under today. Live fast, die young, leave a good-looking corpse." She paused. In any other case, I'd have inserted a charming comment. I just waited for her to finish. "Honey, I struggled with a lot of demons through four marriages. Through 'em all, I found the music my one joy. I wrote me more than a hundred songs in the basement, some of which you're hearing right here. My last man was kind. Gave me all kind of space to find myself. Truly a gentleman among gentlemen. I owe a lot to him."

"What happened?"

"So tell me. Your whole family is musical, but you aren't?"

"That's the story. What about that last husband?"

The way her lips flared up from long, seamless creases into almost heart-shaped lips on a cartoon kissy mouth hinted at a mischievous teenager. The crow's feet around her eyes pointed like arrows at her wishing-well pupils. My cock throbbed.

"Your name is Vivaldi."

I nodded.

"Bet that was tough." She rested her hand on mine and stroked my knuckles.

To that very moment, I had been convinced how tough my life had been. Always picked on by my siblings for my inability to play music, I was like the geeky kid struggling in a family of athletes. Asked to work at a rather prestigious musical magazine because of my impressive knowledge of all things musical combined with my writing abilities, I declined. Music had not been my friend, so I took this job at a dying local newspaper. "In truth, I had it pretty good."

She tilted her head. "I better get to that third set."

"I—I have more questions."

"Don't you fret. I'll be back."

She ripped into her guitar and belted out the vocals for another set. This time, she plied even more from that Les Paul Junior, with those long, strong hands. Her powerful voice caressed the room, now nearly empty. The passion of her performance didn't dwindle in the least. At closing, one of the few that remained brought up her old album. "Jesus, darlin' where did you find that relic?"

The man folded his hands nervously. "I bought it new."

"Oh, you're a doll." She signed it. The man blushed.

"May I?" The rightful owner handed it to me. Adrian had indeed been skinny. Her hair had been straightened and was cut short around her angular face. They'd put a tight silky purple blouse on her to make her eyes appear even more exotic and to showcase her high, full breasts atop her slim chest. Her skin was warmly tanned and buttery.

"You're more beautiful now." I suddenly worried she'd think it was just another line.

Her brows lifted like a draw-bridge.

I shrugged. "Well, you are."

A soft, sweet smile like I'd not seen on her face opened. "Thank you, darlin'."

"Um, listen Adrian. I haven't, um, asked all my questions."

One knee pressed between mine. "I was hoping you'd say that."

A fresh hard-on stretched my zipper. She took my hand.

"It's such a beautiful night. Look at them stars." She reached around my waist. Her sandals, laced in her fingers, bounded off my hip. She stopped and turned me to face her. She grabbed my chin firmly and smiled. "Damn, you're fine looking." She kissed me hard and rested one hand on my bulge. "How far is your apartment, Brendan?"

If I wasn't tone deaf, I'd have been able to calculate how many octaves my voice rose when I squeaked, "Half mile."

"Why, your hair's bright as the mornin' sun, Brendan, and your eyes are bluer than the sky." She traced my cheeks with her powerful fingers, the stiffness of her calluses tingled. She kissed my body as she removed one garment at a time before she even untied the scarf around her hair.

I lay naked on the unmade bed while she slowly drew her jeans down. Her thighs were shapely and tapered to similarly endowed calves. I reached out but she pulled away, and teased as she peeled that top. She held my hands over my head and straddled me in her bright pink panties. I kissed up and down her stomach, all around her breasts and savored her sweat.

She finally pulled down her cotton panties and lay back on the bed, knees pointing to the ceiling. I parted her pubic hair and stared in those eyes while I tasted her with long strokes punctuated by short flicks of my tongue. I inserted one, and then two of my fingers into her.

"Hon, you do know your way around a woman."

73

Body yes, but I was learning things so fast I couldn't keep up. All I could do was continue to drink her, press my tongue inside her as she rocked in time until her hips crushed my face and she shouted out an orgasm. "Oh, honey, come here." She opened her arms in a V as if funneling me up her body. I suspended above her and she gave me the most beautiful smile as her thumb and forefinger circled the base of my cock to guide me inside. We made love slowly, like a ballad. I lowered down onto my elbows where our faces nearly met. We kissed from time to time, deep to shallow to deep, then lingered in each other's hard breaths.

It was not urgent, not explosive, not desperate. It was relaxed, a slow steady ascent through strata after strata. I had never seen a more beautiful sight than her beneath me. When her face blossomed, and her voice uttered vibrant orgasmic notes, I could no longer restrain, and I pounded hard in her until I came in wave after wave.

She stroked my back as I pulled breaths atop her.

Fade to black.

Adrian was pressed tight to my back when I awoke. She still smelled of sweat and smoke and the evening spring air and a bit of me.

Bad as I had to piss, I didn't care as she turned me on my back, straddled me, and took me inside. She pressed my body tight to the sheets, parted my thighs with her toes and rocked her hips in perfect time. She pushed my fingers to her clit and I helped her to another deep orgasm. She collapsed slowly, pumped on me until I came as the burgeoning sunlight washed the pale curtains. I rubbed her back and hips and sides and thighs. I hadn't had enough of her, wondered if I ever could. "Um, look, Adrian, I didn't finish my interview last night."

She gave a rare look of discomfort.

"I mean . . . I . . . don't really have anything tying me to this town."

"Huh?"

"Well, you know, if you'd like, I mean, I could go . . . with . . . you . . ."

"No." She traced her finger around my chin. "You're a fine and handsome man, an' no hard feelings, but I don't fancy any man cluttering my bed night after night. Remember about all those guitars?"

"But you got your Les Paul Jr." I'd have married her on the spot if she'd asked.

"Men and guitars have similarities, but a lot of differences too.

Truth is, honey, I'm married to my music. That's what I learned through all this. Lucky for me, he ain't the jealous type." She gave that infectious wink. "Unfortunately, he don't keep me in the style to which I'm unaccustomed, but that's my cross to bear. I love him somthin' fierce." She patted my cheek a little hard. "You ain't so bad though."

My heart was broken but I couldn't stop laughing.

"I can drive you back to your motel."

"S'a gorgeous mornin'. I reckon I'll walk." She didn't look back as she started down the road with her left spaghetti strap draped down her upper arm, and her sandals in her hand as the fresh, orange sun reflected in the silver strands of her hair.

When she disappeared from view, I found a copy of her CD on my coffee table. I put it in my boom box, and realized that everything she hadn't told me, and some things I didn't ask, was there in her songs.

It's not smart for the writer to come off as a part of the story, and you don't get to be much more part than I was. I poured all the energy of losing Adrian into how I described her music and an unflinching telling of her tale. I found that fan from the night before and scanned in her album cover. He was nice enough to bring me an old-school cassette copy of it, too, and some photos of her performing that pivotal night.

No one was more surprised than I when the wire services picked up the article. Adrian and her band grew in the public eye. She got a nice Wiki page, some fan sites, her own website, a MySpace with 22,362 friends and climbing (yours truly as a Top Eight friend,) and a nice indie CD making its way up the ranks at Amazon.

She moved on to auditoriums. It seemed Adrian's lover was taking care of her properly.

I never did get that date with über-hot Jenn. I made it clear to Talia we were done. I left town a few weeks later, and took the job at that music rag.

Guess I'd come to terms with Adrian's lover too.

Comfort Food

Donna George Storey

One bite of that butterscotch pudding and suddenly I knew everything was going to be all right.

If one of my more sensible friends had been sitting at the table with me, she would have told me the pudding had nothing to do with it. The new, buoyant sensation in my chest was the natural outcome of a relaxed vacation by myself at a charming country inn. The crazy grin on my face, the almost-sexual quickening of my breath was but a long-delayed visceral understanding of all the work I'd done in therapy over the last year. There was no need to wallow in misery any longer. Dylan's affair and my subsequent decision to divorce him were only symptoms of our buried grief for the real death of our marriage years before. It was time to move on.

However, since I was alone and had no need to be reasonable, I knew the epiphany was all in the pudding. Perhaps it was the creamy smoothness caressing my tongue like satin? Or the bottomless depth of flavor: caramel, tropical vanilla, and an almost floral, sweet cream, all mixed together with something else mysterious, alluring, even addictive?

Whatever the reason for the magic, at that moment, I was very glad to be alive.

When I finished my dessert, resisting the urge to lick the bowl clean, I waved over the pretty waitress.

"Does your chef give out recipes? I'd love to make this pudding at home to remember my vacation."

"Actually, I'm new here. I'm not sure," she said, blushing. "I'll ask Joseph."

I gazed out the window overlooking the lodge's perennial garden, wondering what trials of the spirit awaited that fresh, young thing in her life ahead. Or would she be one of the fortunate few who enjoyed the thrill of love without tasting its sorrows? Did such a person even exist?

I was still lost in my reverie when I became aware of a stocky male form in a white chef's coat standing beside my chair. Already my nerves were singing from the warmth of his body, his scent of cumin and olive oil, but when I looked up and met his sky-blue eyes, my pulse skipped two beats. "Joseph" was younger than I expected.

"I'm glad you enjoyed your dessert," he said.

"The pudding was exquisite," I said, pleased at the strangely sultry depth of my voice. "I'd love to have the recipe as a souvenir of my stay here."

The boy chef hesitated. I took advantage of the pause to drink in his smooth skin kissed with a touch of five o'clock shadow, the sensual yet determined mouth. Beneath his chef's toque, his chestnut hair was tousled and very touchable. And who wouldn't be enchanted by those cerulean eyes boring into my soft, secret places more pleasurably than my favorite ice-blue dildo?

Here was a tasty dish indeed.

Finally he spoke. "Again, I'm delighted you liked it, but I'm afraid I don't give out my recipes."

I'm not quite sure what possessed me then. I'd spent most of the last year either sobbing or staring off into space in a self-pitying gloom, but suddenly a fire I'd thought was dead forever sparked to life.

I tilted my head and smiled. "You remind me of my great-aunt Patricia. She was a fabulous cook, and I know she seduced more men with her culinary talents than many a beauty queen. But tragically, she refused to share her recipes. They all died with her. Isn't it a shame to deprive the world of your treasures?"

Joseph folded his arms. "I'm planning on being around for a while."

"It might be a lonely existence. Pleasure was meant for sharing."

"That's the price I have to pay," he replied saucily. "But I will tell you one thing. When you make pudding, never use ultra-pasteurized cream. The processing kills the flavor. Just plain pasteurized is what you're looking for. Start with quality ingredients and you can't go wrong."

I shrugged. None of this was news to me. "Thanks for the tip."

"My pleasure." He emphasized the last word ever so slightly. "You have a great evening now, ma'am."

"Hey, wait," I called after him. "At least tell me what kind of vanilla beans you use."

He paused, mid-step.

"It's Tahitian, isn't it?" I continued. "There's no mistaking those floral notes."

Joseph wheeled around, his eyes glowing with new respect.

"You're right," he said, "I do use Tahitian vanilla beans."

"That didn't hurt, did it? Now I'd guess you use brown sugar, but the flavor's so rich, it could be caramelized white."

He smiled. "Sorry, no comment. I'm onto your tricks, ma'am."

"You haven't seen anything yet." I met his gaze. He *was* a luscious young fellow. "Maybe you'd better get back to your kitchen before you divulge any more professional secrets."

Pudding aside, it had been a long time since I'd enjoyed anything as much as making that boy blush.

That night, in my bungalow tucked away at the far corner of the mountain resort, I finally convinced the baby-faced chef to spill all.

It was perhaps too easy in the end. Boys that age will do anything to get their rocks off, and at forty-four I knew all the ways to bring young men to their knees.

But that was dessert.

First came the appetizer: peeling off his sauce-streaked chef coat, and the Coldplay T-shirt he wore underneath.

"Give me the recipe for that pudding," I demanded as I ran my hands over his broad chest and shoulders.

"My apologies, ma'am, but there's nothing you can do to make that happen." His words rang with conviction, but his eyes fluttered closed.

"Oh, no?" I raked my fingertips over his biceps and circled my way down over the sensitive skin of his arm to his wrist.

He sighed.

I grasped his large, sturdy hand—that chopped and stirred and coddled ingredients into wondrous, life-changing elixirs—and brought it to my lips. Taking his index finger in my mouth, I slowly sucked it down, like a cock. He whimpered and shifted his weight. I let his finger float in the soft, liquid heat of my mouth for a moment before I used my tongue on him, flicks and swirls and lapping strokes, a little preview of the things I intended to do to another long, stiff part of his anatomy.

"There's more of that if you tell me the recipe."

"No . . . I can't . . . I . . ."

Smiling mischievously, I took his fuck-you finger in my mouth, fellating it with all my skill until I swear it stiffened and quivered in release. All the while, he was mewing and purring, sweet feline sounds of pure submission.

My blood was roused and I pulled off, licking the drool from my lips. "You like that, don't you? But what you really want is for me to do the same thing to your cock."

"Yes." His voice was hoarse with need.

I knelt before him. His cock was so hard, the fly was practically splitting open from the throbbing pressure. I unbuckled his belt and yanked down his trousers and briefs. My eyes narrowed in hunger at the vision of that ruddy sausage rearing up between his thighs.

"What a delicious hunk of meat. God I want to suck it."

"Please," he whispered. "Your mouth is so hot and wet. When you licked my fingers, I thought I was going to come in my pants."

"But you'd rather come in my mouth?"

This time his "yes" was a low, beseeching moan.

"You know what you have to do first," I taunted him.

I saw a single tear of frustration roll down his cheek. "I'm sorry, I can't tell you. It was my grandmother's special dessert. I promised her on her deathbed I'd never give it to a stranger."

"Don't you think we'll be pretty intimate if your dick is buried in my throat? Even Granny would have to agree." I wrapped my hand around his cock and pumped slowly. The shaft thickened and swelled, and the head was so red and weepy, it threatened to burst like a ripe fruit.

"All you have to do is give me that recipe and you'll get the blowjob of a lifetime," I cooed.

Now his legs were shaking and he was panting like an animal. "Oh fuck, all right. Suck it and I'll tell you. Just suck it, please."

I touched the flat of my tongue to the sensitive spot beneath the head. His whole body shivered.

"For eight servings you start with a cup of brown sugar . . ." The words caught in his throat.

"Don't hold anything back now," I warned him, unzipping my own jeans and jamming one hand down between my legs.

"Okay, it's *dark* brown sugar . . . oh, God, keep licking it, please."

I gave him one long, wet swipe of my tongue from shaft to head.

"Mix in five tablespoons of cornstarch . . ."

I closed my lips around the helmet of his glans.

"Press the cornstarch into the sugar with the back of a wooden spoon . . ." He swallowed the words in a groan as I sucked his stocky shaft all the way inside.

Shifting the hand I've wedged into my jeans into the proper position, I started to strum my clit. I was so hot and swollen down there, I knew it wouldn't be long.

"Slowly stir in two cups of milk and two cups of heavy cream, not the ultra-pasteurized kind though, and . . . oh, fuck, oh . . ." He thrust his hips and pawed my hair as he shot his own dish of sweet cream pudding into my mouth . . .

This was the image that finally pushed me over the edge as I fingered myself on my bed, my body wracked by a series of spasms that made me thrash so wildly, the mattress creaked in protest.

It had been a hell of a long time since I'd come so hard.

I laughed softly as I stretched my shaky limbs like a cat. I was soaked in sweat, and my palate tasted faintly of semen, although I couldn't even remember the last time I gave Dylan a blowjob. For so long, sex for me had mostly been with my hand, give or take a few mechanical rebound fucks with Dylan's old friend from his college days who "always had a thing for me." Just to prove I could still do it.

I was surprised at how much I missed the sensation of cock in my mouth.

That boy chef had served me up another very sweet surprise this evening. I wondered if I'd ever get the chance to thank him properly.

When I opened my eyes the next morning, I half expected to see Joseph's face on the pillow beside me. No such luck, but I did I find myself with a new and very welcome companion: a burst of desire to *do* something.

After a quick breakfast—a peek through the kitchen door revealed the morning cook was not Joseph—I decided to use my last day of vacation to take advantage of the "twenty miles of beautiful hiking trails" around the resort.

With a sunny August sky cut by a cooling breeze, the weather was so perfect I could have ordered it off a menu. Thanks to the pudding and the fantasy blowjob, all of my senses were heightened. I reveled in the shapes of each leaf growing along the path, the sound of the birdsong, the clean scent of baked earth and oxygen-rich air. And of course, all the time I was thinking of Joseph. What was he doing now? What experience in his brief life made him wary of sharing his recipes? He was a cook who clearly enjoyed eating. Would his cock be as solid and sturdy as the rest of his body? And most intriguing of all—would his semen really taste like vanilla cream pudding?

Thirty years ago, I would have called these obsessive musings a crush, but I was wise enough now to know it had nothing to do with Joseph himself. It was all about me. I was a woman who could feel and want and enjoy life's sensual pleasures. My desire made me more interesting to myself.

I must have walked for over an hour in a daze of lust when I wandered into a clearing to find the very object of my dreams standing before me. For a moment I thought I was hallucinating, but a few blinks reassured me that it was in fact the real Joseph, looking especially fetching in his off-duty jeans.

When he saw me, he seemed equally flustered.

"How did you find this place?" If I didn't know better, I'd say the boy was afraid.

I noticed then that the large metal bucket at his feet was half full of dark berries. We were standing in a wild blackberry grove, which Joseph, with his secretive nature, probably hoped to keep to himself.

The image of myself as a culinary predator amused me, and I laughed. "Don't worry. I'm not stalking you to get that recipe. I was just trying to work up an appetite for dinner. Are we having blackberry cobbler tonight?"

Joseph laughed, too, and returned to his work, his lusciously large fingers closing around the fattest, darkest berries with impressive speed. "There won't be enough for a cobbler this late in the season. I'll probably do a blackberry sauce for the rice pudding."

"Oooh, rice pudding? You can have your fancy, flourless chocolate torte any day, give me a good dish of homey rice pudding, and I'm in heaven." I hadn't meant to sound so much like a gushing teenager, but I was telling him the truth.

"You like comfort food, then?" he said, his expression warming noticeably.

"I suppose I do. And you like to make it?"

"Very much. It's not as glamorous as fusion or the Chez Panisse rip-offs, but I think there's a lot of potential in home-style cooking. Actually, I'm talking with some investors now about opening my own place in the city. Diner food, but raised to a new level."

"That sounds wonderful," I said. "I'm sure it will be a great success. Everyone needs comfort, right?"

"I hope so." He smiled at me for just a little too long, and then turned back to his berries.

The silence between us pressed down on my flesh like a warm hand. I was so hot for this sweet young thing, I could barely breathe. I was thinking up a way to make a graceful exit before I actually pounced on him right there, when Joseph spoke again.

"Are you in the food business? You seem to know your ingredients."

"Me? No, it's just a hobby. Although I haven't cooked much since my divorce," I blurted out, and then blushed. As if the boy would even care if an old bag like me were attached or not.

"Well, I was impressed," he said. "Do you mind doing me a favor—I'm sorry, I didn't catch your name?"

"Natalie . . . Natalie Weston. And you are?"

"Joseph Sokolsky," he nodded politely. His mother had certainly raised him right. "So, Natalie, would you mind tasting a few of these berries?"

"Sure." I plucked two berries from his outstretched hand. My fingers brushed his palm, sending a jolt of lust straight to my pussy. I forced myself to breath slowly. "What am I looking for?"

"Just taste it," he said, his eyes fixed on my face.

I popped the fruit in my mouth and chewed. My eyes shot open in surprise. "Oh."

"What?" Joseph leaned toward me.

"They're fabulous. I don't think I've ever had blackberries so sweet. I can taste the slow sunshine in them, the work of Nature's patient hand. You could never get something like this in a store."

"I couldn't have said it better myself." His smile was sunshine in itself. "Well, I'll definitely be using these in a sauce tonight then. If you like it, I'm sure the less discerning guests will eat it up."

I blushed again, dizzy from the compliment. Funny how I was worried about the difference in our ages, when at that instant, I felt all of fourteen.

The hike left me famished, and I decided to have an early dinner. Not to mention I figured I'd have a better chance for one last chat with Joseph before the crowds descended.

I sauntered past the hostess's podium and peeked into the open door of the kitchen. Two sous-chefs were busy at the stove, and the waitress was dropping lemon slices into pitchers of ice water. Just then, Joseph himself appeared beside the young woman with a spoon in his hand.

"I need a guinea pig, Jackie. It's the sauce for the pudding."

He eased the spoon into her mouth like a mama bird feeding her baby.

"'S good," she murmured, her mouth still full.

He clucked his tongue. "All you're gonna give me is 'good?'"

She giggled. "No, I mean great. Everything you make is wonderful."

Joseph punched her lightly on the arm. "That's why you're my favorite waitress. Hey, it's almost five-thirty. You'd better get your pretty self out there to hand the hungry lions their chow."

"Lions"? "Chow"? The insults snapped me out of my voyeur's trance and I made a quick retreat to the lobby. I was blushing again, but with a new emotion: unadulterated shame. How ridiculous I was to imagine a boy like him might actually think I was special. Joseph was quite simply a ladies' man. Females were just toys to bat around in his big, clever paws. The young pussies were for teasing and fucking—he'd have that girl in bed before the end of the week, no doubt. Flirting with me was just a passing amusement, just to show he could charm us all.

My first impulse was to slink back to my room. However, my stomach was growling so badly, I decided to take a short walk around the grounds then come back when I could blend into the surroundings.

Unfortunately, the dining room was full when I got back. Jackie seated me at a table near the kitchen, where I caught frequent, and now unwelcome, glimpses of Joseph at work through the swinging door. It was childish of me, but I bypassed the chef's recommended specials—risotto cake with prawns and pistachio pesto, summer vegetable galette with green beans ala Nicoise—and went for the pedestrian salad with roasted beets and goat cheese.

I forced down the greens with little enjoyment, and then asked for the check. To my surprise, Jackie slipped a large plate in front of me instead.

"Compliments of the chef," she murmured.

I stared down at the plate, which immediately brought to mind a modern painting. The composition was artful indeed: a small, molded rice pudding crowned with two whole blackberries, floating in a crisscross net of glistening indigo sauce.

Under any other circumstances, I would have been salivating in delight, but now I just wanted to cry. "I'm sorry, but I'm not feeling well. I don't think I can eat this."

She whisked the plate away, but soon returned with a carefully folded paper bag. "Joseph asked me to wrap it up for you in case you're feeling better later."

I instinctively glanced toward the kitchen. The door opened just a crack to reveal Joseph's frowning face gazing out at me.

I bit back a smile.

Apparently, I had the power to hurt him too.

As soon as I got back to my room, I tore open the bag and ripped into the paper box inside. The waitress—or Joseph—had thoughtfully included a napkin and a plastic spoon, but like some wild beast, I pinched off a chunk of the rice pudding with my fingers and jammed it into my mouth.

The moan that escaped from my lips made me glad I'd retreated to my private lair. It was, quite simply, the most delicious rice pudding I'd ever eaten in my life. The texture was mousse-like, rich with cream but airy as a cloud. I tasted a kiss of rum, a heartier vanilla than the day before. Mexican perhaps? I'd only gotten a mere ribbon of sauce in my first mouthful but it did indeed taste like the essence of summer sunshine.

Joseph might be a recipe-hoarder and an incorrigible flirt, but when it came to pudding, the guy was a fucking genius.

Hurt pride and misdirected lust were mere distractions in the face of such greatness. I knew then what I had to do. But first I savored the pudding slowly, smacking my lips, purring my approval, scooping up the remnants of sauce from the box with my fingers and sucking them clean.

It was near ten o'clock when I walked boldly into the kitchen and asked for the chef. The remaining assistant pointed me to a small room in the back corner.

Joseph looked older sitting at a desk covered with papers and charts, his brow creased with concern.

"Sorry to disturb you," I said, "but I just had to tell you the rice pudding was amazing. The best I've ever tasted."

His lips stretched into a grin. "I hope that means you're feeling better?"

"Much better."

"Well, tomorrow I'm making chocolate pudding, updated for more sophisticated tastes. I'd be curious what you think."

"Oh, I'm so sorry I'll miss it. I'm leaving in the morning."

His face crumpled.

"I'd ask for the recipe, but I learned my lesson," I said, forcing a smile.

"Speaking of that, I have something I'd like to say in private. Do you have time for a walk?"

With the way his eyes sparkled, how could I refuse?

Out of habit, I started strolling toward my bungalow and Joseph followed. He didn't speak until we were well away from the main lodge.

"I've decided to give you the recipe for the butterscotch pudding," he announced.

I actually gasped. "You're kidding, right?"

"No, I'm not. I've also decided to tell you why. Even though you might think I'm kind of a creep."

"I can't imagine that I would," I said softly.

"Well, I've been sort of watching you over the past week. The first day at dinner you looked so sad and thin, but you smiled when you ate my food. As the days passed you looked . . . happier. I thought— well, maybe this will sound stuck-up—but I thought maybe my cooking was helping you feel better."

For a moment I couldn't speak. My chest ached, but sweetly, as if he'd reached inside and soothed my sore heart. "Actually, I have been going through a rough time, and your food did comfort me. When I tasted your butterscotch pudding last night, I knew I was going to be all right. I wanted to thank you for that, but I didn't think I'd get the chance."

"No, I should thank you. It's nice to make a difference. Sometimes I wonder if anyone even notices," he said.

"I noticed."

"I appreciate that. So, I'm going to give you the recipe, but I'd prefer if you don't let anyone else know about this."

We'd reached my bungalow and I paused before the door. "Of course. Do you mind if we do it in my room so I can take notes?"

The words slipped out before I realized my proposal might have a less innocent interpretation.

But the way Joseph smiled . . . Well, I suddenly knew everything was going to be all right indeed.

At first we both behaved in a civilized manner. I sat at the desk and wrote the recipe down on the hotel stationery while Joseph stood beside me and dictated. Yet, like the night before, his warmth, his scent, made it hard to concentrate on my task.

When I stood up and thanked him again, he didn't step back. We were standing so close I could have licked him.

"How old are you?" I asked.

"Twenty-six."

"I'm old enough to be your mother."

Joseph just smiled and said, "But you're not."

Then he leaned down and kissed me.

His lips were satin, and his mouth tasted like cream and vanilla and sex, and I wanted to taste him everywhere, just like my fantasy the night before. But it wasn't at all like the fantasy, because Joseph didn't stand passively while I undressed him and sucked his fingers and then his cock. He backed me up to the bed and laid my body over it, as he might arrange the day's special on plate. And so I was the one who submitted, who closed my eyes and sighed, who shivered when he took my nipple in his mouth and licked and sucked with consummate skill.

I was the one who confessed, in a voice hoarse with need, that I wanted to fuck him so badly, but I didn't have any condoms.

"What's the problem?" he replied with a smile. "After all, we both like to eat."

That's how I found myself with my ass propped on a pillow and Joseph's face buried between my legs. Not surprisingly, he was a master at this kind of dining, too, the ultimate multi-tasker: flicking my clit with his tongue, while both hands tweaked and pinched my sensitive breasts. He made me so wet, my juices flowed down over my slit, soaking the pillow. But I didn't care, I knew no shame. I came in record time, my thighs shaking, my head thrashing, my hips bucking like a cowboy on a bull. Joseph rode it with me, tonguing me to the finish. I could tell he enjoyed his meal from the glistening grin on his face.

I cleaned my juices from his chin and lips with my tongue and told him it was my turn to eat.

Joseph's cock was medium-length and thick, a perfect mouthful. I ate him like an ice cream cone, savoring his musk and spice. His groans and sighs told me I hadn't lost my skill. Then I got the naughty idea to ask if he liked a finger up his ass when he was getting a blowjob. To my surprise—and delight—he confessed that he'd never done that before, but he was always interested in experimenting with new ingredients.

At last, I could thank him for the pudding in a way he would remember.

Wetting my forefinger in my mouth, I teased him in that sensitive spot behind his balls, tracing a slippery trail back along his crack to his secret, puckered hole.

"Push open for me," I whispered, easing my fingertip into that tiny, delicate mouth. His hard-on twitched and I pushed farther, gentle in my defloration. I took his cock between my lips and ran the tip of my tongue around the crown. His shaft swelled against my lips, hard as a marble rolling pin, but that made it all the easier to glide up and down, up and down. When his breath quickened, I crooked my finger forward—*come here, come here*—and a few strokes later, my dessert arrived. Tonight's finale was, of course, hot jets of cream splashing against the back of my throat accompanied by a garnish of low, animal moans. I made sure to swirl the chef's special sauce around my mouth before I swallowed. As always, it was exquisite, something only he could make.

Definitely a dish to remember.

And so, although I promised not to share the recipe for the butterscotch pudding, I don't mind passing on the secret for an even sweeter ending to a good meal. I guarantee it will make you very glad you're alive.

**Chef Joseph's Creamy Cougar Pudding
(serves two generously)**

Ingredients:
1 brawny, tireless, boy chef
1 fortysomething divorcée with a sweet tooth

Garnish with:
1 hotel bed with extra pillows

A package of condoms purchased from the men's room in the hotel lobby for the next round

Mix both ingredients together well until they release their natural juices.

Repeat as desired.

Illicit Desires

J.C. Wesner

"Oh! Yes, God, more, more, Javier!" She growled, as her manicured nails furiously rubbed her clit. He let out a mighty roar as he thrust into her once more, roughly, his cock twitching with his release.

She sighed. "Oh, thank you, Javier," she said as she moved off of him. She walked to the open balcony door, slipping into a silk robe. She looked out over South Beach with a smile. Movement caught her eye and she watched him travel across the bed. He really was a beautiful specimen. He stood and stretched, pulling the condom off and slipping it into the trash can in the bathroom.

She traveled over to her Prada bag and pulled out a fifty before she walked back to him. "Here. Thank you for your fast and prompt service."

He looked at the money and grinned as he slid his pants back up. "Sí, gracias, Señora Summerton."

She smiled at the waiter as he nodded. "Your food should still be de right temperatura," he said, bowing his way out of her suite.

She lifted the lid and smiled at the lox, bagels, and cream cheese that sat upon a bed of lettuce. *Thankfully I decided not to do the egg white omelet this morning. No doubt it would have been cold by now.* She smirked to herself as she sat down to enjoy her breakfast.

She was everything she ever wanted to be: successful, brilliant, wealthy, and now she was heading out for a grand vacation aboard a cruise ship. Here, her smile slipped. *With my father and wife number . . . what is it now? Three? Four?* She had lost count.

The worst thing for her was the fact that his new bride, Naomi, was eight years her junior. That was a disgrace. The horror. If she had known *that* was what he would have brought back when he went to New York on business, she would have went herself instead of traveling to Italy and finding that beautiful Italian boy to fuck.

She hurried about her morning, eager to get to the ship and attempt to enjoy herself. *At least I'll be able to find something to keep me occupied aboard ship. Perhaps even a few 'somethings.'*

"My father is an idiot!" She shouted into her phone to her best friend Chelsea as she rode in the hotel's limo toward the port of Miami three hours later. "First he marries this trollop, can you believe she had a kid at fifteen? What the fuck is *that* about? And *now* my disillusioned father insists we go on a family 'vacation' to bond or some shit." She sneered into the phone. "Honestly, Chelsea, I swear to God . . . the man has gone senile."

"What about this woman? Is she a gold digger? Should I have my P.I. try to dig up dirt on her?" Chelsea, like a good friend, asked.

Nicci snorted into the phone. "No. On the contrary. She's Mother fucking Teresa."

"What about the kid?" Chelsea asked.

"I haven't met him. He's quite studious, from what I hear. He's pre-med. I think he got a scholarship."

Chelsea laughed. "Yeah, with your father's money."

"Ugh. Don't remind me. Listen, I'm here. I have to go be 'one' with my family now. I'll talk to you when I get stateside or if I just can't take all the gooeyness anymore."

Chelsea laughed again. "Have fun, Nic."

"Certainly. Because this is my idea of fun."

"Well, at least there are a lot of dicks in the sea."

Nicci snorted. "Chelsea! You made a joke!"

"Ha. Ha. Bitch."

Nicci smiled. "I'm going to miss you, Chels. Really."

"I'll miss you, too, you whore. Go out and find the prettiest cock in the place and ride it for me, won't you?"

"I always do," Nic said as she snapped her phone shut.

The droning sound of her father's ring-tone brought her out of her musings as she looked about her cabin. She looked at her phone and sighed. "Yes, Daddy?" she asked in answer. He was always 'Daddy' unless they were at work. Then he was "Dave," or "Davis," his given name. They didn't mix business with family. Most people found that hard to believe, but then, they hadn't lived with the man. It was easy to be just like him when she didn't have a mother to soften the blow.

"Hello, darling! We were wondering if you'd join us. We're up on the pool deck."

She hid the annoyance and said, "Sure. Just give me a few more moments to freshen up. I just arrived."

He chuckled. "Let me guess. You found something to distract you this morning."

Too much alike, equals the fact that he knows me too well. She smiled. "Well, you know how I like a good Cuban in the morning, Daddy."

He laughed his boisterous laugh and said, "Fine, fine, get cleaned up. We'll be drinking Mai Tai's and enjoying some of the Miami heat."

She took her time, but she finally dragged herself up to the eleventh floor. She grabbed a drink from one of the roving trays, giving her room number to charge it to, and she sipped, taking in the sights. There were quite a few people on deck already. And that's when she saw *him*.

God, he was beautiful. Blond hair, with just a hint of curl to it, strong, lean swimmer's body, long legs, longer than even her own thirty-four inch inseam. That was a plus. She'd fucked a lot of men shorter than herself, and it had its attributes, but there was just something about a man taller than she that got her clit tingling and her La Perla panties wet.

She licked her now-dry lips and took another sip of her drink as she moved toward him. *Forget family time, I need to be riding him. Now.* She moved with the air of a jungle cat stalking her prey. She had just about reached him when the crowd parted . . . , and she saw him standing, talking to her father.

What! She stopped dead in her tracks. *Perhaps he's just a waiter. No need to be alarmed. You know how Daddy meets new friends. Everywhere he goes he sees someone to talk to. That's all.*

She swallowed hard at the slight sense of panic and began moving her feet again. She put on a smile and walked up to her father. "Daddy," she said, ignoring the beautiful man standing beside him.

"Hello, Nicci! I'm so glad you could join us," her father said.

She kissed his cheek. Davis Stuart Summerton III was a statuesque man in his own right. He held a degree of poise and charm that reflected his Southern roots. With his soft accent and his deep baritone voice, he had the ability to calm a room with ease.

"Hello, Nichole," Naomi said demurely from where she sat next to Davis. "We're really excited you were able to take the time off to join us."

Nic smiled, for her father's sake, at least. "Yes, well, I *do* have a slave driver for a boss. But when he demands I take a vacation, I have to listen."

Davis guffawed. "Nic, you're too much like your old man."

She smiled at him, a true smile this time. "Hey, like father, like daughter, correct?" *Only I have enough common sense not to marry everything I fuck, unlike you, dearest Daddy,* she added silently.

"Oh, Nicci. I want you to meet someone," Davis said.

She turned expectantly to the god standing beside them. "Nic, this is Carson McNeill."

She opened her mouth to say something sexy when her father dropped the rest of the bombshell: "Your newest step-brother."

Fuck, she though. *This is just fucking great . . .*

Nicci avoided her family as much as she could the rest of the day, excusing herself while she got a handle on whatever the hell it was she was feeling. *You can do this,* she said, preparing for dinner. *It will be easy. He's just a man. He's nothing. He means nothing. Chelsea is right. There are a lot of cocks in the sea. Just because you want to ride your step-brother is inconsequential.*

She blew out a breath. God, how she wanted him, though. To feel those muscular thighs beneath her as she rode him, to feel those large hands with those long pianist's fingers dipping into her hot, wet . . .

She let out a growl and went to her suitcase. She ripped open the velvet bag and pulled out her vibrator. He was her newest toy, guaranteed to get her off quicker than anything else she'd had. She didn't like to lave attention on herself, preferring to have a man do it for her, but time was short and she needed to go. But she also needed to relieve this pressure she was feeling in the pit of her stomach. She flopped back onto the bed, her fingers doing the walking as she eagerly thrust the dildo into herself.

"Ahhh!" She cried as she felt the familiar stretching as she accommodated the large size of her toy. She needed this, needed to get off before she saw *him* again.

He's just a man, Nic. He's nothing, she thought as she turned the dial up to high and began fucking herself.

But he's a beautiful man, she argued as she let the vibrator thrust within her.

And you've had many beautiful men before. Just this morning you had Javier. She pinched her nipples thinking about him.

But Javier didn't have those *hands and* those *shoulders and* that *ass.*

She pictured him, and then Carson, and his vision, along with her large, pink aid and her fingers gripping her tits, sent her flying over the edge.

Her head fell back and she panted. She had just gotten off. But she felt so far from satisfied. *Ugh. I need to find something. Tonight.*

Dinner was a torturous affair. From watching her father and his wife making goo-goo eyes at each other, to having to sit next to Carson, she felt certain she was in the epitome of hell. After dinner, she tried to excuse herself, but she was caught by her father. "Come join us in the lounge for a dance or two."

"Daddy, I'm tired. I just got in last night from Cairo and—"

"For your old man?" he asked.

She sighed. "You can guilt me into anything, can't you?"

He grinned. "Well, I'm your father. I've taught you everything you know. But I keep a few tricks up my sleeve in reserve."

She laughed and grabbed onto his arm, kissing his cheek. It had been an odd transition going from father and daughter to business associates. They had made it, but a few feelings had been hurt along the way. Now they had finally figured it out and enjoyed each other as family when they could.

He led her in a dance around the floor and they clapped when the house band ended the song. They went back to the table where Naomi and Carson were now sitting, and both ordered another drink. Naomi asked Davis for a dance and he eagerly stood once more, sweeping her into his arms.

Nicci swallowed hard. Now it was down to just her and Carson.

"They look happy," he said softly. His voice sounded like the angels singing. It wasn't deep, but soft, almost lilting, while still having the very common New York accent.

She snorted. "And he has been with his other wives too."

"You don't agree with this?" he asked, surprised.

"What my father does behind closed doors is his business. I just don't understand why he has to marry every woman he feels the slightest inkling for. It would only be too easy to just fuck her and leave."

Carson's hands fisted. "That's my mother you are talking about."

She patted his hand, the thrill of it going up her spine. But she knew she couldn't like this boy, couldn't woo him to her bed. There were certain rules she'd made with herself, and fucking her step-brother surely must be one of them. "I mean no offense. I just can't understand what they can have in common."

"You don't know her," he insisted.

She shrugged. "She's younger than I am, Carson. Surely you must see the irony in that. He married someone younger than his daughter. That's—it's just too much for me."

"You know what you are?"

Her perfectly-arched eyebrow rose.

"You're a hypocrite."

She laughed airily. "Moi? Surely you must be mistaken. *I* do not marry everything I fuck. I've never even *been* married."

"Exactly." He spat. "You haven't been married, so you don't believe in true love, but you're a hypocrite because you enjoy fucking things younger than you too!"

Hmmm . . . Seems like Mommy Dearest has been talking about me behind my back. She smiled at the thought. "Honey, you go, live your life, and then you come back to me in about ten, fifteen years, and tell me that you won't end up doing the same thing."

"I believe in true love," he said softly.

"You're young. Youth makes you believe in the concept. Experience quashes that dream."

"Yeah? Well . . . , well, you're just a sad, bitter, old hag!" And with that, he stood, downed the rest of his drink and stalked out into the sea air.

"Oh, dear, where did Carson go?" Naomi asked as she and Davis walked back up to the table.

Nicci grinned. "I believe he was tired. He must have gone to bed." Davis pulled Naomi back to the dance floor, but Nicci bit her lip. She didn't *mean* to antagonize the boy, but he had such ideals. And calling her a hag? She had to admit, it hurt. A lot.

The rest of the week was spent in much the same fashion. They got together once a day, for dinner, and afterward, some dancing or drinks. Any time they were alone together, Nicci and Carson traded barbs and argued from why the Atlanta Braves are better than the New York Yankees to why one should enjoy Picasso's paintings as opposed to Da Vinci's. Nicci hated to admit it, but she had begun to enjoy the verbal sparring. She wondered if Carson did as well.

Two nights before their cruise ended, Davis and Naomi called it an early night. Carson smiled at Nicci as they stood from the dinner table. "Shall we head to the lounge anyway?"

She grinned. "Sure. Why not? I can school you on the proper Scotch to drink now that you're old enough."

He laughed. "I've been twenty-one for the better part of a year, but I've always been able to hold my liquor. And I *know* which Scotch is the best."

She laughed as well, and they headed toward the bar. Three hours later, they were both just a *tad* tipsy as they made their way out of the lounge and out into the sea air. "It's a beautiful night." Nicci said as she took in the large moon in the clear sky.

"You are beautiful," Carson said softly.

She laughed. "You're drunk, dear boy."

"I'm not a boy," he said with the slightest hint of a pout.

She laughed again. Everything seemed humorous to her tonight. She knew she shouldn't have had that last drink. "You are more of a boy than you are a man, sugar." Her accent slipped in, the Southern twang coming into full effect from the alcohol she had consumed.

"I'm more than man enough," he stated defiantly.

She licked her lips. "Really? Prove it."

That was all it took for his lips to descend to hers. She let out a moan and his tongue thrust into her mouth. His hands were all over her body, and she craved more. She needed him. Like air, like sweet, blessed oxygen, she needed him. "God, Carson . . . ," she managed as his mouth moved down to her neck.

"I want you, Nicci. I've wanted you since the first time I saw you."

"I'm older than your mother," she stated.

"I don't give a fuck," he replied as he ripped the top of her dress open, one perfect breast peeking out. His mouth traveled down to it and he suckled her nipple into his mouth.

She let out a little whimper, and he pulled away from her suddenly, tugging her dress back into place. "My room, now," he snarled as he grasped her hand and pulled her back into the hall.

They had been drinking in the bar on the fifth floor, and it was rather convenient as their rooms were also on the same story. He pulled her down the long hallway to the end, where the master suites were situated.

She was giddy with nerves, an oddity for her, and she wracked her brain to figure out why this felt wrong. But the drink was affecting her thought process and she was just going with the feelings as he fumbled the key card in the slot and pushed open the door.

He grabbed her, pulling her to him once more as he freed the same breast as before, lavishing it with attention.

"Oooh . . . Carson! You've done this before?"

He smirked and licked his way up her neck. Once there, his tongue flicked her ear. "I've fucked my fair share. And trust me. I know what I'm doing."

His voice caused her panties to dampen further as he backed her into the bedroom. "You're mine, all mine," he said between kisses.

"At least for tonight," she reminded him.

He smiled. "Oh, you may find you want to keep me when I'm finished with you."

The thought caused her heart to race.

He pulled the dress off of her, revealing only her matching panties. His eyebrow quirked. "Are these expensive?"

She gasped as he tossed her to the bed. "Yes," she breathed.

"How much?" he asked.

She swallowed hard. He looked much like a predator. His beautiful blue eyes had darkened to almost black in color. "One-one hundred fifty-five dollars," she whispered huskily.

He smirked. "It's a shame."

"Why?" she asked.

He tore them from her body, ripping both side seams and tossing them to the floor. "That's why."

He pounced right then, and his tongue dove into her dripping pussy.

She screamed and grasped his hair, tugging him toward her further. "Oh, fuck, Carson!"

"Yes." He pulled away. "Scream my name. I want to hear you screaming as you cum."

His tongue continued to thrust into her roughly, and she was almost at the pinnacle when he pulled away. She growled at him, and to her surprise, his fingers slipped into her, curling just so to hit that mythical G-spot most men didn't know about.

"Oh . . . SHIT!" she screamed as his teeth clamped down on her clit and she poured forth.

He drank her greedily, lapping her clean before he smirked again and moved away. "That was fast. You're quite responsive," he purred.

She was panting for breath. Even though she had spinning class three days a week, there was something about an orgasm of such magnitude that could leave you gasping for air. "Well," she managed, "You're rather good at that."

"Why, thank you," he said as he tugged the shirt over his head.

He is *beautiful,* she thought as he kicked off his shoes and slipped out of his pants. His cock was standing long and thick and at attention for her. He walked naked without a bit of shame, not that he should, to the bedside table and pulled out a condom.

She licked her lips, eager at the thoughts of her hands on his dick and said, "May I?"

He nodded. "Be my guest."

She took the condom from him and slid it on his length. His eyes rolled back in his head, and he shivered slightly. "Like that, big boy?"

His eyes opened lazily. "Not as good as I'll enjoy your pussy."

Her eyebrow shot up. "You are a bad boy, aren't you?"

He moved to her then and knelt over her, his body aligning with hers. "You haven't seen anything yet, sweetheart."

"I'm waiting," she said, a bit of a taunting tone in her voice.

He didn't wait any longer and thrust into her.

Her nails dug into his back as she cried out, "Oh, God."

"Nope, not God, but close."

She looked up at him and laughed. "Fuck me, Carson," she purred.

"My pleasure, Nichole."

There was something about the way he said her name, the way he began to softly move in and out of her that caused her to reach her peak before she thought possible and all too soon. She had her legs wrapped around him, thrusting herself into him all the harder. But he wouldn't move fast. He thrust with languid strokes, tempting, teasing her, until she was growling. "Please . . . Carson . . ." She was closing in on whining.

His smile was brilliant as his teeth caught her bottom lip. "Please what?" he asked innocently.

"Please . . . move faster," she urged.

"No. I'm rather enjoying this."

She tried to push him away, push him onto his back, *something,* but he would not budge, just continued to slowly, sensually rock into her. He was driving her quite mad. She'd not met a man his age with as much patience as he had. Usually it was a quick fuck and that was it. But he was taking his time and it was insanity she now felt. "Carson!" she finally screamed, "FUCK ME!"

He paused and pulled away so that they were only connected by their sex. "You want me to fuck you?"

"Yes!" she shouted.

He nodded. "Alright, then." He pulled away, but only long enough to roll her onto her stomach. He grasped her hands and pulled them behind her back, holding them in place. "How hard do you want it?" he asked with intensity she didn't realize he possessed.

"Hard."

"Very hard?"

"Almost as hard as you can," she told him.

He paused just a moment before he said with authority, "On your knees, bitch."

She got onto her knees with some difficulty, as her hands were still held tightly behind her back. He pulled her upper body flush with his, and he licked the shell of her ear again, his other hand plundering any bit of her skin he could find. "I'm going to fuck you so hard, you'll never forget it. You'll always want it to be me. Every young stud you fuck from now on will have *my* face on him. Do you understand?"

She wondered if she was dripping onto the linens. She felt like she should, as turned on as she was. "Y-yes," she replied. She wasn't used to not having the upper hand. Giving away some of her control excited her.

He shoved her back down to the bed, one hand holding hers tight behind her back, one shoving her head down into the mattress. "You asked for it," he reminded before he slammed into her.

She cried out and immediately came.

He started thrusting harder and harder, and she felt herself clenching him, rolling from one orgasm to the other as he continued to pull them from her. She felt his hand leave her head to slap her ass instead. She groaned and felt another orgasm threatening.

The hand traveled over her body, massaging her buttocks, and she cried out as that hand dipped to her clitoris, tempting the little nub of flesh he found there.

He was beginning to make noises as well now, and it turned her on even further as she felt one more release coming. "Come with me, over the edge, Carson," she pleaded. "Come. Now!"

He let out a cry of his own as he bucked into her wildly.

She screamed one final time and fell over the precipice with him.

His body went slightly limp as he released her hands. He kissed her shoulders and down each knob of her spine before pulling away and placing a kiss to the apple of each of her buttocks. "Thank you," he muttered as he stood on shaky legs to remove the condom.

He plopped back onto the bed and blew out a breath. "Damn. Now, that was one hell of a way to welcome me into the family."

Too Many Buffalo

Randall Lang

The midday sun blazed in the Oklahoma sky blistering everything beneath. Kenny Cheshewalla was accustomed to the heat, and he knew well the shimmering, asphalt road between his home on the Osage Tribal Lands and Pawhuska. Today he was making the trip to pick up parts for an aging oil well pump, one of many that he managed for the Tribal Authority. It was a routine trip until he noticed a woman standing beside a silver luxury car at the side of the road, cell phone in hand. He slowed and pulled his pick up truck behind her car.

As soon as he opened the door of the truck, the scalding air hit his face. The woman stood with her back to him, the cell phone pressed into her ear. He walked between the vehicles and a quick glance at the right side of her car revealed two flat tires. Not wanting to frighten her, he stood by the rear bumper of her car until she turned around and noticed him.

"Ma'am, you're obviously having trouble."

She flipped the phone shut and walked toward him. Her carefully tailored tan suit and brown, lizard-skin pumps looked desperately out of place along the dusty road.

"I hit something about a mile back. Whatever it was must have been hard and sharp. It punctured two of my tires. My cell phone is useless out here, and it looks like I'm stuck."

"Not any more, ma'am. I'll get you fixed up and on your way as soon as I can."

His confidence impressed her. He appeared so young, early twenties at most. His copper skin accented the angular features that appeared carved by the harsh wind and weather. As he drew closer, she could better see his dark eyes and shoulder-length black hair. He wore several string necklaces with colorful beads about his neck. His broad smile brought her comfort as he extended his hand.

"Hi, I'm Kenny Cheshewalla."

"Kenny, thank you for stopping, I'm Elizabeth Wharton." She noted the roughness of his hand, the leathery skin contrasting to the softness of her own. He surprised her when he took charge of the situation.

"Elizabeth, I'd like for you to go sit in my truck, out of the sun while I get these wheels off. I'll put the spare on one and leave the other on the jack while we go into town for the new tires."

She removed her dark glasses, uncovering her brown eyes and carefully maintained brows. Kenny noticed the age lines at the sides of her eyes and the few wrinkles in her face.

"Kenny you are a lifesaver. I don't know what I would have done if you hadn't stopped." Her practiced smile of perfect teeth was something he had not often seen. Elizabeth retrieved a briefcase from her car and retreated to Kenny's truck. The shade and cooling air were a relief from the heat. The hard vinyl seat felt strange to her, accustomed as she was to the more comfortable leather. The interior of the truck interested her with its gritty, basic, and completely masculine nature. She looked at a feathered and beaded amulet that hung from the rear view mirror. In her mind, she wondered how many young women had surrendered to Kenny's charms in this truck. Finally shaking off such intrusive thoughts, she opened the brief case to review information for her evening meeting.

Kenny smiled when he opened the clean and orderly trunk of her car. The spare tire and jack sat unused and in showroom condition. As he set about his work of jacking up the car, the image of Elizabeth dominated his thoughts. Rarely had he seen a woman of such beauty, style, and self-confidence. He pictured her face, with the pale skin, brown eyes, and hair that fell softly to her shoulders. He figured she was '50-something,' twice his age and more, yet he felt an intense attraction to her. He struggled to control his 'young man's lust' and continue with his work.

She looked up from her work to see Kenny walking toward the truck with a wheel under each arm. The buttons of his shirt gapped as his muscles strained under their load. In a moment, he climbed into the driver's seat and smiled at her. His worn jeans were covered with dust and his shirt marked by the dirt and rubber from the tires.

"We'll go into town and get these tires replaced, then you can be on your way."

Elizabeth nodded a mute reply.

Suddenly she felt an inexplicable sadness at that thought. Something inside of her was contented to stay with this handsome, young man. She remembered enjoying the same strength and appeal in her former husband before life's pressures and the years dissolved the bond between them. The truck pulled out onto the road and passed her crippled car.

"So what brings you to these parts? We don't get many strangers around here."

"I have a meeting tonight with the board of Pawhuska Hospital. I sell medical equipment, and they had inquired about an MRI machine."

"You must travel a lot."

"A lot," she confirmed.

"Are you married?"

She was taken aback by the personal question until she saw Kenny's innocent expression. "I was, for twenty-eight years, to a surgeon. I was selling medical equipment when I met him, and we married. After he decided that he'd rather have a thirty-year-old emergency room nurse than a fifty-year-old homemaker, I went back to work. Two years later, here I am."

Detecting the nerve he had struck, Kenny quickly apologized.

"It's all right. We had two children; both are educated, grown, and married. Three grandkids, all are doing well. I could have retired on the settlement, but I enjoy the travelling."

"There must be more interesting places to travel to than Pawhuska."

"Define 'more interesting'."

Her remark caught Kenny unprepared and he struggled to answer. "More glamorous . . . more things to see."

"Certainly, but so what? I've seen glamorous, and I've seen plain. I'll take plain. I go to hospitals and doctors' offices where they buy my equipment just to have the absolutely newest of everything. They buy it, not because they need it, but so they can say that they have it. Half of the time, they don't even have people trained to use it, or doctors who know what it does. I love them dearly and gladly take their money, but there's no satisfaction in it for me. Tonight when I meet with the people in Pawhuska, I know that their doctors need the equipment that I sell, and they will put it to good use. They will have busted their asses to scratch together federal and state grants, local donations. I've known some communities to hold bake sales and other events to collect money to buy what they need. Those are the kind of people I want to work with, and the company I represent does everything possible to see to it that they get what they need. So I'll take Pawhuska over some spoiled, private hospital any time. Now, what about you, Kenny Cheska . . .? Sorry, bad salesman, I forgot how to pronounce your name."

"Che-she-wal-la. The pure Osage words have been lost, but my parents say it meant something like 'too many buffalo' or 'too many cattle'."

"Well to me it means, 'nice guy who rescues stranded woman'." Tell me about Kenny."

"Oh, nothing interesting there. I've lived here all my life. Finished high school and had no interest in college, so I joined the army. I did my four years and came home. Now I work for the Tribal Authority maintaining a few creaky, old oil wells that spit out a couple hundred gallons of crude each month. Just enough to justify keeping them going."

"Wife . . . girlfriend?"

"Nobody serious. I date a couple of girls but I'm really not ready to settle down."

"Are you happy here?"

"I got to see some towns when I was in the army. I even went to Germany. Those people live squashed together in little villages. There's not much land that's not mountains or river valleys. Much too crowded for me. I like it here where there's room to spread out."

"Yes, Kenny, I can't picture you in an apartment building in some big city. You just wouldn't fit."

They pulled into the tire store and Kenny unloaded the wheels. As she looked around, she noticed a men's clothing store just up the street of the small town. Kenny returned, now empty-handed.

"I've got good news and bad news."

"Yes."

"They have the tires to replace yours."

"Yes . . . but?"

"They're $210.00 each."

"That's about right."

Kenny's eyebrows rose. "Elizabeth, I run sixteen-inch, eight-ply tires on this truck and I pay about $70.00 each. I think they're hosing you."

"You've never owned a Mercedes have you?"

"No."

"Just relax, that's normal."

"It's your money."

Elizabeth smiled back at him.

"I have to go pick up some well parts. It'll take me maybe half an hour. Will you be all right?"

"Yes, I'll be fine." He turned to leave when she called after him. "Kenny!" He stopped and turned. "What size pants do you wear?" He looked at her strangely.

"Thirty-six waist, thirty-two long."

"Shirt . . . large?"

"Yes."

"Thank you."

He still appeared baffled but turned and climbed into the truck.

Kenny returned later to find the two wheels with shiny, new, black tires sitting outside of the service bay. Inside Elizabeth sat in a chair working as two older men across the room sat admiring her legs. As soon as Kenny walked in, she gathered her papers into the briefcase.

"Is everything finished?"

"Yes."

"Good. We'll get these wheels back on your car and you'll be on your way."

"Yes, thanks to you."

She followed him out the door where he loaded the wheels into the back of the truck. When he climbed back into the driver's seat, he noticed the plastic bag she now carried.

"Looks like you did some shopping."

"Yes, there were a few things I picked up."

"Oh, OK."

Elizabeth was grateful to see her car still intact on the side of the road. Kenny pulled behind the car and set about changing the wheels. She watched him, kneeling in the dirt and sometimes laying flat to position the jack properly. Sweat soaked his hair, and she could see the wetness marks on the front and back of his shirt. Before replacing the rear wheel, he took off his shirt. Elizabeth's breath caught in her throat. As he lifted and twisted to put the wheel onto the car, his muscles rippled in a symphony to her eyes. His corrugated abdomen ended at the large, shiny belt buckle of his jeans. She watched enthralled as he worked. Finally, he carefully put the jack and spare tire back into her trunk, making sure that the cover was smooth. After closing the trunk, he took his shirt from the ground, wiping his head and chest. She swallowed hard at the sight as he approached. Opening the door, he handed her keys to the car.

"There you are, Elizabeth, good as new. You should be glad you wouldn't be stuck in this truck with me. I probably smell like a buffalo."

"Or 'too many buffalo'." She gathered up her things and opened the passenger door of the truck. "Kenny, I can never thank you enough for what you have done, but I'd like to try. I have a reservation at the Black Gold Motel in town and I want you to follow me there.

His face suddenly stiffened and a lump appeared in his throat. "Elizabeth, you don't owe me anything."

"I understand that. Just follow me . . . please."

"Of course."

She walked to her car and opened the door, releasing a blast of stored heat. The bag and the briefcase went into the back seat, and she removed her jacket before sliding into the seat. The hot leather felt like it was melting her back as she started the car and put the air conditioning to maximum. She used her jacket to protect her hands from the hot steering wheel before closing the door and driving away. She watched in the rear view mirror as Kenny pulled out behind her.

It took just a few minutes for her to register and get the room key. Kenny had parked beside her car. He seemed nervous and stiff as he carried her suitcase along the numbered doors, finally stopping at the correct one.

The room was cool and fresh, and offered a dark shelter from the baking sun. He put her suitcase onto a dresser and watched as she put the bag and her briefcase on a table. When she turned toward him, he looked almost frightened. She methodically hung up her suit jacket before walking toward him. As she approached, she could see him stiffen.

"Kenny you can relax. I haven't killed or eaten a man for over a year. The medication seems to be working quite well."

He finally broke into a smile. "I'm sorry. I've never been alone like this with a beautiful woman before."

She turned to the table and picked up the plastic bag. "Kenny, you all but ruined your shirt and pants while helping me, so I got you some new clothes. I want you to try them on, but I'll be damned if I'll let you do that without taking a shower first."

He finally smiled. "I can understand that."

"So head for the bathroom. After you've showered, I'll hand you in clean clothes and you can dress.

"Am I going 'commando'?"

"You did say size thirty-six?"

"Yes."

"No 'commando,' but I hope you like boxers."

"I don't know. I've always been a 'tight white' guy."

"You'll get over it."

She sat on the bed as he kicked off his boots and removed his socks. He turned and walked toward her as he slowly removed his shirt. As each button opened, she felt her body reaction to him increase. When finally he slid off the shirt in front of her, he seemed to be aware of the effect he was having upon her. Free of the shirt, he held it in one hand.

"Oh, that is better. I hate when a shirt gets all sweaty and sticky." His pectoral muscles flexed and a ripple passed down his washboard abdomen. He offered her the shirt.

It was now she who was stammering. "Eh . . . no, Kenny. Just throw it over there onto the sink."

He tossed the shirt and stared back at her with a grin as he opened his belt buckle and unsnapped his jeans. "Do these go in the sink also?"

"No . . . um . . . you better take those off in the bathroom." She hadn't been so wet since her water broke before childbirth.

"OK." He turned and walked to the bathroom, closing the door behind him.

"Oh my *God!*" she gasped to the empty room.

Soon she heard the water running and the shower engage. She took his new clothes from the bag and laid them on the bed, admiring the black jeans with the decorative stitching on the back pockets and the new western shirt with more decorative stitching. *That should work for an Oklahoma cowboy. Nice but with just a touch of color, attractive but completely masculine.* It was the silk boxer shorts that tilted her balance. She held them in her hand, feeling the soft, slippery silk as it moved over her fingers. *Who am I kidding?*

She kicked off her shoes and she peeled off the no-longer-crisp blouse. The panty hose slid away quickly and joined the growing pile on the bed. In her excited state, she fumbled with the bra, feeling like a fool when she couldn't get it loose, finally resorting to the "spin-it-around" technique. The wet-to-touch panties slid to the floor, and she kicked them away. Leaving only one dim light in the room, she opened the bathroom door and turned off the light. In the darkness, he called out.

"Elizabeth, the lights are out, are you all right?" When he heard no answer, he started to call again. "ELIZA . . . beth!" The shower curtain opening interrupted him and he moved forward as she stepped into the tub behind him.

"You were so dirty I thought you needed someone to wash your back." Her words were slow and sensual.

"Yes, oh, God . . . yes."

The quiver in his voice confirmed his nervousness. She found his tone stimulating.

"Give me the soap."

He turned and fumbled in the darkness to find her hand. Suddenly he reached for her, wrapping his arms around her and pulling her against him. His lips made a clumsy attempt to find hers but instead glanced off her forehead. Calmly she pushed him away.

"Let's get you cleaned up my strong buffalo."

He reluctantly released her and turned around. She began to wash his back and shoulders, allowing her hands to trail down his arms. Her touch sent shivers through him and his muscles involuntarily tensed. Feeling his muscles flex beneath his smooth skin was sending tingles through her as well. She squeezed her legs together to scratch the growing itch.

He extended his arms and leaned forward against the front wall, entranced by the feel of her hands moving upon him. She worked in circles down his back, her hands taking pleasure from the feel of his flesh. When she reached his tightly muscled ass, she could not resist kneading with her fingers. She heard him snicker and felt him flex.

She straightened up again and pressed her body against his. He shivered at the contact. She whispered into his ear, "You have such a nice ass . . . an ass that I'd love to sink my teeth into."

"Please . . . do it!"

"No, my darling, not yet." She pulled her body tightly against his back, reaching around to wash his chest. She soaped with one hand and rubbed with the other as she explored him. Her slippery fingers pinched his nipples until he squirmed. He gasped at her touch.

Her hands continued downward, soaping and swirling his rippled abdomen while she pressed her diamond-hard nipples into his back. Her fingernails carved trails of pleasure into his flesh. The lower she reached, the more his body stiffened. His gasps became louder and deeper. She paused, generously soaping both of her hands before plunging between his legs to capture his balls. His head reared and he cried out.

"Your balls are large, my gallant one. I like large balls that make your sexy, tight pants bulge." She lifted and massaged him as he now gasped openly. She paused again to soap her hands before dropping the soap and grasping his stiffened cock.

He cried out and shook while she slowly slid her hands up and down his length.

"Oh . . . Oh, God . . . it's never . . . I've never . . . Oh, *God!*"

She remained silent but was equally excited. His cock steamed in her hands, its intense hardness an unfamiliar experience after so many years. She felt heady at controlling his wonderful device and relished the feeling of holding it tightly in her hands.

"Your cock is so hard . . . and so long. I love the feel of it."

"Yes! Oh, God . . . please . . . oh, yes . . . OH!"

Fighting her own desires, she released him and backed away, leaving him stunned. She reached through the shower curtain and pulled a towel from the wall rack before stepping from the tub.

"Where are you going? Wait . . . please, come back." She could hear his desperate pleas as she quickly dried herself. In the darkness she felt her way back to the light switch. Her eyes revolted against the shattering fluorescent light that left her squinting back toward him.

"Finish your shower, my love." She closed the door and finished drying the water from her body. Through the closed door she could hear him calling to her.

She wrapped up in the towel and turned off the remaining light, leaving the room shrouded in darkness except for the glow of sunlight escaping around the edges of the window curtain. She stretched out on the cool bed to savor the excitement she had experienced by bringing her handsome, young man to the edge. In her mind she heard his sounds, his cries and pleas, and relived the feel of his body. Her hand trailed between her legs to find abundant wetness and extraordinary sensitivity. Years of marriage had dulled sexual excitement for her, and she was surprised and pleased by this newfound intensity. It had been many years since she has desired a man this badly.

When he opened the bathroom door, the burst of light briefly flooded the room. She lay silently as he approached wearing only a towel around his loins. Even in the near darkness she could see the lust in his eyes. When he stepped between the beds, she rose to meet him and fell into his arms. He crushed her to him, his towel falling to the floor. His lips found hers in a furious storm as his strong hand grasped her hair and pulled her head to his. His tongue forced its way into her mouth and explored it wildly. When finally he loosened his grip they parted slightly.

"I've never had a woman do this to me! I've never wanted a woman so badly!" He began to pull her toward him again, but she surprised him by sitting on the bed, leaving him standing with his rigid cock jutting before him.

She looked into his eyes with a teasing smile. She knew that her actions were making him crazy with desire, and she was enjoying that. She lifted her hands to his chest and slowly drew them along his body until she again held his cock in her hand. Her calm demeanor contrasted to his excited state.

"Have you been with many women?"

"Some . . . maybe four of five."

"Were any of them older than your mother?"

He swallowed hard. "No."

"Did any of them suck your cock?"

He seemed rattled by her unexpected question. "Well . . . uh, one did."

"Did you like it?" She continued slowly stroking his stiff cock.

"Yeah, it was wonderful." Now he was more nervous and excited than ever. She was enjoying her play with this inexperienced young man. Suddenly she stood up and pushed him back onto the other bed.

"Well you're gonna like this a lot better." She knelt between his legs and pushed them apart. Her hand grasped the base of his cock while her mouth lowered to engulf him.

He began to writhe and to moan. He panted frantically, and his head thrashed from side to side. She took him deeply into her mouth and held him while her tongue teased. Then she withdrew very slowly leaving him with his hands clawing the bed covers. When she reached the top, she plunged deeply again and very slowly slid up his length. Now he lay whimpering like a child. After the third time she stopped, sat back, and looked at him.

"Now you will cum for me."

Her head dropped down again and her mouth covered the head of his cock. She began to quickly suck hard and release as she slowly moved up and down over just the head of his cock. It was only seconds before his hips arched, and he howled like an animal. Warm fluid began to shoot into her mouth. When he lay quiet, she slid her lips from his softening cock. She stretched out on the bed beside him and ran her fingers through his hair. His eyes were wet, as if he had been crying.

"My God, Elizabeth, I didn't know a woman could do something like that to me."

She chuckled, "My dear, there are so many things that you don't know."

He turned and crawled up beside her, his face pleading. "Then teach me . . . please. I'll do anything. I didn't know it could be like that."

"There are things that you must discover on your own. With a pretty, young bride who loves you, and whom you love. You will have many years to discover how to please each other."

"I want to please *you*, as you did me."

"And you shall, my love. You are young, and I knew that you would cum quickly the first time. But you will also recover quickly, and we will have a wonderful union."

He grabbed at her towel, ripping it from her body and spinning her up the bed as it pulled loose. He lunged at her, turning her toward him and covering her body with his. His lips were frantic against hers. He rolled back, and his hand found her breast. His touch was clumsy, but his excitement alone began to recharge her body. His lips slid down to sweep up a swollen nipple. His warm lips and enthusiastic sucking sent electricity through her body. He moved downward leaving a wet trail behind. As her body reacted more and more, she thought less about his inexperience and more of his actions. He slid from the bed to the floor before grabbing her hips and unceremoniously pulling her to the edge of the bed. His face disappeared between her legs, and she felt his tongue mindlessly busy against her,

"Kenny . . . Kenny, slow down. What you want to do isn't that hard."

He sat back, looking embarrassed. "I'm sorry. I've never done this before."

"Yes, Kenny, but slow down, just relax."

He smiled and moved forward as she lay back. "That's it Kenny, lightly. Tease me baby, make me want you. Yes . . . oh, yes, like that, now go deeper. That's it . . . long strokes." She twisted her fingers into his hair and guided his head as her hips began to pump. "That's it, Kenny, now up at the top. Find the bump. There . . . feel it? Oh! Yes . . . there. Oh! There! Right there! Oh, Kenny!"

Kenny was learning fast, and her excitement was building rapidly. Soon he was a bird on the wing following only her chorus of, "YES!" when he hit his mark.

As Kenny's rapidly improving efforts continued, she felt the tightening within her body that had become unfamiliar of late. She lay gasping and crying, eyes clamped shut, as the sensations became more intense, a burst of white light sent her crashing on waves of pleasure. Repeatedly the pulses wrenched through her. When finally she lay panting and drained, she felt Kenny crawl up beside her. She rolled to him, and they kissed. When they separated, she stared at him through dreamy eyelids and smiled.

"You learn quickly." She rolled onto her back and spoke to the ceiling. "Kenny, I have to admit that it has been a while for me, and that was pretty damned good."

He propped up on his elbow. "Then we should make sure the magic doesn't escape." His hand slid over to toy with her nipples.

Her hand crept across his body to find his cock stiffening again. It required only minimal encouragement to restore it. She surprised Kenny by rolling over, straddling his hips and placing her hands of either side of his head. Her hips slid down to rub her dripping pussy against his cock. She stared into his eyes and smiled.

"Kenny, do you like to fuck?"

He looked startled when she used the unexpected word. "Yes, ma'am. I love to . . . fuck."

"Then, Kenny, let's fuck." She raised her hips slightly and reached down to position him. She stared directly into his eyes as she slowly dropped down. Her mouth fell into an 'O' while Kenny's eyes became wide and his mouth fell open. She smiled at him again as she settled completely onto him.

"Oh, God, that feels so good!"

She remained silent as she sat up and her hips began to rock. *How long has it been? Three years . . . four years? I had forgotten how good it feels.* She snapped out of her thoughts to look at Kenny below her, his hands now caressing her breasts. He was exciting to her, and now he was filling and pleasuring her.

"See, Kenny, it doesn't have to be fast. Just relax and enjoy it. You have such a nice cock. From the first time I touched it I wanted to feel it inside of me. And now you are inside of me, and I love it."

Kenny listened and smiled. "When I saw you, out on the road, you looked so classy. I never dreamed that I'd have this chance. God, you are *so* good!"

She rode him slowly as they chatted, occasionally exchanging a laugh or a kiss. Eventually she began to feel that exciting tightness.

"Kenny, it's time to change gears." He looked up, mystified by her remark. "Sometimes it does have to be fast and hard, and I want that now." She lifted from him and moved on hands and knees to the edge of the bed. She stuffed a pillow under her head as she raised her hips into the air.

She felt his warmth when he moved behind her, standing on the floor. His hand was on her hip and his fingers parted her. Suddenly, he was inside her again. He slammed into her, holding himself deeply within her. She moaned in response.

"How about this?" Raising and lowering his hips caused her to moan loudly. He pulled back before slamming into her and pounding her frantically. Her cries were broken each time their bodies collided.

"O-H-H-H Kenny! O-H-H-H Y-E-S-S-S!"

He slowed briefly to catch his breath. "Say the word, Elizabeth. Say the dirty word!"

"Please . . . fuck me . . . Kenny!"

"Again, Elizabeth, say it again!"

"Fuck me, Kenny! Oh, God, Kenny, fuck me hard!"

He slammed into her with powerful thrusts that shook the bed. He lifted one foot onto the bed and resumed his assault. This seemed to re-energize her cries. "Y-E-E-E-E-S-S!"

"Maybe just a little deeper." He unceremoniously shoved her forward before he stepped up onto the bed and squatted over her, holding her shoulders with his hands. The sound of flesh meeting flesh filled the room. Elizabeth's hands clawed at the covers while she buried her face into the pillow. Her muffled cries served to drive him on as he crashed faster and faster into her hips. She was unprepared for the intense orgasm that swept through her. Her body convulsed beyond anything she had ever experienced, sending shock waves through her while her muscles clamped down onto Kenny. She felt helpless as her body convulsed. The light and sound disappeared leaving her suspended as if floating.

He buried his hands into her hair and pulled her head back from the pillow. His deep, animal growls drown out her cries as he spilled his seed deep within her. When finally he stopped, she collapsed, and he fell on top of her. They lay panting and perspiring until he withdrew and rolled beside her. He lay facing her, looking at the hair spread partially across her face. He gently reached over and brushed it aside.

"Elizabeth, did I do all right?"

She started to laugh, slowly at first, then harder when she rolled onto her back. Kenny looked confused when each time she turned to him, the laughter would start again. Finally she calmed enough to turn to him and touch his face.

"Kenny, you have no idea how good that was."

Another shared shower washed the perspiration and body fluids away. She sat in her bra and panties, watching him put on the new clothes. He especially liked the silk boxer shorts and the unfamiliar slippery feel against his legs. The pants fit well but she worried that the shirt might be too tight until the last snap closed.

"You're one nice-looking cowboy."

"Thank you, ma'am, and you're the most amazing woman I have ever met. Can I buy you dinner?"

Her face suddenly changed. "No, Kenny, you can't."

He looked stunned. "Why not?"

"Because I'm hosting four members of the hospital board for dinner before my presentation." She walked away and finished dressing.

"How about afterward? You're coming back here aren't you?"

"Yes, but I'm leaving at 5:30 in the morning for a meeting near Dallas."

He looked shocked. "But I must see you again! I must!"

She took his hand. "Kenny, you're a handsome, young man and a gentleman beyond your years, but there is no future for us. Baby, I have a son and a daughter who are both older than you. Kenny, you have to get on with your own life, and some day you'll meet that pretty, young girl that you'll marry. Sweetheart, what we had today was wonderful, but that's as far as it goes. You need to go home now and move on with life."

"I'll never meet another woman like you. You're everything I could ever want."

Her eyes looked into his. "And in fifteen years? When I'm old and gray and my tits hang to my navel, what about then? You'll be in your thirties and have no children. Your parents will be thrilled about that. Kenny, my sweet, young buffalo, we had a fling. An exciting, magical fling that we'll both always remember, but it's over, and there is no more. So kiss me, then gather up that bag of dirty clothes and go home. Somewhere in Oklahoma waits that pretty young girl whom you will love and marry, and you must go find her."

His look of disappointment was heart wrenching, but he kissed her. Then he turned and collected the bag of clothes before walking to the door. At the door he stopped and turned. Suddenly his face changed,

"Wait here, I'll be right back." Before she could say anything he dashed through the door. When he returned he carried the feathered and beaded amulet from his truck. He handed it to her.

"This is called a dreamcatcher. The elders say that it will catch your dreams for you. This one brought me you, and that was more of a dream than I ever could have asked for. I figure that it's done everything it can for me, now I want it to catch dreams for you."

Her eyes began to tear. "Thank you, Kenny. I'll always treasure it, and it will remind me of you."

He kissed her one last time and closed the door as he left.

In the years to come Elizabeth would spend many hours staring through the car windshield as the thousands of miles flew by. Each time she looked at the dreamcatcher hanging from her rear view mirror, she would smile as she remembered her handsome young buffalo.

Get Up, Stand Up!

Madeline Moore

It should be the happiest night of my life, and it would be, if it weren't for the boy on my fire escape, crouched like a gargoyle, with as miserable a countenance as any stone beast I've ever seen.

It's the night before my wedding and even though it's not my first time down the aisle, it'll be the first time I remember. Plus, this time I'm marrying a handsome, intelligent, wealthy man and my dress is amazing. It's *awesome*, in the vernacular of the young.

I'm not young, but he is—the boy, not the fiancé. The boy's cock is as magnificent in its solidity and endurance as a rock. The thought of it makes my cunt ache. I've been spoiled over the last six weeks. I've indulged myself and now I must suffer.

If I wanted to, I could claim perimenopause has played a part in my behavior of late. My girlfriends point to my sixty-year-old boyfriend and his freakin' *commitment issues*. They didn't even have to see Guy to declare him good for me. Of course, they've been cruising in a pack and feeding on the young for awhile now.

I refused to join the cougar brigade. When they tried to make me go a-prowlin' I said no, no, no. I had a much bigger fish to fry. Now look. An engagement ring on my finger, the pre-nup signed and sealed, and a boy on the balcony. My bad. I'm pushing frickin' fifty and I feel ridiculous.

Tea's on! I tap at the glass doors, smile and hold up a tea cup.

"Come in." I mouth the words. "Talk to me." Tilt my head. But I know he won't respond. This is a silent, passive protest. All the talking is done, he said, and he was right. Try as I might, I'll never convince him that our time is up.

His blue eyes stare, two sapphires set in stone. They stream rain and, probably, tears. His black hair is matted to his head. His face is flushed. He's likely sick by now. I have to do something, but what?

They're so stupid, the young. When I told him that he'd said, "I'd rather be stupid than cruel."

The first thing I said to him was, "You come down out of that tree!"

The first thing he said to me was, "You're not the boss of me!"

In retrospect, everything was mapped out in those two sentences. I would play at taking care of him (while fucking him senseless) and he wouldn't do what he was told (while fucking me senseless.)

I sit down at the table, pour a lone cup of tea and contemplate the list of phone numbers I've been staring at for the past few days, ever since he moved from my bed to the balcony. There's the police, known in these parts as La Sûreté du Québec, and a mental health crisis line. My girlfriends. Plus Ash, Mr. Potato Head, Willow, Big Balls—these are names and numbers I nicked from Guy's cell phone the night I brought him home.

All of my fiancé's phone numbers are on speed dial, of course, though there's no need to drag him into it at this late date, now is there? Brian is a developer. He owns undeveloped land all over Canada, and properties all over the world. I'm a physiotherapist. I own my condo.

We met when I treated his bad back at the swish physio centre where I work. We're both bilingual Anglo-Quebeckers so right there we had plenty to talk about. The relationship took off beautifully, stalled after about six months, and then continued crawling forward.

Thus was the state of affairs one fine, summer evening six short weeks ago. I had the sunroof open on my Beetle, enjoying the breeze and basking in the last of a summer sunset. Brian and I were meeting at a posh restaurant for a night of fine dining followed by sex, which I was very much looking forward to. My cell phone rang. When I picked up, Brian said he had to stay late to meet with the Châteauguay contractors about "the kid up the tree."

I'd heard about the protest of course but hadn't paid it much mind. There are plenty of acres of protected forest in Quebec; indeed we have the Châteauguay Conservation Area. It hadn't seemed too terrible to mow down a few adjoining trees to put in a soccer stadium, and Brian stood to make a healthy profit which of course I was all for. But I hadn't heard about this boy until now.

"How long has he been up there?" My voice was modulated. When dealing with Brian my default state is "patient," this is not always an easy one for me to maintain. But it's essential.

"I don't know, months," said Brian.

"That's crazy! What about his legs?"

Brian laughed his evil developer 'nyah ah ah' laugh. "We start clearing tomorrow, kid or no kid."

"But he could be hurt." Tears actually sprung to my eyes. Partially because I was pissed at Brian and not giving him even a hint of it was making my blood boil, but also because here's a young, idealistic man with no one to stand up for him, or to him, and make him stop. When I was young I did my time in the Marches, but I never risked my life, and if I had, someone would've stopped me.

"So dinner's out but if you want to come by around eleven I'd love to see you. Annie, I miss your lovely mouth." Sounds nice, but what he really meant was, "I'll be too tired to make love but you can always suck me off."

"We'll see," I purred. "I miss your . . . mouth . . . too." I rang off before steam could start whistling out my ears. "Fuck you, pal," I hissed.

I drove to Châteauguay.

The protest was a fair distance from the parking lot, which was hell in my heels, which I wouldn't even have been wearing if I hadn't been en route to a date. Pissed. I wasn't talking out loud but inside I was spouting the worst string of expletives I knew: mother fucking cock sucking prick shit dick-for-brains, and such. Words I stopped saying out loud long ago but that lurk in my brain, ready to leap to my lips at the first sign of frustration. Fuck.

Sunset's gorgeous in Châteauguay and I knew the area well. Back in the day we used to build illegal campfires and sit around singing and swilling homemade wine and smoking dope. I was a "back to the lander."

It turned out just as well that I was dressed like a lovely lady. When I reached the stand of trees where the protest was taking place, the police were herding Mr. Potato Head and Fern Gully and the rest of that motley crew off the premises for the night and would've made me leave, too, but I said I was the kid's mom and had come to take him home. They left me alone, under the butternut tree.

I yelled, *"Parle-toi l'englaise?'*

He yelled back, *"Oui,"* which in Quebecois sounds like, "Wah."

Then we had our first exchange, after which he gently pushed a leafy branch aside and stared down at me. Long, dark hair, lanky body all scrunched up. A wistful face, as the young so often have, pale, unlined, sharp cheek bones and a soft, sensuous mouth. Big, baby blues, baby.

I swear. I hadn't been planning anything beyond the rescue, maybe a little physio, a hamburger platter, and a bus ticket or something, until our eyes met. But as we stared at each other in the twilight, something stirred in the pit of my stomach.

"I don't have anywhere to go,' he said.

"You can come home with me," I replied.

He shimmied down the trunk of the butternut to plop in a bony heap at my feet.

"You stink," I said. I leaned low to get his arm around my shoulders and hauled him up. "Pee-yew."

He teetered, almost falling. I clutched him tight. "Yeah, but *you* smell great," he said, as if one cancelled out the other. He patted the smooth bark of the tree. "She's old and disease-free. A real beauty," he whispered. His voice trembled.

I resisted the urge to say, "Just like me." Instead I whispered back, "I know, baby. It's going to be okay."

He really did have trouble walking, which I thought was horrible but he found "trippy." When we got to my place, I helped him into and out of the elevator, into my condo and straight to the main bathroom. I stripped him like a professional, giving no outward sign that the sight of his tight, young flesh made my blood hum and my clit stand at attention. He was too dirty for a bath and too unsteady for a shower so I left him sitting in the tub with the shower pounding down on his head.

I contemplated throwing his clothes into the washer but in the end I bundled them up and dumped them down the trash chute. I searched his pockets first. They were empty. All his worldly belongings, it seemed, were contained in a filthy jute shoulder bag. I made a quick survey of its contents, copping those phone numbers from the cell, happily taking note of his habit of regularly giving blood (clean!) checking his I.D. for his age, (legal!), and tsking over a couple of chubby reefers (as if there weren't a few skinny joints of hydroponic tucked away in my lingerie drawer.)

The story is that when Cher laid eyes on Rob the bagel boy she said, "Have him washed and brought to my tent." I knew that was what I was doing, but I was still pretending my motives were pure.

"Straighten your legs," I ordered when I was back in the bathroom. Yum Yum, sang my body in response to the sight of him stretched out in my tub. Young, young, yum, yum. I averted my eyes.

"Tub's too small."

"Do your best. Now flex your toes. Can you feel it in your calves?"

"Sorta."

"Do five flex and relax reps. Ready? One. Two. Three. Four. Five. Relax."

"You have a beautiful voice."

"*Merci*. Again. One. Two. Three. Four. Five. And relax."

"Will I walk again?"

"Yes."

"Will I play the piano?"

I laughed. "No."

"I'm clean now," he said. "Get in."

"You think?" I looked at him. His cock waved a solid, friendly hello. The sight of that majestic hard on struck me dumb.

We exchanged a long look. Mine said, "I'm almost fifty, *chéri*," and his said, "*De rien*."

So I dropped my button-through dress. I was wearing a black satin push-up bra and thong (sixty-year-old men love a thong on any woman's body, even a perimenopausal one) and lacy stay-ups that were riddled with runs from my trip into the forest.

"Ooh la la," said Guy. His cock got bigger; the head got thicker and started turning purple.

Desire hit my crotch so hard it hurt, like a cramp in my clit.

"I haven't even touched you," I whispered. I was awestruck. Honestly, I hadn't seen a cock that big and hard and blatantly horny since I quit trolling the gay porn sites. As for the real thing?

Years, baby.

"You have a beautiful voice," he said. "And a bootylicious body." He licked his lips.

I stripped off my bra and panties and stepped into the tub, positioning one foot on each side of his slender, boy hips. Then I simply lowered myself onto that magnificent member. I didn't even spread my labia with my fingers, instead letting the heat-seeking head of his dick shove them aside to find my seriously aching hole.

"Christ," I muttered as my opening stretched happily to accommodate him.

Water hit the back of my head and poured over us both.

"*Oui*," (Wah) he said. He sighed like an old man, long and slow, and closed his eyes.

I kept mine open, watching the guileless grin that spread across his face as I slipped down another inch onto him, and another, until he was fully inside of me, encased by the wet satin walls of my cunt. My lips and clit nestled in his straight black pubic hair.

He humped up.

I gasped like a girl.

He did it again. Again. Again.

I started trembling all over. Usually I need a little help to make it all the way to euphoria, by which I mean wine as well as foreplay, but not this time. I was about to start howling, and even the sight of my belly wrinkling between my navel and my pubic hair didn't faze me.

"Fuck it," I hissed. I leaned forward a little, so the head of his cock rubbed my G-spot.

His eyes opened. "Cool," he said. He cupped my breasts, thumbing my nipples.

"How long can you fuck like this?"

He shrugged. "Forever, if you like." He humped up again.

I made a strangled little noise.

Guy let his right hand trail down between my breasts, over my belly, to my mound. Again, his touch was gentle. He used his thumb to make lazy little circles around and over my clit. "Or we can come now, and then come again later, and then come again later and . . ."

"Uh huh." I was nodding in slavish agreement. I shifted to a kneel.

He guided my head to his. Our mouths met in a sloppy kiss, sloppy because we were eager and the shower made it hard to breathe, not sloppy because he was young or demanding. He pressed my head to his skinny chest and he fucked and fingered me until I really did start howling and shaking and grinding and coming like I hadn't had an orgasm in years. I was scared I might squeeze him right out of me with the force of my clenching contractions, but he was as solid as ever inside me.

"Stop!" I tried to wriggle free. "I can't stand it!"

"Sure you can, *chérie*," he murmured. He just kept on going, fingering and fucking me as if I hadn't just come, until I did it again, as hard and long as the first time.

I lay plastered against his chest, half-delirious with delight. "You come!"

"I did," he said.

"So quiet," I marveled. "And gentle. And patient."

"I have to be these things," he replied.

I climbed off him and out of the tub with as much grace as I could muster. Then I helped him out of the tub and wrapped him in a bath sheet. We were both a little unsteady.

"Why?"

"Hmm?" He leaned on me. He looked exhausted.

I leaned back. "Why do you have to be quiet and gentle and patient?"

He looked at me with the sad eyes of a weary warrior. "I think it's going to take a long time to save the planet."

When I woke in the morning he wasn't in my bed. We hadn't had sex again but I knew he'd spent the night, because every so often we'd curled into spoons and I'd felt his hard-on pressed against my bum.

It crossed my mind that he, and possibly my electronics and jewelry, might be gone, but I wasn't surprised to find him in the kitchen, naked, gazing at the screen on my laptop and stuffing his face. I'd fed him all the non-meat stuff I could come up with before putting him to bed, but now he was back at it with a vengeance.

"Morning," he said. "I made tea." He gave me a dazzling grin.

"Great." Who needs coffee when you've got a boy toy in your kitchen? I felt buzzed.

He held up a bubble wrapped package. "Mind mailing this for me? It's a solar-powered cell phone. A prototype. I have to return it now that the protest is over."

"It's over?"

He nodded at the screen. I bent to take a look. My robe slipped open so his face was brushed by soft cotton and even softer skin. He rubbed his cheek against my breast.

There was Brian in a hardhat, amidst a swarm of chanting young protesters. The only girl, presumably Willow, was being dragged away by a cop. In the background, the bulldozers were busy.

"That's my girlfriend," said Guy. He pointed to the girl.

I pointed to Brian. "That's my boyfriend," I said.

"No shit. What does that make us?" He gave me an amused look. "Romeo and Juliet?" He shrunk the window with a click of the mouse. Now we were staring at my desktop, icons dotting a vast expanse of beach. "What's this?"

"Negril Beach. Jamaica. I went after my high school grad, intending to stay for two weeks. I stayed for two years."

"Cool. Rastas are okay," he said. "But I don't believe in God, or Ja, or whatever. I'm a pantheist. You cool with that?"

"I'm cool with you," I said. "I'm sorry about Châteauguay." I closed the laptop. "How can I make it better?"

Guy grinned at me and patted his lap. His erection grew under my adoring gaze, like a time lapse photo: no hands, no mouth, no cunt or ass or even whispered compliments, just my gaze, urging it to thicken and lengthen and pulse with power.

I sat on the table, instead. "Show me you can walk."

Guy stood, walked stiffly but quickly to the tea pot, poured me a cup of peppermint tea and brought it to me without spilling a drop.

"Beautiful," I cooed. I meant it too. The restorative powers of the young always amaze me. I can get three kids walking in the time it takes me to get an oldster prepped to begin.

Guy tugged at the belt to my robe as I attempted to drink my tea.

"Careful." I tipped up a pinky in a display of daintiness and sipped.

He nuzzled my ear. I shivered. He took the cup from my hand. "Tea time's over," he said.

"We gotta be quick," I whispered in his ear, before biting the lobe.

He parted my knees and stepped between them. As the head of his cock touched me, I shivered again. He slid into me as easily as if we'd been lovers forever. When he was fully inside we kissed. Then he cupped my ass with his hands and started fucking me furiously.

"Goddammit!" I shouted when I came, which was like three minutes later. My fingers were busy torturing my clit, just above the tunnel Guy was pounding in and out of. Together we were like some kind of pneumatic machine that thrusts and contracts at the same time. "Goddamn good!"

"Mmm . . . ," was the only noise he made. He froze, his eyes flew open, and that dynamite grin that announced, "I'm coming," spread across his face.

I hugged him tight until he was done.

"I gotta go," I said. We shared a long, lovers' kiss. "Will you still be here when I get back?"

"Want me?"

"Yes."

"Okay. I'll cook. We can fuck before supper."

Work was a blur. I was capable and considerate but the only bone I *really* wanted to manipulate wasn't available. Dumb thoughts like that struck me as hilarious; I kept having to stifle the girlish giggles bubbling in my throat. I wanted to go home, badly. Not because I was afraid he was stealing my stuff or answering my phone (which

I'd forwarded to my cell anyway, as always.) Because I wanted more fabulous sex with Guy. My clit twitched at the thought. My groin burned.

Brian didn't call, which was par for the course. He was punishing me for not showing up at his place like a good little cocksucker. I didn't bother plotting how long to make him stew before giving in (I'm always the one who gives in when we get into one of these little *contretemps*.) He could stew till the flesh dropped right off his osteoarthritic bones, as far as I was concerned.

When I got home the condo was redolent with yummy smells.

Guy was lying on my brass bed, still naked.

"What 'cha doin'?" Suddenly I was shy. Who was this lovely, lanky, blue-eyed boy?

"Slow cookin'," he said. "C'mere."

I started tearing off my clothes.

"Slow –w –w . . . ," he said. "Tonight we take our time."

I paused with my pants halfway down my thighs, not because he'd said we'd go slowly but because the difference in our ages suddenly overwhelmed me. He was used to younger, tighter, smoother, more flexible bodies. I had to counter that with my years of experience. Whatever his girlfriends had done to or for him, I was going to do better—and dirtier. A woman my age doing a boy his age was pretty depraved already. So, if I was going to take a dip in the depravity pond, why not dive in deep and wallow in it?

There were a few things I hadn't learned until my thirties and a few more that I hadn't discovered until my forties. I had a repertoire to draw on that'd more than make up for my few wrinkles and no-longer-quite-so-perky breasts.

Talk was one of them. I stepped out of the pool of my pants. "You have a magnificent cock," I told him.

He grinned and waved the member in question at me. "*Merci.*"

"Inside me, it feels *fantastique.*"

"Is that where you want it? Inside you?"

I leaned forward and doubled my arms up behind me to unhook my bra. That way, my breasts would be at their best when I exposed them. I said, "Later," and flung my bra aside. "For now, I want to get to know it better."

"Help yourself," he offered and tucked his hands behind his neck.

That pose inspired me. Brian liked to play bondage games once in a while, with me the one getting tied up. It'd be a nice change to reverse roles. I went to the dresser and returned with a coil of soft, white cotton cord.

Guy's peepers widened.

"You'll like it," I promised.

He looked a bit uncertain, but he held still while I took a few turns around each of his wrists and looped the cord through a rail of the bed's head. I took a bottle of strawberry-flavored oil from a nightstand and anointed my palms, and then poured more oil over the head of his cock. "It's flavored," I told him. "For my benefit." I let my fingertips run up the underside of his shaft. "So smooth." I gripped him and squeezed. "So hard."

"How else would it be, considering?"

I ignored that and continued with a loose-fingered stroke, base to head. "Nice?" I asked as my palm glossed over his knob.

"Mm."

Good. Forming words was becoming harder for him. My strokes alternated, firm, and then loose. "Your cock, being so thick, will press my tongue down and rub against the roof of my mouth. I'll be able to feel its pulse."

"Cool." The beginning of that beatific grin played across his face. "You're a lot of fun, Annie."

"*Merci.*"

I dipped my head a little, as if about to take him in my mouth. Instead I breathed words onto his shaft. "I'm going to make it *so* good for you, Guy, and when you finally climax, I'm not going to swallow your hot cream."

"Huh?" His eyes, which had started to close, flew open.

I grinned. "Not till I've savored it. I'm going to let it sit in my mouth for a little bit. I'm going to suck air, like you do when drinking a fine wine, to release the bouquet."

"Jesus, Annie . . ."

I stroked him slowly, sometimes full-fist, sometimes just one finger and my thumb. "Look at me," I ordered. My other hand went to my breast. I rolled and teased one nipple to aching hardness. "I like to have my nipples played with."

Guy jerked his arms and shrugged helplessly.

I shrugged too. My hand dropped to my thong. Two fingers slid under it. Guy's eyes followed them. "I like to play with myself too. Do you mind?"

"*Non.*"

"My clit's buzzing. I'm going to make it ready for you."

"And I'm going to make it wait."

"Really?"

"I'm going to make you beg me to fuck you."

My pulse quickened. Such a smart boy. Such a fast learner.

"Good." Still softly pumping his shaft, I stood up and wriggled out of my thong. Two fingers bracketed my sex and spread to fully expose my hot pink nub.

Guy licked his lips.

"You like?"

He nodded.

"And I like your cock, your long, thick, hard cock."

A dewdrop appeared in its eye. I licked it off.

He groaned.

"Nice," I said, and squeezed another drop out. "Yummy."

"Your mouth?" he asked.

"Not yet." My fingertips worked inside my cunt and carried a smear of my juices to his lips.

He tried to follow my hand as it retreated but the cords stopped him. The long muscles in his thighs flexed. "Please?"

"Please?"

"Let me come?"

"Already?"

"I'll still be able to fuck you."

"I know." I smiled. "Guy?"

"Yes?"

"Wanna try something new?"

"Such as?"

"Such as this." I went to work with my mouth, just lips and tongue at first but gradually taking him deeper and deeper.

He chuckled. "Silly, I've had blow-jobs before."

"Mm?" My fingers were still slick with the oil. I rimmed his anus slowly, and then applied pressure.

"Ah?"

I slid in to my first joint, and then my second. There it was, that hard, little walnut. As I rubbed it, his rigid cock thickened just a little more inside my mouth. Ready to burst.

Guy tensed. His shaft swelled in my mouth and started to spurt. His climax seemed to surprise him. A prostate massage will do that.

I sat up and parted my lips, letting him see his cream in my mouth and on my tongue. I drew in a long, steady breath and exhaled.

"Dirty, dirty girl."

I smiled, breathed in again, breathed out, and swallowed. "Now," I said as I released his bonds, "you do me."

He pounced. One minute I was in charge, the next I was helpless. He pinned me to the bed. His arms were surprisingly muscular when tensed. I struggled a little, thrilled to discover he was so much stronger than I.

"Maybe I should tie you up," he muttered. "But there are other ways to tame a filly."

What started as a giggle turned to a moan as he buried his head between my legs. His mouth surrounded my nether lips; his tongue slowly traveled up between them, dipping into the hole and out again and circling my clit at the conclusion of each languid lap.

My legs began trembling. "Please," I whispered. "Stay on my clit?"

He ignored me.

I put my hand to his head, marveling at the texture of his black hair. So fine. So thick. I stroked his head, and any thoughts of trying to make him do it my way vanished. It was perfect. His tongue tasted me, tortured my entrance with shallow thrusts, found my clit, circled, and then abandoned it, only to start again, from the bottom up.

Perfect.

When I came, it was as if he'd pulled the orgasm from deep within me with his lips and tongue. As if he'd sucked it to the surface and set it free.

Before the last paroxysm had shuddered through my body Guy was mounting me, his cock as hard as ever.

"Goddammit!" I whipped my head from side to side as a fresh wave of desire rolled through me.

Guy propped himself up, his hands on either side of my head, and gave it to me good. Hard. Good. So hard. So good.

When I came I locked my gaze with his, using his baby blues to keep me from exploding. Then his eyes closed and he grinned wide and said, "Yesss . . ." and I knew he'd climaxed too.

I wanted to keep him forever but life's not like that. I could clothe him, and feed him, and fuck him, and I did. But I couldn't keep him. Life goes on, things change. Boyfriends resurface, suddenly insecure and looking for a commitment. Life is strange.

And so we come to the eve of my wedding. I dial a number, and in surprisingly little time, Guy's ragamuffin gang shuffles into my condo, led by the suspicious and spunky girl named Willow.

In the end he goes quietly. They convene on the balcony, in the rain, for a few minutes of intense conversation. When they return he's among them. Back where he belongs. Willow picks up his jute bag and slings it over his shoulder.

Guy stops in the doorway. His voice is anguished. "What about love?"

Words fail me. His friends surround him, protecting him. They leave. The door closes.

I step out onto the balcony and stare at the stars and the full moon.

Tomorrow, I'll be a Mrs. Again. The night after that, I'll be gazing at the constellations of a different hemisphere. Brian is taking me to his villa in Negril for our honeymoon. If everything works out between us, it'll be ours. If not, well, then it'll be *mine*.

A few nights after that, I'll slip out to find the taxi stand my friends have told me about. You can get anything you want there, for a price. A ride around the world.

"What about love?" I wink at the moon. "Gonna get me some sweet, young, midnight love."

It might just be the rain blurring my vision, but I swear, the lascivious bitch winks back.

Sally Jean, the Dishroom Queen

Bill Brent

That's how these problems always start: Just some bright idea I had.

It didn't seem like a big deal at the time. I just wanted to make the rent. That's all, honest. It was nearing the first of the month and I really didn't want to explain to Ol' Grizzly Jowls—my nickname for my ancient landlord—why mine was, um, not completely existent.

Plus, it was a grim, raw day, which always gnaws at my crotch anyhow. And there he was, shivering in the breeze: Wastrel-Boy, huddled in the doorway of my—formerly our—apartment building. He looked up at me imploringly as I approached with my key.

"Sod off," I growled, in what I hoped was a fair approximation of his new girlfriend's British accent.

"Can we talk?" he pleaded, the annoyance creeping into his voice. One hand went for my pepper spray.

"I said get lost," I replied, "And don't come back, or I'll go to court." I pulled the lobby door until it locked behind me, grateful that Ol' Grizzly Jowls had re-keyed the front entrance so promptly.

He banged on the glass door, which told me all I needed to know. She'd already given him the bum's rush—nice going, new girlfriend.

As the elevator door shut smoothly, sealing me off from Loser Boy's rage, I prayed that my landlord was out for the afternoon. He'd done enough for me already this month. His apartment was directly above that entrance, and I sure didn't want him to witness my ex's unresolved mama drama.

In any case, I didn't have Slacker Boy's share of the rent. Not that he'd given it to me more than half the time anyhow.

No second chances for loser boys.

So right then, I made up my mind: No matter what it took, I would make the rent by the fifth of the month. Penalty-free living was my goal. No late fees. And there's nothing like pissing me off to get my grim determination going full-bore. According to Mom, I have been this way for every one of my forty-four years.

Double-locked inside, with the chain bolt on, I poured myself a Fresca and sat down to fully digest the reality of my predicament. Even with my check coming in on the third, I would still be exactly three hundred ten dollars short. Sure, I could ask Ol' Grizzly Jowls for some leeway, but that would just give the leering old letch an edge over me. Somehow I knew he would use it to unfair advantage.

No penalties.

I picked up the phone and dialed.

"Hello, Myrna?"

"Sal?"

My frustration came tumbling out. "Yeah, it's Sally. Look, I know it's after hours and all, but it's an emergency. Can you get me some temp shifts doing evenings for the next couple of weeks or so? I don't care where. I'll do anything, even bedpans at the VA. You know the story with my ex. I just need some fast extra cash to make rent and here it is, already close to the first."

I could hear the tumblers clicking in Myrna's mind during the long silence. "Anything, hmmm?"

"Yeah. Seriously."

"Okay. There's usually some slots open in the dishroom out at the University. You know, the one that's by the dorms there? They contract out."

"Washing dishes? Sure, I'll take it."

"Okay. Lemme look up the details as soon as I get in tomorrow morning, and I'll ring ya back, okay?"

"Phone me, text me, send carrier pigeon. Anything. You're an angel."

"Okay. Talk t'ya in the morning."

Myrna pulled some strings and got me started the very next night. Soon I was on the fourth evening in a row of moonlighting. My day job performance was already suffering, and now I had full-blown dishpan hands. As my blisters and calluses increased, my resolve was weakening. I called Myrna during my lunch break.

"Hello, Myrna?"

"Hey, how's it goin' at the dishroom?"

"Oh, you know how it is," I sighed wearily. "My blisters have blisters. I just need a reality check, friend to friend. Tell me again why I don't need a live-in boyfriend to cover half the rent."

"Because when two people try to run each other off the road, it definitely means that the relationship is over."

"Oh. Right. Thanks."

Emotional intelligence has never been my strong suit.

There are four stations to cover in your basic cafeteria dishroom: (1) scraping (grab trays off the incoming belt, remove utensils and receptacles, dump everything else in the trash can); (2) spraying (hit those puppies with a high-pressure hanging hose); (3) sterilizing (load that junk into giant spiked trays for the dishwashing machine); and, finally, stacking (grab the finished trays, unload the cleaned-up crap, and sort it onto the rolling stainless cart for return). Repeat this grubby, mind-numbing ritual ad nauseam.

My co-workers all had mock Mafia names: Scott the Scraper, Stan the Stacker, and Roosevelt the Hose. Roosevelt was a gravelly-voiced, gray-haired guy who had been there since Year One. Dishwashing supplemented his true passion, which was playing jazz trumpet when he could score the gigs. Sometimes he had to trade shifts or take off for up to a week at a time to do a brief tour. Rosie was a relic of the bygone days when positions like his were unionized, or at least grandfathered in by rules and regulations that no longer applied to the likes of us newer, highly replaceable dish-droids.

Since I was the only female on staff, I was promptly christened "Sally Jean, the Dishroom Queen." My middle name isn't really Jean, but Roosevelt had to rhyme everything, so I went along with it. He was always singing at the sink, too, and due to this charming habit, along with being the only staffer remotely close to my age, he won my sympathy and trust.

The other two guys were college-aged. Nothing special, but perfectly fine as counterparts for this grungy gig. The first week, I caught Stan giving me the once-over one time too many. I had to admit, he was kind of cute, but the way he stared at me was pretty off-putting. He wasn't obnoxious about it, just kind of . . . hungry-looking. So I ignored him but filed this away for future reference.

For a lame-ass, just-beyond-minimum-wage assignment, this one sure begged for a lot of accoutrements, none of which were provided by the management, natch.

Everyone else in the dishroom wore cheap tennis shoes. There was rubber matting over the floor by the big sinks, but the rest of that linoleum was slick. At the end of the first week, I saw Scott the Scraper take a tumble—all three hundred fifteen quivering pounds of him. He ripped out his pants and bloodied his shins. He shrugged it off, but I knew that had to hurt—and that I'd be spending part of my weekend shopping for black, rubberized, knee-high boots with anti-skid soles, expense be damned.

Visions of food flying into my eye didn't sit well with me, either. So I also made a trip to Dollar Hardware for a pair of those clear plastic goggles, the kind that house painters wear.

That's where I spotted the clincher: elbow-length, black rubber dish gloves. Thick ones. Fleece-lined. With reinforced fingertips. ON SALE. Oh, I couldn't stop myself. I just had to have 'em. My blister-crazed days would soon be put to rest. After all, there was still about twenty dollars on my credit line.

Next Monday evening, I was back in the trenches, decked out in all my fresh finery. It was a whole new game on now, and so it was Stan the Stacker who first gave me my next Bright Idea—that perhaps I could pick up a bit of extra cash by providing the guys with a bit of a floor show.

"Drool much, Stan?" I taunted him, when he walked in to spot me pulling racks off the sterilizing machine in my new warzone-ready attire.

That was when I realized I'd been bopping my hips in time to Scott the Scraper's boom-box, which was belting out Robert Palmer's "Addicted to Love." The perfect peep-show song.

To make matters even steamier, I had worn a halter top, having discovered that steaming dish racks and heavily covered flesh did not mesh.

"You do look pretty good in all that black rubber," he admitted.

"Then why are you staring at my tits? That's a cotton top I'm wearing."

"Oh. Sorry," he muttered.

"No. It's okay. Frankly, Stan, I'm surprised a guy like you would be interested in an old broad like me." By now, though, I was stretching and rolling my torso around for the full-on effect. Jiggling, even. Stan gulped and I saw his Adam's apple jump. I suspected it wasn't the only lump of his leaping just then.

"I think you're, uh, beautiful," he admitted.

Something about the way he said it. Be careful, Sal, I told myself, you're playing with fire here. A very young, out-of-control fire.

Just then, Roosevelt's old lady came strutting in. The boom-box oozed into Cyndi Lauper's "Time After Time." It was the perfect segue out of this awkward moment. I started swaying to the rhythm, taking Stan's hand and pulling us both into the center of the room. Heck, the shift was winding down anyway, I told myself, so why not a bit of fun.

I rolled my shoulder back and peeled down a strap. Just a quick peek of bare shoulder. Then off came a glove. I held it out to Stan, and he caught on, grasping the other end and using it to reel me in. He twirled me around a time or two, and just for good measure, and I twirled him back. All in good fun, I thought.

Afterwards, I was in the ladies' changing room. Roosevelt's girlfriend was out in the hall when he emerged from the guys' side. She didn't think I could hear her. Probably didn't even know I was on the other side of the hollow-core door.

"Who's that crazy old bitch?" she demanded. "The one with the strip-tease?"

"Just a friend of a friend," Roosevelt replied. "Been working here two weeks now."

Fuck it, I told myself. *I'm done here, and I'm not waiting around.* And so I blew through the door. His girlfriend looked as if she'd just been electrocuted.

"You two have a beautiful evening, hear?" I leaned in and said to her, mock-conspirator-style: "Take him home and make him happy, okay?"

Roosevelt smiled, sly. He winked at me. "See you tomorrow night, friend."

They say that most of the stuff we keep represents not our actual self, but rather, our aspirational self—everything we wish for, everything we hope we will become, the "I" that we want to project into the world for others to see, rather than the small, actual selves that we are.

I wanted everything having anything to do with Loser Boy out of my house. Well, out of my tiny, cramped apartment. See what I mean? The house was aspirational, existed only in my mind. The actual *space* we'd shared was claustrophobic to the point of suffocation. I wanted out, but I couldn't leave. The only way out was to go further in. Can't run, can't stay. So in we go.

The sex had been hot and hard, fast and furious, and frequent enough, right until he moved in. But the moment he moved into my space, standard penetration sex was out. Boy lives on his own; dick gets hard. Boy moves in with me; dick goes soft. That's all it boiled down to, really. Why couldn't we have been honest about it then? Did I remind him that much of his Mom? What was it?

He was on top of me, pushing to get in. Man-on-top, woman-facing-up had always been the least successful position for us. We knew our goose was cooked then. At least, I knew. We would never have a "normal" relationship. If a young stud like Duck Boy, Chicken Boy, what-the-cluck-ever boy, couldn't keep it up—or rather, up and pointed down—and stick it in, then how the hell was the rest of the relationship supposed to work?

I should have quit him then. Or, rather, if I'd been honest with myself, I would have quit him at the first possible moment. Or had his stuff shipped somewhere else. Back to his folks? Anywhere but here.

We tried other things. Anal did nothing for me, but I gave it a game go. It worked great for him, but he was too wide for me back there. Facing up at him; facing down from him; it didn't matter. Spoons? Yawn, next. Standing at the kitchen counter? Those dishes need to be done. I started to resent him for being a slob. Me + Loser + Anal + Kitchen = Angry. Not good.

Talk therapy for couples wouldn't have worked. He was too stupid and I was too smart. Oh, I know it's all but a cliché to say "older-woman-smart, young-stud-dumb," but that is truly how it was.

"You need to not talk while we're having sex," I told him one evening. Smiling.

"Why not?" he challenged me.

"I don't know." Kissing. "Just try not to, okay?"

Silence.

"You don't like it when I talk dirty to you?"

"No. Not really."

More kissing.

"But you used to."

"Things were different then."

"What do you mean, 'different'?"

I bit my tongue. Took a breath. Counted to five.

"Well?"

"You weren't living here then." There, I'd said it.

By then, not only had he stopped, his dick had fallen out. Again.

"You want me to leave, then?" It was a threat, not a serious question. Manipulation tactics. Fucker. Non-fucker.

"Yeah, I do."

The only thing that works reliably against manipulation tactics, in my world, is raw, unfiltered, brute-strength honesty. At least, that's what I think. But there I go again, thinking.

So that left oral sex. His dick in my mouth. More tolerable than anal, but never long enough to get him off. I had no stamina for oral. He still ate me out, but he didn't like that anymore than I liked anal, I could tell. So instead, I started to get off on the thrill of making him do something he didn't really enjoy. Sign number two that I should have just quit us then. Why do I ignore my intuition? Maybe I'm just not a relationships gal. Fuck.

It's always been a matter of economics, you know? Always. How many jobs have I been fired from because I asked one too many questions, the wrong question, the right question to the wrong person at the wrong time?

Washing dishes was brainless. Therefore, perfect. Too bad it totally sucked blue-ass donkey balls as a career track.

These guys knew they had me with the over-exposed Eighties music. The next night, Scott's boom-box was playing "Legs" by ZZ Top when I walked in. Oh, man, I had to put an end to this, toot sweet. I smirked and managed to keep from cracking up.

"Listen, I'm just here to do a job, okay? Just like you."

They actually looked crestfallen.

"Oh, all right." I glanced into the hall, just to make sure the coast was clear. "Start it up again."

Start with the strut, I thought. *The sexy strut is always the first and most important part of every routine. It's all about being provocative.* I'd learned a few things about sensuous stripping in a Learning Forum workshop many years ago. *Now work those gloves.* It was all coming back to me now. I tell you, it was tough to look slinky, peeling off those thick rubber gloves, but I managed. My butt bounced in time to the boom-box. Okay, maybe the butt-bouncing was a bit more provocative than I'd intended to be, but it felt fun and fine. The instructor had told us that you have to give any routine your own personal stamp.

They applauded when I was finished. I curtsied, and then shook my no-longer-rubberized finger at Scott: "Just don't ever play 'Private Dancer,' or this shtick is over for good."

I had to admit it was fun. Some small part of me craved the attention too. Hell, if I couldn't afford nice stuff anymore, if I couldn't have a lover . . . at least I could have semi-cute, young, male admirers. Life could be worse, I told myself. Somehow I knew that Stan was making a beeline for his bunk and whacking off a load every time the shift ended, but what harm was in it, really?

Believe you me, it was not easy to strip without heels, exposing flesh below my shoulders, or any other number of girlie-show basics, but I did okay. Until I walked in at the end of the week to find the boom-box missing.

"Scott's out through next week," Roosevelt informed me. "Laid up in bed. Twisted his ankle on the steps!"

"Oh, well. In that case, no show tonight, guys. There's no box to work with."

And still, I had dragged in my own boom-box to Monday's shift. Music-free Friday had been a bore. I guess we'd all gotten used to me.

By now, I had a fairly well set routine, although I varied it a great deal. For instance, I liked running my hands over my trunk and ass. It may not sound sexy when I say it like that, but let me assure you, there is not a centimeter of flesh on my curves that does not belong there. Pushing forty-five, I doubt I could have held down two gigs otherwise.

One shift, I doffed my hairnet and tossed it at Stan the Stacker. He sniffed it, not entirely in jest. Hey, just one more prop to fling into the audience, right?

"I'm gonna take this home and send it to my mom right away for laundering," he joked.

"Then I'll just make it dirty again," I purred. "Why not put that postage money in my tip jar instead?"

I held out the plastic, foodservice peanut butter jug I'd prepped for the occasion. I knew that at some point, it would make more sense to start charging for this routine, and that night had finally arrived. Would they go for it? There was a long silence.

Then two reluctant bucks went into the slotted jug.

"Happy now?" he leered.

I just put my finger tip into my mouth and spun around.

Bolder now, I carried the peanut butter jar over to Dan, Scott's temporary replacement. "Put up or shut up," I sweetly smiled.

"Huh?" he replied.

"It's a game around here," Roosevelt explained. "Our Lady of the Sterilizer puts on a bit of a show for us at the end of each shift, and now I guess we tip her." Rosie was playing along! Maybe it was a musician thing.

So I traced my rubber-gloved finger down Danny's torso. He reached into his pocket and pulled out a soggy dollar bill, placing it into the tip jar.

I visited the dollar store to stock up on cheap hairnets. I started playing with my hair a lot more during my set. I guess I do have great hair. Personally, I'm not so crazy about it, yet it has always seemed to drive guys wild.

My fan base started showing up during my third or fourth week of dish duty, just one or two at first, every several nights, but then more steadily. Just the guys' friends, mostly from the dorms. They sneaked in through the back door, which Roosevelt had somehow managed to de-alarm, starting about twenty minutes before the end of the shift. By twenty till nine, we were just finishing up, and the rest of the staff had cleared off. It was left up to us to kill the lights and lock up.

By ten minutes to, the dishroom took on a completely different feeling. A speakeasy vibe, like from an old gangster movie, with about ten guys, and occasionally a girlfriend or two. Maybe those guys hoped their girlfriends would warm to the idea and put on a private show later, just for them? Scott had assumed bouncer duties, once he'd returned. He would put up the plastic rope and posts that we sometimes used earlier in the shift to keep the other staff out, whenever there was a major mop-up. Every guest had to literally toe the line.

Two songs a night, and then I was done. That was my entire set, usually running just under ten minutes. There was three extra minutes for an encore, if the crowd demanded one, and then we were outta there.

What had started out as a lame joke about some ditzy old broad behind the scenes in the dining center had turned into a pass-the-hat fan club. I couldn't believe the tips. Twenty, thirty—one night I broke fifty dollars in tips. I locked myself behind the ladies' room door, counted it, and cried.

Looking back, I cannot imagine how we got away with this for as long as we did. Pure dumb luck? The sheer unreality of the setting, I suppose. Who'd a thunk?

Roosevelt had a lot to do with it, I think. Foodservice has a blinding turnover speed. Yet Roosevelt had been on staff for years and gained each successive manager's implicit trust. The old guy had charisma and confidence to burn, along with the cred that comes bundled with gray hair. Why should any manager worry, much less hang around until the dishroom clowns were finished? As our evening shift supe, Rosie had a lot of clout. Plus, he seemed to have eyes in the back of his head for anything amiss.

Yet nothing seemed amiss the night we got caught. Luckily, it was a slow night. Still, any unauthorized visitors were grounds for instant dismissal. I knew that.

I posed with my hand angled daintily atop my bent knee, propped against a rolling dish cart I had locked the wheels on.

I pouted. My hand went to my butt, elbow pointed at a rakish angle.

When I arced backwards across the cart, the guys went wild. Scott held out a dollar and I went for it, shoulder shimmying up, as my boots gripped the floor securely.

Walk as if you're on a tightrope. Step up and bend at the knees. That shows off the calves.

One foot in front of the other, and then get the hips involved.

The guys looked *very* involved. I knew right then that I had them by the balls.

Use the cart like a big feathered fan. Put your foot up on the first shelf.

Place the body in beautiful, angled positions to show off its contours.

Run my hands up my leg, across the fishnet, plucking a bit at the string and teasing the guys further. Roll the shoulders back, now. The guys were clapping in time to the beat. Not too fast, guys.

Roll the hands up the body, above the head, pose, and show off the torso.

Elbows akimbo, lean back against the doorway, arms above the head. The guys stomped, cheered, and whistled.

I lay back across the front of the sterilizing machine. The stainless steel strip. *Pose with one foot on the stool. Now step up.* Last rack of dishes emerging from the guts of the machine, the dark, watery tunnel. Through the rubber flaps now, and out the mouth of the machine.

Perfect.

I took the cue to straddle the opening with both legs spread apart, so that that last rack had to emerge between my outstretched legs. Glistening, still steaming, it inched out slowly as if I were giving birth to the damned thing. As I shoulder-shimmied, I'm sure I looked more than a bit ridiculous. As if giving birth to a tray full of Melmac wouldn't. But then again, I've noticed that whatever we women perceive as ridiculous regarding the act of sex—and all that it touches—most men find highly arousing. Go figure.

And that's when Don, the evening manager, walked in. Fuck! He'd never stayed past eight-fifteen before.

I stood up straight and kicked the machine to a stop by pressing my toe against the big button. "Hey, there, Boss," I said in my most confident, comfortable voice.

You can bluff your way out of any situation in life, I have found, if you act like you know what you are doing. Stripping is about teasing a reaction out of your audience. It's not only about how you move, it's about the look, and the energy. Good advice to remember, wherever you walk in life.

"What the hell is going on here?" he demanded.

"Just having a bit of fun," I purred. "You can see that the last of the dishes are clean."

"Get down off that thing."

"No problem, Boss." I smiled sweetly and dismounted. I hoped he wouldn't notice the big bucket of bucks.

The only thing to do was to go with it. Go further in. So I started bumping and grinding like my job depended on it, which quite probably it did.

I think the only reason I could go so brazen on Don was because I just didn't care. My desperate need for this job a few short weeks ago was, by now, strictly for a lark. I'd grown to like the guys, and yeah, I would miss the tips, but frankly, if I was fired, I'd just go looking for another dead-end job. My rent was paid.

"Hey, lighten up, Mr. Don. We're just having some fun here. That's all, honest." I knew I was repeating myself, but who cared. I figured he wasn't listening anyhow.

"So what about this?" he demanded, pointing at my peanut butter bucket.

"Oh, do you have a problem with me making a few extra bucks on dishroom time? I've got an elderly mom to support, you know." That was a lie, but it popped into my head. I always say, whenever your ass is in a sling, run with anything that pops into your head.

That's when I realized that the music was still playing, and my butt was still bopping. Nervous habit. Go further in, then. I toned down my moves, though. I marched in time to the beat. Shook my hips to the ka-choom, kuh-kuh-chee!, but not too much. Shook my shoulders and did a few moves I dimly recalled from the "Rhythm Nation" video.

"Turn that thing off," he snarled. The boom-box snapped off. Scott opened the emergency exit, and the guests scattered into the night.

I surrendered my hairnets and gloves to the Dishroom Gods. Of course, Myrna and I had a grand old laugh about the whole affair, once I called her and explained what had gone down. Luckily, we had just found me a better deal on an apartment, thanks to the Old Girls' Network.

"I don't know how you could stand it for so long anyhow," Myrna laughed over salad and iced teas, after I'd settled into my new digs. "Women always hate that gig. It's that creepy young guy. They all complain about him."

"Oh, he's just got a thing for older women," I shrugged. "I think he'll get over it someday. Or not. He seems a little tortured about it.

In any case, if it hadn't been for him, I wouldn't have gotten the bright idea to turn the dishroom into my own little burlesque theatre. Still, I can't hold that against him, really, even if he did turn out to be sort of the Judas of the Dishroom."

"Cafeteria food is its own form of torture," Myrna replied. "The horrors of dorm food and mandatory meal plans. Oh, the stomach-cringing stress."

"Yeah, I was always a microwave dormie myself," I admitted. "I never ate that crap while I was working dishroom, even when I was running late from my day job. I always kept some healthy snacks in my bag."

"Well, in that case, I hope your taste in boyfriends improves to match your taste in food," Myrna cracked.

"I can't help myself, Myrrh. I just know there are some young puppies out there, worthy of my bosom . . ." Oh, how we both howled at that. "Maybe someone should develop a Learning Forum workshop on how to keep it fresh with the young dudes. It's a thought. There's gotta be a market for that."

"It's a thought." Myrna could see the wheels turning. "Oh . . . don't you *dare*."

"Hmmm. Now, I'll bet that's one way I could meet some hot young studs."

Myrna scoffed.

"You know, the kind who are well-adjusted!"

She leaned back, looked at the ceiling, and just shook her head.

Just some bright idea I had. That's how these problems always start.

A Taste of Ginger

Adriana Kraft

"There's a handsome young man checking you out!"

"Where?" Ginger Nelson didn't dare look around the sweeping bar to where Annette James pointedly stared. It wasn't Ginger's idea to come to this swingers club. That was Annette's doing.

Apparently it was one of Annette's frequent weekend haunts. Ginger thought she knew her co-worker better than that, but they hadn't really started doing things together socially until recently, after her divorce. This was why she'd agreed to this crazy idea in the first place. Today marked the final divorce decree. She was a free woman again—at fifty-five.

"Don't be so uptight," Annette cautioned. "He's a hunk and he's really looking you over."

"He's probably looking at you," she groused, staring into her wineglass.

Annette giggled. "No way. He doesn't even know I'm here. You could at least peek at him. That's why we're here, to look at the guys."

"That may be why *you're* here." Ginger groaned. "I know. I know you didn't force me to come with you tonight. But—but this is different than I expected. The music is too loud. People are making out right by the bar. They're all so young. And I feel so old." She tried not to wail.

"Nonsense! You're overreacting. There are plenty of people here our age. But don't dismiss the younger guys so quickly." Annette squeezed her friend's elbow. "I bet the guy undressing you at the end of the bar doesn't have a single gray hair on his body."

Frowning, Ginger cocked her head sideways enough to peer out the corner of her eye and catch a glimpse of the far end of the curved bar. "I don't see anyone. I only see a guy with a couple girls draped over him."

"Exactly. And his eyes are on you. Think of the girls as accessories. They're no competition. Not with you."

"I'm old enough to be his mother," Ginger gasped. "And those girls are hot. If they were any hotter, the skimpy outfits they're wearing would go up in smoke."

"And you don't think you're looking pretty damn sexy?"

Ginger tugged on the short skirt that had climbed way above mid thigh. She knew better than to touch the satin blouse that dipped dramatically between her boobs. She just hoped to God they stayed in place. There was no way to wear a bra with this outfit Annette had talked her into. She wouldn't feel much more naked if she was naked. At least she'd inherited her mother's boobs—very little sag for her age. That was more than many of the younger women could say. That was quite obvious.

"Oh my," Annette purred and waved at a blond man who'd just entered the bar area.

He waved back, beamed a smile and headed their direction. Ginger groaned again. The guy looked like he'd just showered after playing a game of baseball. Mid-thirties, maybe. He was taking his time getting across the room, stopping to pat a guy on a back or give a girl a hug. The man was a social gatherer. Not her style. Not her type. And way too young. She panicked for a moment thinking maybe Annette had set her up with the guy.

"Hey, babe," the blond fellow said, kissing Annette on the cheek. "Didn't know for sure if you'd be joining us tonight."

"I'm here," Annette said breathlessly. "Jack, this is my friend Ginger. This is her first time at the club."

"Welcome to the club," Jack said, grinning easily. "Didn't know you had a girlfriend." Jack nuzzled Annette's neck. She tipped her chin down and moaned softly.

"Not that way," Annette said at last. "We work together at the university. We're celebrating. Her divorce is final today."

"Congratulations."

Ginger flinched. He was shaking her hand before she knew it. "Thank you," she murmured.

"Sexy outfit." Jack glanced back at Annette. "So you want to play?"

"Of course." Annette slid off the barstool. She glanced from Jack to Ginger. "You do know the bedrooms with the round beds we saw on the tour aren't just there for people to take naps?"

Unable to speak, Ginger nodded. She gulped and glanced quickly around the bar. "You're going to leave me here? Alone?"

"You're a big girl. You can handle it. Or," Annette arched an eyebrow, "you can come along and watch."

"Hell," Jack interjected, "she can join in if she wants to. There's plenty of room on the bed."

Ginger blinked. Annette wasn't saying no to Jack's proposition. She stood there with the oddest grin. *Oh my God.* Ginger swallowed hard. "Maybe another time," she demurred. "I'll stay here. You won't be all night, will you?"

Annette laughed. "Jack may look virile. And he is. But he's not an all night kind of guy. Give me an hour or so. You okay with that? I didn't know if he'd even be here tonight."

"I'll be okay. Like you've said many times, I'm a survivor. You two go have fun. I'll be waiting when you're done."

"Thanks," Annette said over her shoulder as she led Jack out of the bar toward one of the bedrooms.

Why did she feel like she'd just sent the kids off on a date—a racy date—warning them not to be late? Because that's what she'd just done, damn it. She nodded at the bartender to refill her wineglass. She might as well enjoy what she could. A fine wine usually helped calm her soul.

She tried not to think too hard about what Annette and Jack were up to. On the tour she'd seen the bedrooms with round beds and ceiling mirrors. This place was definitely set up for swingers out for a night of fun. She'd never seen a sex swing before, although she'd heard of them. It had been unoccupied so she still didn't quite know how it worked.

And then there was a Sybian that made her vibrators look like they were made for amateurs. A redhead had been using the Sybian as if she was riding a bull or a young stud. She'd risen upon and down enough so the observer could see the machine's pulsating dildo work its apparent wonders. The girl was clearly an exhibitionist. Ginger hadn't realized she might be a voyeur until she began to cream watching and listening to the girl. Annette had suggested giving the machine a try once the redhead finished, but Ginger shook her head. No way in hell would she get on that apparatus. She sipped her Cabaret Sauvignon. Maybe she could rent one. Maybe in the privacy of her bedroom. It did look like a wild ride.

Sipping her wine, Ginger stole a peek down the bar. The dark-haired guy and the two hotties had gone. She snickered—Annette thought he was interested in *her?* So much for that theory.

"I appreciate a full-bodied . . ."

Startled, Ginger nearly slipped off the stool. A strong hand settled on her shoulder, steadying her. Embarrassed, she stared up into dark brown eyes. "Oh, my. Where are your girlfriends?"

She hadn't said that. Had she? Puzzlement turned to humor on his face. Yes, she'd definitely made a fool of herself. Well, it wasn't the first time.

"May I sit down?" The voice, while well modulated, wasn't as deep as she'd expected.

Trying to seem self-assured, she nodded. From where he stood, he had a clear view down her too-flimsy blouse to watch her nipples blossom. Well, at least he couldn't see her toes curl or her loins tighten. She shut her eyes briefly as he pulled the stool out next to her.

She did have at least an hour to kill. There wasn't anything wrong with sharing conversation with the guy. She thought of Annette and Jack. There wasn't anything wrong with what they were doing either, but that was them and this was her. She'd recognized that look on Annette's face when Jack invited her to join them. Ginger had her share of girl/girl flings in college to know what was behind Annette's smile. Why hadn't she noticed that before? Wouldn't Annette be surprised to learn she was much more attracted to her than she'd ever be to a guy like Jack?

"Hey." A knee grazed her bare thigh. "I know I can be boring at times. But the ladies usually don't go to sleep on me right away."

Ginger's eyes popped wide open. "I'm sorry," she stammered. "I didn't mean to ignore you."

"You seemed to be doing a fairly good job of it. Can we start over? I'm Nathan Samson. I haven't seen you around here before. I've noticed your friend in here several times, but not you. I think I would've noticed."

Ginger shook his extended hand, aware that he was flirting. She hadn't been flirted with by anyone for decades. She'd had plenty of men before Harold, but not since they became engaged. It took her way too long to discover Harold had been playing around for years. And he'd finally found his "true love"—a twenty-year old cheerleader at the university. She didn't doubt the girl would have Harold hung out to dry before long. But that was his problem, not hers.

"So you do have a name?"

"I'm sorry. Again." She heaved a sigh. "I'm not accustomed to talking with strangers like this. My name is Ginger." She hesitated. "Let's just leave it at that."

Nathan nodded. "That's fine. Ginger is a nice name. As I said when I first tried to get your attention, I appreciate a full-bodied wine."

Feeling herself flush, Ginger gave him a small smile. She'd thought he was talking about her, and he knew it. "Yes, a quality Cabernet is definitely full-bodied and robust. So you're a wine connoisseur?"

"I like wines." His lips curled into a smile. "I'm a connoisseur of most things full-bodied."

"Oh." Her cheeks heated. He *had* been talking about her. It was a long time since she'd engaged in this kind of repartee. Too long. She decided to take up the offensive. Wasn't that supposed to be the best defense? And she suddenly felt the need for a good defense.

Nathan Samson was indeed easy on the eyes—dark hair, Roman nose, solid chin, and penetrating brown eyes. How could he be so young? How young was he? Way too young. Annette had led a mid-thirties guy out of here just minutes ago. But that was Annette. She swallowed. And this was her. And there was no misreading the lust growing in those brown eyes that didn't hide their appreciation for a particular full body—hers.

"Where are your girlfriends? I thought they'd have you in one the bedrooms by now."

He chuckled. "Why would you think that?"

"They were draped all over you. Isn't that every guy's fantasy— two girls satisfying his every whim?"

"Whoa, lady. Draw your talons back in." He gave her a brilliant smile. "I do like a woman who isn't afraid to use her fingernails but . . ."

She scowled taking in his meaning.

"Besides. That really depends on the women."

"Huh?"

"Being with two women can be fantastic, but they have to be the right two women."

"Oh." She glared at her wine. She'd gotten them into this discussion. How could she get them on safer ground? "How old are you?" She'd blurted out the question without warning—herself, or him.

"I'm twenty-five." He pursed his lips. "Not that it matters, but how old are you?"

"Fifty-five," she squeaked. "God, I *am* old enough to be your mother."

His fingers slid along the top of a bare thigh. She swallowed hard but couldn't find the energy to pull away.

He leaned over close to whisper in her ear. "Ginger, when I look at you I don't see my mother."

She didn't have to look to know he was again looking down her blouse at her breasts. Damn Annette. No, she'd wanted to attract a man tonight—or at least, to tease one. This was her night to howl. But she'd wanted a silver haired man with a silver tongue. Not a boy younger than her youngest child.

"And," Nathan continued, "I love how your nipples have grown twice in size since I've sat down here. Maybe they're not as disinterested in me as you think."

She pulled away and laced both hands around her wineglass for security. She had a decision to make. How far was she willing to go with Nathan the Youngster? His hand slid up her inner thigh. She tried to breathe. How could she have forgotten his hand? She'd been so eager to get away from his whispered words and warm breath.

"Why did you come to the club?" he asked softly. His hand stopped. "Don't you find me a little bit attractive? I think you're the most gorgeous woman in the house."

"But I'm so old," she protested, half heartedly.

"I love playing with an attractive, sexy, mature woman. Don't you want to play with me?"

She couldn't prevent a giggle. "Well, I can't argue with the mature part." She peeked around the room. As the night wore on more couples were becoming quite bold. More than one woman had her boobs bared and was grinding her crotch against a man. She wet her lips watching one woman gyrate between two men—one in front and one behind.

Following her line of sight, Nathan coaxed in her ear. "They're having fun. So can we." His hand started moving higher again.

She grabbed his hand before he found what he was searching for. "Not here. This is too public."

"Of course." Nathan stood and took her by the hand before she could change her mind. "I know a room that has plenty of privacy and is classy, befitting a lady like you."

Ginger inhaled and took one more swallow of wine before throwing caution to the wind. She rose up on her toes to whisper in his ear. His fresh clean smell only served to embolden her.

"Hope you won't be disappointed. I've never done anything like this, so I'm not promising anything." She swirled her tongue around his ear. "But if you want to play with an old lady, who am I to stop you? I may be a little rusty, but I think I remember how the game is played."

She knew it had to be the wine talking, but she didn't care, not now. Maybe in the morning. But probably not even then. Playing with Nathan Samson had to be better than spending the night staring at her divorce decree.

She leaned into the young man with his arm around her and let him guide her from the bar. She'd been married to Harold for over thirty years. Now she was about to step out into a sexual void with a man who hadn't even been alive when her father walked her down the aisle to hand her off to Harold.

Ginger squared her shoulders and boldly slipped an arm around Nathan's waist. She didn't need an escort this time. She wasn't looking for marriage or 'til death do us part—which had been a bad joke. She squeezed Nathan and blinked at the hardness of his abs. Tonight was hers for adventure. A sexual romp. No more, but certainly no less. She was ready—no, eager—to test a younger vintage wine. She only hoped she could keep up with her young charge.

He stopped in front of an open doorway. "You ready?"

She peered into the dimly lit room. The covers of the round bed were invitingly turned down. Tentatively, she stepped into the room. An uncorked bottle of red wine stood on a nearby stand. She recognized the brand of the pinot noir was from a prestigious winery. "The most sensual, erotic of wines," she murmured, waiting for Nathan to close the door. "You weren't counting on me turning you down, were you?"

"Perhaps unbridled optimism is a sin of youthfulness," Nathan admitted. "You haven't answered my question. Are you ready—for me?"

"Maybe more than I realized," she whispered, reaching for the top button of her blouse.

"No," he said, covering his hand with hers. "Let me. I want to unwrap you slowly like the quality gift you are. Thank you," he whispered, kissing her brow, and then her eyelids.

At last his mouth slanted across hers. She rose on her toes, eagerly accepting his kiss, deepening it, letting him to know she suddenly wanted him as badly as he wanted her. Yes, she was ready. Past due, actually.

Ginger lay on the luxurious round bed staring at the ceiling through half closed, half clouded eyes. Had it been only minutes or hours since they'd entered the room? She hadn't anticipated such patience—no, such sweet torture—from her young lover. After removing her clothing with great care, Nathan had escorted her to the bed. She'd lain on the bed and watched him strip for her. She'd gasped at the sight of his cock springing forth in search of a home. While he was above average size, it was its eagerness bobbing about searching for her that had her mesmerized.

She'd leaned over and curled her fingers around it, pleased at the stifled groan emanating from Nathan's lips, but he had shaken his head and pried her fingers loose. And then the nibbling had begun— from the top of her head to her toes. She'd whimpered without embarrassment as he explored her entire body as if he were determined to memorize its contours, its textures, its taste. He'd turned her over and back again.

Catching their breath, they'd sipped pinot noir from the bottle. Glasses seemed like an unnecessary barrier. And then she'd bathed Nathan with her tongue as thoroughly as he had her. His pecs and abs were amazingly firm. Although she hadn't dwelt there long, his tightly veined cock had filled her throat nicely. But the most memorable moment, the one she'd keep with her long after this night had finished, was the moment when she'd gently slipped one of his testicles into her mouth and he'd called out her name. Did a man ever have a more vulnerable moment?

More wine had passed their lips since then and now she laced her fingers through Nathan's dark hair as he suckled a breast while rhythmically probing her interior heat with two fingers. She couldn't remember if she'd ever been this turned on, this open. She'd worried whether she'd have enough natural lubrication. By the time he'd finished nibbling on her flesh the first time around, she'd been seeping like an underground spring. And there was no sign of slowing down.

"Oh," she moaned.

His fingers quickened. "You've had plenty of little waves." He lifted his head and smiled. "Come for me. I can't wait any longer. I want to hear you come for me."

Unable to speak, she nodded. He placed an index finger across her lips. She took it into her mouth and suckled. His fingers in her vagina curled upward, searching. She lifted her hips to help him find what they both were searching for.

"Oh, my God," she screamed, bucking against his fingers. She thrashed from side to side.

Nathan never paused. "Come for me, Ginger. Come for me."

"Good God, I am. For you." She did her best to keep her eyes open and locked on his as he watched her intently. The explosions began as searing ripples. She held out her arms. "I can't do this alone. Hold me, please."

He cradled her with one arm while still probing her most sensitive spot. She ground against him searching for more. Unhinged, uninhibited, she demanded more. Her squeals pierced the room. Her body shuddered with a rolling orgasm. She couldn't feel his fingers. She gulped. There they were again, tapping her core like they knew she was still building. "Holy God," she screamed, digging fingernails into Nathan's back.

"Come for me, Ginger," he insisted. "Don't hold back. Let go."

"Uh. I am. Uh, huh." She couldn't keep her eyes closed. She strained against him, and then she released. Built up tension, built up hopes and dreams of years past . . . even built up thoughts escaped as she flowed over his fingers—the keys that had helped her find release. At last she managed to murmur, "Enough."

She drifted away reveling, relishing. She wasn't sure when he'd withdrawn his fingers, but when her focus returned he was cradling her with both arms.

Repeatedly, he kissed her forehead. "You were wonderful."

"That was pretty amazing." She felt her cheeks warm. Fucking him could hardly be more intimate than this moment.

He offered her the bottle of wine. She sat up against the headboard, sipped and then swallowed deeply. A mixture of cherries and chocolate flavors swept across her tongue. She looked up and frowned at Nathan, who was ripping apart the casing of a condom. "Don't you want me to do you? Orally?"

He shook his head and reached for a tube of lube on a stand. "I may be a patient man, but," he gave her a mischievous grin, "if you get your warm mouth around him one more time he's going to be a goner. He can wait another time for that."

"Another time?" She arched an eyebrow. "You think we're going to be together again?"

"Why not? You're enjoying yourself, aren't you?"

"Of course I am. This is beyond my dreams."

"Then why wouldn't we see each other again?"

Her breath caught somewhere in her windpipe. She shook her head. "I hadn't thought about it."

Nathan stretched out beside her. His encased penis stood so tall and proud, Ginger thought maybe it was this image that had inspired the saying *strutting like a proud cock*. She reached out and patted the object of her attention. "This isn't a good time for thinking."

Chuckling, Nathan scraped his knuckles across her cheek. "From what I gather, it's been quite a while for you. Why don't you get on top? Then you can set the pace."

"Me?"

He nodded. "I want to watch you fuck me."

The word *fuck* unsnapped something deep inside her. Her pulse raced. Without speaking, Ginger moved to straddle him. Rising up on her knees, she positioned Nathan at her entrance. His eyes widened as she slowly started to take him in.

She blinked. Even as turned on as she was, she had to go slow.

"Damn, you're tight," he moaned.

She closed her eyes and settled a bit more. She didn't want to break the mood by telling him that her three kids had each been delivered Caesarian. And now this young man was the beneficiary. She paused, moaned and gave him a weak smile.

"Over halfway," he murmured. "What a beautiful sight."

She nodded. "She'll open for you. It has been a long time. Oh my," she muttered settling astride him. "There."

"You got him!"

She smiled at Nathan's exuberance. Had he really doubted she could handle him? She shifted from side to side. Carefully, she flexed upward a bit and let herself slowly sink back down. Satisfied that she had Nathan where she wanted him, she leaned back to give him an even better view. "Now watch carefully. I want you to watch me fucking you."

His nostrils flared and his lips parted as she simply flexed back and forth on her knees.

"Jesus. Your clit is so big."

"Thought you might appreciate that." She reached down and stroked her clit gently, matching her movements over his cock.

"Christ, lady. You've got me right on the edge."

Ginger stopped suddenly. "Thought that might be the case." She sat straight up and without warning began rising and lowering over and around his penis. She raised her arms above her head. His eyes shuttered. "No, watch me!" she ordered without pausing. "Watch me fuck you."

"Oh, hell. You've got him."

She laughed as Nathan's hips churned, slapping against her bottom. Showing no mercy, she slammed against him knowing that she was claiming his essence. Only briefly she wished the condom hadn't been necessary. At last she closed her eyes and let herself soar. They continued to pump and strain, torso pounding torso. Their voices merged. Vaguely she knew he must be finished, but she didn't want to stop. Not yet.

And then she felt him tapping on her exposed clit and she shattered. She collapsed into his arms. Neither of them spoke for the longest time. His hand slid rhythmically over her backside. Her breathing slowly steadied. She licked the side of his neck. He was salty with sweat—the perfect after-lovemaking liqueur.

At last she felt him stir beneath her.

"I hate to be so mundane, but we probably should yield this room fairly soon. I'm surprised no one's knocked on the door yet."

"Oh." She stared at him, trying to sort out where they were. "Oh my God! Annette! What will she think? How long have we been in here?"

"Almost two hours."

She started to pull off of him but he held her firmly in place. "Annette was going to be ready an hour ago."

"She can wait a few more minutes." Nathan pecked at her lips. "I expect she'll be quite happy for you."

Ginger didn't doubt that. "Still, we should be leaving. Like you said, some other couple may want the room."

He flexed his hips and his semi-hard cock seemed to find new life. She shook her head. "I'm exhausted. You may have to carry me out of here." She blushed, suddenly aware that sounded way too intimate.

"Shh." He slanted a finger across her lips. "You made magnificent love to me. We fit so well together, don't you think?"

She tried not to think.

"So when will you be ready for me to make love you?"

"What?" she squeaked. "Isn't that what we've been doing for the last two hours?"

"But I want a turn on top. I want to make love to you doggie style, standing up, sitting on a chair, in a park, in my car . . ."

"Hey, I'm not a teeny bopper. And I never said there'd be a next time."

"You said you'd think about it."

She had said that when she'd offered to blow him. She hadn't quite gotten around to that.

"Don't you wonder what it would be like to milk my guy dry with your mouth like you just did with your pussy?"

Her mouth watered. She nodded and grinned down at his plaintive look. "I'll meet you here next Saturday, nine o'clock."

"I'll be here waiting."

With aching muscles and a slight feeling of remorse, not because she'd gone to bed with Nathan but because they wouldn't have another opportunity for an entire week, Ginger got dressed trying not to make eye contact with her young lover. He'd grown equally silent. Maybe he was having second thoughts.

She smoothed out her skirt and waited for him to open the door. She'd have some explaining to do to Annette so she'd better be prepared.

Nathan pulled her into his arms one more time, and they kissed like lovers of any age trying to get a lasting memory to carry with them until they met again.

He backed away. His eyes clouded. "I'll meet you here next Saturday, but not again."

"What?"

"I know you'll need time to think about it, but after next Saturday I will want to take you out to dinner and have a regular date like two lovers who are sorting out who they are and what they might have."

"But my age . . ."

"Is only a number. Besides, I've been thinking I might need someone older and wiser to help keep me in line." He winked at her. "How are you with a paddle?"

"A paddle?" She tilted her head to the side, slowly grasping his meaning. "I've never tried that."

"But you're never too old to learn, right? Be adventurous. Give me a chance. Give us a chance."

She tried to hide a smile but failed. "I'll think on it. Will a ping pong paddle work?"

She didn't wait for a reply but opened the door herself. She had to get out of there before she said too much, too soon. Stepping into the hallway, Ginger squeezed Nathan's fingers and looked directly into Annette's smiling face.

"Thought I might have to come in and help you out if you two took much longer," Annette mocked. "Looks like you might want to crown me a prophetess after all."

Without looking back at Nathan, Ginger brushed past Annette. "Let's go. Prophetess or not, I've got some serious thinking to do."

Illicit Intentions

Keeb Knight

Two weeks before the wedding . . .

"I am so glad you reminded me to pop in here to get this dress for Danielle's party next week." She held it up, as though making a final decision, and then turned around to face the full-length mirror that was directly behind her. She draped the flirty dress over her chest and down her torso. It stopped just short of a foot from the hem of her business suit, which was just above her knees. "Teal is so me," don't you think, Emily?"

"Oh please, Lauren. I think you're full of it. Is that even your size," she said knowing full well it wasn't. Emily owns and operates Mother's Intimate Treasures, a lingerie boutique in Olde City, Philadelphia. "If you're really serious about purchasing that little number, then I have the perfect, lacy, boy short to go with it. You do plan on wearing panties with that outfit, right?"

Lauren gave her a shameless stare. "Panties are so over rated, Em. But I have to keep some of my dignity hidden so let me see what you have. There's going to be a lot of young, ripe men at that party and I need to reel in a stallion."

Emily coughed, as though clearing her throat. "Uh . . . Speaking of stallions," she interjected as she peered over Lauren's shoulder. "Isn't that your future son-in-law, the mechanic, who just walked into my shop?"

She turned around. "Oh, yes it is," she said in a soft, curious tone.

"I don't know about you, girl, but I haven't ridden one of those in a good while," Emily whispered in her ear, as they both looked in his direction like two carnal cougars plotting on one young, fit, innocent man-prey.

"He looks like he's lost. Here. Ring this up for me will you while I help him find his way," she handed her a credit card. "Add the boy short too. You pick."

"L, I believe that's my job to help the lost in shop."

"C'mon, Em. I just want to have little fun, plus I could use a ride home."

"Well, don't tug too hard on his reigns, love. He might just buck."

Lauren turned to Emily as she headed toward her son-in-law to be. "I love it when they buck," she said with an annunciated whisper.

In true feline fashion, she snuck up elegantly and quietly. "Can I help you find something a bit more your size, sir?"

He was a bit startled, but the alluring voice sounded familiar to him. "Uh, yeah," he said as he slowly took his attention away from a sheer, periwinkle teddy to that of the woman whose beauty was as youthful, natural, and fresh as he's ever seen. He was almost a loss for words. *Whoa!* he thought. "Oh, hi, Ms. Thomas," he said looking at her as though he could fuck her where she stood.

Dr. Lauren Xhang-Thomas was a psychiatrist. She specialized in sexual and behavioral therapy. She kept her married name after her divorce, but she let most people call her "Ms. Thomas." She was of mixed decent: part Chinese, part African-American. Her light-sepia skin was like an exotic coffee mixed with just the perfect amount of cream. She had the most alluring honey-brown eyes; her long, raven hair framed her flawless oval face. She was a natural beauty.

"You know if you keep staring at me like that, young man, you might just go blind."

"Well, you're a very stunning woman, Ms. Thomas."

"That's very flattering, Kyle. I may have to marry you myself if you keep that up."

"I'm just surprised to see you."

"I can say the same. So, are you trying to find something for yourself or for my daughter?"

"Funny, Ms. Thomas."

"Just asking. And you do know you won't be calling me Ms. Thomas for much longer."

"Uh, yeah. I guess you're right. That's going to take a little getting used to."

"Don't you worry your handsome face about that, dear. I'll help you get more comfortable with calling me mother, mom, or *mommy*."

"Mommy would be a bit much don't you think?

"No. It just depends on what context is agreeable between the two of us. You'll come to find I'm a very open-minded woman, Kyle."

"So, is that why you're here?"

"Nice segue. I was picking up a little something as well."

"Really," he said as he trailed a gaze over her body, letting his imagination take him quickly where it didn't belong.

"Yes, really."

"Well, I was looking for lingerie for Leila. It was going to be a surprise. And I was kind of hoping I could keep it that way. She can't know we even ran into each other today."

"Aww! How sweet. We're sharing our first secret. I think you can trust me. But I do have a favor to ask."

"What's that?"

"I could use a ride home, if you don't mind? My car is still in your shop."

"Oh, yeah. Sure."

"I'm not taking you out of your way am I?"

"No, No. You're not. I was headed home after this anyway. It's my day off. I'm working Saturday though. I thought I'd run some errands and sneak downtown for a minute. And here I am."

"Yes, here you are," she said as she tried hard not sound too lustful. At the same time her eyes quickly panned down his white, T-shirt covered, diesel chest and back up to his piercing hazel-browns."

"How'd you get to work this morning?"

"I took the train. It's been a long time since I've done that. I forgot how relaxing it could be, not to mention the station is directly across the street from my office. So! Were you planning on giving Leila your naughty gift before or after you get married?"

"Uh . . . ," he paused.

"Don't look so perplexed, Kyle. There's no right or wrong answer. I was just curious. Anyway, I can assure you I'm pretty good at keeping a secret. Let me help you pick something out."

"Okay. Sure."

"I see you know what color she likes. That's a good start to a marriage. Hmmm . . . It also looks like you're drawn to the floaty and flirty teddies, huh," she said as she turned her attention to him with an enchanted look on her face.

"I just want to show her I can be romantic."

"I could just gobble you up! You are so perfect for m—my daughter. Come. Follow me. I think I can find the perfect two-piece for her, plus I know her size."

"Great!"

He followed her to the rear of the shop. He couldn't help but watch how she walked with such sass, style, and sexiness all in one pendulous motion. All this going on in a business suit that had to be tailor made.

When they made it to the back wall of the shop there were two full racks, one above the other, of lace-trimmed, solid-to-sheer lingerie in various styles and flavors. Any one of which could set the mood for seduction. In a matter of seconds of her thumbing through the bottom rack, Lauren picked one out and handed it to him. "Here you are. This is the one."

He looked it over. Front, back, and through it—literally. "Are you sure about this one?"

She leaned into his face, took the tip of her forefinger, placing it under his chin, bringing his attention to her alluring, almond-shaped, long-lashed, honey-browns, her lips nearly touching his as she spoke succinctly. "Trust me on this, sweetness."

"This one it is then," he said.

"Very good. Let's go take this over to Em and have her ring you up."

At the register Emily scrutinized the intimate sleepwear of choice and nodding her head in approval. "The Bleu Ballerina baby doll is an excellent choice, if I may say so. I love this shade of blue. Leila is going to love this."

"Thanks." He turned his head to Lauren. "And thank you for helping me pick this out. You did me a big favor," he said.

"Anytime."

"Guess I better get you home. It's almost five. We doing want to get stuck in Friday rush hour traffic."

"Oh, no we don't that to happen," she said as they grabbed their bags, and she looked back at Emily with a mischievous look on her face. "Bye, Em!"

"Bye! Come again. Be good."

"Always."

A little after seven in the morning, and she'd been awake at least half an hour before, she turned onto her side, her elbow wedged in the pillow, her lush breasts cascaded naturally one on top of the other. Her rich, dark-brown nipples looking like they were dipped in chocolate were already semi-hard. She lay there quietly studying his young, handsome face as he slept. She had already stolen the black silk sheets, leaving him totally uncovered. She couldn't resist the dish that lay before her—all 6-foot-4-inches of his bronze, muscular physique. She leaned forward and with her free hand she took her forefinger and placed it gently on his agape mouth, stroking his top lip, and then the bottom. Without pausing, she traced the deep separation between his muscular chest. She dwelled there for a moment, admiring how defined he was. She then continued down the paths that lead her to his cobblestone abs. When she strummed her fingertips back and forth across each one, she felt a tingle throughout her body. He stirred a little just as she reached his navel, nestled arrogantly between his well-developed, vascular thighs. It was as though his vulnerable cock could sense her approach as it began to show signs of life.

His eyes slowly blinked open. He looked down to see her finger gently stroking the belly of his cock.

"What are you doing? And what time is it," he said.

"I'm getting him ready," she said.

"Getting him ready? Shit! What time is it?"

"Five after seven," she replied.

"Huh?" he shouted as he quickly raised his head off the pillow, looking over her shoulder at the clock just as it digitally moved to six minutes after seven. "I thought you set the clock to alarm for five-thirty. What happened?"

"I didn't bother. You had a long night. I thought you could use the extra hour to recharge," she said seductively as she gently kneaded his heavy balls, at the same time looking him straight into his hazels.

"Why'd you do that, Leila? You know I have to be at work by eight."

"I thought you might want to stay in for a morning fuck."

He looked at her with a confused look on his face. "We fucked for damn near four hours last night. Aren't you tired?"

"Not in the least, baby," she said, shaking her head as she leaned in to kiss him on his full lips.

"Leila? I have to go to work, and then we're having dinner at your mom's house after I get off. Remember? Not to mention you got a flight to catch after that."

"Well, that's what good sex does to me, Kyle. It makes me want more of it. Sometimes I wish I could share what we have with the world."

"Sometimes I think you're certifiable. Maybe you need set up an appointment with your mother," he said annoyed as he rolled out of the bed.

She watched him as he padded naked across the floor to the bathroom to get ready for work. "Can I come, baby?" she teased.

"No. I'm already late."

"Your loss," she said smiling.

She reached for the phone on the night table beside her and started dialing. "Kyle, what time should I tell my mom we're coming over for dinner!" she yelled.

"About five-thirty!" he shouted just as he turned on the showerhead.

"Hi, Mom. You up?"

"You know I'm up, honey. I just got back from my morning jog. What's up?"

"I don't know how you do it. Anyway, I was just calling to let you know we'll be over for dinner around five-thirty. Is that okay?"

"That's fine, dear. I'll be done cooking before then."

"Okay, great! Oh, Mom! Did I leave one of my uniforms over your house—the navy blue blazer and matching skirt?"

"Yes, you did. I had it dry cleaned for you along with some of my clothes a few days ago. Why?"

"Thanks. I need it. That's my retro flight attendant uniform. They want us to wear it again out to Chicago tonight. I'll just change into it when we come over."

"So how's that fine man of yours doing? Tell him I'm going to pick up my car later this morning. Maybe I'll see him."

"He's fine. In more ways than one!" Leila gushed.

"Oh, well excuse me," she said. "You'll have to tell me all about it later."

"There's so much to tell. I don't know if you have the time."

"I do have a couch downtown if you want to make an appointment."

"Everybody's got jokes this morning. 'Bye, mom. See you later. Love you."

"'Bye, honey. Love you too."

"Kyle, could you be a dear and pass me the mashed potatoes? Please?"

"Sure, Ms. Thomas. Here you go."

"Thank you," she said as she took the bowl from him. She sat directly across from Kyle. Her eyes peered up at him for a second or two as she dished out a couple of scoops of the mashed potatoes onto her plate. "You've been very quiet, Kyle. You must be really enjoying my food."

"I'm definitely enjoying this," he said with his mouth partially full. "You can definitely throw down, Ms. Thomas. I'll give you that."

"Oh, thank you, Kyle," she said glancing over at her daughter, Leila, who sat next to Kyle. "That's how I won Leila's father's heart. Well, for the most part, that is. It took a little more than just my cooking to reel him in," she said winking at Kyle.

"Okay, mom. Let's not go there. We're eating. Please!" Leila injected.

"Why not? We're all grown folks here. Right, Kyle?"

He looked up from his plate at Ms. Thomas' alluring smile then he turned to Leila. "She's right, Leila. We are grown. It's not like—" He cut himself short. "Well, never mind."

Leila stopped her fork just short of her mouth and turned her head to Kyle. "No, finish what you were going to say, Kyle," she insisted.

He hesitated.

"I want to hear what you were going to say. You might as well finish. I will stare at you while you eat until you do."

"Go ahead, Kyle. What were you going to say," Ms. Thomas asked curiously.

He looked over at Leila. "I was just going to say it took a lot more than your cooking to win my heart. That's all."

"Kyle, I'm an airline attendant. You know damn well I don't have the time to cook. So why are you complaining now?"

"You see that? No. I'm not complaining. I knew it."

"You knew what, Kyle?" Leila said.

"That whatever I was going to say wouldn't come out right. Anyway, all I'm trying to say is that you won my heart by being who you are as person, the whole package, and not because I was won over by some succulent, mouth-watering meal you prepared."

"Aww. That's so sweet," Lauren said looking over at her daughter. "I think you've got yourself a great catch, baby."

"Yeah, that was a good come back, Kyle," Leila said cutting her eyes at him.

Kyle made no eye contact with Leila as he put one of the last pieces of mouth-watering filet mignon in his mouth.

"Succulent isn't it, Kyle," Lauren said with a cunning smile as she studied the movement of his mouth and sensuous lips.

"Mmm-hmm," he responded nodding in agreement.

"Kyle, Leila, I want to apologize for bringing up Dorian. It's just that seeing the two of you together brought back a few memories. It's been over a year now since the divorce, and there are times when I miss his being here at the dinner table eating with us, even though half the time he wasn't here anyway."

"Don't worry about it, Mom. No one said being divorced was a cakewalk. You still have to take it one day at a time."

"Thank you, baby," she said affectionately as she clutched her daughter's forearm. She then drew here attention to Kyle. "Yes, Dorian being an airline pilot took a lot of getting used to. Like father, like daughter. They're always on a flight out to somewhere. So, Kyle, I hope you've been adjusting to this lifestyle with Leila always being away from home days at a time."

"It can be hard to deal with sometimes. Anyway, she's usually just a phone call or a text away. That kind of makes things a little easier," he said throwing a smile over to Leila.

Leila smiled back, leaned over and pecked him on the cheek.

"Well, baby. On that note, you know I have to finish getting ready for my flight tonight out to Chicago," Leila said as got up from the table, supporting herself on Kyle's shoulder halfway up and out of her chair. "And I won't be back in town until Monday morning unless my schedule changes."

"Yeah, I know," he said.

"Don't look so sad, baby. You can hang with my mom this weekend. She's not doing anything. Are you, Mom?"

"No, it just so happens I'm not. I just have to run a few errands in the morning then I'm all yours, Kyle," Lauren said as she lightly brushed the tip of her foot against his leg underneath the dinner table.

He ignored it. "Well, then I'll stop in at noon. Maybe I can help you with some chores or something."

"Great! You see. Now at least that way I know you won't be getting up to any trouble," Leila said as she stood up from the table adjusting her clothes and giving him another peck.

Kyle looked over at Lauren and received a friendly smile and a wink in return from his future mother-in-law. His cougar-in-heat future mother-in-law. He looked to see if Leila caught that, but she had already headed out of the dining room on her way upstairs.

Lauren, with her elbows on the table, leaned forward as she perched her chin on top of her interlaced fingers, gave Kyle an unwavering stare. "So, what can you and I get up to this weekend, Kyle?" she asked as she kicked off her shoe underneath the table, lightly rubbing her toes alongside his calf, slowly raising it to his knee, extending the ball of her foot between his legs, and pressing it against his quickly aroused cock. His jeans suddenly began to feel a bit tight.

He grabbed her foot with his right hand. "Umm . . . Ms. Thomas, I don't know what your intentions are, but—"

She pulled her foot out of his grasp and skillfully planted it back into his crotch. She tapped her foot along the length of his hardening cock.

"Hmm. That's funny. He seems to know what my intentions are. How come you don't?" she asked as she began to fondle his cock with her toes through the unforgiving denim of his jeans. "It feels good doesn't it?"

"What's wrong with you," he whispered. "Are you okay?"

She removed her foot from his crotch, put her shoe back on, got up, made her way gracefully around the table, and stood behind him where he sat. She leaned over him, wrapped her arms around his neck, her breasts pressed firmly against the top of his broad shoulders. She positioned her lips less than an inch from his left ear.

"I know you want fuck me, Kyle," she whispered. "You've wanted to fuck me for a while now. I see it in your face all the time. Don't deny it."

"What are you talk—"

"Sssh! You know damn well what I'm talking about. I know when I'm being mentally fucked. It's so obvious. It's a damn shame I can't feel what goes on in your mind because I'd probably like some of the freaky shit you got me doing inside that handsome, young head of yours," she said as she slid her hand down inside his shirt, copping a feel of his tensed pecs. Her lips were practically nibbling on his earlobe. "From the feeling I got from my toes a moment ago, I'm willing to believe there's some potential there. So, if you're game, I can help you sow your oats." She circled her fingertip around his nipple before releasing him from her not so motherly hug.

She walked out of the dining room, but not without giving him something to think about: a little extra sway in her hips accentuating the fullness of her curvaceous, bodacious bottom.

Kyle almost got whiplash watching her as she left the dining room. The way she walked was almost enough to make him come to rigidity. She was right, though. He's had plenty of explicit thoughts of fucking her. But he never thought a day would come where he'd actually be called on it. He had no idea he was that damn obvious.

"Leila!" Lauren shouted from the bottom of the stairs. "Were you planning on driving your car or taking a taxi?"

"I'm driving since I'm already running late, Mom," Leila, shouted as she headed back downstairs.

"Do you want us to come with you," Lauren said looking at Kyle and he looking back at her while she said it.

"No, no! I'll be fine. I'm going to work, not on a vacation. You both can stay here and relax. Enjoy each other's company. In a couple of weeks I will be on vacation and he's all mine," Leila said as she came down the stairs dressed in her navy blue two-piece uniform, accented by her white-collared blouse flared over her lapels, and her silver name badge pinned over her left breast. She walked past her mother over to where Kyle was now standing under the archway between the dining room and living room. She gave him a tight hug, looked up into his deep browns and kissed him on the lips. He stood at least a foot taller than her—and her mother. "Oh, I am going to miss these delicious lips of yours. I love how they just gobble me up," she said as she wiped off the bit of lipstick that smudged his mouth. "Doesn't he have a pair of the most gorgeous lips, mom?"

"They're very nice. Even from where I'm standing," Lauren replied.

"Is that all you're going miss is my lips, baby?" Kyle injected.

"Oh, be quiet. You know I gonna miss you too."

"I'm going miss you, too, baby," Kyle said giving her a kiss and a hug in return, placing hands at the small of her back and pulling her in close.

"You better get going, dear," Lauren said.

"Alright, alright," Leila said heading to the door, grabbing the telescopic handle of her suitcase that she left at the bottom of the stairs and rolling it behind her. "Take care of my man," she said as she kissed her mother on the cheek.

"You don't worry about him, honey. He'll be just fine under my tutelage." Her nipples were getting hard from what she was actually thinking, knowing a few places where those delicious fucking lips of his could be put to good use.

"Mom, don't you go trying to change him," Leila said, waving goodbye to both of them as they stood at the door to see her off. Kyle stood behind Lauren, and they both waved back.

"Make sure you call when you land in Chicago," Lauren motioned, simulating a phone with her hand up to the side of her face.

"I will. 'Bye." Leila got into her car, backed out of the driveway and drove off.

There was complete silence for about a minute after the goodbyes were said and the front doors shut. They stood before one another as though they were about to get into a gun drawing contest to see who was going to make their first move.

At forty-plus, Lauren looked liked she could be her daughter's older sister. Genetics played a great part in her youthful look. Her figure didn't lack, either. She had the full package: taut, ample breasts, a small waist, and a shapely bottom complimented by the most gorgeous silken legs.

Those feline-like eyes of hers penetrated his. He felt a sensation run throughout his body as he looked at her for what seemed like the very first time. And of course it wasn't.

She remained at the door facing him and began to unbutton her blouse.

"Leila, is barely at the airp—"

"Sssh," she said taking a hand away from her blouse and placing her fingertip on his lips. "The only thing these lips should be doing the next time I hear a sound coming from them is the lapping sound of you licking my kitty."

She continued to undress in front of him. She tossed her blouse onto a chair not far from the door. It didn't take long before she got down to her bra, which she unhooked at the front. He was unable to avert his eyes. Her breasts spilled out of the deep cups of her bra. He looked at them with adoration. Firm with dark-tan areolas with the most prodigious nipples he's ever seen. It was a uniquely beautiful contrast to the complexion of her skin.

She unzipped her skirt from the back, tugged it down her hips and legs, letting it drop and puddle around her feet. She wasn't wearing any panties. Surprise, surprise. Her fleshy labia and the lightly trimmed, silk-soft black down of her pussy made him even more excited.

She stepped out of her skirt moving in closer to Kyle, who stood there with his lips parted in awe of her. She took notice of this, fingered her moist pussy lips, and brought her hand back up to his mouth. "Say, Ah!" she simulated the motion with her own mouth while inserting two, pussy-juiced fingers onto his tongue.

He played along by grabbing a hold of her wrist, licking, and then sucking her fingers like they were little Popsicles. He sucked the length of them down to her knuckles, hollowing his checks before pulling her fingers back out, showing her he got every last bit of her sweet, vaginal nectar.

"Ooooh, good boy," she said with appreciation. "There's more where that came from, you know."

With her free hand she tugged at the center of his shirt. "Off!" She ordered.

He started to unbutton his shirt while she started unbuckling his belt, but at the same time she slid her hand inside his boxers before actually unveiling his immense appendage. "My, my! He is a big boy isn't he? Will it get bigger than this because I think I might need two hands."

"One way to find out," he said in a cocky tone.

While she caressed the length of his cock and his heavy balls, Kyle did away with his shirt and let his jeans drop to the floor.

She was taking him all in. The body of twenty-five-year-old Kyle Chance was very lean, muscular, and sleek in a beautiful, masculine way. The long lengths of the muscles in his arms stirred as he bent towards her to shimmy his jeans down. His bare back rippled with the slightest movement. He looked like he could have been hired to pose for an anatomy chart.

Her hand was still towing at his cock when he started peeling off his boxers. She looked down in anticipation and couldn't believe her eyes. Feeling it and seeing were two different things. "Oh my mother-fucking God," she said in disbelief.

He slowly removed her hand from his semi-hard cock, but not without a little playful resistance on her part. The skin all over his body seemed to pulsate as he began to take some initiative. She stood quietly watching the bunching of the muscles in his arms as his massive hands palmed her breasts, roamed down her belly, her back, and her buttocks. He paused. Her ass was fully rounded with long, sweeping lines and curves. He was truly admiring her shape and could feel the blood scrambling to his cock making him even harder. His hands continued down the backs of her thighs as he lowered himself to the full view of her womanhood. His eyes were level with the moist folds of flesh between her thighs.

She shifted her legs apart, moving and balancing herself on her fire-engine red, fuck-me high-heeled pumps. Kyle looked up at her with a salacious gleam in his eyes. Hers pierced his with a commanding look.

"Filet mignon, baby," she said as she cupped the back of his head, pressing his face towards her treasure of pleasure. She could feel his warm breath against her wet labia folds. This sent a trill up her spine. Her breasts heaved.

He no longer hesitated and pressed his mouth to her glistening vulva. It was about to be on.

Lauren suddenly thrust her pelvis forward while she guided Kyle's hands to her hips so that he could wrap his arms around her waist and get more of her meaty labia in his mouth.

Sensing her excitement incited a twitch in his cock with more than an anxious anticipation of giving her a thorough dick down. He slipped his tongue between her MILF-lips as high up as he could stretch it, lapping up her love-juices, which made this cougar purr with pleasure.

"Oooo! Oooo! Oh, fuck!" She purred under her breath, falling back against the door, gripping the doorknob in attempt to hold herself up. "Goddamn, Kyle, is that tongue of yours as long as your cock too?" she gasped as he licked her from slit-to-clit, sucking it hard between his tongue and teeth. "Oh, yes!" she screamed as her eyes rolled back into her head, her grip on the doorknob gave and she had no choice in the matter. Her knees buckled, and she slowly guided herself down to the floor before she let go of the knob, which was now above her head.

Relishing her pussy with every ounce of his ravenous mouth, Kyle bent forward in a kneeling position pulled her backwards. His tongue was still deep inside her, detailing her velvety vaginal walls. He easily took each of her legs from the backs of her knees and wrapped them around his neck, holding her up by the round, ample flesh of her heavy ass-cheeks which fit nicely into his massive hands. The only part of her body that touched the floor of the foyer was her head and shoulders.

Her clit was gorged and he could feel it swelling in his mouth. He flicked his tongue against it harder, faster, relentlessly drawing on her bud in an orgy of sucking. Making her scream even louder than before, moans of pleasure passed her lips in staggered, gasping fashion, falling into a sexual seizure. Then came the shuddering, her vagina flushed with thrilling waves of ecstasy. Feeling the powerful orgasm searing through her, she looked up between her thighs and watched as Kyle sucked and swallowed her juices of orgasm as she writhed and gasped on the floor. She didn't expect it to come this fast and unexpectedly like a surprise visit from a dear friend showing up at one's door, it was most welcome—sometimes.

The doorbell rang. And rang, and rang in rapid succession. *What the fuck*! Lauren thought as she quickly rolled off of Kyle's shoulders. They looked at each other for a moment. "Who is it!" she yelled in the opposite direction down the hallway as though she was a distance away from the door.

"Hi! It's me, Miss Ella from next door. Are you all right in there? I heard a lot of screaming and thought I'd check on you to make sure you were all right."

Lauren was already up on her feet peering through the peephole. Her home was a semi-split twin where only the front half of the house was attached to her neighbor. She grabbed her blouse and slipped it on quickly, buttoning only a few buttons, and then cracked open the door to talk and at the same time hide her partially-naked body behind the door.

"Oh, hi Miss Ella. We'—I'm just fine. I was just trying out this new workout DVD I ordered last week."

"It sounds like it's working out fine," Miss Ella said panning what she could see of Lauren. A braless, hard nipple poking against the thin cotton material of her white blouse, some thigh, and the well–manicured, candy-apple red toenails of her right foot which adorned a fire-engine red, high-heeled pumps. She smiled and nonchalantly brought her attention back to Lauren, watching the lies fly out of her sex-flushed face.

"Oh, yeah it is working out just fine. And I do apologize for the noise, Miss Ella. I was just really getting into it, and I must have gotten carried away. I'll try and keep it down. I really appreciate your checking up on me, though."

"Oh, dear. Not a problem at all. We neighbors have to look out for one another, you know," said Miss Ella raising her chin and a hard stare from under her eyelids.

"Yes. I agree. Well, 'bye now. Thanks again," Lauren said as she started to close the door. Miss Ella turned away to walk back to house next door. But then Miss Ella suddenly turned around.

Lauren noticed this and cracked the door back open. "Yes? Is there something else, Miss Ella," she asked.

"Yes. When you're done fucking that handsome dark knight you have in there, send him over to me for a few, so I can get my scream on too," she said with a wink and a one-toothed grin on her face.

"'Bye now, Miss Ella!" she said slamming the door shut and shaking her head.

"So . . . Are we done?" Kyle asked, waiting behind Lauren with his blessed glory hanging in a neglected, semi-hard state.

"Huh?" She responded as she locked the door and turned around. When she saw him standing there a good four feet away, she couldn't help but think how beautiful this man was butt naked. Just the sight of him could have induced another orgasm if she let it. The sweat glistening off of his muscles gave him a nice, sexy, smooth sheen. She wanted to lick him the fuck dry.

"Turn around," she said.

"What?"

"You heard me! Turn around. I want to see everything."

He turned around. His shoulders were broad, and his back was wide with a V-shape, a narrow waist, a high ass firm and round. "You are such a fucking beast. When they made you, they made the mold. We need to take this upstairs. Give me a few minutes then come on up to my room."

As he entered the room there she was, laying on her back, butt-fucking naked on a king-size bed with a wrought-iron bed frame waiting for him.

He walked over to the bed, climbed in and over her. She grabbed his arms, her nails digging fiercely into their long strands of muscle and pulled him down on her. Her lips pressed onto his full, welcoming lips, initiating a deep and passionate kiss causing her nipples to harden and stab into his chest as her breasts heaved.

"Kyle, Kyle," she breathed incessantly, as if she had been saying his name forever and day.

He shifted on her, his hip grinding on hers, the flesh of her belly billowed and swelled under him. The rigidity of his rock hard, ebony rod was painfully pleasurable as he could not wait any longer to fill her desire.

Her hands moved round to his back, her arms locking him to her, their legs intertwined. Her eyes were heavy lidded, her mouth open in a moment of bliss. She seemed more beautiful in her heat of passion than he had ever seen.

"Kyle," she breathed. "Don't fucking tease me! Give it to me! Give mommy what she wants so bad!"

It was nothing but a word. Kyle positioned himself between her thighs and slid his throbbing, bull cock into her aching cunt, as she writhed with lust.

She worked her pelvis up and down to get more of him in her, grabbing a hold of his tight, muscled buttocks, urging him into her wide, open thighs. She met each of his thrusts with moans of pleasure.

Kyle felt like he was in pussy paradise. He wrapped his hulk arms around her body, and with a strong, swift, full stroke, he drove his girthy cock into her.

Lauren gave a strangled gasp as she felt the dull pain of his entry. He seemed to split her in all directions. He was biggest man she'd ever accommodated, but she would never let him know it.

He thrust into her again, splitting her farther and farther apart as his thickening cock coursed up into the core of her body. She wanted him to fill her. She wanted him to make her ache, sore, crippled. This magnetic man for now was hers, his mind focused on her and the satisfaction of her body.

Kyle soared into her with an unleashed ferocity and felt a tingling in every sweating pore of his body where it touched her; his chest against hers, his thighs brushing hers. He gasped out his breath, crushing his lips over her face, over all those beautiful, fine features that made her a woman.

Writhing under him, moaning her ecstasy, Lauren was in a bitch-heat of passion, pulling her thighs back to her breasts, almost to her shoulders, wriggling her heart-shaped ass so he could really drive it home. Kyle was impressed with this move and wallowed in his raging lust. His hand roamed over her skin, holding the flesh, which at that moment in time belonged to him.

She spread her thighs to the max, forcing herself to endure the erotic pain, which accompanied the ecstasy, moaning with a pleasure under the impalement of his thick, virile cock. His crushing, aggressive weight seemed to be almost forcing her through the bed. The heavy wrought-iron bed frame bounced, rocked and creaked under the furious rhythm of their illicit intercourse.

She felt inside her stomach a sort of growing restriction of breath, a stirring sensation ran throughout her body, which seemed to grow and grow as though she was heading to a point of no return as his heavy cock surged into the velvety wetness of her lustful womanhood.

His name seemed to mix with the animalistic noises of her moans. She strained toward him as she panted, and the gasps became a continuous low-pitched moan that suddenly changed to abrupt screaming as she pushed her belly up at him. Locked in lust, another wave of warm ecstasy overtook her being, sending her over the edge.

Kyle wanted to make this woman completely his in this moment. Passion made his head swim, his eyes glaze. With sweat pouring off his forehead, he slowed his strokes to thick, precise, grinding penetrations behind which every working muscle in his body flexed and surged.

"Oh, God, yes! Keep fucking me just like that!" she screamed.

Kyle wanted this woman he had beneath him—all of her. He reached down in front of him and got a hold of one of her rolling breasts. He leaned forward and adeptly took his mouth to it, sucking hard on her erect nipple, his tongue flicked diligently at the sensitive tip.

This sent an uproar sensation to her already swollen clit. "Ooooh, you fucking bastard! Don't stop!"

As the bed hammered against the wall and Lauren screamed her filthy bliss, Kyle's thoroughbred cock began to throb beyond his control. It was as though it had its own heartbeat. He felt the overwhelming weight of sensation gathering deep from the root of his being, trying to find an outlet. His breathing became short, unrestrained gasps. He began to breathe all her names with every thrust. "Ms. Thomas . . . Lauren . . . Mommy, I'm about to be your goddamn daddy!"

He got used to her holding her stare at him. And now was no different. This time she was literally talking with those honey-brown eyes of hers. But she decided to speak for them anyway.

"Lay it on me, Daddy," she grimaced, her eyes focused steadily on his as she interlocked her silk-soft legs tight around his waist. "Give mommy that big daddy-dick!"

Inside him there was a hot, burning sensation boiling in his loins. His entire body began to quake.

"Yes, Kyle. Give my mommy that big, fucking, daddy-dick of yours!" a familiar voice shouted from behind.

He whipped his head around in shock at hearing the voice. "Leila?" Right then and there he changed his mind, but his cocked balls didn't, and neither did Ms. Thomas.

She tightened her grip. He had no damn where to go, but up in her accommodating pussy.

He suddenly came hard and long. A weekends worth of his life-giving fluid, spurting in a series of volcanic climaxes, his eyes steadily transfixed to Leila's as he groaned and uncontrollably bucked, emptying his aching balls into his future mommy-in-law.

Leila turned to her mother. "I came back for my locker key. So, how was he?"

"He was everything you said he was, baby. And then some," Lauren replied with her legs still locked around his waist.

"Oh, good. I'm glad."

"Thank you for sharing him with me."

"You're welcome, Mother. I knew Kyle would be more than willing to attend to your needs without my having to ask."

"What the hell is going on?" Kyle said dumbfounded.

"Oh, Kyle relax," Leila, said. "I told my mother how unbelievably great the sex was, and I thought since I owed her one, I'd loan you to her for the weekend. Oh, and thank you for the baby-doll teddy. I can't wait to see it."

He turned to Lauren who shrugged her shoulders. "What happened to keeping secrets?"

"We have no secrets, Kyle. Sorry." Lauren said as she loosened her grip.

He backed up off the side of the bed and walked right passed Leila. "You're both crazy," he mumbled as he left the room.

"Crazy for you, Kyle!" Lauren shouted.

The two women looked at each other then started laughing.

"Are you still going to marry him?"

"Hell, yes! That's prime beef!"

Shelly's Mom

Jolene Hui

I am a cougar.

I fully admit it.

My daughter was the first one to call me such a thing because of the way I acted around her fraternity friends. On the couple of occasions when I visited her at college, the fraternity boys serenaded me. "Shelly's Mom," they sang, instead of the popular song "Stacy's Mom."

Maybe it was because I had my daughter fairly young. I was twenty-four when I had her; twenty when I had my son, so I was a mere forty-three-years-old when I first made my way to her sorority house. Was that too many numbers to keep track of? Well, they do say age is just a number. I tend to agree with that saying.

Nothing happened with any of the fraternity boys that year. They were a little too young. Most were only nineteen. I seemed to be most attracted to men in their twenties. Thrice divorced, I'd realized that finding love was not easy. So instead of finding love, I decided appreciating a hot, young body was the better option. Also, younger men had more energy. As an energetic woman, I needed someone to keep up.

The summer Shelly graduated from college she was twenty-one and so were most of her college friends. I offered to have a party for her but her friend Lucy's parents had a large house better equipped with the perfect summer party backyard for something of this sort.

Lucy's mother was going to be out of town but she entrusted her summa cum laude graduated daughter to have a responsible party. Plus, Lucy's mother Ellen and I were friends.

"Helen," she asked me, "could you please keep an eye on the party?"

Shelly's father Pete was planning on helping me out, but he ended up vacationing with his girlfriend who was, of course, in her twenties. Sure, it's "normal" for a man to date younger women, but when a woman does it, she's labeled. I could deal with it, though. I was proud to be a cougar.

I sorted through my recipe box a couple weeks before the party. These college kids would be easy to host. I'd get some hamburgers and hot dogs and some chicken breasts for the calorie conscious. A fruit salad, green salad, potato salad, and chips would top off the meal nicely. I'd always liked being a mother and planning parties.

Since I always loved it, I took my time planning this one. And— lucky me—the party wasn't even at my house.

On party day, I'd selected a nice, lime-green, two-piece swimsuit with a matching wrap for when I tended to the grill and served. I'd invited fifty college students over to the house and left the invitation open for any of their family members to stop by if they wanted.

I'd recently quit my job as a nurse and started teaching at the community college but, luckily, had the summer off. It made me feel even more young and carefree than I already did. I couldn't remember the last time I had an entire summer off.

My son was nice enough to help me decorate and setup the party, without even one complaint. I had to give it to my kids, even though they sassed me enough; they at least still loved each other to help out with each other's functions.

"Give me that Tupperware of chicken," I demanded of my son when people started trickling in through the backyard gate.

I grabbed a pair of tongs and adjusted my sunglasses. Shelly cranked music. She'd been working on the perfect playlist on her iPod for days. My long, brown hair hit the middle of my back. I was blessed with only a few wiry gray hairs and a thin but curvaceous frame, yet I still felt like a mother hen to all the bikini-clad girls walking into the pool area. The recently-graduated college boys even looked a tad bit young to me, but when a hot, slightly-older looking guy walked into my line of sight, I almost burned my fingers on the grill.

"Yowsah!" I yelled it a little too loudly. I put my first three right fingers in my mouth as a reflex to the burn. My sunglasses slid down my nose a bit. Through the sun I saw the hottie turn around. We made eye contact. He smiled. I dropped my tongs.

I stood there staring at him with his fingers in my mouth, a very Lolita-ish look.

His light-brown hair looked bleached by the sun. He was shirtless in green board shorts, his smooth chest tanned and muscular. He was lean, but looked like he surfed. Defined muscle tone riddled his lanky body. It looked like he was accompanying Lucy and Shelly's friend Paco. Paco had just graduated with a business degree.

The noise from his flip-flops as he walked away snapped me out of my daze. I flipped the chicken breasts and tossed some burgers and dogs onto the grill. I tried to keep my eyes on what I was doing, but I couldn't help but try to find those green shorts again in the crowd that was slowly becoming larger.

"Go get some more soda and refill the cooler, please!" I yelled at my son who had gotten in the pool and was flirting with some bikini-clad co-eds. Despite most of the guests being over twenty-one, I wasn't into serving alcohol at someone else's house.

"This marinade is great," said a girl in a teeny polka-dot bikini.

"Thanks." I gave the fruit salad a quick stir. The kiwis, strawberries, and peaches smelled delightful. Nothing really beat a summer fruit salad—aside from the vision that planted himself in front of me just as I looked up from stirring.

Fine blonde hairs danced on his lower abs under his belly button. The laces on his board shorts were bright white. My eyes followed the trail of blonde hair in between his pecs to his smiling face.

"Can I have a burger and a breast?" He asked.

I wanted to say something flirty and maturely Mrs. Robinson to him but nothing came to mind. My spatula found a patty and set it on his plate. "Don't you want a bun?"

"No thanks. I don't like buns," he said.

As juvenile as my connotation was, I still laughed aloud at myself.

The Adonis in front of me laughed as well. "Hey, I'm Marshall," he said.

"I'm Helen," I said. "Shelly's mother."

He genuinely looked shocked, "No way. I don't believe it."

"Believe it."

He was opposite of my last boyfriend. My last boyfriend, Mario, was dark, with black hair and brown eyes. Mario was also muscular, not lean like this surfer boy and definitely not as tall. Marshall was at least six feet tall. I could only see a hint of his eyes behind his sunglasses. His nose was strong and large.

"Thanks for the breast," he said.

I laughed. "Do you want some potato salad?" I touched his hand. Instead of answering my question, he looked at my fingers on him.

I pulled away, not wanting to rest too long on his skin.

"Nah, but I'll take another breast." He left his hand on the table.

"Save some for everyone else," I said. Boys will be boys, though. And I didn't want him to leave hungry, so I put another on his plate.

"Hey, quit flirting and give me a dog." Paco walked up next to Marshall. I was used to Paco being around. He was one of Lucy and Shelly's friends from college that I knew. "Isn't he a little old for you anyway? He graduated like three years ago, Helen." Paco laughed and squirted ketchup and mustard on his bun.

"As long as he's under twenty-five, he's OK in my book!" I decided I might as well joke around with them.

"Eh, he barely makes the cut. You might have to stop talking to him in December," Paco said.

So he was twenty-four. Marshall took a scoop of fruit salad, gave Paco a little salute, and took off toward one of Lucy's friends. I watched him walk away.

"Close your mouth, mama!" Paco was always good at figuratively slapping me across the face

I snapped out of my Marshall daze and gave Paco a dirty look. "Oh, eat another hot dog, ya punk."

As if on cue, "Stacy's Mom" came on. Everyone immediately turned toward me and began to cheer.

I shook my head when they replaced "Stacy" with "Shelly." I couldn't be positive, but I think Marshall kept his eyes on me the whole time.

The rest of the night floated by smoothly. I abandoned the grill eventually, sipped on Diet 7-Up, and meandered through the crowd. I asked a lot of the college grads what they'd be doing for a living. A lot of plates, napkins, and cups had been left on tables so I walked around with my sunglasses keeping the hair out of my face

I wished Ellen were home to keep me company. Shelly turned the music down like the good daughter she was. People started to trickle out as it got dark. I suspected everyone was headed out to the bars to drink. My son had abandoned ship hours ago. He had to work in the morning so I forgave him for leaving me alone. As I picked up the last stray fork, I looked up to see Paco and Marshall sitting on lawn chairs. Shelly and Lucy were inside with their boyfriends.

"Need a hand?" Paco asked.

"Oh yeah, now that I'm done, I surely need a hand," I said and set the plastic bag down.

Marshall's eyes glowed through the dusk. He was wearing a

hoodie now, with the logo of his alma mater on it.

"Well I'm gonna go hit the pool table," Paco, said, standing up.

"Thanks for your help," I shouted to him as he walked away.

"So, Helen," Marshall finally spoke. "Do you need help?"

"Paco already asked me!" I glared at him. "I'm gonna take this to the garage if you wanna go with me." I hadn't even meant to hand him an invitation. I walked toward the garage, swaying my hips a little more than usual. My flesh started to turn goosy in the cold evening air. Marshall must have noticed.

"Do you want my sweatshirt?" he asked. Before I answered, he peeled it off his sexy body.

We were in the garage in the dark. Instead of just handing me the sweatshirt, he decided he should try to put it on me. I giggled as he tried to pull it over my head. I started to feely silly. I couldn't stop laughing even as he pulled my arms through the sweatshirt. My infectious laughing made him start laughing. I tried not to roll around on the ground but had to crouch down to laugh my stomach hurt so badly. I could feel my hair was in disarray around my face. The full garbage bag was right beside me on the ground and I lightly leaned into it.

"You're leaking," he yelled in between his laughs.

"Huh?" I leaned into the bag more.

"You're leaking!!!!"

I looked down to see a rush of root beer pouring out onto the concrete.

"Shit!" I jumped up, still laughing. This time, I leaned on Marshall, who had also jumped up.

Our laughing subsided. I leaned into him more—into his neck this time. I smelled his skin. It smelled good. I couldn't help but put my lips lightly on his skin. His body froze. I kissed him up the neck to his jaw line and to his chin until we were facing each other. He was taller than me but I was up on my tiptoes kissing his chin.

So gracefully and almost automatically, he tilted his head down to meet my lips.

I slid my arms around his bare waist, feeling the heat from his skin through the hoodie. Our kiss deepened, our bodies moved against each other.

The garage door slammed. I pulled away. He'd kicked it shut while kissing me. He was obviously good at multi-tasking.

I started to get dizzy, but he held me closer.

"Dude, we need to get go. My brother needs my car . . ." Paco's voice trailed off.

I hadn't heard the garage door open again. Marshall and I separated. I felt my face blush. "Oh, sorry," Paco said when he realized we were in the middle of something.

"No worries," Marshall mumbled. I noticed he couldn't make eye contact with Paco. "Let's go," he said.

I felt frozen and didn't know what to say.

"I'll get my hoodie back from you another time," he said. They walked off, leaving the door open behind them.

I disposed of the bag and walked back to the pool area. I sat on the lawn chair and looked at the stars, my arms wrapped around my body. His smell was on the hoodie. I inhaled it.

I felt silly for the next few days. In the evenings, I'd put his sweatshirt on and sit outside. During my time off from work I tried to relax and recuperate. Shelly had been living with me during her last year of college. As soon as she'd graduated, she'd moved out and I was left with an empty nest.

For once in my life I had peace, quiet, and time off to relax. But what I really wanted was another rendezvous with the surfer boy.

Two weeks passed and I considered calling Shelly to get Paco's number so I could track Marshall down. My prayers were answered on Wednesday when I was in the middle of making a sandwich for lunch. Trashy romance novels, sandwiches, and lemonade were my life lately. It reminded me of my teen years. The doorbell startled me.

My heart nearly stopped when I saw Marshall standing there.

"Oh! Hi!" I definitely felt silly.

"Hey, what's up?" He smiled. He was wearing his sunglasses again.

"Come in," I said, not even sure why he was here, but pleased all the same. I was glad I'd used my best-smelling shampoo the night before.

He accepted my invitation. He brushed past me and stopped at the edge of the entry way and the living room.

I closed the door and silently led him to the couch. His hands slid behind my back. His lips went to my neck. His warmth rubbed off on me through his soft, thin, blue t-shirt. I could feel his muscles rubbing against my breasts. I tightened my arms around his shoulders and returned the kiss to his neck.

"Is anyone here?" He whispered.

"Just you and me," I answered.

177

We slid to the couch, kissing furiously. I'd been thinking about him since our encounter that night in the garage. He seemed like he'd been thinking about it too.

I was glad I had a reclusive urge and not left my curtains open this morning. Probably better that I didn't broadcast my sex just yet.

I wanted to feel exactly what he was packing. I slid my hand to his crotch and felt the stiff mass. He let out a little moan and pulled away from kissing me.

"Well you don't mess around, do you?" he said with a pleased look on his face.

As a reply I unbuttoned his jeans and slid the zipper down. He put his hands up under my shirt and unhooked my bra while kissing my mouth. My pussy was more than wet and ready for the cock I pulled out of his boxers. With a tad bit of effort, I pulled down his jeans. He rolled on top of me. He pulled my shirt over my head and threw my bra to the floor. He moved from on top of me to shimmy my pants over my hips so that I could kick them off. There was no more need for comments as we got naked.

One thing I loved about younger men is how they were always prepared. Marshall put on a condom so fast I hardly noticed he had taken his hands off me. Seconds after, he used his strong arms to flip me over on my stomach. My tits pressed against the soft couch. He found my wetness with his middle finger and slid it in and out. Even though I couldn't see him, I felt his warm body looming over mine. I didn't need a warm up.

He shoved my legs apart with his knees and put his cock inside me. He stayed inside for a moment, leaning over to kiss my shoulders.

I buried my face in the couch pillow under my chin. He moved in and out of me swiftly but lingering just enough to tease my swollen clit.

He pulled me up to my knees and reached around, still inside me, to play with my clit. I tried not to buck against him uncontrollably.

I'd never had a younger man so in control before. Marshall knew exactly what he was doing. I loved that he was dominant in bed. I held myself up and threw my head back in pleasure while he fingered and fucked me.

My knees dug into the couch. I thanked myself for getting the expensive and sturdy couch. We rocked back and forth in a quick steady rhythm. Sweat started to bead up on my forehead. His slick crotch bumped against mine.

I needed briefly to see Marshall's face. I craned my neck, damp tendrils of hair stuck to my forehead. Our eyes met. He sucked on his thumb. I opened my mouth knowing what he was going to do next. I screamed when I felt it plunge into my anus. My cunt exploded around him. I kept coming as he fucked me and fingered my ass. I buried my face in the pillow.

"Fucking hell!" I yelled. The cushion muffled it.

Finally he pulled his thumb out and pushed himself deep inside me. I felt him explode. His fingers gripped my hips.

My thighs were covered in my juices when we parted. I felt slightly bashful.

"Hey beautiful, are you blushing?" Marshall spoke while he put on his boxers.

He was right. My cheeks were warm.

"You want your hoodie back?"

"Trying to get rid of me already? I'm still practically naked!"

I laughed and made my way to the bathroom to wipe myself down. That was the best adrenaline rush I'd had in a long time.

When I got to my bedroom to grab the hoodie, Marshall was there waiting for me, still in his boxers.

"I think you should keep the hoodie," he said.

For some reason, that touched me.

"That's really sweet," I said.

And because I couldn't resist his smile, his abs, and his thumb, I put my lips to his chest and my hands on his tight ass.

Cruising for C-men

Dona Lee

Cougar: Sleek, graceful predator

There's no doubt about it. The fresh sea air, the freedom and luxury of the ship, everyone dressed in scanty summer clothing, a cruise made a woman feel like . . .

"Oh, hell. I feel like getting laid," Cindy said to her friend Margaret.

"I know what you mean," Margaret Harrison replied as she continued to unpack her suitcase. "But all the men are here with their wives. I was checking them out when we were boarding."

The cabin, 2926B, seemed smaller than pictured on the brochure. Nevertheless, Cynthia Parker intended to make the best of this vacation. She hadn't had one in so long. Thinking about it she realized it had been . . . three years. Three years looking at the same eight walls: the four in her apartment and the four at work.

Her husband, the worthless dog, left her the year before, and she dove into her work to compensate for the lonely nights. It earned her an award and a promotion, but did little for her social life or her emotional state.

"I don't care." Cindy tossed her sleek, coifed mane in frustration. "I want something hard in me. And nothing at the buffet table has any appeal."

Margaret chuckled. "Girl, you are so bad."

"Sure, whatever. Are you joining me?"

"I think not. I've got a little something going on the side."

"You do? And you didn't tell me about it?"

"Well, this is a little too close to home. I thought it best to avoid any complications."

"But I'm your BFF. How could you keep anything this important from me?"

"He's . . ."

Cindy stopped unpacking and leaned forward. Margaret stared out the portal and showed no signs of continuing her sentence. Cindy became impatient.

"Girlfriend!"

"What? You know him, okay? It's best if I don't say."

Cindy made one of those noises as she sucked in her breath. "It's Murray from the office. Isn't it?"

"Stop. I can't say and I don't want to. If you're really my friend you won't make me."

"Okay, but before this cruise is out, I'll put enough food and booze into you to make you want to talk."

"The last time you put something into me I told you everything."

"I remember," Cindy sighed. "But we were both too tipsy to enjoy it."

"Are you about done playing with your silkies? Or is that your way of trying to make me horny?"

Cindy looked at the small pile of clothing she'd brought. She packed lightly in the hopes she'd not need clothes most of the cruise. Still the task of taking them out of the case and placing them in the small dresser seemed daunting.

"I want to go topside and see what's available to play with."

"Then quit fooling around and let's go."

"I've got to change first," Cindy said, pulling her shirt over her head and clipping on a bikini top. The flowery skirt remained.

On deck, people of all ages roamed about dressed in brilliant, tropical colors listening to the reggae beat of the band. A few played shuffleboard while others swam in the pool, drank at the bar, or caught up on some rays and generally tried to subtly do what Cindy wanted to do, only without appearing to want it. Cindy chuckled.

"What's so funny, girlfriend?" Margaret asked.

"All these people want the same thing I do. Only they want to play this silly game and look like they don't *really* want it."

"That's the way the game is played, honey."

"Not me. I want to wear a neon sign that says: Slut Here! I want action and I don't want to have to dance first."

"Cindy, girl, you've got it bad."

"That's what I keep trying to tell you. Expect fireworks. Expect them soon."

"Yeah, just be careful. Fireworks can burn your fingers."

"Hey, this is a cruise ship. And I plan . . . to . . ." Cindy's voice trailed off and she slowed her walking pace, leaving Margaret out ahead—talking to herself.

"What the hell are you doing?" Margaret walked back to where Cindy had come to a complete stop. She followed her friend's gaze. "He looks about twenty. Now what the hell would you do with a twenty-year-old?"

"Everything," Cindy whispered.

"Well, that can wait. Let's get something to eat first. You'll need your strength if you're going to ride a young buck like that."

"But what if I miss out on my chance with him?"

"He's not going anywhere, Cin—I mean, Miss Slut. We're on a ship. Besides, he works here. Check out the duds."

Cindy scanned the young man's clothes. He wore the traditional white of a cruise ship employee. She realized Margaret was right. He'd be around to devour at a later time. To confirm her decision, Cindy's stomach chose that moment to growl.

"Okay, okay," she said, more to her stomach than to Margaret. "We'll eat something."

Sitting in the crowded galley, Cindy watched Margaret pile food high on her plate. The buffet table stretched down the center of the room and disappeared around the corner of the center galley.

"Have you ever noticed how much better the food tastes on board a cruise ship?"

"Unless you get food poisoning like those people did a few years ago," Cindy retaliated.

"Come on, seriously. Don't you think everything tastes better?" Margaret inquired around a mouthful of shrimp cocktail.

"I don't know. Maybe it's because we're on this ship and everything just *seems* better."

"Want to talk about your young cabin boy?"

That shut Cindy up for a moment. With no further ammunition to fire back, she settled. "Okay, the food's great. Feel better now?"

"So tell me, darling, you don't *really* plan on going after that young boy, do you?" Margaret asked with sincerity. "That's just asking for trouble."

"Are you my conscience, now?"

Margaret hesitated. "Well, at least remember to bring condoms with you."

"Way ahead of you, girlfriend." Cindy reached down into her little pouch and held out several small square packages.

"Jesus! How many you got there?"

"You've heard the word 'stamina,' right?"

Margaret laughed and stood.

"Where are you going?" Cindy asked.

"I'm going to go work on my snappy jokes for when you come back walking bow-legged— like you've been on a horse all day and night."

"Thanks. I can always rely on you to keep me humble."

"What are friends for?"

At that moment, the purser walked by. Both women noticed his ass and stared. Cindy dropped her fork. Margaret sat back down. She looked at her friend.

"A part of me is almost envious," Margaret said with a sigh.

Cindy came back to her senses. "Don't be envious yet. He could be a complete dud between the sheets."

"Is that going to stop you from going there?"

"Hell no!"

"I'll expect details."

"Perv."

"Hey, vicarious is better than no life at all."

"But you said you had something going," Cindy reminded.

"Sure, but it's not like *that*. I can still dream about it, can't I?"

"Hell," Cindy confessed, "you could still *go* for it."

"I couldn't."

"We're on a cruise. What happens here stays here."

Margaret hesitated as if she were giving it a great deal of thought. "Thanks anyway. I'm trying to be a good girl."

"What for?" Cindy waved a dismissive hand. "That stuff is for kids. I'm forty-three years old. I'm too old to worry about conventions, and too young to roll over and die."

"Okay, okay. Go get him and stop talking before I have to slide my hands inside my pants right here at the table."

"I'll see you later—for dinner, maybe?"

"Get out of here, you cougar."

Cindy turned to walk away. "By the way," she added, turning back to her friend. "Don't go back to the cabin for a while."

"You are so sure of yourself."

"Look at me." Cindy pointed at her lack of love handles and flat belly. Continuing the display motion with her hands, she brought them up and waved around her 38Cs. "How could he resist this?"

"I'm finding it difficult myself," Margaret said eating another shrimp from her plate that she'd missed.

"Go play shuffleboard, you old fart." Cindy chuckled. Margaret offered some muffled retort, but she'd already walked too far away to hear.

Cindy followed the boy up to the bridge. Civilians weren't allowed inside, so she waited outside, admiring the expanse of the ship, looking down from the high perch. She tried to act casual, nonchalant.

He exited before long and she took up the pursuit, or was it stalking, once again. He seemed very busy, visiting cabins, apparently solving a multitude of guest problems. Then he entered the Engine Room.

Cindy found herself standing casually in hallways and against railings all over the ship, like some amateur sleuth tailing a suspect. She chuckled a little as she realized how she must look to others. *And what would Margaret think?*

When she began to doubt finding the perfect opportunity, her prey slipped into a storage room. That gave her the chance she'd hoped for. She quietly slipped in behind him. The room looked much larger than she'd expected. Stacks of "ship stuff" crowded the space forming narrow walkways.

"Hello."

"Huh?" He turned, startled. "You aren't supposed to be in here, ma'am."

"I know. I just got so lost." She took a step toward him. He didn't back away. That was the sign she'd hoped for—the signal he wasn't afraid of her touch. So she did. She ran her well-manicured fingernail down the length of his exposed arm below his short sleeve and swirled it in his palm. He flinched, but Cindy sensed excitement and surprise rather than offense.

"What's your name?"

He gulped so hard she heard it. "Ch-Chester, ma'am."

"Call me Cindy." She stepped so close her breasts touched his chest. "You look tense, Chester."

"I . . . don't think we should be . . ."

"How old are you, Chester?" she asked, stepping back to arm's length.

"Tw-twenty-two, ma'am. I mean, Cindy."

"You're going to do what I say, right?"

"I, uh . . ."

"Pinch my nipples."

"Wha . . . ?"

"Do it."

Chester reached his hands up and waved them hesitantly in front of her breasts but didn't touch her. She leaned into his hands, and he had little choice but to feel them, but he didn't move. He just let them rest in his hands.

"I said, pinch my nipples. Do it now!"

Startled, Chester searched the bathing suit top for signs of her nipples. Then he pinched a little. Frustrated, Cindy grabbed her bikini top and pulled it down so her tits bounced out and Chester could get at her skin.

"Now," she said in a whisper, "pinch them. Hard."

Chester's eyes stared down at her exposed chest, and he breathed in deeply. His hands found their mark and followed her instructions all by themselves. Wrapping her hands in his hair, she pulled his head toward her.

"Come on, babe. Suck on Cindy's breasts."

He obeyed, running his rough tongue across her flesh and nibbling her erect nipples until Cindy couldn't resist a moan. Her mind clouded with need. She needed him. *All* of him.

With a little effort she forced him to his knees. Once in place, she slid off her panties and raised one sandaled foot onto the crate behind him. Raising her skirt for total effect, she lowered her pussy to his lips. She didn't need to instruct him further.

Cindy kept her pussy shaved clean so he had no trouble whipping his tongue all around on her lips, over her clit, and into her hole. Throbbing, she felt an orgasm building and approaching. For a moment she worried about only one leg supporting her full weight. Only for a moment, and then her knee buckled as the orgasm wracked her body. Chester supported her weight, slowly folding her over the crates.

Her juices flowed as the spasms ran through her entire body, but Chester continued to lap at her. Quivering, she stood still as he licked her inner thighs, cleaning her off. *What a considerate young man*, she thought.

He thrust his tongue inside her again. She hadn't expected him to be so bold. And he didn't stop there. Without warning, she felt his tongue slide back, further back, and into her other hole. The sudden anal attention brought her quickly to the brink of another orgasm. She collapsed against the crates enjoying sensations she's never relished before. The pulsing orgasm clenched his tongue, and she pushed into it wanting more. *Ohmygod, ohmygod, OH MY GOD.*

Her feet barely touched the floor as her belly and breasts lay flat against the crates. She faced sideways watching the wall, slowly catching her breath. Cindy heard him moving, but couldn't see him, nor did she have the energy to look. Her flowered skirt had fallen back down and she felt him raise it up. A breeze wafted across her crotch and gently cooled her burning core. But only a little.

She felt his tongue again, sliding the length of her, from clit to asshole. He licked like his ice cream pop was melting. He quickened his pace and Cindy breathed deeply. She hadn't thought she had another orgasm left in her. She was wrong.

He thrust into her, deep. Surprised at his aggressiveness, she opened herself wider to his fullness. He pounded his meat into her with the energy only young men can muster. This was why she'd pursued him.

Cindy just lay there, receiving him, accepting him, enjoying him. But he pulled out of her completely. She felt empty, abandoned. It didn't last long. She felt him pushing back in, but in the other hole. She'd been anal-ized before, but had never really enjoyed it.

But this was heavenly. She felt another orgasm building rapidly. She slipped her hand down to her clit, playing it to the beat of his pounding. She sheathed him and the sensations cascaded one on top of another. Pushing here, probing there, she knew she'd walk funny afterward, just the way Margaret predicted. But at this moment, Cindy didn't care. She's tolerated the teasing to savor this encounter.

The orgasm hit her, leaving her feeling like she was being pounded with a warm, heavy hammer made of marshmallow. Still, her young stud hadn't come. He continued to pound at her and all she could do was lie there, flaccid, complacent, willing, smiling.

When she felt him explode inside her, she noticed a feeling deep down, the beginnings of another orgasm, but she felt too tired to make any effort.

Chester rested on top of her, allowing himself to get soft while still inside—a feeling she enjoyed almost as much as the orgasms themselves. But all too soon he flopped out with a little pop and she rested, closing her eyes and drowning in the ecstasy and the erotic odors. But just when Cindy thought the moment might be perfect, Chester spoke.

"I'm . . . uh, sorry, ma'am. I don't think . . . "

Cindy rose and turned toward him, placing a finger on his lips. "Shhh."

"But I—we just—"

"I know, and it was great."

His smile grew and so did another part. Cindy admired his size, realizing he'd had that thing inside her. She saw something else. He'd worn a condom. Lost in the fantasy, she'd completely forgotten, but he hadn't. *When the hell did he manage to put that on?*

Cindy reached down, pulled it off him, and he sprang to renewed life. Despite her satisfaction and exhaustion, she didn't think it wise to waste such a beautiful thing. She sank to her knees and faced it. More a weapon than a tool, she kissed it with her lips and tongue. His arousal aroused her in turn, dampness spread between her legs again—not that she'd truly dried out from the first encounter.

She could taste the latex of the prophylactic. It had no appeal, but his flavor lingered as well. Cindy savored it. Soon he'd offered her more flavor. She managed to catch it all, not wanting any to go to waste. Now she felt ready again and hoped he could manage to do something—anything for her.

She touched him gently and noticed he wasn't completely lifeless. *Damn! Young stuff.* Cindy helped him don one of her condoms for round two. She climbed up on the crates and lay back, raising her skirt and then her legs. Without any words exchanged, he followed her unspoken request explicitly.

He climbed atop her, grabbing her legs and thrusting them back so her knees almost became ear muffs. He slid into her, pushing inch after inch. From this angle Cindy couldn't believe he would fit it all. He buried himself to the hilt, bottoming out inside her, holding her legs up with his strong arms.

His steady pounding rhythm quickly drove Cindy out of her mind with need. She began to chant, "S-t-a-m-i-n-a, ah!" like some pornographic cheerleader getting gang-banged by the whole team.

Cindy knew there was another orgasm within her, and she felt it rise, like a tremor deep in the California ground. Not only did Chester hit all the right spots, satisfying her needs, but the view from this angle drove her to devious heights of perversion, and ecstasy was the only possible outcome. As that feeling rose higher and closer, she braced herself so she didn't buck completely off the crates, and still Chester showed no signs of slowing.

The wave slammed her harder than anything she'd ever experienced before. The mystery and taboo of this younger man pushed her nearly to unconsciousness as the waves kept coming. Cindy didn't feel done. More orgasms hit her like she'd stuck her orgasm button into a ceiling fan and the blades kept hitting it over and over again. She couldn't stop it, and she wasn't sure she wanted to.

Despite his youth, he was quite expert at pile driving. He used the full length of his man meat to impale her and thrust just a little deeper each time. Cindy couldn't catch her breath. She lost track of time.

When Chester finally came, Cindy felt the swell of his head inside her. This filled her up even more and she had yet another orgasm. She'd already had so many, she feared they might keep coming even after he finished and pulled out of her. How would she ever be able to walk normally again?

Looking at his watch, Chester rapidly pulled up his pants. "I-I have to go," he stammered, apologetically.

"We'll see each other again." She dismissed him with the ominous leer of a woman planning on returning for seconds.

Chester offered a half-weak smile and left the storage room with an almost imperceptible wave and a lingering glance over his shoulder. Cindy lay there, her pussy hanging out, feet down but knees apart, letting the air in to cool her off. If another man walked in and made a move, she didn't think she could find the strength to fend him off.

But eventually she managed to get up, pull herself together, and hobble back to her cabin. Margaret returned hours later and immediately recognized the look of satiation on Cindy's face. She expelled a deep sigh and sat on the next bed. "I take it you managed."

"Oh, yeah."

"And he's gone?" she continued, looking around the cabin.

"We never made it back here."

"Oh." Margaret looked resigned. "Tell me all about it."

So Cindy did. She explained every detail. She described with her hands. She closed her eyes and envisioned each moment as she relayed her tale of lust fulfilled. When she finished, Margaret appeared as exhausted and satisfied as Cindy.

"I wasn't sure before, but now I am."

"Sure of what?"

"I'm envious."

A knock on the door interrupted them. Margaret opened it to the room steward. He leered oddly at her and handed her a note. She opened it, read it slowly, and began to laugh until tears ran down her cheeks.

Cindy struggled to sit up. "What? What is it?"

"'Would lady from cabin 2926B please report to room 2038 on Continental Deck immediately. I have fresh sheets'. He's ready for seconds," Margaret teased.

"Oh, my God. I can't. I'm still sore."

"He tore you up that bad?"

"Honey, you know me. If I could be there, I'd be there. I'm done in." Then she added as an afterthought. "Why don't *you* go?"

"Who, me?"

"Why not? Tell him you want the lights out. Once it gets going, who cares if he notices or not? Besides, you're a lady from 2926B."

"I couldn't do that. Besides, it's so . . . wrong."

"Yeah," Cindy sighed, smiling like a cat that had lapped up all her cream. She bounced her head back down on the pillow. "It certainly was."

"You're still in the moment, aren't you?"

"I haven't been used like that in decades."

Margaret sat quiet, staring.

"Go. Take care of my boy for me. When he finds out you're not me, tell him the truth and I'll see him later."

"You think I could?"

At that moment, Cindy knew she had Margaret hooked. Perhaps by the end of the cruise they'd both do him together. "I'll never tell," she said to the back of the door.

A Great Commute

D. L. King

It was a long commute to work each day. Same subway station, same time every morning; you get used to the same faces and the same boring routine. Although you see them every day, you don't actually look at the people—at least not overtly—you just file their presence away. It's important to maintain as much privacy as possible, preserve personal space as long as you can because you know it won't last.

There was the woman with the outrageously expensive, imported leather, work bag and the two little girls she had to deposit in nursery school before continuing on to her office; the two little girls who whined and pouted the entire time. There was the older gentleman, with a twinkle in his eye, who would smile and offer his seat to whatever woman was standing closest; the very large red-haired woman in the tight suit and pink sneakers who took up two seats (but sure as hell didn't pay two fares); and the thirty-something guy who was completely wrapped up in his new wife or girlfriend; I wasn't quite sure which. They'd keep their heads close as they chatted, hanging on the pole, staring into each other's eyes. He'd kiss her before his stop, and once he left, she'd close her eyes and smile, and then bury her head in a magazine for the rest of her commute.

Lately, I'd begun to notice a young art student on the platform. I'd see him sporadically. He dressed in torn, paint-spattered blue jeans and tee shirts. He carried one of those tackle boxes, the kind that was full of art supplies, rather than fishing tackle. He looked to be in his early twenties at the most, with shoulder-length, dark-blond hair that would benefit from a good brushing, or maybe practiced fingers run through it. His eyes were light. Green? I hadn't been able to get a long enough look to know for certain, but god, he was pretty.

I'd begun to watch him surreptitiously, and occasionally I would catch his eyes meeting mine for a split second before he'd look away. The idea that he might have been interested made me smile, after all, I must be twice his age.

I work hard at keeping my shape. I have a commanding presence and people tend to think I'm much taller than my four-foot-11-inch petite frame, but still, I could've been his. . . mother's younger sister.

He always got off three stops before me. If I was close to the doors, I got to watch that really nice ass exit the train. That day I happened to be standing just in front of the doors, and as I was drooling over that squeezable bottom and fantasizing about reddening it with my hand, he turned around, grinned, and waved. I had no choice; the only possible response was a wink and a smile.

Two days later he rushed into the train, just as the doors were closing. He seemed to search the car, finally catching my eye. He smiled, and then looked away. As I had a seat, I opened my paper, eventually forgetting about him. When the doors opened on my stop, I left the train as usual and began the walk to my office. As I walked down the street, I heard a throat clear behind me and felt a hand on my arm. Adrenalin pumping, I turned around, ready to punch the guy, and saw my artist.

"Hi, um, my name's Justin. I was just wondering, I mean, would you like to get a coffee?" he managed to stammer. He looked a little reticent. Perhaps he realized how close he'd come to being laid out on the pavement.

I looked at my watch and realized I'd be late for work if I didn't continue on. "Yes, thanks. I would," I said with a smile. I continued walking and he followed. I led him to a Starbucks around the corner. After getting our coffees, we took seats at a corner table.

"Anne," I said, offering my hand. "Don't you have some place to be? A class or something?"

"Don't you have work?" he countered.

"I thought this might be a better use of my time." I took a sip of coffee. "So Justin, I'm thinking I'd like more than coffee. What about you?" I gazed at him, trying to gage his reaction.

Justin fidgeted in his seat and began to blush just a little. "Ah, yes ma'am, I mean, Anne. I think I would."

"Ma'am is fine, Justin. You can call me Ma'am if it makes you more comfortable. Shall we?" I got up and walked out the door, turned right and continued around the corner, sure Justin was following me. I had a small boutique hotel in mind. It wasn't far, and

I had a corporate account. I stayed there on occasion when I worked late rather than make the commute home.

As we got closer to the hotel, I turned to see Justin following three steps behind me. I took his hand, drawing him parallel, and put my arm around his waist.

"Good morning, Ms. Shepherd, nice to see you back with us," the doorman said as we entered. I could feel Justin's intake of breath when he saw the lobby.

"Don't worry, you'll be all right. I'll just be a minute," I said, leaving him to try to look without gawking.

We had the elevator to ourselves and as soon as the doors closed, Justin closed in for a kiss. And what a lovely, sweet kiss it was. His tongue gently prodded my lips open and so sweetly explored my mouth as a hand tentatively slid its way up my body to my breast. I allowed him to continue in this manner until we reached our floor. As the doors opened, I wrapped my fingers around the front of his belt, inserting them between the leather and the denim, and then gently pulled him after me down the hall. I held him like this while I opened the door, and then pushed him into the room, still holding onto his belt.

Once inside, I closed and locked the door behind us. Pulling him along behind me, I opened the bathroom and looked inside—'cause that's what you do—and then continued on into the room. All this time, Justin hadn't made a sound. I backed him up to the king-sized bed and forced him into a seated position. Removing my fingers from his belt, I stroked his crotch and felt the growing bulge in his pants. Giving it a squeeze, I buried my face in his neck and inhaled.

"Mmm, you smell nice. You must have headed for the train fresh out of the shower."

"Yes Ma'am," he said, shivering as I licked his jaw.

"Be a good boy and get out of those clothes while I call my office."

He looked at me with those big, beautiful eyes and a hint of a smile and took his shoes and socks off. He still hadn't said anything other than 'yes ma'am' but now I could see a bit of playfulness coming out. He stood before me as I picked up the phone and punched the buttons. Taking off his shirt, he was encouraged by my response. I practically swooned when I got a look at his tight chest and flat, hard stomach. Running my fingers over those washboard abs while I spoke to my secretary and listened to my messages, all I could think about was finding where that treasure trail under his navel led. He was definitely a tasty young man, and I took great pains not to drool.

He watched me while he slowly undid his jeans, and then slid them off as I finished up with my office. He wasn't wearing any underwear, and his cock sprang to attention as soon as his pants cleared the area. I wrapped my fingers around it as I hung up the telephone receiver.

"If you don't mind, we'll just let this be mine for the next several hours," I said, pulling him towards me. I took my jacket off. "That all right with you?"

"Oh yes," he said, as my fingers returned to lightly stroke him. He reached for the buttons on my blouse but I gently took hold of his wrists.

"No, Justin, I'll tell you when and what you can touch." He didn't seem to know what to do with his hands, so I suggested he place them behind his back. He was very good at following instructions, and I noticed precome had begun to gather at the end of his cock. How delightful.

I always keep what I like to call my emergency overnight kit in my bag. You never know when you'll need something, and it would be such a shame if you didn't have it. I pulled my purse over and took out a frumpy-looking cosmetic bag. I opened it and dumped its contents on the bed: several condoms, a travel-size bottle of lube, and a vibrating anal plug.

Justin coughed and said, "You always carry that stuff around with you?"

"Oh yes. I believe in being prepared. Aren't you glad? What would we have done otherwise?"

"I have condoms," Justin volunteered.

"That's very commendable, but do you have personal lubricant or a vibrator?"

"No, but do you really think we'll need those things? I'm sure I can make you wet. Well, I mean, uh . . ."

"My dear, you've already made me wet. The lube's for you, as is the vibrator." I absolutely loved the expression on his face as I pushed him onto the bed, that combination of confusion, a bit of fear, and excited anticipation.

I shimmied out of my tight skirt, leaving my garter belt and stockings on, along with my plain black thong. I unbuttoned my blouse, exposing a sheer, black, lace brassiere and saw Justin's cock jump in anticipation.

"Justin, be a dear and fold the covers all the way down. Make yourself comfortable on your back, in the middle of the bed," I said, shrugging out of my silk blouse. "Oh, no, Justin. Keep those pesky hands to your sides for now," I said when I saw him begin to reach reflexively for his cock while he watched me.

He actually sat on his hands, poor dear, to keep from touching himself. "Scooch down a bit, away from the pillows, so that I can get behind you. Do you like the smell and taste of pussy?" I asked him.

He assured me, in no uncertain terms, that he did.

"Mmm, that makes me very happy," I said as I lowered my damp, thong-covered mound to his nose. I could feel him slide his hands out from under him and I caught him by the wrists before he could grab my hips.

"Mmm, mmm, mmm, Justin. No hands, remember?' I felt him whine into my pussy as I placed his arms back by his sides.

'Do you like my scent?' I asked him, rubbing myself from side to side against his nose.

He mumbled something I couldn't quite understand, but he managed to nod his head. I leaned over, sliding down just a bit and suggested that he tongue my wet thong. He eagerly complied, pushing his tongue against me in a very practiced way.

"You're not bad at this, Justin, for such a sweet, shy boy. I might even say you're pretty good. Seems you've had some practice."

"Yes ma'am," he mumbled. "I love to eat pussy."

"Well then," I said, "you go right ahead." I pushed the brief fabric covering my cunt to the side and lowered myself completely onto his mouth, hearing and feeling a muffled grunt. Leaning forward, I made sure I wasn't blocking his nose, which rested in the crack of my ass. I could feel his breath tickling me as he began to use his tongue again. He was really quite skilled, and between little shivers, I complimented him on his technique.

The room became suffused with his musk as his cock dribbled more precome; copious amounts of it ran down his shaft to gather on his balls. I couldn't resist running a finger through the sticky coating on his sack, which led to fondling and massaging. He had such a lovely pair of balls: large and nicely formed. I could feel the skin becoming taut and feared I'd lose him too soon, so I let him go and rose from his face.

"No, don't stop," he blurted. His face was wet and shiny with a combination of saliva and my juices from the bottom of his nose to his chin. The juices were running off the sides of his cheeks, as well.

"That was very nice Justin," I told him, "but I have something better in mind. Turn onto your stomach and get on your knees. That's right, with your bottom in the air, just like that. I think you'll like this," I said.

I put lube on my finger and pressed it against his anus. He jumped away.

"No, Baby, don't be scared," I said. "You're just so sweet. No one's ever done this with you?"

"No, ah, ma'am. I, um . . . I'm not sure . . . well, that is . . ." He kept clenching his ass and moving it away from me, but without actually getting out of position. "I never did . . . I don't think . . ."

"All right," I said, stroking his bottom gently, relaxing him. "I want you to trust me now. You're just a sweet, inexperienced boy."

He made noises of protest. "Yes, I know, you've had lots of experience," I said in a placatory way. "But, let's assume I know a bit more than you, in this instance, okay? I know you'll like this. Trust me." He began to relax and tacitly agreed by pushing his rear end out in a deliciously submissive manner.

"Good boy," I said, as I massaged lube around his opening. He moaned a little as I added more lube and slowly pushed against his sphincter again and again, teasing the opening until I finally inserted my finger slowly, a fraction of an inch at a time. I reached under him and found that, although he had softened a bit, his cock was still semi-erect. I gently stroked the back of his balls and cooed to him as I slowly slid my finger in and out, a bit deeper each time.

After a while, I felt him begin to hump back against my hand, trying to achieve a deeper invasion. His cock was steel hard once again as I chuckled and said, "If you don't like this, we can stop."

"Oh, god, no. Don't stop, please," he begged, continuing to rock against my hand.

I added more lube and inserted a second finger, widening him a bit more. He grunted but continued to push back against me, and he whined his displeasure when I withdrew my fingers altogether.

"So you like that after all, do you? Don't worry, Justin," I said. "I won't tell." I slowly inserted the plug, past his sphincter, all the way to the end. Once his muscles had closed around the neck of the plug and it was well seated, his breathing calmed. He jumped and froze when I turned it on.

"Oh, man!" he moaned.

I got him turned over on his back again and made him open his eyes so he could look at me as I wrapped my hand around the base of his cock. "Having a good time?"

The poor boy couldn't speak. He laid there, eyes wide, staring at me, panting heavily and smiling. "Thought so," I said.

Squeezing the base of his cock, I told him he'd better not come. Each breath was a whine, but I continued to hold him with one hand while I put a condom on him with the other.

"I want to get at least a few good strokes out of you," I said, lowering myself onto him, but keeping my hand around the base of his cock. Once I had settled myself on his shaft, I removed my hand and just sat.

"I can feel the vibration in your ass through your cock. So yummy."

As I began to move slowly, I placed his finger by my clit and told him to earn his keep. Amazingly, Justin was good at that too!

He told me he couldn't hold out much longer, and as I was on the verge, too, I let things take their natural course. I could feel his entire body vibrate right before he came. He tensed and pounded into me twice, and then shook under me. His orgasm wrenched a lovely, deep, guttural moan from him.

Lying next to him, after turning the vibrator off but leaving it in, I played with his hair. "Justin, how old are you?" I asked.

"I'm twenty. Why, does it matter? Um, listen, can you take that thing out of my ass please?"

"No, not at the moment, dear, let's leave it where it is for now." Changing the subject, I said, "You seem to know quite a bit about how to please a woman. Just how long have you been having sex?" I asked.

His hand began to stray toward his cock and the vibrator protruding from his ass. I caught it and brought his arm around his body and held it to his side. "No. Do you want a spanking? Now tell me how you learned to use your mouth and hands like that."

"I like older women. Older women teach you stuff, you know? Older women know what they want and make sure they get it.

"I'm not really into girls my age, but when I have had sex with them, they don't seem to want to talk about anything. I don't think they know what they want. Well, if they do, it's not like they'll tell me.

"Older women are much sexier and they aren't afraid to teach you things. Like you . . . I mean . . . I wasn't implying that you were old or anything . . ."

"That's all right, Justin. I am older than you. Actually, I'm more than twice your age, and yes, I do know what I want," I said, as I slowly twisted the vibrator in his ass.

"I'm glad you're open to learning new things. I'm sure you'll learn a lot today. For now, why don't you turn over on your stomach and I'll give you a nice massage?"

I put a pillow under his hips and turned the vibrator on low. As I began to massage his balls, the most lovely, gentle moans issued from his throat. I looked at the clock. Wonderful. It wasn't even noon yet. We had all day.

Sherry

Doug Harrison

To the Cougar Women in my life:
Memories of you swirl through archetypical
mists of time and distance.
My gratitude for your empathy,
passion, guidance, and love.

Another Saturday evening. And I didn't have to rummage around bars for some action. My friend Thelma was hosting a pansexual play party in the waterfront district. A first for her, but her experience and connections in the kink community, coupled with her authoritarian presence, guaranteed a successful event. Besides, I always managed to enjoy myself, regardless of the venue. I donned 501s, denim shirt and boots, stuffed my leather bag with appropriate attire and a few toys, slid into my suburban sedan, and drove across town. The city towers sparkled across the harbor as I entered the warehouse neighborhood.

I found a parking space under a street lamp a few blocks from my destination, trading the increased protection of my brightly lit car for the decreased personal safety of a longer walk. No stranger to karate, I nonetheless sallied forth with a can of red pepper spray in my pocket. I stood tall and strode briskly, careful to hug the sidewalk's edge, away from deep shadows and dark doorways, and peered between parked cars like an insurgent expecting an ambush. I only jumped once, and chortled when I realized that the sounds assaulting me from a grimy dumpster were a rat family's nocturnal picnic. I arrived at a nondescript door illuminated by a dull, red light bulb, without seeing another human, or even a black cat. A late-model Porsche was parked directly in front of the entrance, its pristine black body shimmering under a street lamp.

I pummeled the wooden door with my knuckles; the doormen at these affairs usually paid more attention to the action in the play area rather than to their sentry duties. Surprisingly, the peephole squeaked open almost immediately.

A gruff voice assaulted me. "Get lost, kid."

"I'm over twenty-one."

"So what?"

"My name's Brad. Thelma's guest."

A shuffle of papers, a grunt, and the door swung open on shrill hinges. I jumped sideways and entered. A grizzled guard dashed into the cool night air, checked the black car, glanced up and down the sidewalk, and rushed back inside. He bolted the door shut, put a checkmark against my name, and shoved the clipboard at my face.

"Sign here."

I scrawled my signature, and skimmed the list of attendees. The sentry scowled and yanked the clipboard from my hand. We each took a step backward. My eyes blazed. I puffed out my chest, and rested one forearm on my toy bag and my other fist on my hip. My nemesis scanned me head to toe. His eyes settled on my bag, he formed a half smile, and finally held out his hand.

"Welcome. My name's Tom."

I returned the handshake, but not the half smile. "For the record, I'm pushing thirty. Now, where do I change?"

"Locker room's over there," Tom answered as he threw his thumb toward a dimly lit doorway. "Hope you brought your own lock."

"Always do," I said and turned away. I come face-to-face with a scurrying Thelma who braked rapidly despite her three inch spike heels.

"Brad! I was hoping you'd show up. Don't mind Tom. He's getting used to his new job."

"He needs more practice."

Thelma guffawed, I chuckled, and we fell into each others' arms.

"It's been a . . ." we exclaimed in an impromptu duet.

"Ladies first, Thelma," I said.

"Haven't been called that in a long time."

"It's not a woman's profession that entitles her to be called a lady—it's the woman herself."

"Spoken like a true gentleman, Sir!"

We both howled. A few heads turned our way, not from annoyance, but in appreciation of unrestrained laughter.

"What've you been up to? Thelma asked.

"Well, I've been knocking about the city, doing my usual thing, and—"

A cascading tenor voice shrieked at the upper limits of its range. "Thelma, over here! Quick!"

"Damn. Some newbie probably can't untie his shoe. Catch you later, Brad. You know where the changing room is?" I nodded. "Drinks against the far wall. They're on me. Tell 'em Thelma sent you," she bellowed over her shoulder. "I know you'll have a great time!"

"Thanks," I shouted back as she disappeared into the crowd.

I entered the makeshift locker room. Coed, as usual. Still, I wasn't used to this. A double-decked train of lockers leaned against a long wall. Light from an almost-full moon made its way through a narrow window above the lockers and fought two small light bulbs at either end for the brightness trophy. Must have been the boiler room. A few wooden chairs were scattered about. A musty smell, not quite disguised by pot smoke, hung in the air.

I found an empty locker, grabbed a chair, and collapsed onto it.

"Whew." I slid my bag between my feet, stretched, locked my legs, and crossed my arms over my chest. I looked around.

Not many people. Yeah, it was still early. Two women, one chunky, one thin, stared at me as they removed their bras. Chunky turned away and unfastened her straps, while her partner did a subtle strip tease, wiggling her hips as she slowly lowered her garment. I returned her smile. A group of men huddled in the far corner, the obvious source of the pot smoke. Raucous laughter followed the pipe around their circle, along with coughing and hacking. Several of the men had changed into leather outfits: a vest here, chaps there, and a few studded, leather thongs that attempted to sparkle in the dim light. Two wore street clothes and there were no toy bags at their feet. Voyeurs? If so, Thelma would boot their asses out, pronto. We were here to add energy, not drain it.

A straight couple had finished their preparations. She wore a black corset that thrust her ample breasts toward her chin and boots that stretched up her thighs and almost grasped her bare pussy. Her partner wore red leather wrist and ankle cuffs that matched his collar and briefs, including dark blue piping. He picked up their toy bag and followed three paces behind. Two guys searched for a locker, giggling arm in arm, each carrying a huge toy bag. They couldn't possibly work through all the crap in their bags. Still, be prepared!

I stood. Vest off. Denim shirt off. Leather arm bands already in place. Vest on. Boots off. 501s off. Leather jock already in place. Boots on. I shoved the locker door shut, secured it, and put the key in a zippered pocket in my toy bag. On with the show!

I crossed a lounge area and walked past the bar. I'd pass on the free drinks for now. Couldn't take a leak in the middle of a scene. Still, if I wanted to piss into or onto someone . . . well, that would take care of it.

The huge play area had probably held semis in better days. Or maybe it was an old warehouse. Or both. The walls were draped in black cloth. The nondescript disco music was loud, but not overwhelming; you could actually hear yourself think. Better yet, you'd be able to hear your partner's breathing and gasps of pleasure and pain. I wondered if the disc jockey had ever played for an event like this. But, after all, it was San Francisco; he had probably seen just about everything.

The area was well-equipped with the usual paraphernalia: crosses, slings, T-bars, fuck benches, mattresses, and cages. Thelma had done a good job. Must have called in lots of favors. A few pieces were conspicuous with their elegance, highly-polished walnut instead of plywood laminate. A dungeon monitor paid particular attention to the activities at these stations.

I observed a few scenes: flogging, no-escape bondage, let's-look-pretty bondage with multicolored ropes, play piercing. I tarried at a group grope where numerous appendages protruding from a tangle of bodies reminded me of an overcrowded crab tank on Fisherman's Wharf.

By far the most intriguing scene was located in the center of the room. A spot light shone directly onto a metal cage. It was two feet wide, three feet tall, four feet long, and was constructed from metal bars spaced five or six inches apart, including the top. It had a swinging door at one end. An effeminate brunette sat scrunched at the far end, his hands and torso secured by ropes, his legs stretched in front of him. He couldn't reach his hard-on. A redhead was prostrate on all fours, his ass protruding up and out through the cage's open door. He was nibbling the captive's toes in slow sequence. Yuck! Not for me, especially after I noticed the captive's bright red toenail polish which, incidentally, matched the color of his fingernails. But, I supposed, being plowed from behind by an eager blonde Adonis spurred Red on. I considered extending the conga line by fucking Blondie, but a heavyset woman with white hair approached and began pummeling Blondie's ass with a ping pong paddle in time to his strokes. Oh well.

I scratched my head and began a slow walk around the perimeter in search of a partner, male or female, or perhaps both. I smiled and flirted. Halfway around, I halted, removed my vest, and tucked it into my bag. I resumed my cruising and sensed that someone was watching me. I scanned the crowd, but couldn't pinpoint my observer. I moved back into the pack.

Finally I plunked down onto an empty mattress, and leaned back on my elbows. Whatever was going to happen would happen all in good time. I closed my eyes and relaxed, and let myself slide into a dark, peaceful world.

I opened my eyes, how much later I don't know, feeling refreshed. This, of course, meant extra horny.

Again, I felt two eyes staring at me. Only this time, directly ahead. A ravishing redhead in a black pants suit and white blouse had captured me in her gaze. I almost blushed.

She was dressed as though she was about to chair a business meeting. What was she doing here? Another voyeur? No, not if Thelma could help it. What was going on?

I stood up, conscious but nonetheless proud of my almost-naked torso. I tried to subtly square my shoulders, sauntered toward her, and stopped at arm's length.

"Hello, my name's Brad. Nickname's Puma."

"And I'm Sherry. A Cougar. How interesting." She held out her hand. No ring, nails well done, light polish, gold bracelet, not from Woolworth's.

"You have me at a disadvantage." I stared at my crotch.

"On the contrary. I like my men totally naked, particularly a man who's comfortable with both men and woman. But you look good in that leather jock. Leg straps set off your bubble butt. And the snap-on pouch acts like a chastity device." She smiled provocatively. "Waiting for the right person to yank it off."

I stared at her outfit. "What brings you here?"

"Thelma's an old friend. Let's just say we've shared occupations in the past. I offered to help her out with this event, her first, to loan her, shall we say, some furniture, to give suggestions if needed, to kick ass, if warranted." Her delicate, but throaty, laugh bode authority. "We've been planning this affair for some time now." She cocked her head and waited.

"Same thing," I replied, "I mean, not the same business, er, well, I mean, we're old friends and I'd like to support her endeavor."

"I'll bet you could turn a few bucks by turning a few tricks, Mr. Sexy Man."

I achieved a full blush.

Sherry leaned into me. "Let's continue the discussion at my place." She stroked my crotch.

Goose bumps erupted on my body. "I'd like that. I'd like it very much." My cock quivered in its leather cage.

"Good. I'll leave now and warm the place up for us." She handed me a red card with gold embossing. I looked at the address and tried not to raise my eyebrows. "I'll say goodbye to Thelma, and be on my way."

"I'll walk you to your car," I offered.

"Not to worry. I'm parked out front." She gave my arm a light tap and walked toward the bar.

I stared after her. "Wow!"

She and Thelma whispered a few words, and then hugged. Heads turned as Sherry made her way through the crowd.

Thelma plunked her forearm across the bar's damp wood, and leaned into the bartender. He looked up from the beer glass he was wiping, followed her gaze as Sherry strode through the open door, and nodded. I hurried to the locker room.

I changed and put my right foot into my left pant leg only once. I dashed to my car, glanced at my San Francisco map, nodded, and fought my way through downtown late night traffic to Pacific Heights. My car had enough gas to haul me there, but my net worth wouldn't permit me to roost. The tops of the twin towers of the Golden Gate Bridge, red lights throbbing, rose through the fog, which glowed with yellow and white light scattered from the bridge's spires and roadway. Surreal. Almost like a theatrical production. Lost in my tangle of thoughts, I hadn't turned on the car radio, set permanently to my favorite classical station, or stuffed the impatient jaws of my CD player with my opera-of-the-day selection.

I turned into an upscale neighborhood and searched for Sherry's address. I stopped peering at numbers when I noticed a brightly lit yard and house in the distance, a beacon in the otherwise dark neighborhood. Although closely spaced, the homes were huge, and enclosed with brick, stone, or iron walls; most sported signs proclaiming vigilant security systems in bold, black letters. I pulled into the lone, open driveway and rolled to a stop before a three-car garage attached to a two-storied brick house. It was obvious that the rear windows commanded a splendid view of San Francisco Bay and the bridge.

I stepped from my car as an iron gate rumbled behind me and clicked shut. So, locked in for the night. The front door, dark-brown oak sporting lustrous, brass hinges, swung noiselessly open and Sherry stood impassively framed. I quickly took in the small, well-manicured lawn bound by precisely-trimmed hedges. An alabaster bird bath held court in the geometric center of the yard, circumscribed by a well-weeded bed of cheerful petunias. Lucky birds. Statues of Venus and David guarded each side of a small portico. Where's Cupid? In the bedroom, I'd bet.

I barely noticed that Sherry wore tailored black leather slacks and a white, sheer, scooped-neck blouse before she stepped forward and threw herself into my arms.

"Welcome, sexy man!" She nibbled my ear and ground her crotch into me, searching for my erection.

I ran my hands through her hair. "I should blush."

"Assuredly," she teased. "The neighbors are probably staring at us from their second story bedrooms."

My body jerked.

"It'll do the old fogies good. Let's give them something really scandalous to gossip about."

"Like what?"

"Like seeing your car here tomorrow at noon, and like this!" She bit my lip.

"Ouch!"

"Did I hurt my big, tough man?"

"Careful or I'll put you over my knee and spank you right here."

Sherry put her hands on her hips. "Or vice-versa. Come in." She grabbed my hand, tapped the door shut with the tip of her red shoe, and led me into a small marble foyer.

My eyes widened. "I should have worn my tux," I said.

"Clothes don't make the man," Sherry countered through a she-devil smile. She turned into the living room and said over her shoulder, "Let's have a drink."

"You have a stunning home. My compliments on the decorating."

Sherry settled onto the couch, and patted the cushion next to her. I sat.

She took a deep breath. "Women have a habit of making their fortunes through marriage. I stumbled into mine through non-marriage. I had a client, a young bachelor, who died suddenly from a new disease they didn't understand then." She lowered her eyes and continued. "He was bisexual—as far as his family was concerned, that was worse than being gay. They disowned him." Sherry looked back at me. "The family didn't need his money, owned an oil company or something, but they sure didn't want his bucks going to the likes of me. Surprise! They couldn't contest his will." She brushed a finely woven silk pillow.

"Quite a story," I said.

Sherry nodded. "All that was a few years ago. But I'm still attracted to younger men, especially ones who know their way around. Thelma told me about you." She threw a disarming smile my way. "Let's drink to the night," she proposed, "and to our new friendship."

"I'd like that."

"Do the honors." Sherry passed a bottle of chilled Harvey's medium dry to me. "My favorite," she said.

I set the bottle on a precisely-folded, white linen towel, twisted the corkscrew into its target, and teased it out with a pop.

"Done like a pro," Sherry said.

I poured. We balanced on the edges of our cushions, knees brushing, and our glasses touched in a silent toast.

Sherry raised her glass to her lips, stared through the wine's silky red surface, but didn't sip. The shade of her lipstick matched the color of her nail polish, and the tip of her nail seemed to vanish into the amber liquid as she slid her finger silently along the rim of the crystal goblet. She raised her head and aimed her radiant eyes at me. "Tell me about yourself."

I sipped, swallowed, and sat back. "Very good wine. No wonder it's your favorite."

"I'm glad you like it." Sherry paused and rejoined. "I'm waiting."

I held her gaze as I leaned forward and planted my elbows on my knees. "Where to begin? There's so much."

Sherry didn't hesitate. "Begin at the beginning. You're a man who comes to the point."

I sat up. "And you're a woman who knows what she wants."

"And knows how to get it." Sherry languidly took her first sip of wine, set the glass on the end table, and kicked off her shoes. She

205

crossed her legs underneath her and sunk into an amalgam of colorful pillows.

I sat upright and stared out the window as I collected my thoughts. I turned to Sherry and spoke in a low, deliberate voice.

"I suppose you could ask, 'How did a shy, Catholic kid from a small, conservative, New England factory town become a bisexual sadomasochist?' I have from time to time. But, I'm not sure I can analyze, explain . . . Hell . . . as some self-proclaimed pundits would say, *rationalize* the situation. Why even try? I'm no therapist. In fact, some of the weirdest people I know are therapists and psychiatrists."

Sherry nodded and cocked her head while raising her eyebrows.

"Yep," I responded, "I've had sex with more than a few of them." We both laughed.

"I was born in a small town in Connecticut. Mom was Catholic and Dad a Congregationalist. So, no surprise, I was raised Catholic, and traipsed through baptism, communion, confirmation, confession. Should be called 'captism,' and then we'd have a more accurate description, and four C's to boot!" We both snickered.

"Mom questioned my decrease in piety when I was a freshman in high school. I didn't think it showed. She never found out that I drove around town rather than attend Mass when I borrowed the car on Sunday mornings. Thank God I never had an accident!" Sherry's quick laugh gave way to a pained expression.

I leaned back and crossed my legs, one ankle over the opposing knee. "I went to college, married, and had two children. My wife and I finally divorced because 'we weren't bringing out the best in each other.'"

Sherry again nodded. I continued.

"I found myself in the Bay Area after a few job changes. Then I explored my sexuality. My nascent kinkiness emerged. So did my bisexuality." My body tightened.

Sherry placed her hand on my knee. She waited until I relaxed and tapped the tip of my nose with her index finger. "Come sit over here, between my legs."

Sherry spread her legs. I did as requested, sunk into the rug, and leaned back against the couch. She ran her fingers through my hair and massaged my scalp.

"Hmmm, that's nice," I moaned.

She slid her hands down my neck and kneaded my shoulders. "You're tight here." She flicked her finger against my back. "Take off your shirt," she ordered.

I shucked my shirt and she gave me one hell of a massage, even from that position.

"Nice, smooth back."

"Yeah. I shave what I can reach, get occasional help for the wisps I can't."

She reached around and slid her hand through the forest on my chest, followed by a quixotic, "Mmmmmm . . . "

She resumed her two-handed kneading, which eased into caresses, and my head sunk to my chest. Her next remark jolted me from my reverie.

"Have you ever been fucked by a woman?"

"Huh?"

"I mean with a dildo, a strap-on, silly."

"I thought only dykes did that."

"You have a lot to learn, Mr. Stud."

"I guess so. Is this considered Sex 101 or the advanced course?"

"It's whatever we make it to be. But enough of labels. It's just good, old-fashioned fun." She looked at the bulge in my jeans. "I see you're intrigued."

"We both are."

"Great! Go upstairs and use the bathroom at the end of the hall—it has a douche hose—while I freshen up." She leaned over and rubbed my crotch. "I'll fetch a few marital aids and wait for you in the master bedroom."

I climbed the circular staircase humming, "When the Saints Come Marching In." I cleaned out, but not leisurely, my established procedure accelerated by curiosity and excitement. I dried off with a huge, fluffy, white terry cloth towel, draped it around my flanks, and found my way to the master bedroom. I was about to be fucked by a woman. Would it count as losing my cherry a second time?

Sherry reclined on a red velvet fainting couch, her pale skin illuminated by a Tiffany lamp. I thought of a Renaissance painting—all that was missing were two or three cherubs. No, it couldn't be a Renaissance painting, not with a Tiffany lamp. Perhaps a Victorian painting, yeah, that was it, Victorian. No, Tiffany came after that, in New York, wasn't it? Well, then, a classy Upper East Side bordello—but the cherubs would have to go—perhaps a cupid or two. I halted in front of Sherry, hands fidgeting, eyes darting about the room.

She laughed. "Shy, are we?" She looked at my towel, which hung from my waist to my ankles. "Come over here, Mister."

I edged toward her. She leaned forward and yanked the towel off in mid-step. It disappeared into a shadowy corner.

"That's better," she purred.

My hands flapped at my sides. Sherry sat up.

"Gonna make me work for it?" she asked, eyebrows raised. "All the way over here, Mister."

I stepped as close as possible, my horizontal dick bobbing in front of her nose. She put her arms around my thighs, and drew me closer. Surprise! No blow job. Instead she stood and issued a command.

"Kneel and put your elbows on the couch. Don't worry, it's not a prostate exam . . . well, somewhat, I suppose."

I did as ordered and peered over my shoulder. I still hadn't conquered my awkwardness when my doctor told me to bend over his examination table, and, of course, marriage had never been like this. Sherry smiled and gave my butt a love pat.

"Relax," she cooed. I stared at my knuckles, took a deep breath, and closed my eyes. I felt droplets of sweat forming on my brow, lining up in precise formation to jump onto Sherry's pristine couch. I wiped my forehead.

"Don't worry. The cleaning service will take care of it. Again, relax!"

Cleaning service? Well, it went with the place. Must be a gardening crew also. I tucked my arms under my chin and cradled my head like a lazy cat.

"At last." Sherry spread my ass cheeks, careful not to scratch me with her long finger nails. "Nice asshole," she cooed, "and nicely shaved, too." Then her tongue went to work.

I was surprised at how proficient she was. Her technique was better than most guys'. I wished I could lick pussy as expertly as she rimmed. I wondered if she was bisexual and had rimmed other women. Or, how many men she had done. She moistened my hole with long strokes of her tongue. Then she nibbled the perimeter as a prelude to running her tongue around in ever deepening circles. Finally, what else can I say? she fucked my hole with her tongue. She seemed lost in her mission. My legs began to tremble and she slowly withdrew. She gave my butt a second and final love pat. I slumped into the couch.

"Yummy," she chortled. "Great tasting butt." She sat next to me and raised me to a sitting position with her index finger. Two flutes of white wine waited on a marble table. We drank silently, thighs and hips touching. I shivered. She fashioned yet another enigmatic smile.

"Follow me." She rose and I trailed behind, conscious of her full attire and my nakedness. But any embarrassment had vanished. She led me to a closed door, probably over the garage, swung it open, flicked a light switch, and stood back.

"It's the old billiards room. I didn't have any use for it or old fogies with cigars. So I converted it into a dungeon. For old time's sake." She laughed. "But I kept the pool table. Great for bondage."

I wondered about the balls and cue. Walnut paneling matched the veneer of the table and other furniture and equipment: a bondage bench covered in black leather with eyehooks protruding every six inches along the frame; a shelf displaying leather hoods ranging from slight sensory deprivation to total encasement; pegboards with coiled rope of various girths, lengths, and colors; more pegboards with collars and gags, and wrist, ankle, and thigh restraints; multi-drawer cabinets concealing God-knows-what; two gleaming, circular stainless steel chef's potholders, from which hung floggers, cats-o-nine-tails, crops, and signal whips. A T-bar dangled in the center of the room, its suspension linked to a motorized rack and pinion. And, of course, mirrors everywhere, including the ceiling.

My eyes were drawn across the deep-pile, black carpet to empty territory against the far wall. Sherry followed my gaze.

"I loaned my cross and fuck bench to Thelma. But we'll make due." She ran her finger up my spine. "To the center of the room," she ordered.

I positioned myself under the T-bar and held out my wrists. Sherry paused.

"Eager are we?" she asked.

"Eager and curious," I replied. "Well?"

Sherri frowned. "I like my men to be willingly submissive. To squirm while I fuck you, yes; to have the option and pull away, and not, even if it hurts. Oh yes."

I nodded. "You want me to continually give myself to you."

"You understand."

"I understand. I don't agree." I stepped toward Sherry. "I want to surrender myself to you all at once. And then sink into your power."

Sherry's eyes softened. "You've bottomed, but never really submitted, have you?"

"You understand, Cougar. Take your Puma, now!" I knelt, lowered my head, and held out my wrists.

Sherry put one finger under my chin and gently raised my head. Her eyes sparkled from the moonlight reflected in the mirror.

"I'm glad I can give you this," she said softly, and then whispered, "Puma."

She released my head.

"Thank you, Mistress."

Her eyes misted. "And thank you."

"Now, down to business." She shook her head, squared her shoulders, and looked every bit the senior executive. Or Domina. "Stand!"

She turned away. Soft music pervaded the room; an indeterminate, meandering melody supported by a subtle, yet driving bass. She soon returned with two fleece-lined wrist cuffs. She cinched them on my wrists and locked them to the T-bar. A whirring sound followed and my hands rose as far as possible while still allowing my feet to touch the rug. She stepped back and admired my taut torso. "This is how I like my men—helpless."

I moaned.

"You like this, don't you?"

I looked at my crotch. "More than you can guess."

"I don't guess. I know."

Sherry leisurely unbuttoned her blouse, folded it neatly, and placed it on the billiard table. She smiled, undid her bra, and wrapped it around my neck. Then she kissed me. Deeply. She grasped my dick between her thighs.

"Feels good," she said. "Very good."

She dry humped me for a few seconds and backed away. Her breasts were small, tight, and well formed. Her nipples were perky, probably as hard as my dick. I stared at the tattoo over her left tit.

"I'll tell you about that sometime. Perhaps, maybe, you'll get a matching one."

Before I could respond, she removed her shoes and placed them beside her blouse. Her hips gyrated and she did a slow half turn as her pants slithered to her knees. She bent over, wiggled her butt, and removed her slacks. As I had projected, her narrow hips supported lanky, perfectly formed legs. Not *Playboy* material, but my type— runner's thighs and calves. She tossed her slacks toward the billiard table, but they only made it to the floor under the side pocket. She laughed and pulled off her panties. These went over my head. "Smell good, Puma?" she cooed.

I nodded. She stretched the crotch across my mouth.

"Taste good, Puma?"

Again I nodded.

"Enjoy," she ordered.

I breathed deeply and tried without success to make sense out of the sounds assaulting me. Finally I felt Sherry close by. I heard a droning noise, like a plane approaching. Only it landed on my chest. Clippers!

"No," I shouted into her panties.

A slow, deliberate swipe across my chest. I shook my shoulders.

"Don't wiggle, or I'll nick your nipples."

"Why?" I squeaked.

"Why not? You'll look great with a smooth torso. Maybe I'll even oil you up."

"I'll look weird at the gym."

"Particularly since I won't shave your legs. At least then you could pass for a swimmer or a model."

"Fuck."

"You could shave them yourself."

"Never!"

"Quiet." Buzz, buzz. One pec smooth. Sherry swirled her finger tips over it, landing on my nipple, which she fondled. I groaned.

"Maybe I'll even take you to the country club pool Sunday afternoon."

"Fuck."

"After I lock my exquisite, yet masculine, collar around that strong neck."

"Aah."

"Show you off."

My dick stirred.

"You'll be marked—mine."

My dick jumped.

"And the high school girls will giggle."

My dick drooped down.

Two pecs smooth. "Whenever you peer into a mirror, which I suspect is often, you'll think of me."

"And blanch."

"After tonight, I think not."

She finished and stood back. "My own David, sans fig leaf. I should leave you here." She laughed. Then silence. Maybe she had left.

Sherry eventually returned. She threw the bra over her shoulder and grabbed the panties. I snarled and tossed my head to and fro like a puppy playing with his favorite rag while she yanked them off. She stood before me in stiletto heels, legs spread, and hands on hips, bright eyes perched over a wide grin. She sported a black leather jock-like harness that held a tan dildo.

My eyes widened.

"Is my big boy frightened?"

"It looks so large."

"I have larger ones. This is the beginner's model."

"It looks so hard."

"Harder than a guy's dick, yes, but I'll go easy on you. At first."

I took a deep breath.

Sherry covered the dildo with a condom and lube and stepped behind me. She gently inserted one, and then two, and finally three greasy fingers into my butthole.

"You've had dicks up here, haven't you? Don't be shy—no secrets between us—well, perhaps a few. I can figure it out. You're either tight or you're not."

"I've had a small toy or two up there." I paused. "And, yep, butt fucked too. But not much."

"We'll soon find out what you can really take."

Sherry put one arm around my belly and guided her cock to its target. I grunted as the rubber head penetrated my asshole.

Sherry grabbed my hips with both hands and pushed the dildo to its limit. I shrieked.

"It's okay, it's okay. The worst is over. The best is yet to come."

I tried to step away, but she dug her fingernails into my thighs. She began with gentle prods that soon became urgent lunges. Then she started pumping. After awhile it wasn't so bad. In fact, it almost felt good. But my hard-on wilted.

"Don't worry," Sherri reassured me. "Nobody stays hard while they're being pounded like this."

I relaxed and started backing into her thrusts. Her groans became gasps. Her panting turned into wheezes. "Fuck, this feels good on my pussy. Yeah, bang your butt into me, Stud Boy."

I didn't need further encouragement. I loved riding her dick and pushing her into further screams of delight. "Go for it, Stud Woman!" I shouted. Our voices rose to higher and higher pitches as our screams intertwined into meaningless gibberish.

"I'm coming, I'm coming," Sherry shrieked. I gave a final push, she gave a final thrust, and she yelled, "Fuck, fuck, fuck!"

She held me tightly for a few minutes, our torsos lubricated by a coating of sweat, as the aroma of sex dispersed into the room.

Sherry withdrew with a loud pop.

"Ouch," I yelped.

"So sorry."

"It's okay, it's okay," I babbled. "The ride was worth it."

Sherry lowered me to a sitting position and gave me water through a straw. We grinned at each other.

"Wow," I said.

"Double wow," she countered. "How are your wrists?"

"Fine, thanks for asking."

"Good. Ready for more?"

What could possibly follow? I nodded assent, the motor whirred, and I ascended, but not to my taut position. My feet were on the floor, and I could bend my knees. Quite a bit, actually.

Sherry glanced at my nipples. They're sizeable, due to numerous play sessions and self-inflicted abuse. She chose a pair of nipple clamps that I had never experienced, let alone seen, and dangled them in front of me with a mischievous grin. Inch long brass talons covered with black plastic protruded from a two-inch long black cylinder a half-inch in diameter. The talons were closed by rotating the cylinders which were joined by a twelve-inch chain of compact, stainless steel links that sparkled even in the dim light.

She circled each nipple with a talon, the cylinder adjacent to my body and pointing down, and tightened the clamps while holding my gaze. She watched me go from grin to gasp and stopped just before I entered the pleading and praying stage. She chose wisely. The clamps would keep me hard indefinitely, prancing midway on the tightrope that stretched from *Why bother?* to *Get those damn things off me, now! Please?* How had she known? Well, that's how she had earned her living.

She knelt before me and grabbed my balls with one hand, and the base of my swelling dick with the other. At last! My blow job! Then she disguised my prick with a blue condom. She rose. Our eyes locked.

"I'm so wet, lover boy," she said before kissing me. She grabbed my hips and pulled me into her. I gasped. Then I started pumping. Oh yeah, did I pump.

"That's it. Give it to me, Brad. Give it to me hard, real hard."

"Fuck, yes!" I answered.

Sherry loosened her grip, but not all the way, and we charged into each other, both of us a mirror image of the other's frenzy. We repeated our motions, over and over, a tangle of flesh and lust.

Then Sherry leapt up, threw her arms over my shoulders, and locked her legs around my waist. Her boobs dug into my nipple clamps.

"Ohmygod," I bellowed.

Our pumping dissolved into churning as she hung onto me. Fuck! Double fuck! What a sensation!

Cuffs notwithstanding, I was able to grasp the bar with both hands. I threw my legs behind me and we swung. Two sluts on a trapeze. I wriggled my prick as much as I could, Sherry pumped as much as she could, and we flew. Oh yes, we flew, we soared out of the building, above the neighborhood, through the dark clouds, and into the starry night.

"I'm coming!" I gasped.

"Go for it, Brad, I'm with you!"

I watched us from the side of the room as we came together in a welter of screams and wild oscillations.

I landed, none too gently. Sherry slithered off. We stared at each other, too dazed to speak or move. Sherry lowered the boom and undid my cuffs. She led me to a love seat. I collapsed and she fetched two snifters of brandy. We lifted our glasses in a mutual toast, trembling hands notwithstanding.

"So many firsts tonight," I said. "You took me into uncharted territory."

Sherry put her hand on my thigh. "You inspired me to travel there, gorgeous young man with a sharp mind."

I smiled and placed my hand over hers. We sat in silence for a few minutes."So, you must really like older women." Sherry's tone of voice mixed question with tease, admiration with trepidation.

"Well, I, er, uh . . ."

"I know, I know," Sherry said, camouflaging my embarrassment. "You go where passion takes you."

"I guess you could say that."

"And where your good looks and charm lead you."

I blushed. "You're very flattering."

"You deserve it. Let's take a swim, have breakfast, go for a walk. It's Sunday. We'll see what happens."

"You know damn well what will happen."

"I sure do." Sherry stood and hoisted me to my feet.

Mine for the Night

Brenna Lyons

"Are you ready, Doctor?" the ancient woman in the doorway asked, a gleam of jealousy in her eyes.

Sondra ignored it. Late in her eighties, the handler was old enough to have had her pick of men before the plague had struck Earth. The wrinkled hag was old enough to have been married and have had a man to herself, or nearly to herself, for many years before the plague killed him off. She might even have raised a son to adulthood before he was lost to her. If she hadn't, the crone was a fool who'd squandered her chance, and Sondra had no time for fools.

At forty-five, Sondra had had her first man less than five years earlier. She was one of only thirty thousand of the remaining quarter billion women on Earth young enough to bed a man who'd had since the first had been saved by the very process she'd helped created to repopulate the world.

Moreover, Sondra had worked her ass off to save the world. It was a small reward she reaped for it.

As if her gimlet stare had clued the handler as to how out of line her petty emotions were, the elder woman shifted uncomfortably and cleared her throat, her face going a deep crimson.

Sondra straightened the files on her desk, making a show of ignoring her. "I am indeed," she finally answered.

The handler withdrew, and the door to the male habitat closed behind her. Sondra set about her preparations.

She unbuttoned the top few buttons on her blouse to show the edge of lace and cleavage. The rest of the time was spent in busy work: fluffing the pillows on the bed in her combination office and apartment, smoothing the blankets, and setting nonessentials off the desk. Since every man reacted differently to his reintegration into society, she never knew how the first time would pass, and it was better to be safe than sorry.

Sondra straightened at the knock, her slit hot and wet already. "Come in."

Oh, he will come in. They always did.

The man was more enticing in person than he'd been on the monitors. Then again, they usually were.

Three months off the suppressants, he had gained muscle, and a light smattering of male curls decorated his broad chest. Sondra's mouth watered for that first taste of twenty-five luscious years of uneducated male specimen. Since half of the group they'd tried to mature at twenty-three had perished, she dared not move the process back further.

He tipped his head, half in greeting and half in challenge. "You wished to see me, Doctor?"

His life was full of handlers and doctors, women too old to have real aspirations of bedding a man and who had no wish to lose their comfortable positions by acting inappropriately around the young men they tended to. His newfound aggressive tendencies would make him bristle at yet another doctor in his life.

She motioned to a comfortable chair. "Sit. Please."

He—*Benjamin*, she reminded herself.

Benjamin folded himself onto the chair, seemingly strung tight. "Am I in trouble?" he asked.

Sondra feigned interest in the file she'd left on her desk, though she'd memorized it in the two days she'd been watching him. "You've been in several altercations with other students."

It wasn't unusual. They had to suppress testosterone production until the engineered virus timed out and died off at sometime close to twenty-three or twenty-four years old. When the suppressants were taken away, and the testosterone production rebounded, the young men often suffered violent mood swings.

Benjamin ground his teeth, his eyes hardening, proving himself a veritable throwback to the times when men were hunters and providers, the times before men were pampered and protected by the females who needed them so desperately.

"Am I in trouble?" He annunciated every syllable, warning that he would chance fighting with her and finding himself tranqued in the process.

She smiled, trying to put him at ease. "Not at all, but I may be able to help you."

A look of surprise turned wary. "In what way?"

"Aggression is a symptom of—"

"You're saying I'm sick?"

Sondra set the file aside, assessing his reactions. She'd never invited a quad in and had the male prove unstable, but there was a first time for everything, she supposed. Even with all the psych evals, they could be wrong.

"Not sick. Your body is changing." It was a given he'd noticed it. "You are in a transition phase."

"Transition to what?" His words were economical, nearly clipped.

"Full adulthood."

He hesitated and then nodded.

"You will have noticed other symptoms. You've increased in muscle mass." *It will feel so good when he's thrusting inside me.* "You've grown body hair." Sondra panned her gaze to his lap. "Erections."

Benjamin darkened but didn't reply.

"How often do you come erect, Benjamin?"

"Ben," he snapped back at her.

Sondra raised an eyebrow at that. "You've chosen to shorten your name?"

"If I am adult, I have that right." His chest and shoulders tightened down in preparation to fight over it. It was time to defuse the situation.

"Of course you do. I simply hadn't been informed that you'd done so. I meant no offense."

He relaxed again, crossed his arms over his chest, and grunted his agreement.

"Now . . . How often do you come erect?"

Ben seemed to consider it. "Five . . . times a day."

Sondra knew he was lying. Most of them did. She'd seen him on the cameras. He had a healthy male response of more than double that number in a day. "Only five? Perhaps we should start there."

One brow went up in something resembling shock, but he didn't respond.

She sat on the desk in front of him, close enough for him to smell her musk. In this stage of the testosterone storm, scent would be a powerful motivator. As if in confirmation, his cock thickened slightly. Ben lowered his hands to his thighs, and his eyes dilated in arousal.

"Do you notice anything in particular that brings you erect?" Sondra added a note of invitation to the question.

His gaze slid downward then flicked back up. So, he was a leg man, but he didn't want to admit it.

Sondra raised one leg and planted it between his parted thighs. Ben stared at it, swallowing hard. His cock hardened further, going thick and heavy behind the soft, medical center lounging pants he wore.

"Excellent response," she noted. "Touch, Ben."

His dominant right hand skated up his thigh toward his cock.

"Do you want to touch yourself?" she asked. "Or do you want to touch me?"

His breathing went harsh. Ben's hand settled on her foot. He stroked back and forth, circled his fingers around her ankle, and moved upward.

"What do you feel?" she prompted.

"Soft. You're so soft."

Sondra stared at the impressive length of his cock, licking her lips. "And you're hard."

"Is that right?"

Very right. "Yes, it is."

His hand passed her knee. Ben paused at the hem of her skirt, meeting her eyes as if seeking her reaction to him going farther.

"Touch, Ben. Touch everywhere you want to." Her inner muscles clenched in anticipation. "Taste everywhere you want to." A vision of his long, auburn hair brushing her body as his tongue played between her spread legs sent a trickle of moisture down her perineum.

"Taste?" His voice went rough at that, and his brown eyes dilated until the black pupils were more dominant than the iris.

"Perhaps we should divest of clothing," she suggested.

Ben stood, towering over her. Sondra untied his lounging pants and pulled them down, letting them pool around his ankles. He kicked them away, his body fairly vibrating for more. Sondra wrapped her hand around his shaft, stroking up and down. Precum leaked from the crown, and she licked it off. His shout was sharp in the newness of the sensation, and she took a moment to suck at him before she released the tip and sat back.

He stood, his eyes closed, seemingly shocked into stillness. Sondra leaned toward him, laying a lick over one male nipple . . . and then the other. Ben gasped, arching his back.

"Undress me, Ben. Touch and taste."

He was aggressive. Whatever came next was sure to be a wild ride.

The first few buttons on her blouse opened smoothly. The next two ripped away in his haste. Sondra didn't offer instruction or correction. When she chose an aggressive one, she planned to lose clothing in the process.

Ben grasped the edges of the blouse and pulled, and Sondra arched toward him, aroused by his raw need. He yanked the blouse off her arms, then dragged her chemise up and off, leaving her nude to the waist.

One large hand kneaded at a breast, and Sondra leaned back on her elbows. He stared in fascination, his gaze flicking this way and that.

Her breasts weren't as perky as a younger woman's, she knew. Sondra had produced her required male child by insemination, after all. Perhaps he would enjoy the young quad member's breasts better, but tonight, he didn't know any other woman's body.

Even when he was presented to the quad, the women would have no hetero physical experience. Other women, even with strap ons, or computer-driven neuro-stim weren't the same as sex with a man. Sondra was experienced in things his quad wouldn't learn without years of experimentation and research.

She could have had one of the first surviving males and all the children he could offer her. But at forty, Sondra hadn't wanted another child, and it would have been a waste to accept the government's offer and not return it with children.

In the end, she'd requested a night with two men a week, before they were presented to their quads. The government had snapped at the offer, and nearly a dozen of the other scientists had taken her lead. As the one instrumental in identifying that the virus would die off if not activated by a given time, she'd been moved toward the top of the list, second only to those who'd formulated the suppressant to keep the men safe.

Ben lowered his head, licking at her nipple as she had his. Sondra gasped in pleasure. Her nipple hardened, and he stared, his cock jerking and bobbing.

She didn't tell him to suck it. Ben was aggressive. He would get there on his own. He wanted to discover her textures for himself, without being led there.

As if in confirmation, he suckled hard, wringing another gasp from her. Ben didn't stop there. He moved down the soft plane of her belly, unclasping her skirt and pushing it away. Then he trailed his mouth upward to her neck . . . and then her mouth.

Sondra pulled her feet up, planting her spike heels on the edge of the desk. Ben cupped her knee, working his way up the unexplored length of her leg.

He hesitated at her slit, touching with trembling fingers, moaning. "So different."

She threaded her fingers in his hair and drew his mouth down to hers. Ben's breath was hot and moist on her lips. He didn't question what she intended; the aggressive ones rarely did. Ben started experimenting with touches of his lips against hers. His lips parted as hers did, and his tongue tangled with hers.

Ben's venturing fingers slipped through her slit, and Sondra groaned into his mouth, encouraging him. He thrust them deeper, stretching her pussy around them.

His mouth left hers. "I have to," he gasped out. His whole body shuddered and shook in restraint.

"Have to what?" It always challenged an aggressive when she played coy.

"Touch myself." It came out from between gritted teeth.

"You've already tried that. I thought you wanted help." She was taunting him, pushing him into something hot and mindless.

His expression hardened. "Your mouth," he snapped, locking on the taste she'd already given him.

Sondra kept her voice low and calming. "Not this time. There's something else you need. Something we both need."

Ben started to question her, stopped, and looked at the fingers impaling her, moving them in and out as if in consideration.

"That's right," she invited.

His fingers eased out, and Ben spread her slit, staring in wonder. Another encouragement emerged as a shout as he stroked his cock inside. His hands closed on her hips, holding Sondra still for his nearly desperate thrusting. Some men were clumsy their first times, but Ben moved like the trained athlete he'd proven himself in competition with the other men.

In moments, he was cradled in her arms, his cum jetting into her, his harsh breaths fanning her mouth. She hadn't come this time, but before the night was over, she would. They rarely lasted long the first time, but the testosterone rebound gave them stamina, and they were willing to learn the things that gave women pleasure as well as finding their own.

Ben's breathing evened. "Oh, Goddess," he grumbled. "What was that?"

Sondra smiled. "Just the beginning, Ben. I have so much more to teach you."

His cock bucked against her inner walls. "Your mouth?"

"That can be arranged." But she would have her climax first.

"Goddess, yes."

"We don't have to stop now," Ben teased.

You don't have to. Sondra shot him a sly smile and tucked her blouse into her skirt.

He pushed from the bed and sauntered to her, his cock semi-erect and all too appealing. Her slit dampened at the idea of Ben taking control of the situation. Her fascination with the thought allowed him to do so.

In a dizzying move, she was laid out over the couch, her skirt around her waist and Ben's tongue playing along her slit. Sondra cycled her hips up and down, too shocked to protest the move.

Ben took it for permission. His tongue thrust inside, finding the rhythm he'd only just learned she loved.

Sondra licked her lips. She could have had a man like this every night. His quad wouldn't have Ben or another man if it weren't for Sondra's work at saving them.

Still, it wouldn't do to have him lagging when he got to Jenice. She moved to sit up.

Ben planted one large hand on her chest and forced her back down. He ate ravenously, driving Sondra toward an explosive climax.

I can't let him have sex with me again.

She could take advantage of his fervor to take one more climax for herself. But how would she convince him not to continue to his own release?

Her rising body made the answer clear to her. "Make me come, Ben," she panted out.

He doubled his efforts with a growl that brought her hips off the couch.

"Make me come, and I've got a surprise for you."

Ben had a thirst for learning. As often as he'd taken Sondra in whatever position they'd been playing in, he'd demanded new experiences. Overall, he'd be a delight to his quad. And the promise of another new experience would likely stay his hand.

If it didn't, Sondra wasn't going to fight it. If Jenice and the rest of the quad weren't happy about it, that would be just too bad.

His tongue was a delight: fluttering, thrusting, stroking along every sensitized line of her pussy. Sondra closed her eyes, giving herself over to the aggressive tendencies in him. Every male was different, and she was lucky enough to be able to sample a wide variety of them.

"Goddess, yes," she breathed, tunneling her hand in his hair.

Ben was diligent, rocketing her toward release. Until Sondra had her first, she'd believed the crones were lying about how good it was. Now she knew better.

Her pleas for him to continue degraded into moans . . . and then screams of climax. She went boneless, warm waves of serotonin and endorphins flooding her system.

Ben covered her with his body, parting Sondra's lips in a forceful kiss. His cock teased at her seam, and Sondra wrapped her arms around him, urging him on.

He eased back. "The surprise," he demanded. "I think I've earned it." His eyes challenged her to deny it.

Sondra bit her lower lip, reminding herself that her night with Ben was over. "Help me up. I'll take you there."

His smile was wide, and his eyes glittered. Ben pushed off her and lifted Sondra to her feet. She directed him to wash his face. It wouldn't do to have him go to Jenice without that much. While he complied, she straightened her skirt. When he returned to her side, Sondra took his hand and led him into the far corridor.

There was no worry that anyone but Sondra and Jenice would see Ben walking the corridor nude. The access corridors to the quad habitats were locked to anyone but the three scientists on this wing, and it was Sondra's day to move a man to his quad.

But Ben wouldn't know that. To her surprise, he didn't balk at his nudity in the corridor. Perhaps it was an aggressive show to him. Perhaps it was a challenge of some sort.

Ben furrowed his brow, staring at door after door. "Where are we going?" That was a challenge.

She smiled. "You like sex."

He groaned, his cock twitching at the mention of it.

"You'll have sex every day, Ben."

He went fully erect. "With you?" There was something cautious in that.

"Very quick, Ben," she complimented him. "You'll have a quad . . . four women. You'll cycle through them, one a day."

His breathing went ragged.

"Unless you convince them to take you together as a treat, in pairs or more."

"Goddess, yes," he whispered.

Sondra glanced down at his cock, considering indulging in one last taste. She drew her gaze away. It would be better to send him to Jenice in a fervor.

"Your first is named Jenice. The others are Tamra, Emmie, and Rose." *In that order, the order I chose for him.* "They were chosen to match your personality. Jenice and Emmie will let you take charge. Tamra and Rose are going to offer a challenge."

It was more than that. With the advances in genetics and endocrinology, the women in his quad and Ben would be appealing to each other. Nothing was left to chance.

He licked his upper lip. "And how long will I be with them?"

"Every day."

Sondra avoided promising him forever. Since the geneticists were actively encouraging home-groups to agree to swap males once all four women had a child or two from their first male, she wouldn't promise he'd spend his life with a single quad. Ben was adventurous. If he and his quad agreed to it, he might have three or more quads in his future.

"And you?" he asked. He was a perceptive one. Ben would keep his quad on their toes.

"I get first taste of other men."

Ben seemed to consider that and then nodded. He didn't question if he was just another cock to her.

Sondra had a well-rehearsed answer she usually dusted off in answer to that question, but Ben wouldn't have been given that answer. Yes, all the men were special in their own ways, but Ben stood out, even among the most memorable she'd bedded.

"And will this be my . . . home?" It was a word they'd been taught, the place they'd reach after their forced isolation.

She shook her head. "This is a temporary placement. Once you and your quad are settled into a true home-group, you'll all move into your permanent home."

It was a safety feature that the newly formed home-group would live in the medical center habitats, under full monitoring, for three lunar months. After that, they were transported further behind the safety walls and away from the women still waiting for men to mature.

Sondra stopped at the appropriate door, and Ben took a calming breath. He slid her a sideward glance and nodded his readiness. She punched in the security code and opened the door.

Apparently, Jenice had been too excited to wait for Ben to arrive. She was on the bed, working a vibrator in and out of her body. Ben stared at her, swallowing hard, his cock thickening further at the sight.

Sondra leaned closer to him. "She's been waiting so long for you. They all have. This is all they've had . . . self-gratification, machinery, and other women."

He replied with a stiff nod. Ben strode to the bed, placing one knee on the mattress at Jenice's hip. The young woman startled, her eyes opening and then widening, panning from Ben's chest to his cock, then up to his face.

His fingers closed around the vibrating shaft and yanked it free, bringing her hips up in surprise. Ben tossed it away without turning it off, and Jenice's legs spread in an instinctive move.

"You don't want that, do you?" he purred. Without waiting for her response, Ben positioned himself between her thighs.

Jenice shook her head, gasping out a negative response to his question, even as she stroked her hands over his chest in seeming disbelief.

Ben thrust inside her, and Jenice screamed in delight. "This is what you need," he informed her. "This is what we both need."

Sondra slipped into the corridor and headed back to her lab. Her report to the quad would include some of the sexual positions and tastes Ben seemed particularly interested in, including group sex.

An hour later, her report filed, Sondra stared at her computer. Ben and his quad were on full monitoring; she could watch if she wanted to.

It took her only a moment to discard that idea and move on. It wasn't healthy to obsess over a single man. There were thousands more in the medical center's male habitat, on suppression and being educated for the life of ease they'd live, or weaned off the suppression and maturing into the sexual beings the Goddess had intended them to be.

Instead, she took a long, hot bath and returned to her desk. There were eighty-four men left in this month's cycle. Five of her sister scientists had already chosen their next men, leaving seventy-nine files for Sondra to peruse.

She deliberated only a moment. Sondra had chosen two aggressive males in a row. It was time to choose something different.

The psych evals beckoned, and she pored over them for hours. Three stood out from the rest, and Sondra ordered the camera feeds on them. The second proved to be what she was looking for, and she entered her call for him before one of the others could.

Zak was a lean male who'd chosen to wear his golden hair cropped short. He was relieving his sexual needs under the shower spray, his strokes slow and precise, and his grip almost tentative.

Sondra slipped her fingers through the split in her robe, stroking herself in time with his movements. She closed her eyes, envisioning Zak coming to her.

He would be less sure of himself than Ben had been. Zak would have to be seduced.

Sondra would order him to disrobe and lay on the bed. He acquiesced to such commands from the doctors and scientists. He wasn't one to question them or challenge them, as Ben would.

Her 'examination' would involve bringing him up with a hand job and straddling him to take his cock inside. Though it would be new to him, Zak would follow her orders straight to climax.

Zak would need guidance and teaching. He would need to know about his quad early in the evening. He'd need to have the goal of learning to be gentle with them.

Climax came soft and sweet, much as it probably would with Zak in her bed and body.

In the afterglow, Sondra punched up the files of his matched quad and started coding the invitations to report to the medical center for matching. A quick scan of their fact sheets showed one very experienced and aggressive woman, two of moderate experience and somewhat introverted . . . and one who'd remained virginal to the match.

"How unusual," she murmured. Yes, a virgin would be the perfect first of his quad for Zak. He'd want to learn, if for no other reason to make her first time a memorable and pleasurable experience.

Sondra ordered his quad's introductions to ease Zak into his home-group. That accomplished, she sent the missives off.

This evening, four excited young women would meet each other and Sondra. They'd be shown carefully selected vids of Zak: competing with the other men, grooming, sleeping . . . and relieving his needs. They would have two days to settle into their temporary quarters and their relationships with each other. Then their rotation with him would begin.

"But before then, he's mine for the night."

To Make It That Way

Emerald

When people tell me I seem different now, my stomach clenches for a moment. At those times, there are two things I know: first, that they're right; second, that even though I am aware of precisely why, I could never explain exactly what happened to make it that way. It was, and still is, an enigma in my life.

I was twenty-one when I met her. Three of my friends and I were standing outside one of the bars we went to all the time when she pulled up in a black Toyota and stopped at the curb right beside us. I glanced over, and her eyes fastened on mine with an expression I couldn't begin to decipher. It was an expression I would come to know well. It meant that she was seeing me, really seeing me, and she saw something I needed that she knew she could give me.

"You," she said to me. Her voice was sweet but had an edge of command that made me jump even as she smiled. I moved forward to her open passenger side window and looked down at her.

She nodded at the bar. "You going in there to get laid, sweetheart?" I just stared at her, at a loss for what to say. Behind me, I could hear my tipsy friends shuffling and murmuring.

Her smile grew wider. "Why don't you come with me instead?" She kept her eyes trained on mine, and I grew no less stupefied as the seconds ticked by. I thought I hadn't understood her correctly, and I didn't give the idea that she was serious more than a second's— an elated second's—thought. She lowered her voice and made her intentions perfectly clear.

That's when I got nervous. I wasn't into casual sex—had never had it, actually—and sex in general, much as I craved it, made me shrink back in fear that I wasn't doing something (anything) right. My shyness had kept me from having it as much as I could have, and I had only slept with two women. One was my girlfriend right after we graduated high school, and we had waited so long that my performance anxiety was camouflaged among the closeness we had developed. The other was a girl I had dated a year before for a few months, and I attributed the fact that our sex had never been fantastic to my own inadequacy.

Now a woman whose expertise I could only imagine sat in front of me, already fucking me with her eyes and expressing unambiguous interest in me. Petrified, I said the first thing that came into my mind:

"Um, don't you think we should go out or something first?"

She laughed out loud, a spontaneous, hearty laugh that I knew was not mocking me. She shifted into park, smiled at my friends over my shoulder and called to them.

"Do you guys mind if I borrow your friend for a while? I'll see that he gets home safe and sound," she said with a wink after they'd bumbled forward to crowd around the window. When my buddy Jake finally came to his senses and made some reply, Cole, whose name I didn't yet know, placed her graceful hand on the gearshift and nodded. "Hop in, darling."

I did, and she shifted the car into drive and took me to her house.

Thus began what seemed like a sudden double life for me. I still hung out with my friends on weekends and most other times we usually had. But sometimes I disappeared for a while. I often lost track of time when Cole summoned me—or, considerably less often, when I called upon her—to get together for one of our fervent, marathon, phenomenal sex sessions that left me feeling like the rest of the world had evaporated or that we'd stepped onto another timeless planet for a while. Not many people even knew about her, and those that did didn't hear much about her. She slipped in and out of my life like an intoxicating scent, not there for long, but hitting with such force it left an impression that time has its work cut out to erase.

She lived by herself. No pets, no plants, no evidence of any live entities to which she was responsible for other than herself. I hardly said a word as she drove us from the bar to her house that night, and she let me sit in silence, a quiet, serene smile on her face as her wrist rested casually on the top of the steering wheel, her eyes settled on the road in front of us.

After she led me inside, she threw her jacket over the back of a dining room chair, turned, and offered me her hand. "Nicolette," she said simply, her lips opening in a smile. "You can call me Cole."

Her smile seemed to be knowing, sly, rather Cheshire Cat-ish, and I couldn't imagine of what secret she was in possession. She was gorgeous: striking peach complexion, tall graceful figure, blond hair cut in a way that seemed to invite pieces of it to fall sexily in front of one eye. I had wondered then how old she was. I didn't know yet that she was forty—and I never would have from her appearance.

"I'm Zack," I said, immediately disgusted by how weak my voice sounded. But her smile didn't waver. I glanced around me. In the bathroom down the hall I saw a corset and several pairs of stockings hanging from the shower rod. She saw me looking.

"I collect lingerie," she explained, moving in front of me to the kitchen.

"Lingerie. That's interesting."

She smiled. "I'm glad you think so. Some of it requires hand washing, which is why it's in there. Would you like some tea?"

Tea? It didn't seem to fit the occasion. She reached into a cupboard toward a high shelf and glanced back at me. Her thin sweater slipped a bit over her shoulder and displayed a slender black strap.

I nodded and moved back into the dining room, suddenly so nervous that I didn't even want to be around her. Much as this situation could lead to something I certainly wanted, I was so scared right then that I just wanted to be somewhere else. I would have preferred by multitudes to be home in my boxers playing video games.

I heard her shriek and stepped back into the kitchen.

"Shit," she said, looking down at her shirt. Water had bounced off the side of the tea kettle and splattered all over the front of her. I stared at the dark wet splotches, almost covering her breasts and splaying up to her neck.

Christ.

"I'm going to have to change," she said, smiling at me as she headed toward the stairs. As she ascended I caught a glimpse of her sweater being pulled over her head and the shiny black camisole underneath it.

If I had been a little more sure of myself, I would have followed her up to the bedroom and ripped off the rest of her clothes. Even despite my nervousness, the urge was uppermost on my mind. With a deep breath, I turned toward the door just as she reentered through it, and we almost collided. She gave me a glittering smile and moved past me to attend to the kettle.

I tried to catch my breath.

She'd put on a black, oversized, button-down shirt. The top two buttons were undone, and when she turned to take the kettle off the stove, the collar slid to the edge of her shoulder. There was no strap this time.

That's when I felt myself get hard. I wanted to walk up behind her and rip her shirt the rest of the way off, grab her tits and—

"Sugar?" her voice cut into my fantasy.

"Huh? Sugar. Yes." Maddeningly, I blushed as I looked down. It was funny how I could clearly imagine what I wanted to do to her, but standing right there with the immediate opportunity to, I was scared shitless to try.

Suddenly I noticed her little smile as she watched the white grains slide into the steaming liquid. Something that had vaguely been swirling in my consciousness solidified: she knew precisely the effect she was having on me. My eyes narrowed. Did she enjoy the way this was tormenting me?

"Cream?" She turned what appeared to be innocent blue eyes to me again. I looked back at her, and the urge to kiss her became literally overwhelming.

"Yes," I said, and moved toward her before I could stop myself. I pressed my mouth to hers and felt her tongue slide against mine. I pushed her back against the counter and wrapped my arms around her waist.

That was the end of what I initiated. She took over from there, dropping us both to the kitchen floor and straddling me as she pulled her still-buttoned shirt over her head. She was naked underneath, and the memory of that first glorious view of her full, round tits and the way she ran her fingertips over her nipples, can still make me hard. She had a condom in her jeans pocket, and she fucked me right there on the kitchen floor before any nervousness in me had time to catch up.

I was never sacred to make a move with her again, which she later told me was her objective.

Much as Cole was obviously in charge of our sexual encounters, and just about everything else it seemed, she loved to be dominated, and she was teaching me things I'd never even thought about rough sex.

"Pull my hair," she said once as we stood in her living room, her blue eyes trained on mine. I noticed again the effortless sweetness in her voice even amidst the edge of command.

I reached up and clasped a handful, giving it a hesitant tug.

"Pull it," she said as she reached up and gripped my forearm, snapping it back once with a speed and brevity that surprised me.

I swallowed. I pulled again with the same sharp, no-nonsense force I had felt her use.

Her eyes glimmered. "Better. How do you like that?"

She looked at me steadily. I wasn't sure what the right answer was.

Knowing my thoughts had become so common it was hardly surprising anymore when she said, "I'm not looking for a 'right' answer, Zack. I'm looking for *your* answer."

I wasn't sure what that was either.

"I like it because you like it," I finally said.

She nodded, eyes locked on mine.

"And I like it because . . . I don't know why," I faltered.

"Did it make you uncomfortable?" she asked, and somehow I knew despite her neutral countenance that if I said yes, she would never ask me to do it again.

But it hadn't. I mean, it had, but it hadn't because she liked it. I wouldn't have dreamed of doing it on my own. I told her as much.

"Appropriate." She gave another short nod. "It wouldn't be something you should do if you didn't know someone liked it. There are a lot of things like that. Many of them you'll be doing with me. How do you feel about spanking?"

"What?" I immediately blushed at such a stupid answer. It wasn't like I hadn't watched porn. I knew some people were into spanking. I just hadn't done it.

"I don't know," I said. "It seems . . . violent or something. Or degrading." Yet somehow I knew it wasn't, knew it was different. But I wasn't sure how, and some part of me seemed unable to reconcile it with that conception.

Cole's eyes glinted. "Sex," she said, "has the potential to encompass all human experience. All the nuances, all the understood and not understood, may be experienced through sex. And that means there's a whole realm of it we're not going to understand. It's beyond our common forms of understanding." Her eyes bore into me like steel. "But it's not beyond our experiencing."

After a moment she broke her gaze, and I noticed I had started breathing again. I also noticed my cock was rock-hard.

"The key," she said, lifting her water glass from the end table near where we stood, "is in awareness, respect, openness, authenticity. We don't have to understand it all, as long as we are aware of ourselves. As long as we respect our partners. As long as we approach with openness what is happening between us. As long as we are authentic in our dealings, our experiences, our examinations. If something is uncomfortable, be aware of that and see what it teaches you. If it feels inauthentic, stop doing it. "

"That wouldn't account for a lot of abusive situations where sex is concerned," I countered. "Lots of people may think they're aware of and like what they're doing, but it hurts someone else or is even criminal."

"Yes," she agreed, setting her water glass back down. "But that means at least one of those pieces is missing."

I pondered that, as she didn't appear inclined to expound. She moved toward me and caught my mouth with hers, and I caught my breath at the suddenness, at the heat zipping through me like lightning at her touch. She backed me up against the couch until I fell onto it, my hands groping her breasts. She pulled my cock out of my jeans and dropped her head, sucking with fervor, going after my cock as though she was possessed, like she was taking something from it she needed.

With a final pump, she paused, running her tongue up the length of my shaft. Her cat-like eyes gazed up at me with a hard lust and a hint of something else glowing in them. Abruptly she stood up on the couch, towering over me as she pulled off her shirt and stepped out of her jeans. Underneath them she wore an impeccable red lingerie set, glimmering bra, thong, and garter belt with rhinestones embedded around the rims and matching stockings. I caught my breath.

Cole didn't need lingerie, but she sure knew how to use it.

I was still tingling from the cock sucking she'd just given me, feeling practically euphoric but awaiting instructions. I watched her, not knowing what she was going to demand of me.

She threw her jeans aside and stood above me on the couch, one foot planted on either side of my thighs. Her gaze rested on mine as each garter was individually undone and the garter belt, thong, and bra slid off one by one. I broke eye contact to look at her naked pussy above me, and then quickly flicked my eyes back to hers.

"What do you want, Zack?" she asked, breaking the silence.

What did I want? What did she mean? The question was a departure from the order I had been anticipating, and I didn't know how to address it.

I saw the smile in her cobalt eyes before it reflected in the curve of her lips. It was that same smile, the one I'd seen when she'd pulled up in her car outside the bar that night, the one she'd given me when she'd first told me her name, the one she'd flashed as she'd gone up to the bedroom to change out of her wet shirt. The one I never determined what lay behind, that was always the same for her but seemed to bring such a wild variety of things out of me. The one that, to this day, may still be the strongest mental image I have of her.

"What do you want, Zack," she repeated, a statement this time. "Why are you waiting for me to tell you what to do? Do you think that's your job? Being told what to do, and then doing it? What do *you* want?"

I swallowed. To be told what to do *is* what I wanted. How else would I know?

Cole continued to stand above me, her naked pussy shimmering. "Yes, I know you feel like you don't want that responsibility." The smile was still in place. In a lithe movement she sank down onto me, straddling my body but not taking me inside her. She leaned forward.

"But you have it anyway."

I looked at her tits, naked and easily within reach in front of me. I wanted to grab them. She was watching me. She ran her own hands lightly over her breasts, a lock of blond hair falling in front of one cat eye.

"I'm not always going to be here to tell you what to do, Zack. Trust yourself. What you want is just as important as what anyone else wants." She looked at me. "Do you understand?"

I grabbed at her, shoving her hands out of the way and squeezing her tits, sitting up a little to yank her down on top of me. Indignation and embarrassment rose in me as I felt uncertain, wanting to show her for once that I knew something she didn't. I wanted to show her I could know what to do, that I could do something on my own.

I reached up and grabbed her hair, and she expelled a hot breath as I yanked it back and turned us over, pushing my body on top of hers. I reached for the one of the condoms from a pile on the coffee table and tore it open. When it was on, I grasped at her throat, administering a firm choke hold like she'd shown me how to do not long before. I met her eyes as I reached for her dripping pussy, hot molten liquid covering my fingers just like the heat from her eyes covered my entire body. I circled her clit like she'd taught me until she came, my body trembling almost as much as hers when I finally pulled my hand away.

I pushed my cock into her and pounded, feeling the same way Cole had looked when she had sucked my cock moments before—like I was possessed, needing something that was inside her as I drilled into her. She screamed my name, clawing at the cushions around us. I yelled as I came, something I had never done before and panted as I collapsed on top of her.

She was panting beneath me. As our breathing slowed, gently she reached and touched my cheek. The unexpected tenderness gave me pause. I lifted my head and met her gaze.

Only once did we run into each other unexpectedly in public. Some friends and I had decided to stop at a coffee shop near her neighborhood on the way home from a concert. I saw her as soon as we walked in. Momentarily paralyzed, I didn't know what to do. For some reason I felt uncomfortable mixing the two sides of my life: the Cole side and the non-Cole side. It was like they represented two different selves for me, and I didn't know yet how to put them together.

Concentrating on a notebook on the table in front of her, she didn't see me as we ordered and sat at a booth on the opposite side of the cafe. Jake finally noticed my distracted state and, when he followed my eyes, recognized Nicolette immediately. Since two of the guys we were with hadn't been there the night I'd met her, Jake enthusiastically filled them in while I sat in conspicuous silence. Suddenly everyone at the table was pushing, wondering why I wasn't going over to see her. Comments about how hot she was intermingled with pointed urges for me to approach her. Finally I knew I'd rather go talk to her than listen to their horseshit for another second.

She looked up at the sound of her name. I stood in front of her. She smiled slowly, and suddenly I knew she had known I was there. She looked me up and down before re-meeting my eyes.

"Hello," she said pleasantly, motioning toward the chair across from her. I sat. I tried like mad not to fidget nervously, but I know I failed.

"Here by yourself?" she asked. Her eyes sparkled. She knew I wasn't.

I considered lying to her but decided I would be neither convincing nor comfortable with that. Instead I shook my head and said what I hoped sounded casual, "Nah, I'm with some friends." I indicated them with a jerk of my head.

She nodded, that maddeningly knowing smile on her face.

"Hmmm." She tipped her chair back and smiled wider. She was about to embark on some spiel, I could tell. Just once I wanted to tell her that I already knew what she told me, or thought it was wrong and could give a good reason why, or that I'd already tried it and it didn't work. Each time, in fact, I braced myself to give her one of these responses, but each time she managed to convey things in a way that was so obviously true that I couldn't try to dispel it without looking utterly stupid. I was never good with bullshit anyway. I would end up mad and glaring at her, at that knowing smile, small and subtle as if it existed just for me, and just want to smack her, and soon we would be wrapped together naked, sweating and squeezing and screaming . . .

"Let me guess." Her voice interrupted my thoughts just before my cock got hard. My thoughts veered from the hot to the dull as I focused my attention on her smooth monologue. "Your friends saw me and recognized me. You are in one of your serious moods, and possibly due to some ambivalent feelings of which I'm unaware, you felt uncomfortable encountering me in public when you were with your friends, whom you probably haven't told much about me." She winked as I glowered at her. "But they teased you and made you feel stupid for passing up the chance to come over here when it meant you'd get laid, so you came over even though you didn't really want to."

I don't know how the fuck she knew everything. I hated it that my behavior was so easy to predict. I didn't know if it signified a weakness of mine or a strength of hers.

"Why would you think that?" I thought my voice sounded decently defiant, and I was proud of myself.

She glanced down at the drink she was holding and chuckled. "I have supreme confidence, Zack, that someday you'll learn not to let other people dictate your actions," she said as she looked back up.

I glared at her, and when she smiled again, I got pissed at the same time a jolt of arousal shot through me. I clenched my jaw and tried to look away, but my eyes locked on a blond wisp of her hair that fell across her cheekbone. I wanted her. Now.

She held my gaze. In the span of a few seconds, all but the active desire to fuck her became distant priorities in my consciousness. My cock strained against the zipper of my jeans, and I wanted her to yank it out and take it in her mouth right there.

She stood and swung her purse over her shoulder. She must have packed up her things sometime during our conversation when I wasn't paying attention. She looked down at me.

"Let's go."

I stood up and followed her without so much as a glance back at my friends. She led me to her car in the back of the dark parking lot and opened the back door, nodding for me to get in. After I did, she climbed in after me and shut the door, reaching up front for the lock button.

When she turned back to me she immediately grabbed my zipper and yanked it down. In seconds my cock was out in the cold night air, and her gaze rested on mine for just a second before she dropped her head and took the length of it to the back of her throat. I groaned and grabbed her hair. She started sucking hard and fast, and I was going to come if she didn't stop soon. I pulled her hair gently, and she rose off me as I throbbed with the urge to explode.

I looked at her, breathing heavily, and she pulled a condom from her pocket. She seemed to carry them wherever she went. She watched me as she unrolled it slowly down my cock. Then she sat back on her heels for a moment and looked at me. Even in the dark I could see that smile lurking in her features. It was almost as though I could sense it by now.

Just as I was about to say something, she moved forward, and I thought I heard a low chuckle just before she straddled me, hiking up her skirt and pulling her thong to the side. I reached up and pulled her down on top of me, pushing my hands under her shirt to her flesh. She rode me hard, moaning into my neck as I slid my hands under her bra. Then she sat up, blond locks swishing around her face as she bounced on top of me. I closed my eyes, knowing I was going to come if I looked at her. I heard her gasp, and when I opened my eyes she was working her fingers over her clit, getting herself off. I grabbed her thighs as I came then, too, shuddering as she bucked and squeezed around me.

Cole climbed off me and reached under her skirt to reposition her thong as I grabbed a tissue from the box she conveniently kept tossed around her vehicle and took the condom off. She reached behind her for the door handle, and in seconds we were standing back in the parking lot again.

She chuckled. "Thanks, Zack. Go on back to your friends." That beautiful smile was on her face as she gave me a long kiss. With a wink, she opened the car door and climbed in, leaving me to pick up my thoughts where they had left off back inside at her table.

I learned a lot from Cole. Some of it I think I haven't even realized yet. I still think about her even though I haven't seen her in almost a year. Once in a while my friends still mention "that hot older lady you slept with for a while." But they don't understand. What they do know about it is merely the surface, nothing of what was underneath, where the two of us were—and where no one else could see. I have no idea where she is now, but every time I stand outside that bar or find myself in the parking lot of that cafe, I remember her indescribable smile and how, for a time, she directed it at me. It's hard to say whether the omniscience she exuded in my eyes was really there or whether it was the youth and naiveté in me that displayed it, in reflection, only to me. I still can't convince myself that Nicolette wasn't something special, someone who has that intangible ability to see inside people and know what they need. Maybe she thought I didn't need her anymore. The emotional investment in me made it impossible to see if that was true. It seems to me everyone needs her.

Sometimes I wonder what I meant to her life. It's hard to imagine I had anywhere near the impact on her that she had on me, but I suppose it's impossible to say. It's just another one of the mysteries that, as intimately as I knew her in some ways, I will never know about Cole. By now I don't yearn for her anymore, and it isn't even painful, which was once hard for me to imagine. I still hold out hope that someday I'll get to see her again. I've finally come to accept what somewhere inside me I've always known: If she wants it to happen, it will.

Her Apolonio Smile

Trish DeVene

Kate had her eye on the checkout boy since she'd first seen him run across the lot. He'd been wearing a black store uniform and ran with smooth assurance from the automatic doors to his car. He stood at the back passenger door, fidgeting with something she couldn't see. The slim young form of him had locked her throat—his narrow waist, belted pants, and the gentle slope that raised heat in her face. Then he'd run back across the lot, to the store, and she'd followed.

Now, as she sat in the meeting room in the high-rise at 123 Hamilton, she ran her left thumb along the crease of her labia hidden by her blue pantsuit. The marketing director pulled up another pointless PowerPoint and her clit swelled under her fingers.

She didn't believe in love at first sight, wasn't interested in love at all. She was forty-three, divorced five years, and in no way wanted a new relationship.

What she *did* want was that boy at the supermarket.

"Kate, we're heading to Draco's for lunch." The meeting had ended and the marketing assistant just had to ask, again. "Coming?"

Coming? Nearly, she wanted to say. The lights had come back on and she brought both hands back to the table.

She shook her head. "Working through lunch today," she said.

From the corner of her eye, she saw Matt roll his eyes. She was past forty and unmarried. That meant she was a lesbian or cold, hard bitch. That was their opinion and she heard it in the insinuating jokes. What she wanted to tell them was that just because she didn't want them, didn't mean she didn't want men.

"Drinks at Bon Suite after work then?"

She couldn't suppress the smile as she said no again. "Shopping tonight," she said. Her underpants were soaked. Maybe they could smell it. Could men smell a woman on the prowl?

For the past six weeks Kate kept working her way into the new checkout boy's lines. She could paint these two suited co-workers a picture; lash their leering and disdainful eyes with what real beauty was. Beauty named Polo.

Daniel stood in the doorway beside Matt. His hand crossed the opening. Was he daring her to duck under?

"Did you ever see beauty so exquisite it was painful?" she asked

His body slackened. "Maybe," he said. The exit cleared as he fumbled to recall what beauty meant at all.

She needed the bathroom on the 29th floor. It was hardly ever used because the tenants had moved out. Ever since seeing this boy, her memory played images of him from morning into the night. She needed constant release.

"You got a guy stashed away somewhere, Kate?" Matt called. "Always with that Mona Lisa smile." That's what really bothered them. Like sperm battling their way to the egg, these two sensed her desire. Did they imagine that one day she'd admit to them her desperate need? The prudish librarian come undone?

She wasn't a prude. She wanted sex, not ownership, not conquest.

She wanted Polo at the local grocery store. He was young, eighteen or nineteen at most, but the initial moments of guilt she'd felt flashed and passed when he had looked at her with those hazel-brown eyes—serious and more deadly than she'd imagined for someone so young. He was Latino, with a shine to his high cheekbones, and his full lips broke easily into an even, white smile. At the cash register, while he tapped and scanned, she'd imagine the taste of his black silk hair where it nibbled at his brown neck. His profile hinted at soft slopes, satin skin, a color she couldn't name—sienna was too orange, umber too dark—something created by sun but holding the mystery and quiet of dusk.

He was beauty in its highest form.

When Polo's smiles at her became more frequent, when he began insinuating himself into her space as well, she took it as acquiescence; perhaps not complete reciprocation, on his part, but acquiescence was enough. She wasn't interested in love.

At the day's end, she had to pass Daniel and Matt once more. Matt leaned against the copier, twirling his key ring on his finger. Her breasts felt tight against her blouse, nipples sharp after the quick climax in the 29th floor restroom. Let them smell her desire. Their crass leering and clueless superiority could never touch it.

She turned back to them at the door. "Did you ever witness grace in the simplest actions?"

Polo maneuvered about the store between service desk tasks, cashier, and bagger with nonchalant ease; confident in his duties, lithe in his stride. She spent the six weeks learning his schedule, noting when he was at customer service and when he was bagging. While she waited, she continued her studies of him. His name, she found out, was a nickname for Apolonio, a name derived from the god Apollo, god of light. Sunlight pulsed under Polo's brown skin, black hair. He was the wrap of night around fertile heat.

Tonight, he'd be bagging. This would be the day she would accept the bagger's polite offer to help her to her car.

On the drive to the store, Kate kept her hands on the steering wheel. No more rubbing away the desire. She wanted to feel it fully when she saw him. At stoplights, she leaned forward, breasts against the wheel. She unbuttoned two buttons of her blouse to let the cool, evening breeze sweep in.

In the parking lot, she drove once past the window to spot him. Yes, there was the slender back side of him that needed to be licked and bitten. He fluidly gathered boxes of rice, bags of pasta, fit the pineapple alongside the melon, and then in a second was at the next counter, gathering, sorting, as if all matter succumbed to his wish.

She had little to buy, but made sure it was enough for a few bags of packing. The moment she got in line, he abandoned his post at the quick checkout, slit open the first bag, and waited.

She hadn't buttoned the blouse; her breasts felt like waves cresting over the bra. Her hands quivered a bit as she handed over her rewards card. Each time she came, he was more beautiful. She looked at him, the dark sweep of hair over his brow, the equally dark eyebrows and lashes. He was a late-night cognac, molten earth ready to turn volcanic.

The last of the groceries were bagged, one last slip of handle-through-handle and he placed the bags in the cart.

"Would you like help out?" he said with his usual nonchalance, his dark eyes lingering longer than the question demanded.

They all expected "no." She was fully capable of handling her own groceries.

She said, "Yes, if you don't mind."

His brown eyes locked on her. He offered no smile. When he was serious, he lost all boyishness. He wasn't the least afraid. He put the last bag in the cart and steered it toward the door, glancing back once to be sure she was following.

The sun nestled somewhere below the horizon of strip malls, the sky holding the blush of day as night's lavender breath descended. In this quiet light, he seemed not the black dead of night, but dusk, slow and sensual twilight. His lips would be a sparrow's underbelly, his tongue the heart that kept the blood in rapid flow. Blood throbbed low in her as she followed him through the parking lot, watching his easeful stride, wondering how long before she could unlatch that belt that secured him.

Popping the trunk, she brushed by him to grab a bag. Again he looked. His eyes were darker in the evening light. They stared at her, not with naïve questioning, but with assured commitment. If she wanted this, it would happen.

She let him finish arranging the bags in the netted holder and clicked open the driver's door. As he slammed the trunk, he had two options: to role the cart back into the store, or to leave it and come around to where she waited. She sat in the door's opening, legs out, fishing in her purse as if to tip him.

He walked over. "Is that everything?" he said. His left hand rested on the top of the door. It swung a little, and he opened it further, stepping closer. His pants were a black river, rippling, hinting of underwater life. His other hand met the roof of the car. Closer. Her eyes were level with his stomach that would concave when he breathed and released.

She hooked one finger into the top of his pants and pulled him toward her. His body blocked the frame of the store. He closed the door slightly and blocked all but him from her view. Him at the waistline. His belt was buckled in the third hole. She ran her fingers across the leather, slid it from its latch. His breath caught, his stomach hardened beneath the thin cotton shirt, and she put her mouth to the shirt to breathe him.

He smelled like sandstone warmed in sun.

Her breath came back hot. As she undid the buckle, he didn't move. Sound beyond him seemed to fly off with the distant jets, streaming far away. She heard the zipper; she heard another breath.

He was hard, but she didn't release the shaft that pressed against cotton. Raising his shirt instead, she put her mouth to a stomach of satin valleys, burnished fields warmed and feathered with sun. Her hands came around the back of him, holding the slender hips, pulling him closer. When he moaned, she ran her tongue under the elastic waistband. Her fingers slid around, pulling elastic from what it held captive. He was released, the silk tip of him against her cheek.

The silken glans, a millimeter from her mouth.

She withdrew a second and lowered her head so it brushed against her eyelids, down her nose, breathing the deeper scents of him. Lips on his testicles, she exhaled heat on them, flicked her tongue. And when he jerked, she took his hips again and pulled him closer. A fraction of movement would join her lips to him.

Closer. Her first kiss of him: Polo, beautiful youth, something fresh, not yet scarred, no rejections needing recovery, no possessive ownership. Optimistic youth—demanding in its optimism. He pressed closer, his hand sliding down the window. Kate opened her mouth and let him rest in the hollow of it, so he would feel breath, sense moisture without contact. Her tongue would be a bed if he moved again. She pulled back slightly, and then flicked her tongue once on the opening, and again under the ridge. The hand on the car roof tightened, a metal protest against his palm.

Running her tongue down the shaft, flicking again around the testicles, she looked up at his face in struggle. Around him, the world was open, people exiting cars, shoppers rattling carts; inside, his employer waited. His mouth was tight, and when he looked down at her hesitation, those full lips parted. She wanted his mouth, but instead took the shaft in her own. Tonight would be his.

She set the rhythm, and he leaned in. His forehead knocked against the car, his hair a black wing along the roof. And when his gasp released a deep held moan, she felt the semen pulse. Her mouth closed tight around him, and she drank.

When Kate drove away, window down, the evening air smelled like goldenrod and clover. Her jeans were tight against her clit, and it swelled in wanting more of him. She took the back roads, driving toward the black silhouette of trees against lavender sky. She drove one-handed and rubbed at the throbbing painful pleasure between her legs. Her pelvis flamed while the sky doused the day's lingering heat. *Polo.* The road was deserted, and she rubbed faster. At the burst of release, her foot pushed pedal to the floor.

She eased up and whispered his name, pressing her chest against the steering wheel in embrace. *Polo.* He'd be back behind his counter. He'd said, "I have to get back," and his eyes had been worried, but his mouth had twitched a crooked smile.

She smiled now over the arc of the steering wheel.

The next day in the office, Matt and Daniel were a beige blur of chatter that couldn't break the tingling smile. She drank three bottled waters, her mouth around the neck, tongue dipping in. She didn't make it to the 29th floor, climaxing in her office chair under the pressure of her well-used pencil.

When Kate returned a week later to the store, Polo was behind the service desk, bent over, writing something while a customer waited. He was a wash of black, with his hair over his forehead, and as she walked by, he raised his eyes with their black-lash framing. The brown eyes stayed on her while his hand still moved across the paper. He knew what he was writing. He could fulfill many tasks with simultaneous efficiency. He looked away, handed the paper to the customer, and smiled that full, polite whiteness.

This boy had marvelous self-control and nonchalance about his beauty as well as its effect on people. He was young. The world was his.

"Excuse me," she said as the customer turned away. "Do you have a public restroom?"

He stared.

"I have a key." He snatched a string from a hook, a tangle of keys dangling from it, and turned to the service booth exit. She followed him past pastries, past deli, through the scent of rising bread. Tonight, her lips would feel his. The throbbing in her clit rose in a wave up her chest, tightening her throat. Some beauty was exquisite enough to cause pain.

He slid the key in the lock. It clicked. He didn't glance back as he entered. Didn't turn until he leaned against the white wall-sink. One sink, one stall, a silver trashcan below the towel dispenser. And Polo—legs crossed, body one sleek slope clothed in black. His brown hands rested each side of him on the white porcelain. He would make her come to him this time.

Either he hadn't been as innocent as she'd at first expected, or he adapted easily to any situation. Kate felt a smile edging up. His beauty might be painful, but his youthful daring was intoxicating.

"Will they be looking for you?" she asked, as she approached him, as she closed off the space and chance to leave.

He stared again, his head tilted just slightly down so that he looked up under dark brows. His legs uncrossed. He wanted only one thing from her. She wanted only the same in return.

Kate ran a finger over that tight cheekbone, down his jaw line.

There was nothing like the skin of youth. His stare darkened. There was nothing like youth's careless hunger. Her own hunger was too often seeped in questions, examinations, doubts, and tried determination. *How would this feel?* Their legs touched. Her hands found space on the cold white sink, beside his. *What would it mean his lips against hers?* She had to spread her legs around his to come closer. He didn't straighten. He didn't move. Her breasts pressed lightly on his chest.

How would it feel to know those brown eyes? Their mouths were a millisecond away from losing this world. His lips parted. She felt the moan in her throat, a tingling that made her eyes water. *To kiss him.* His breath brushed her lips. She took his lower lip first. And at the touch, pleasure channeled through her, blood rushing to stimulate the nerves of clitoris and canals.

She bit, and then her tongue slid along his upper lip. He was last night's sweet clover and this morning's sun-baked porch. His tongue flicked at hers, and she closed her mouth around his lower lip again. She opened her eyes again to his. There was no other world but him before her. Her hands found the small of his back, pulled his shirt from his pants, and lips parting, found silk beneath her fingers, found satin in her mouth. Tomorrow, she would button up her blue suit, swing that briefcase into the office, and participate in the world that lay beyond them now. But here, the universe was behind Polo's lips, and she wanted it.

Without tongues, they held their mouths open on each other's, waiting for first penetration. As he moaned, she flicked her tongue in. His hands moved off the sink, sliding up her rib cage, around her breasts. He broke the kiss and tugged her shirt up, lifting her bra. His mouth closed on her nipple, hands grabbing her hips, pulling her tight against him. He sucked and she ran her lips, her cheek along his feathered hair.

When he rose again to her mouth, she needed more than one kiss. Kate yanked at her belt, tried to unzip her jeans. His hand that clasped her ribs, slid hard down her waist, over her stomach and dug past the protest of zippers, into the place that begged for him, that had demanded him from first sighting.

His finger flicked at wetness, raising a moan in her, a deep breath in him. His finger slid into the opening, and quickly he turned them, pushing her against the sink, his finger penetrating deeper. Flicking. The jeans slid down. He bent over, his mouth on her breasts, biting her ribcage, a tongue down her stomach, the finger flicking so that she kept backing up on the sink.

She saw only fluorescence and shadow and heard another zip. A struggle of fabric. She reached to help, to stop him, but the finger flickered, inflaming her pelvis, nerves zipping down to the arches of her feet. She kicked off the jeans at her ankles and wrapped her legs around him.

"Polo." His name defined every desirous moan the world could conjure. That satin tip she had tasted yesterday now pushed against her labia. He wetted it with her moisture. She knew before he entered that the thrust would shatter cells and set rivers of fire along her veins. He played a moment at the entry, played and teased, until she grabbed his neck and drew his mouth to hers.

Now. His first thrust emptied his own chest of the long-held, guttural moan. His cry of pleasure was released in her mouth. She held him with her legs, rocking over the sink. She wanted more skin. Fumbling with buttons, she sought his chest, stopping as each new wave of blood shocked her. As her hands met chest, his heart beating under her palm, he pulled her up off the sink, and she rode him down to the cold tiled floor.

Atop him now, his chest bared, his hard penis waiting inside her, she circled his nipple with her tongue. Flicked her tongue across it, and he thrust upward. His hands roamed from breasts to waist, grabbing her again, grinding her over him. They would hear, she thought for a moment. Outside the door, they would smell the climax that poured from her.

She moaned and bit back the sound. There were screams people kept inside. Need that was starved for fulfillment. She followed Polo's rhythm. He was young. He wasn't yet tired of the world's demands. He gave without question, asking nothing in return. He was still the spark that lit the world.

He thrust into her because it felt good. She gripped him, arching back. Sometimes it felt like swallowing the sun, or a royal blue ocean bubbling through. He would smile when they finished, that briefly hesitant but uncontainable smile. And she'd be wearing him home and to the office every day, in the smile they didn't understand, the one that kept her striding forward through every tomorrow they tried to steal.

Polo. He moaned with his final thrust, and his body collapsed, arms spread over the tiled floor. Grace and beauty and surrender. He wasn't afraid. The world was open and she was stepping into it.

You Just Might Get It

Julia Barrett

"Oh, my God! This is so yummy! Thank you. You didn't have to do this, you know."

"Of course I did, Kate. I can't leave a damsel in distress dripping on my doorstep."

Kate put a hand over her mouth to hide her grin. She didn't think it would be polite to smile with a mouthful of sandwich.

"No, I mean this . . . supper. It's really nice of you and it's amazing."

"You saw me make it, it's nothing really. Took all of five minutes."

Kate watched Eric take a bite of his own sandwich. Egg yolk ran down the back of his fingers. Kate looked on, her mouth suddenly dry, as he turned his hand over and licked the bright yellow yolk with a pink tongue. Kate almost licked her lips in response, but she caught herself. She swallowed, hard, instead.

"I'm so embarrassed to be locked out again."

"Not your fault," replied Eric, grinning at her. He reached over and delicately rubbed her lower lip. "Egg," was all he said.

Kate could feel herself blushing.

"These sandwiches hit the spot, but you either have to be prepared to use a lot of napkins or do a lot of licking. And I'm out of napkins."

Kate had been waiting on the stoop, drenched and shivering, hoping for somebody, anybody to show up, when Eric arrived home. For the fourth time in a week, her electronic key card hadn't worked and she was stuck outside the building. She'd run out in the rain to retrieve a book from her car, barefoot, wearing a threadbare T-shirt and baggy jeans, only to find she couldn't get back in. If Eric hadn't come by when he did, she'd have had to walk several blocks to the neighborhood grocery store to call a friend. She'd left her cell phone sitting on the kitchen table, along with a card where she'd written down the security company's phone number after the last time she'd gotten locked out. Eric was nice enough to let her in, for the second time in two days, and kind enough to invite her over for something hot to eat. She'd changed quickly and toweled off her hair, but it was still damp. She felt the wet curls against the side of her face and she automatically brushed them back. She watched Eric's eyes follow the movement of her hand. Kate deliberately looked down at her plate. She picked up a piece of arugula that had fallen from her sandwich and popped it into her mouth.

"So, you're a chef?" she asked, feeling suddenly uncomfortable with her thoughts.

"I was, but I'm not working as a chef right now," Eric replied.

Kate looked up. "Oh? Why not?"

"Coming up with a business plan. Doing some research." He stopped to take a big bite. "I'd like to open my own place, but I need to figure a few things out."

"Such as?"

"Oh," Eric chewed thoughtfully. "Location, size, marketing, staffing, theme . . . maybe. I want to be very cautious. Most restaurants go out of business within the first year. I don't want to be one of them."

"I can understand that," said Kate. "Nobody wants to lose their shirt."

"Oh, I don't know," he winked at her. "I can think of any number of situations where I'd like to lose my shirt."

Kate felt a grin tug at the corners of her mouth. If she didn't know any better, she'd think the man was flirting with her.

"It's okay, Kate, you can smile. You have a lovely smile."

"Yes," she allowed herself a small, self-deprecating laugh. "Just lovely with egg sandwich all over my teeth."

Eric reached a long arm across the table and delicately tucked a stray curl behind her ear. "Yes, even if you did have egg sandwich all over your teeth, you would still have a lovely smile."

Kate shivered. No man had touched her like that in five years. Not since way before her divorce. He was definitely flirting with her. Eric had to be, what? At least ten years younger than she was. God, maybe fifteen. Why was she doing this? Sitting here at a table in a man's apartment, eating his food, allowing herself to be disarmed by his charm, fantasizing about things forty-one-year-old women weren't supposed to do with twenty-something-year-old, very attractive men.

"You're a nurse, right?" Eric asked.

"Yes."

"Just, yes? Not 'Yes, I work intensive care,' or 'Yes, I do oncology nursing'? Just 'yes'?"

Kate smiled again. She couldn't help it. "I don't talk much about my work. It freaks some people out. I'm a hospice nurse."

"Oh, so you see dead people."

Eric's delivery was so deadpan that Kate nearly spit out a mouthful of bread.

"Yes," she laughed. "I see dead people. Where'd you pick up the hospice humor?"

"Friend of mine. She's a medical social worker. I guess you have to laugh or you couldn't do the job, right?"

"You got it," replied Kate. She took a sip of the fresh-squeezed orange juice he had poured for her. She raised her glass to him. "Nice," she said. "I ought to buy myself a juicer."

"No need," said Eric, "You can use mine anytime you want."

Eric lifted his eyes and studied the woman seated across the small table from him. Her damp curls surrounded her head like a halo. The first time he'd seen her, in the window across the courtyard, her hair had been damp, just like this. Sweet. Very appealing. He wondered if she had any idea her kitchen window looked directly into his. Probably not. She'd only moved in ten days ago. Eric assumed she was still busy unpacking. That was one of the reasons he'd invited her to dinner, one reason among many. He wondered, briefly, how old Kate was. It was hard to tell. She could be anywhere from twenty-nine to forty-five. But he wasn't about to ask her and he didn't care. Her age didn't matter to him. Her laugh did. Her big, brown eyes did. Her luscious lips. Her wide, white smile.

When he'd arrived home and found her soaked to the skin and shivering on the stoop, he got to play the hero. That was twice in two days. There was no way he'd pass up an opportunity to spend time with her. He'd hoped she'd accept his offer of dinner, and he'd been pleased when she did. It was no big deal, one of his easy meals: oven-toasted rustic bread with melted gruyere, roasted tomatoes, baby arugula and a soft-fried egg. Simple and sensuous. The sandwich was messy and it required the use of all your fingers. There was a lot of runny egg yolk and licking involved. Eric hoped he could segue that licking into something else entirely.

God, there was a lot to like about her. Not only was Kate easy on the eyes, she was intelligent, articulate, mature, and she appreciated his sense of humor. Plus she blushed at the drop of a hat. Eric found that adorable. She wasn't jaded or flighty, like so many women he'd met recently. He'd bet the farm she hadn't grown up in California. Probably Iowa or Illinois. Someplace rural. An old-fashioned country girl.

"Where'd you come from? I mean, where are you from, originally?" he asked.

"Blair, Nebraska. It's a little town near the Missouri River. I went to school there. Dana College. You?"

"Minneapolis."

"You're kidding? You don't have a Minnesota accent."

"Yeah, well, I worked hard getting rid of that. I can do it if you like."

"You mean like . . . Minnesooooota, North Dakoooooota, ya think? Like that?"

It was his turn to laugh. "More or less." He looked at her plate. "Finished?"

"Oh, yes, thank you. The sandwich was great. I can cook, but I guess it never occurred to me that such simple ingredients could taste so good together." Kate reached for his empty plate and set it on top of hers. "Let me help clean up. That's the least I can do."

He watched as she rose from her chair and stretched. He enjoyed watching. Her breasts were pert. Not large, but pert with perky nipples. Two handfuls. That's all he needed.

"You have a long day today?"

"Not too bad. Really. It would have been better if I hadn't locked myself out. But . . . what can you do? I was sort of hoping to curl up in a hot bath with a good book, but I left my book in the car and then the key . . . well, you know the story." She carried the plates to the sink.

Eric followed with the empty glasses. "You can still have a hot bath," he said.

"Yeah, I guess," she replied, rinsing off the plates.

He set the glasses down on the counter and ran a hand lightly through the chestnut locks that hugged the back of her neck. He watched goose bumps rise as he trailed his fingers along her shoulders, and heard her sharp intake of breath. He waited momentarily to see if she'd move away, but she remained still.

"I mean, if you're interested, you could have a hot bath . . . with me." He lowered his mouth to the tender juncture between her neck and her shoulder and lightly moved his lips over her soft skin. God, she smelled sweet. Like fresh, spring rain. He felt her breathing quicken, and he wondered if she would bolt, but she stayed where she was. He moved his hands down her arms and wrapped his hands around hers beneath the running water. His long fingers twined through hers. She didn't pull away.

Kate raised her head and stared at his reflection in the window. Her eyes were wide. "Eric," she said softly, "We've only known each other for ten days and even at that, this is the most time we've spent in each other's company. I'm not sure . . . I'm not sure it's a good idea."

Eric stood behind her, meeting her gaze in the window. "I think it's a very good idea," he replied. "I've been thinking about it since the day you moved in, and I saw you across the courtyard. Through this very window."

"You can see me?" she asked.

"Just your head," he chuckled, "When you're in the kitchen. I like your hair damp like this. I like the way it curls around your face."

Another intake of breath.

"Eric . . . I . . . what about . . . I mean . . ." Kate began to pull her hands away. "We're not the same age."

"No, we're not," he answered. "And that's an issue because?"

"It's an issue because I'm older than you." Her voice was husky.

"An issue for whom?"

"You? Me?"

Eric kept his voice low. "Kate, if it was an issue for me, I wouldn't be standing here, trying to keep from pressing against you because I'm so hard it hurts."

Staring at her reflection in the window, he watched her eyes close. Her lips parted and a tiny sound, almost a whimper, escaped her. His wet hands left hers, and he wrapped his arms around her narrow waist, drawing her backwards, drawing her close, pressing her shapely bottom against his erection. He wasn't lying to her. His cock throbbed behind the zipper of his jeans, eager and aching to be buried inside the heat of the woman in front of him. If, and this was a big if, Kate would give him the opportunity.

Eric didn't find many women this intriguing at first glance. When he prepared a meal, he refused to settle for anything less than the best quality ingredients available. He felt the same about women. He didn't like drama. He didn't like guessing. He wasn't attracted to gigglers. He preferred a mature woman. One who knew what she wanted, where she was going. A woman who knew her way around her own body, who knew what she liked and wasn't afraid to show a man how to give it to her. Younger women tended to be too self-conscious for his taste. It often seemed to him as if many of the younger women he'd dated acted like being in bed with a man was an audition tape. They tried to turn love making into a performance. A big turn-off for him.

The minute he'd spotted Kate across the courtyard, he felt something. A tug in her direction. It didn't hurt that she had short hair. For some reason, Eric had a thing for a woman with short, dark hair. Not to mention her other assets. She met all his requirements. Kate was smart. She had a lovely smile and a contagious laugh. And she possessed sweet, perky breasts with those eternally erect nipples. They'd poked so enticingly through the thin material of her wet t-shirt when he'd found her on the stoop that his cock had begun twitching immediately. She had a slender waist and nicely-flaring hips, and she possessed incredibly long legs that could wrap around a man while he pumped into her. He wanted those long legs wrapped around him. Tonight.

When Eric pulled her to him, and she felt the ridge of his erection pressed against her bottom, she nearly swooned. A voice in her head spoke up. *How silly that would be,* it said. *Don't swoon. Say yes. When was the last time you had an offer like this? Years ago, lady. Years ago. Say yes, Kate. Say yes.*

Eric turned her around slowly and looked into her eyes. A wet finger stroked her cheek, asking permission. He opened his mouth as if to say something.

"Don't speak," she ordered. "Just kiss me before I change my mind."

"With pleasure," Eric growled, and his mouth descended upon hers. Hot. Hungry. Demanding.

Kate's lips parted beneath his onslaught and her tongue touched his. She felt his hands in her hair, gently but firmly positioning her head where he wanted her, allowing him the deepest access to her willing mouth. Her body automatically molded itself against his hard length. Before she knew it, her arms were around him, her nails digging into his shoulders while the man liberally explored her mouth. Taking his time. Tasting.

Soft sounds escaped her throat. Whimpers. Moans. Sounds she hadn't heard herself make in a very long time, except in her dreams. Eric's mouth left hers and trailed along her jaw line. She threw her head back. He took the hint and nipped his way down her neck, his movements slow, deliberate. His lips warm and insistent. Kate felt his hand on her waist, beneath her shirt. His touch seared her skin as he moved his palm upward, seeking her breast. His hand closed around her, fingers toying with her sensitive tip through the lace of her bra.

"Oh God . . . ," she gasped. "Eric . . ."

In an instant she found herself lifted onto the countertop. Her T-shirt was suddenly pulled over her head and tossed aside. Kate watched Eric use a free hand to tug off his own shirt. She reached for his lean, sculpted chest and felt a ripple run just below his skin as her fingers touched him. With little effort, he undid the front clasp of her bra and freed her breasts.

"You're so lovely," he murmured, staring at her in unabashed appreciation. He lowered his mouth to a rosy nipple. His mouth felt hot against her, and he sucked urgently, rolling the tight bud between his tongue and his palate. Nipping at her. When he licked his way to her other peak, Kate leaned back, wrapping her long legs around his waist, drawing his lower body closer. She heard him practically growl with desire. She could feel how hard the man was as he rubbed rhythmically against her through their jeans, even as he concentrated on her other nipple with the same exquisite attention to detail. Kate's head dropped forward, her breathing shallow, rapid.

"Eric . . . ," she cried, "God . . . yes . . ." Any more of this and she would come right there sitting in front of the kitchen sink, water running behind her.

Eric pulled his mouth away from Kate's breast, breathing hard. He placed a hand on either side of her face and slanted his mouth over hers. He thrust his tongue inside, ruthless. He lifted his head and looked at her, seeing her flushed face, swollen lips, hooded eyes.

"Not yet, lover," he murmured against her mouth. "Not yet. I want to taste you first."

He heard her whimper at his words. God, she made such glorious sounds. He reached behind her and flipped off the faucet. Her legs still wrapped around his waist, he lifted her from the counter. His mouth on hers, he stumbled through the kitchen with her in his arms. He made it as far as the living room where he sat her on the couch and knelt in front of her. With a groan, he unzipped his jeans and freed himself. He ached to be inside the woman. He couldn't remember ever being this fucking hard. But he wanted to taste her. He had to feel her silky skin against his lips. He wanted to watch Kate come before he allowed himself the ultimate pleasure of thrusting his cock inside her. She was so beautiful, with her long legs and her smooth, slender body, and those big, brown eyes that questioned his motives but accepted his actions nonetheless.

He could sense that she was exactly what she seemed . . . a woman who had lived a little. Who had learned how to laugh, how to lose graciously, how to say *thank you* when a man complimented her, instead of asking if some dress made her look fat.

Christ, she turned him on. He felt her hands on his shoulders, waiting for him to make the next move, silently begging him to make the next move. He reached for the snap on her jeans. He stripped them from her, eyes locked on her face. He watched her bite her lower lip in anticipation and smiled when he saw her black, boy shorts. No silk thong for Kate. He very slowly slid his palms along the inside of her satiny thighs. Savoring the feel of every inch. Her legs began to shake as he spread them wider, giving him access and a view of what he was about to do. His thumbs reached the edge of her shorts and he slid them beneath, one on each side, touching the delicate, silk inside.

"Yes," he heard her say, her voice husky with desire. God, she was hot. She was wet and slippery and ready for him. Ready for whatever he had in mind.

Kate felt one of Eric's thumbs slip inside her panties. He slid slowly through her folds until he found her clit. Oh. My. God. He knew enough about a woman's body to know that direct pressure was sometimes too much, especially when a woman was as turned on as she was. He deliberately circled the swollen nub with his wet thumb, a thumb that was wet with her now, instead of water from the kitchen faucet. The second thumb trailed after the first, entering her carefully. Thrusting inside her in a slow, steady rhythm. She tried to keep her eyes open, she tried to watch his face as he watched her, but she found it impossible. She thought she might scream with pleasure. Instead, she threw her head back against the couch and gripped the cushions hard with both hands.

"Eric . . . ," she called.

He bit the inside of her thigh in response.

"Oh . . . God . . . Eric . . ." She arched towards him as she came, hard, against his fingers. It felt like her orgasm went on forever.

"That's it, lover," she heard him murmur. "I want you to come again, just like that, but this time, against my mouth."

Kate heard herself cry out at his words, something unintelligible, as he removed her boy shorts, spread her thighs and lowered his mouth to her. He replaced his thumb with his tongue and ran it over her swollen, sensitive clit, and down to her tender opening.

He lifted his head for a moment. "You taste heavenly, Kate," he said, and then he placed his mouth against her, alternately sucking and licking, nipping at her clit. He slid a finger into her, and then two, while his other hand reached up her body to toy with a hard nipple.

Never in her entire life had Kate experienced anything so sensual, so arousing, so intense. She threaded her hands through Eric's thick hair and followed his movements. There was no need to direct him. He knew exactly what she needed.

Kate heard herself moan wildly as she teetered on the brink of orgasm. Suddenly Eric nipped her and she screamed. She shattered, his tongue thrusting inside her to lap at the tiny contractions. Eric was masterful, she realized from a far, distant place. He was quite simply, a masterful lover.

The woman was delicious. Honey and caramel and Celtic sea salt mixed together. Her response drove him wild and he nearly exploded when she came against his tongue. Jesus Christ, Kate was much woman. Eric laid her down on the couch and impatiently stripped off his remaining clothes. As she watched, he pulled a condom out of his jeans' pocket. He ripped open the package, but Kate sat up and reached for it, stopping his hands.

"Let me," she said.

She gently took the foil-wrapped condom from him and set it next to her on the couch. Her hands stroked him as he stood before her. She ran her palms slowly along both sides of his swollen cock and he closed his eyes for an instant. Suddenly he felt her warm, wet tongue follow her palm, and he groaned from deep in his chest.

"Like silk over steel," Kate murmured, just before she wrapped her hot, luscious mouth around the head of his thick cock, taking in as much of him as she could.

He placed his hands lightly on her head, not directing, just encouraging, letting her take charge. She wrapped one arm around his hips, her other hand carefully caressed his scrotum, squeezing gently, as she sucked the head of his cock with marvelous enthusiasm. He felt like a gourmet lollipop at a specialty food fair. Her tongue was a wonder. Unconsciously, he began to thrust his hips, and she took him deeper. Christ, if she didn't stop, he'd come in three seconds.

"Kate . . ." His voice was deep. "Kate . . . stop. God . . . stop. Let me inside. Now. Fuck. Now."

It seemed to him that she reluctantly pulled her mouth away, rubbing her thumb over his tip as she left him to reach for the condom. She pulled the latex out and carefully rolled it over his jutting erection.

"Magnum," she said, looking up at him with a mischievous grin.

"Too big for you?" He challenged her with a matching grin as he lowered her to the couch.

"Uh-uh," she replied. "Just right."

"Then spread your legs, lover, and let me in."

He lay over her, ran his cock through her slick folds, and pressed against her opening, exactly the position he'd wanted to be in since the moment he saw her. She was tight and he met with resistance. He could tell this act wasn't something she made a habit of. What a shame. A woman like Kate should be fucked, and often. Very often.

He heard her gasp as he entered. He lowered his mouth to hers and licked her lips. "It's all right, lover. Relax. I've got you. It's okay. I won't hurt you. Ssshhhhh."

He felt her muscles loosen ever so slightly and he thrust inside quickly. Impaled himself to the hilt and held very still. She arched against him. He kissed her deeply, concentrating on her mouth, calming her, as he tried to bring himself under control. If he didn't, he'd come in one more thrust just like a fucking teenager. Kate was hot. She was wet. She was tight as a virgin and he could feel her body take him in and surround him as if there was no barrier between them.

Slowly, very slowly, he began to move inside her. He pulled nearly all the way out, hearing her whimper, and he thrust again. She moved to meet him and he rocked against her, watching her thrash beneath his hard body. Her hands clutched at his buttocks, squeezing, pulling him deep inside with each pump of his hips. He moved his mouth to her breast. His teeth tugged at her erect nipple. He growled against her as she practically screamed with arousal. God almighty . . . he hadn't known it was possible to be so hard. He couldn't wait another minute.

"Kate," he panted, "Come with me lover. Come with me."

"Oh, yes," she moaned. "Yes, Eric, yes . . ."

Eric felt his climax begin. He buried his face in her sweet neck and bit down. She clutched at him desperately, shattering beneath him without a sound as he thrust deep, burying himself against the mouth of her womb. Her contractions milked him and he spurted hot and heavy. He felt out of his body for one long, heavenly moment. It was almost as if Kate was the first real woman he'd ever made love to.

Panting, spent, arms shaking, he tried to hold himself above her, but she pulled him to her chest.

"You won't squish me," she said with a smile. "I want to feel the weight of you."

So he lay across her, his face nestled in her soft, sweet-smelling hair, his fingers toying with her still erect nipple. She purred her approval.

"You better be careful," she whispered, "I might just make you do that all over again."

He chuckled. "You read my mind," he said. "Give me fifteen minutes and we can continue this in the bedroom."

"I was teasing," she laughed.

"I'm serious."

Kate was silent for a moment as she stroked his back. "The perks of being with a younger man?" she asked.

He lifted his head and kissed her lovely mouth. "The perks of being with me."

Kate drowsed against Eric's chest. The water in the tub was still warm and she felt deliciously sated. What was that old saying? The third time is the charm? She wasn't certain that the first and second times weren't the charm too. Eric had wrapped one of his arms firmly about her waist while his other hand held her breast softly. She fit into his hand perfectly, as if made for him. Who knows? Maybe she was, at least for this one night. This one night of sensual bliss.

"Eric?" her voice was soft.

"Hmm?" He sounded sleepy.

"I should go back to my apartment."

"Why?"

"Well, so you can . . . I don't know . . . so you can do whatever it is you do."

She felt his chest shake beneath her back as he laughed.

"There's nothing I'd rather do than this," he replied, "With you. Stay tonight. Here, with me."

She turned her head and looked into his face. "Are you sure that's what you want?"

"Have I seemed uncertain about what I want up to now?" He grinned at her.

"No, uh, you've seemed . . . quite certain," she teased.

"Then stay."

"On one condition."

"What's that?"

"I make breakfast. I make the best cowboy biscuits this side of the Mississippi."

Eric brushed her wayward curls from her face. "It's a deal," he said. "That will give us an opportunity to discuss a few other details."

Kate's eyebrows flew up. "Like what?"

"Like, whose apartment we're going to sleep in tomorrow night."

"Oh," laughed Kate, "You plan on sleeping, do you?"

"God," teased Eric, "I've unleashed a beast."

"Be careful what you wish for," Kate commented, a wry grin on her lovely face.

"Because I just might get it? That, lover, was my plan all along."

Inter-Office Men-O

Blue Canyon

The box lowered into the hole with smooth ease, mechanical winches grinding out the support cables. Flowers wilted quickly as tears clouded all clarity. Soon the dirt would begin to fly. And fly it did—right into her face.

Carol woke with a start as the dream faded far too slowly, the same dream—for over two years. Kyle lived with zeal and it infected her, but he'd been gone so long. Her life since became hum-drum and empty.

She forced her eyes open even though some internal instinct told her she could sleep for a while longer before the alarm erupted. Her hair matted to her face, and her hands thrust between her legs as usual, Carol woke in quite a disarray.

Frustrated beyond all sense, she performed her morning ritual in her hot spot, using both hands. Some days she used a toy. And as usual, the empty orgasm just couldn't make up for *real* sex and left her wanting something more. But time flew and she needed to make ready for work. Her boss wouldn't appreciate the smell, a smell that drove her crazy most mornings. It also drove her to the lady's room at the office on several occasions.

"To hell with love," she said to the face she'd secretly drawn on the back of the other pillow with a marker. "I need to get laid."

Mildly sated, Carol rose and washed—only a little, she didn't want to make *all* the smell go away, her boss be damned—and dressed for another dreary day. Her office, only a short bus ride away, always felt so cold and austere, though efficient. Carol thought a nice desktop statue of DaVinci's David would decorate nicely. Then again, looking at that penis all day would probably drive her to the *ladies'* more frequently.

Day in and day out she would come and sit here, performing all sorts of useless and mundane functions for the sake of the bean counters upstairs. And the stack of papers on her desk rose quicker than a New York City high rise.

"How's it going, Miss Blake?"

"It's *Mrs*. Blake, Harry."

"Oh, yeah. Sorry."

At that, Carol looked up from her desk and eyed Harry up and down. She'd always liked his ass, but she couldn't bring herself to get close with such a young man. She'd checked his records. Twenty eight, last month, and firm bodied. Besides, inter-office mingling had been put on the taboo list by the upper echelons.

Still he—

"You look really nice today, Mrs. Blake."

"Be careful, Harry. You're bordering on harassment."

"I think I'm within my rights to say you look good."

Carol wanted to chastise him. On the other hand, she also wanted him to come around behind her desk with her and dive right in. She shook her head and blinked a couple times. When she looked up Harry stood naked in her doorway. She blinked again.

In the ladies' room, Carol used a tiny finger vibrator to drive herself to another fleeting ecstasy as she thought about the young mail boy. She just knew he could drive her into oblivion, if she let him. But maybe she didn't have to.

At that point a scheme entered Carol's brain that rivaled the greatest criminal minds. As she returned to her desk, a devious smile sat on her face. No one noticed. She commonly came out from the rest room with a smile on her face, as if relief had become so imperative, it showed when she got it.

Carol liked her lights dimmed after a hard day at work to ease the tension behind her eyes. A chilled glass of Amaretto often helped. But her true relief would only come if she did, and it had to be with someone else. Self-manipulation would only carry her so far.

But right now the computer called. She needed to do some research on the mail room at her company. Perhaps, if they had an opening, she could research as if she were a potential employee looking the job over.

While that gave her an overview of his job, it lacked specifics. So she shut down the computer and went shopping. There were still a number of things to accomplish in her mission. Granny panties just weren't going to cut it for her task, not even petite lacy ones. She needed thongs.

And while the concept of a thread sliding up her crack didn't sound appealing, it all fit her plan. She had to proceed.

She had everything she needed. She set the plan in motion like a pro. Carol knew Mark Hagedus would be away from his desk all afternoon, so she made sure to send a message to accounting, attn: Mark.

As soon as Harry left Carol's office, so did she. The direct route brought her to Mark's office before Harry so she had time to prepare, though she needed so little. She fought with her skirt's waistband, rolling it underneath to shorten the hem length. Then she quickly dropped her panties to her ankles and hid them, sliding on a thong she'd pulled from her purse.

The shorter skirt made her long legs look ever so much longer. And the all-black suit efficiently hid the love handles she'd begun to develop. Despite her age, people still often complimented her ass so she felt relatively confident about her plan.

Then, as her last step in the plan, she overturned her purse onto the carpeted floor. She bent down and began painstakingly picking up one piece of purse flotsam at a time. That's when the door to Mark's office opened. Carol froze.

No one spoke but she could see Harry's telltale sneakers. She heard the door latch closed followed by another click. *He locked the door!* Carol couldn't help but smile. Still not speaking, or asking permission, he knelt behind her and placed his hands on her hips. Then he pushed her thong aside . . . with his tongue.

Carol closed her eyes and gripped the carpet in her hands as his tongue explored her insides, driving her into one satisfying moment after another. By the fourth or fifth—she'd completely lost count— her eyes felt crossed and a bit of drool dripped from the corner of her mouth. She did her best to retain balance by keeping her hands flat on the floor.

With her legs fully extended, it offered a very accessible position for Harry. He stood and Carol heard a zipper. She waited patiently but it seemed like forever. What could he be doing? She thought how big 'it' might be.

But when it touched the opening to her womanhood she bolted upright and pushed him away.

"You can't."

"What?" he stammered, his arousal standing straight for her to admire.

"I mean, I can still get pregnant."

"Oh. I didn't know." He looked away and then back. "Well could I rub it against you so I don't have to carry this all day?" he asked, indicating his not-so-little problem below the belt.

Carol smiled gently. "Sure. What would you like? I could—"

"If you just bend over like you were, I could rub the head against your lips."

"You sure you don't want me to kiss it and make it better?"

"The other lips, please."

She eyed his manhood and bent back over, prepared to jump back up should he try to put it inside her again. A child is something she just didn't need. But he remained true to his word. He rubbed the length of her, pushing the little button at the top on every pass, driving her crazy once again.

Then the pain hit her.

He entered her. She could feel his girth inside, but he'd gone in the wrong hole. She'd never been taken there before and it really hurt. She wondered if he just . . . missed. He left it sitting in there while she moaned. Her body tensed and clenched down around it. Still he didn't move.

Carol relaxed and it didn't hurt quite as much. Harry began to slide in and out, gently at first. She noticed it felt pretty good. Rocking with him, his testicles slapping against her the whole time, she felt another moment coming. Harry pushed harder, banging his belly against her backside, burying himself completely into her each time.

When the ecstasy hit her, Carol thought she lost consciousness for a moment. When she regained it, she lay on the floor and there was a bit of a mess, but she felt used and satisfied. Harry had put himself away and quickly pulled up his zipper. He left the room without a word.

Carol stood and fixed herself as best she could. She double-checked the floor for purse fodder, or anything else, and quietly left the room, closing the door behind.

That evening, as the ecstasy began to wear off, guilt over what she'd done quickly swept in to take its place. How could she seduce a young boy like him? Okay, sure. He was over eighteen, but compared to her that's still a boy—young enough to be her son.

"What am I going to do?" she asked the face on the pillow.

Oddly mixed in with the remorse, she felt the need calling to her from below. The two opposing emotional states resembled two colors of paint swirled together, with no way to ever separate them again.

Even as she struggled with the morality of her earlier actions, her hand involuntarily snaked down to perform its assigned task. The sheets parted willingly, as did her legs. Before she realized, her fingers did their intimate dance around her entrance and she began to breathe deeply. Her eyes closed. All thoughts of remorse escaped.

At the office she felt very self-conscious. Everyone must surely be aware of what she and Harry did. Of course it had to stop. She forced her mind to focus on the mounting pile of work before her, hoping not only to get things done but keep her mind from wandering back to him.

But soon enough—it seemed to happen so quickly because time flew as she remained busy—Harry walked in to deliver the interoffice mail. Carol forced her eyes to remain on the desk in front of her, as though she focused on no one thing. She bravely fought to control the images flowing through her mind.

"Good morning, Mrs. Blake."

"Harry." She didn't mean to be short with him, but she felt sure she'd lose control if she interacted with him too much.

Apparently taking the hint, he dropped her mail in the tray and left without a word. Carol congratulated herself for the small victory. She'd worn a pant suit today to add protection—not from Harry but from her own desires.

Despite her extensive precautions and her strong mental focus on other things, her hips danced slightly in the chair, swinging from one side to the other. One might think her swaying to music, but the material in her clothes rubbed against her in a tantalizing way. Without realizing it, she brought herself to a quick orgasm right there.

She got up and headed for the rest room once again. Just as she opened the door, she saw Harry enter the store room. She hesitated.

The hallway was empty. She double checked and triple checked. When no one came, she let the restroom door slip from her hands and she made her way to the store room. She quietly slipped in.

Harry showed no signs of noticing her entrance. He worked with his back to the door and did not turn when she approached. She slid her hands around his waist and to the front of his pants. She opened them and released his meaty stick. Harry inhaled quickly but stood still as if caught doing something he shouldn't.

Overcome with desire, Carol dropped to her knees and forced Harry to turn so she could have access to him. She rubbed and kissed and he quickly rose to the occasion. She pounded away like a pro, using her lips and tongue and one hand to finish the job and give him a happy ending. With her other hand she found another moment of bliss inside her own pants, but she didn't miss a beat on Harry. She finished him off and this time there wasn't a mess to clean up. She'd seen to that herself.

She rose and left without a word as he had the day before. She made her way discretely back to the ladies' room. There may not have been any of Harry's mess to clean up, but she still had one of her own. Plus she had to remove the dust and dirt from the knees of her pants.

Back at her desk—more or less pulled back together—she began rifling through her mail and noticed something small fall out. She looked closely at it. A small white business card with only a hand-written address on it, somehow she knew it was Harry's. He was inviting her to his place.

Well, that's never gonna happen.

After work, walking from the parking garage to her apartment, the twist of material between her legs drove her to the brink of ecstasy once again.

Christ! I can't even walk anymore. I wonder if there's something wrong with me.

Horror words like "nymphomaniac" and "slut" drifted through her head. Clinical issues that could cause neuroses or even physical problems seemed suddenly clear and defined in her mind, as if a medical encyclopedia had just opened up in her head. But somehow, even though the encyclopedia kept pointing its accusatory finger at her, she felt normal and healthy.

As she struggled for the key to her front door, the little white card fell out and flitted to the floor like a leaf from a tree. She recognized it immediately, even before she bent to pick it up. She stared hard at it, turning it over and over.

Now how did THAT get here?

Although she couldn't remember actually doing it, Carol felt sure her hands had involuntarily slipped the card into her purse when she wasn't looking. Those hands of hers were getting out of . . . hand. She chuckled.

Inside her flat, she quickly disrobed and took care of the business she often did, disposing of any immediate desire to seek out the address on the card. Nevertheless, as always, the satisfaction fleeted so quickly and left her wanting something more. Something real. Something hard.

A toy? No. They were old news. She wanted something new and fresh . . . , and young. Sometimes she could hardly believe the thoughts that ran through her head. Nothing could come of this except trouble, she felt sure of it. He was so much younger than her and in the office—that always asked for trouble.

But you don't have to do it at the office. Now you know where he lives.

It sounded like a voice in her head, although she recognized it as her own. Had she spoken out loud? Carol thought not. And yet . . .

Before she had an opportunity to make a choice, she found herself walking the six blocks to the address on the card. She looked down to see what she wore; hoping she'd bothered to dress before she left.

A slinky, short number, the color of bright peaches, hung from her shoulder, clinging to her curves. Not entirely flattering. She could feel a breeze which told her she'd not worn any panties. The peaks from her chest suggested no underwear at all. Not a safe way to walk the streets in the city. Fortunately he lived in a safe neighborhood.

Her legs ached and she'd caught a permanent chill, as her *high beams* attested, and yet she couldn't remember the passage of any time. She stood at his door and knocked, brazenly. At that moment, she decided. *Slut* probably suited her more than she would have liked. Nothing could be done about that now. The itch had driven her here and footsteps already approached in response to the knock on the door.

"Mrs. Blake?" he asked with complete surprise.

Carol didn't know why he would act like he hadn't stuck his card in her mail, but she could play along. If that's the way he wanted it. Maybe he had nosy neighbors.

"We are *not* dating."

"Okay," he agreed, standing aside to allow her passage inside.

"We are F-buddies, that's all," she added, stepping over the threshold and into his warmly decorated apartment. "As long as you take care of business for me, I'll take care of business for you. Then we go our separate ways. Understood?"

"Mrs. Blake, I—"

"If I get any feeling that you're falling for me," she interrupted, "I'll leave right away. Do I have to leave already?"

"No."

"Are you falling for me?"

"No."

"Good." She passed her eyes around the room. "Nice place."

"Thanks."

"Which way is the bedroom?" She moved to put her hands on her hips but decided it might look confrontational so she let them slide down her hips. The effect on Harry was quite impressive.

He mumbled something she couldn't understand and pointed. She followed his finger and found the room she sought. The bed had posts, not girlie but dark wood with intricate carvings. Quite expensive looking for a mail room clerk. Her curiosity must have shown on her face.

"My dad left me some of his furniture when he died."

Carol gave the matter no further thought. In one fluid motion she slid her dress up and over her head, leaving herself completely nude for his viewing pleasure. If this was only to be a kind of business arrangement, she saw no need to waste time on useless pleasantries.

She stepped up onto the foot board of the bed—her head nearly touching the ceiling—and spread herself out as if tied, grabbing the top of the posts. Standing on the footboard, she faced the bed like a sensual X between the two posts, waiting and open for his easy access. Though initially the aggressor, she became submissive, a willing slave to whatever deviance he wanted to perform on her body.

Facing the bed, she could not see as he approached. This lent an element of surprise and arousal to the encounter. Her feet hurt, as she stood waiting, longing for his touch, anticipating it, but not knowing exactly when it would happen. She could smell her own desire and she knew he could too.

When his tongue touched her, she looked down toward her feet and saw his eyes looking up at her through her thin pubic hair.

Although he must have had his back arched at an awkward angle, his warm breath in such an intimate place sent her head reeling and she didn't want it to stop. She threw back her head and squeezed her eyes tight shut as she reached for a crescendo, her nose gently brushing the ceiling tile. She felt sure it would be only one orgasm of many that night.

Her head hanging back, she stared at the ceiling through nearly-closed lids, barely hanging on to the posts, as a wave of pleasure surged through her. She felt her own juices flowing and he didn't stop, making sure to clean her as she'd done to him earlier that day.

Carol swam in her mind's ecstasy as he stopped and moved back behind her. She could hear him struggling with his clothes. The moment, the anticipation, stretched out for what seemed like an hour. He stepped up on the bed's foot board right behind her. Reaching around, he held onto her breasts, pinching her nipples. She wiggled in pain and pleasure.

He found his mark with his cock and entered her back door once again. It went in easier this time, she noticed. Less of the pain, more to the pleasure, she welcomed his advance. From this angle, he hit her pleasure center deep inside. She began to build up once again. But something odd happened, something that startled her.

She could feel Harry's tongue inside her again. So who was inside her? She managed to turn her head and saw Harry's smiling face over her left shoulder. Everything going on at once sent her reeling further into ecstasy, and she lost track of her surroundings. An orgasm like a sonic boom blew through her before she had a chance to object.

Harry had another guy there, perhaps a roommate. While she felt embarrassed, the thought of two, hard . . .

When she managed to look down, she saw a pair of beautiful eyes and long, shining, black hair between her legs. Carol pulled away quickly and lost her balance, falling to the bed. When she looked back she saw Harry and a petite, attractive girl standing there, both naked.

"Wha..? Who..?"

Harry smiled. "This is my girlfriend, Alyssa."

Carol felt mortified. "You mean . . . a *girl* licked me?" Carol sat upright on the bed, hugging her knees.

"So you're the woman who took care of my boy while he was at work?"

"I never knew he had a girlfriend."

"Did you ask?"

"I-I'm sorry."

"Don't be. That was the first day in a long while he came home in a good mood. Normally, he's so frustrated from being run ragged by people who think they're better than him. But yesterday he came home with a smile and took me to bed. I thought he might be cheating on me. But I guess he just had a cougar giving him the treatment."

"Cougar?"

"You know," the girl continued, "an older woman after a young guy. You did him up nice, lady. Thanks."

Is that what I am? A Cougar? I'm not sure I like that word. Then again, it does describe what I've been doing.

"But you're a girl. And you licked me."

"You liked it," her smooth voice cooed. "I could tell."

"I've never been with a woman before. I like men."

"You want me to do it again, don't you?" Alyssa whispered, almost singing.

"I . . . no . . . I . . ."

Alyssa grabbed one of Carol's ankles and Harry grabbed the other. They pulled her apart like they were about to make a wish. Carol's head fell back onto the pillows as both heads worked between her legs and both tongues swiped at the tender flesh there.

Carol's eyes closed and she lost track of all time.

Deep Waters

Shanna Germain

"We'll see dolphins for sure today," The Boy says. His name is not "The Boy," of course. He's told me what it is, twice I think, but for the life of me, I cannot remember. His hand is on the motor, jumping a little with each sea wave. He stands in the back of the boat, the wide, practiced stance of someone who spends more time on water than on land, maneuvering the boat with an ease that appeals. I've always liked men who know their tools, who are good with their hands.

"Dolphins? What makes you think so?" I feign interest in the dolphins. No, that's not true. I *am* interested in the dolphins. Somehow it just hurts to admit it, after all this time spent not caring about much of anything. To know that I shouldn't be doing this alone, to feel this bright spark of interest is like a jellyfish sting against my brain. I want to submerge it, blot it out.

The Boy takes one hand off the motor and points to the horizon line. He says something, but I cannot hear it over the motor and the waves and the whirlpool of my own brain. I've never had good eyes—glasses in grade school, and contacts from then on, as soon as I could afford them—but my ears have always been sensitive. Perhaps overly so. I have a sudden fear that my hearing's going. Brought on by middle age. Or grief.

I settle for watching his lips while he talks. He has plump lips, sunburnt just at the bow on top, the very center. I lean against the back of the boat, wrapped in a dark blue terry robe, almost like a bathrobe, but called a "beach cover" and twice as expensive, over my swimsuit, watching him through my sunglasses. He is blonde and sun-bronzed, boy-muscled. I saw his eyes, briefly, when we passed through the shade trees on the way to the boat. He lifted his sunglasses atop his head—they are golden-brown. Nearly as gilded as

268

his shoulders. Something swings from around his neck, thuds against his bare chest with each wave we hit. It's a medium-thick silver chain with a shield-shaped pendant. A crest? I'm not close enough to tell.

He's still saying something, but I can't hear and I don't know if I care enough to ask for a repeat, so I sit back as he steers the boat, letting the waves crash over me when they're strong enough to rise above the sides, sprinkling water over my pale, sunscreened arms.

I lean back and tell myself it's okay, that I can afford this. All of this. This private boat on nearly-uncharted waters. This young boy, shoulders burnt by sun and salt, his bleached lengths shifting around his pretty, unlined face as he motors us through the softly lolling waves. I can afford it without thinking twice.

Of course I can. I am Sam McCade's widow. The one who was only in it for the money. Twenty years. Twenty years of marriage to you, Sam, and fucking, and the way you looked at me sometimes when you thought I wasn't watching. And still they said it. Those glass-green eyes of yours; hooded and dark all the time with desire weaving together into a web of love and lust. It was the same look you had sometimes right before you came, when you'd cup my face with you palms, saying my name again and again as you drove yourself between my soaked thighs. And still. It was all about the money.

The sun's breaking through, battering on my shoulders and legs despite the wind, and I peel away the cloth robe to let the warmth sink into my pale skin. The Boy cocks his head at my gesture, thick lips parting slightly. I can't tell if he's looking at me behind those dark glasses, and if he is, what he might think. He doesn't know who I am—or more likely, he does. News travels like blown ash in small, non-tourist-ridden Hawaiian towns. Especially when a man as publicized as Sam comes here to die. Alone. By choice.

Whether the boy knows who I am or not, I know what I look like. I know that not eating and too much walking have cut down my curves some, made me leaner than I should be; my calves long and tightly sinewed, my stomach concave. I never wanted to be one of those Madonna-women, all odd muscles and tendons where there should be curves, bearing those skeletal smiles. Sam, you never wanted me to be that either.

If you were here, Sam, you would dress me up in heeled boots and the green cocktail dress you bought at Saks, pull me down to your special table at Sur, force-feed me tiny, fat morsels—gourmet cheeses, half-cooked slivers of steak from the end of your knife, bites of torte and crème fresh. You would tie me to the bed after, wrists bound in the impossible figure eight of your favorite leather belt, bringing me to near-orgasm again and again while you left me there, immobile but for the rise and fall of my hips and breath. You would have said something perfect and laughable, like, "I can see the curves of your ass growing. They're beautiful," even as you fingered the tight clench between the globes of my skin, slid in to the knuckle, farther. And I would have come, finally, mouth clenched over the pillow, those curves you loved pushing upward off the sheets into the swat of your fine hand.

Sam, gods I miss you. How you would have loved to see me eyeing this boy, my desire coming finally, to surface, after all those desolate months of dry. So dry that spit and lube and tears weren't enough to keep me going. How my hand would ache, caught between the press of my thighs, trying, trying. And nothing but a dry trench, wetted with a few drops of rain. If you were here, Sam, oh the things you'd do to me to make me well. But you're not here, are you? And so I stretch my too-tight, too-long legs out on the side of the boat and I watch the boy work the motor through my big dark sunglasses.

As though he feels me watching, he turns away from his scan of the horizon. The sunglasses keep his eyes hidden but a pale upper tooth slides forward and catches over the side of his big bottom lip. It's a gesture of both blatant desire and of shyness. The combination forces my breath away in the wind, and my fingers tighten hard against the side of the boat.

"Hold on!" he says, and in that moment, he's all boy. All speed and desire as he revs the engine, zooming us through the water with only a single hand on the motor. The waves pick up, a solid thud-thud against the boat that makes me shiver, and he turns us inward slightly, toward the land, which rises somehow both lush and sharp. The softened shores and weathered rocks contrasting to the razor leaves, the jagged rise of mountains. We ride in silence, letting the motor and the water talk to each other in soft growls and slaps.

It's a long way from the town to the hidden cove where he's taking me, and I wonder about other women who come here alone, if any do. It's dangerous, I suppose, going out in a simple boat like this, no lifejackets in view, with a strange man . . . boy. Grief rides with me in this boat, too, don't think it doesn't, Sam. You're in every drop of water that touches my arm or face or lips.

Despite the grief that washes through me, I feel a sense of

gladness for this sudden desire, to feel again. The slap of the boat seat against my ass as it settles over a hard wave. The drops of water that spray along my sun-stroked arm. The Boy, with his invisible eyes and his mop of damp hair, the way the sea beads off his skin and runs down tiny rivulets that would taste of salt and life on my tongue. The tiny nibble of desire that's starting somewhere beneath my breastbone and rolling down into my stomach.

The boat slows, stops. My body doesn't do either. It's a live, humming thing caught between wind and water, salt and sun. I feel off-kilter, my balance off so that I have to clutch the boat sides with both hands, suddenly afraid I'm going to topple over the edge.

"There," he says. And there is an unhidden delight woven in the single word, in the way his hand guides my eyes across the water. I don't see anything, but my pulse jumps just because I can hear how his has done the same, as though he doesn't do this or see this every day. He cuts the motor and settles his lean hip against the side of the boat. The word for that part of the boat escapes me, although I think I knew it once. I'll have to ask him later. But for now I keep my eyes trained on the path of his pointing finger.

"Can we go to them?" All my breath has been torn away by wind or want, and I sound high-pitched, excited.

"They'll come for us," he says. I wonder how he can be so sure. So certain. And I wonder why his saying that sends another whispered slide of desire up my back. Then I realize it's because the way he said it makes me think of you. He sounds like you. *You'll come for me. Oh, you'll come.* How many times did you whisper that? Until I would come, sometimes, just from hearing you say it. My body trained to ripple and crash at your very words. You didn't even have to dip a finger beneath my wet surface. How many conferences did you go to, when you would call? "What are you doing?" you'd ask. And I'd answer, as I always did, "Just fucking some stranger." Our private joke, pulled out of an article by some pseudo-reporter who'd called me a "treasure whore without a map." That laugh of yours—I craved it almost as much as I craved the throaty growl that meant you were close to coming. "What will you be doing later?" you'd ask. "I'll be coming," I'd answer, a hand already sliding between my thighs, surprised as always at how wet you could make me with just a word. "Good girl," in that low voice. "You will come for me. Oh, yes."

I realize The Boy is watching me, and I wonder just how much of my thoughts are obvious. Or if I've made a noise. I find myself doing that sometimes, Sam, in a way that would make you proud—stepping into the bathroom where you so often fucked me, bent over the sink, my hands flat against the mirror, and I'd discover I was moaning low in my throat. Or find myself saying your name aloud in the store, the sound rising up from my lips, unbidden.

As The Boy watches me, his smile is sweet, so sweet that I want to nibble along his lips, taste his skin and salt. His head tilts toward the side of the boat. I follow his gaze and realize the dolphins have come, as he said they would. I swallow back whatever noise I was making and lean over the side, gaping, my mouth open to the seawater and the splash of their fins. The dolphins are big and sleek and faster than I could have imagined, only slowing as they softly bump the boat. Their skin shines with water, a blue-green-grey that reminds me of wet suits and seaweed and, for some reason, the wet and salted heat of tears. They're gorgeous and playful, jostling each other. Creatures utterly foreign and yet I feel that I know them. I hesitate to say that I feel kin—so presumptuous—and yet, it feels as if I could be. They're alien too, unknown and unknowable.

But then, it seems, aren't we all? Even you, Sam, so see-through in some ways. So untouchable in others. The parts of you hidden away by your need to control. The businesses. Your movements. Your wife. Your body. Even your death.

"So," The Boy says after we've floated in silence for a while, watching the dolphins play and seemingly grow bored, moving out toward other parts of the water, and then coming back to nose at the boat. "In we go."

"Here?" I am momentarily shamed by the fear that slides up through my breastbone and knocks me in the throat. In this dark water, with dolphins and who knows what all, so far from shore? I try to swallow the panic away. What was I expecting? A closed-off kiddy pool somewhere near the shore? Yes, actually.

He doesn't answer, merely points to the snorkel gear that rests at my feet. "Trust me?" he asks. There's a hint of cocky teenager in his voice, but mostly it's overridden by a simple confidence.

Trust him? I don't, but I do.

Still, I want in. I want to be surrounded by that playful banter, come whatever costs may rise. He settles the boat, steps across it to my end and kneels in front of me. His attention is on the gear at my feet. The curve of his neck arches, delicate, before me. The soft hairs that curl at the back. The chain swings against his neck and I can see now that it isn't a crest at all, but a locket. Oddly dainty, with a few filigrees across it. It's old, you can tell just by looking at it. So out of place with all of this young masculinity. Its silver curves beckon my fingers, but I force myself still.

Without seeming to notice, the boy turns and dips the flippers into the water. Then he picks up one of my feet, running his palm along the arch of my foot, sliding the flipper over the toes and heel. It's a practiced movement, one of those ones where someone knows their tools, and watching him do it floods the space between my thighs. He's so close to me there, head bent, fingers occupied with my other foot, I'm afraid he can smell my desire. I have a sudden fear that he's going to lift his head, and nose against the damp space between my thighs like a dolphin.

There is something in his smile as he finally lifts his head, a sharpened curve to his thick lips that makes me wary, but he just lets the smile widen and hands me my mask.

"This one goes like this," he says, settling the mask against my face, nose and mouth covered, the tips of his fingers drawing the elastic over my hair, tucking it around me ears. My head swims, full of vertigo and the momentary feeling of seeing everything, especially his face, through a broken mask. I blink at him, suddenly feeling like I'm the young one, and he's impossibly old. Then the real world slides back in, and he's just a boy, a boy with his fingers lingering in my hair for one moment too long before he stands and motions me overboard with a single movement of his lean and muscled arm.

I slip carefully over the side until I'm in the water, buoyed by salt and surf. As soon as I'm submerged, my hearing seems to come back, full force. I can hear nothing and everything; the waves that crash through my fingers and against my thighs, the roll of stones and shells beneath, the play of the dolphins turning. They've scattered some, but not disappeared. My own heart, echoed and driving, against my ears. The splash of The Boy as he slides into the water beside me.

For a moment, I watch his lean body sliding through the pale blue, and watch the muscles of his legs and shoulders. I can't tell if it's want I feel for him, this wet press between my thighs, or if it's just the ocean, caressing me with her wavy tongue.

He slides off, toward somewhere else, and I turn my attention downward. Everything beneath is black and white and blue-grey and electric orange. Fish slicker by, striped and wiggling. Coral of all colors line tiny hills like trees.

I close my eyes and float, amazed at how everything washes away. I feel part of something bigger than myself, an unimportant cog in a huge machine. As though nothing I do or say matters. Not to anyone. In fact, for a moment, there is nothing else. Sensory depravation of sorts. Is this what you came for, Sam? This washed-away nothingness? This thing you couldn't find anywhere else, not even with me? I choke, thinking my snorkel is filled with sea water, but it's just tears, washing down my mouth.

I don't know how long I spend under there. The Boy stays away, as though perhaps he knows what the water can do to someone. It's like all the mourners who stood on the other side of the grave, not wanting or willing to include me. Not willing to accept my grief as anything more than running mascara to hide behind until the will was read.

What feels like hours later, I pull myself against the boat, dripping and panting. The Boy is already there, still wet himself, his arms reaching down to grasp me by the elbows and help me up. His head brushes my shoulder as I'm lifted, long wet strands of hair graze and sting like jellyfish. I feel bruised and battered, exhausted, as though I've been beaten back to health by a masseuse with too-big hands and a careful understanding of my weak points. I also feel grateful, and alive. My skin is washed clean, my hunger for new tastes and journeys honed by all that time in the quiet depths.

I nod my thanks and practically flop into the boat. He kneels down, pulling off my flippers for me. "You've got a small cut, you know," he says. When I look down, I see the blood sliding down over my knee. It's a slow dribble of color. I never even felt it. "Looks like a clean cut, nothing to worry about."

He grins, those big lips slipping into a slow curl. "Be glad there's not sharks. They'd have eaten you up."

A quiet moment of silence rests between us, heavy as a stone. For a moment, I imagine him saying something out of a movie, like "I'd have eaten you up," and I imagine what I'll do if he says it. Laugh? Groan and pull his mouth to mine? Lift my hips toward him in a silent plea?

He does none of these things. He dries my legs with a dark towel and then presses the fabric to the cut with a hard press of his palm. "It'll stop in a second. It tends to bleed a lot, because of the water."

"Where did you learn that?" I ask.

"I've learned a lot of things." And this is the moment, right here, that could be so fucking cliché, Sam. Like you would have laughed if you were here to see it. But it isn't that way at all, the way this boy slides his sunglasses back into his wet hair, and then drags his gilded gaze right up me, making my skin sizzle and pop. The way he leans in and brushes his lips, very softly, sideways across mine, it isn't a kiss. It's something else.

I want him with a sudden fierceness that makes my soaked skin feel too dry. I want him to slide his tongue between my lips. To feel that sharp press that young boys have, the impossible hardness of his cock nudging between my legs. I ache to throw my legs around his thin hips, to drive him back against the floor of this boat, to ride him and the waves and water until we are both coming. Until I can stop talking to my dead husband in my head. Until I cannot hear him answering.

The boy brushes his lips down the length of my neck. In response, my body, such a traitor, such a horrible, horrible wild creature, arcs up off the seat, presses into the downward curve of his hips as he leans against me. He is as I imagined, all hard-on, throbbing and raging inside the cage of his shorts. Groaning against me, rubbing into me like a creature past curiosity, past anything but want, and I'm opening my hips against his desire, the material of my swimsuit doing nothing to hide my want.

"Stop," I think I say. I mean to say. I'm panting, my tongue and teeth are finding the curve of his ear even as I beg him to go away, and my hand slides down inside the soaked material over his ass, finding the perfect, muscled curve, kneading it.

"Okay," he says, and I realize with sadness that I have said the word aloud. And that, unlike you Sam, he believes it and will abide by it. And somehow I know this is how it should be.

I touch his unlined cheek with one hand, draw my thumb along the burnt, peeling top of his lip. "Just for now," I said. And I realize that what I meant to say as comfort is actually true. That if I stay here long enough, I will have this boy. I will teach him the things you taught me, and I will begin, finally, slowly, painfully, to let you go.

The boat rocks beneath us as he pulls back to his heels. Breathless. Panting. Both of us. Looking at each other, my hand still lingering on his lips.

I shake my head. What am I shaking away? My spent desire? The desire that slides into me again, wanting, even though I've just had him? My sudden, hot shame? Myself? His request for my name and attention?

He turns just slightly and bites my fingers, catching the tips between the edges of his teeth, his golden-brown eyes shy despite his action.

"Oh, fuck." It is all I can say, and it is enough to give us both permission. He leans in, and this time it *is* a kiss and it catches my still-bit fingers between our lips, his tongue glossing over my fingers and lips and teeth. He tastes of fish and salt water and sunshine, bits of earth and air.

I pull my hands away as we kiss, return them to the muscular curves of his ass, and pull him against me until we are both sliding around on the bottom of the boat, wiggling and slippery as fish. I want to suck every bit of his skin into my mouth, to taste him until there is no taste left to him, until my tongue is crusted with salt.

Tucking two fingers on either side of my hips, he slides down, planting his mouth over the fabric between my thighs. I can feel him through the swimsuit, but it's muffled, and I buck my hips, wanting more, burying my fingers in his slippery hair.

"Please." I am groaning, and there is no shame in it. There is barely any noise in it either, only want and breath.

Yet, somehow he hears. He slides the fabric to one side, holding it there as he sinks his mouth against me, a hard suckle over my clit that jolts my hips off the rocking boat. A second later, he's sinking his fingers inside me—two, three? I can't tell—but they move in a slow scissor that opens me, almost painfully, and makes me ripple and shudder beneath him. My hands slide down his shoulders, some part of my mind noting the way the muscles roll and turn even as the other part of me thinks of how young he is, how firm on the bone. I want to ask him where he learned this thing, this thing that men my own age wouldn't know, but his movements have stolen my words, turned them into slippery, uncatchable things.

He pushes himself up over me, fumbling with his swim trunks and I try to help, but mostly our fingers just get tangled in laces and impatience and desire. And then he is free, the thin stalk of his cock rising and bobbing between us. I have to reach out a hand to touch it, the firm bone of it, the pale, golden skin of it.

He grips the base of his cock with one hand, aims for my rising, hungry hips and slides the tip between my lips. I almost say "please" again, but I bite it back, pulling the insides of my cheeks in between my teeth. It is enough to raise my hips into him, to push myself over the long hardness of him, to feel him crack me open and fill me.

We come together, hip-to-hip at first, and then chest-to-chest, and then mouth-to-mouth, his tongue searching for mine, suckling it hard into his mouth the same way he did my clit. His thrusts are slower than I expected, almost leisurely, but the rigid want in his body makes it clear that he wants to much more.

I urge him on—I want to feel him drive hard into me, to send me against the bottom of the boat again and again with an urgency that will bruise me—and he responds without hesitation, arcing his hips down, hands settling to the boat on either side of my shoulder. We move together, thrusts that match the ocean, or create it. He is so silent, and I am so much noise. Grunts and pants and soft, wordless pleas. He slides a hand down between us, catching my clit between his fingers each time he pulls from me, a sharp tug that makes me cry out.

Somewhere inside the pleasure, I think, Are you watching this, Sam? Are you? Is this what you hoped for, this wild lust, this fucking above the sea of your body and beneath the sky of my grief?

And then the boy's cock and his deft fingers are making me come, a wild, rising wave that shatters me like glass against stone, and there is no more thought, no more Sam or me or even The Boy, just a pleasure that slides through me and washes everything else away.

The Boy pulls out with a groan, his fingers milking his climax from him with a quiet shudder and I can only watch, marveling in the milky ropes that pulse from him and spread along my stomach.

After, there is no shame, or guilt. Or even grief. And, forgive me, Sam, but for a moment, I am so glad to be weightless, to have nothing more on my mind than the rough loops of the towel as The Boy wipes my stomach off for me. I would take him again, I think as I watch him, the muscles bobbing in his shoulders, the intensity of his eyes as he watches me. I *will* take him again. Or he will take me, and I will be unthinking and unsinking and I will float above this ocean of grief I've begun to call home.

I open my mouth to, finally, ask his name, when he sits back on his haunches, the towel covering his thighs.

"Ms. McCade?" he says. Of course he knows who I am, I think. Of course he does.

He swallows, and the sound is low and wet. I want to lick his teeth, his tongue, the soft palate of his mouth behind those gates. My fingers push into my lap, stay there, fists heavy as stones, resisting the world's urge to roll and batter them away.

"I'm . . . I'm sorry about your husband." His words rush past me like wind, water, battering my ears.

"You knew . . . ?" Now it's my turn to swallow. My tongue is bloated and logged in my mouth, my throat an impossibly small tunnel. I can't even finish the question.

"I was his guide when he came here. Except, of course, not the last time."

"Oh," I say, but there isn't any sound.

"He talked about you a lot. I know what the papers say, but . . .," his voice trails off. There's something he's trying to grasp, maybe about death, maybe about love. I can't help him with that. I can't.

My throat closes around the only words I can get out. "Take me back, please."

The Boy nods and starts the motor. I let a few fingers trail through the wake as we move forward. The wind slides its fingers into my hair and takes hold, strong and feral as grief. How can we ever know the ones we fuck? The ones we love? How could we ever want to? The secrets hidden in those unfathomable, caressing depths.

Oh, Sam.

About the Authors

Adriana Kraft is the pen name for a married couple writing erotic romance together. Published at Extasy Books and Whiskey Creek Press Torrid, their novels and short stories garner top reviews and are available in e-book and print. Genres include straight m/f, lesbian, bisexual, ménage and polyamory, with both contemporary and paranormal settings.

Longtime social activists, they like to take on stereotypes and challenge social barriers of all kinds. Ageism is near the top of their list and they think sizzling sex isn't just for the young. Something else special is that they're writing for both genders, offering scenes that partners might enjoy together. They often read scenes they've written out loud as part of foreplay, and they hope their readers will, too – or, as one reviewer suggested, keep "a bucket of toys close at hand!" It may take longer to finish the book, but Adriana believes a good book is meant to be savored.

Bill Brent's sex-and-drugs memoir, "This Insane Allure," comprises one-seventh of *Entangled Lives: Memoirs of 7 Top Erotic Authors*. His nonfiction article, "Martin Luther Goes Bowling," appears in *Everything You Know About God is Wrong*. His best-known work is probably *The Ultimate Guide to Anal Sex for Men* (published in French as *Le Plaisir Anal* [*pour lui*]). Bill has completed one novel, about a drug-dealing whoreboy who runs away to join the circus.

Follow Bill's antics at http://www.LitBoy.com.

Blue Canyon has been writing since age 22. Now age 52, Blue is a single parent of six children. They all live together in Florida. As part of a self-improvement program, Blue belongs to several writers' groups including Florida Writers Association, frequently meeting with authors such as Steven King, Tim Dorsey, Don Bruns, Susan Klaus, and H. Terrell Griffin.

Brenna Lyons wears many hats, sometimes all on the same day: president of EPIC, author of more than 80 published works, teacher, wife, mother, member of ERWA, MWW, IWOFA, MFRW, WPM, and Broad Universe. In Brenna's seven years published in novel-length, she's finaled for 11 EPPIES, 3 PEARLS (including one HM, second to Angela Knight), and a Dream Realm Award.

She writes in 21 established worlds plus stand-alones, poetry, articles, and essays. She's a bestseller in indie/e fantasy, horror, and erom. Brenna has been termed "one of the most deviant, erotic minds in the publishing world . . . not for the weak." (Rachelle for Fallen Angels Reviews) Milieu-heavy dark work is practically Brenna's calling card, with or without the erotic content.

Brenna enjoys hearing from people who read her work and can be reached at brennalyons4168@gmail.com

Craig J. Sorensen

A computer geek by day and an author by early morning light, Craig J. Sorensen's short stories have appeared in diverse erotic anthologies as well as print and online magazines. He recently completed an erotic novel, *Augsburg Diary*, based on his experiences stationed at a military intelligence unit in Germany in 1980.

Visit him at his blog: http://just-craig.blogspot.com

Doug Harrison's erotic ruminations, which complement his opera fairydom and offset his PhD in optical engineering, appear in zines, more than twenty anthologies, and a spiritual memoir, *In Pursuit of Ecstasy*.

Doug was active in San Francisco's gay and leather scenes. He is a founding member of Black Leather Wings, a twenty-year old pansexual S/M group with spiritual foundations. He is an Associate member of the Chicago Hellfire Club.

Doug, a.k.a. Brad Chapman, appears in BDSM educator and practitioner Cleo Dubois' groundbreaking S/M video *The Pain Game* as Mistress Cleo's male submissive; this video discusses the "why" of S/M. Doug can also be seen with male, female, and transgender partners, either as top or bottom, in eight other erotic videos. He has also been the subject of professional still photo shoots; e.g., Michael Rosen's *Sexual Art*, and an AIDS Emergency Fund's *Bare Chest Calendar*.

He is the father of two children, a grandfather, and the slave of two delightfully entertaining tomcats. He has a gregarious but firm leather partner, with whom he experiments with the tried and true, the new and delightful, and the concomitant mixture of pleasure and pain.

Doug lives in warm Hawaii (pumadoug@gmail.com), where his most difficult sartorial decision is which color jock or thong to wear.

Dona Lee has completed two novels and is currently co-writing a nonfiction consumer guide for writers, as well as a nonfiction on the homeless, an erotica novel, and a paranormal thriller. She is the editor of *Plotting Success*, a monthly newsletter for the Sarasota Fiction Writers. Last year she was President of Sarasota Fiction Writers, an 80 member local writing group, and has been the leader of Florida Writers Association Manatee, an affiliate of the state group with over 1000 members for over three years. She has won numerous short story contests, two of her nonfiction short stories were recently published in an anthology on family, *Our Family to Yours*. She also writes occasional stories for the local papers on writing and the art community.

Donna George Storey has always found food sexy and sex delicious. She is the author of *Amorous Woman*, a very steamy novel about an American woman's love affair with Japan, which explores every flavor of erotic pleasure the country has to offer. Her short erotic fiction has appeared in over a hundred journals and anthologies, including *Swing!*, *Penthouse*, *Best American Erotica*, *The Mammoth Book of Best New Erotica*, *Best Women's Erotica*, and *X: The Erotic Treasury*. She currently writes a column for the Erotica Readers and Writers Association, "Cooking up a Storey" about her favorite topics: sex, food, and writing. She loves to read—or rather, purr—her work aloud and is producing a series of erotic podcasts.

Read more of her work at www.DonnaGeorgeStorey.com.

D. L. King

The editor of *The Sweetest Kiss: Ravishing Vampire Erotica* and *Where the Girls Are: Urban Lesbian Erotica*, D. L. King is also the author of *The Melinoe Project* and *The Art of Melinoe*. Her work can be found in anthologies such as *Swing! Adventures in Swinging by Today's Top Erotica Authors*, *Girl Crazy*, *The Mammoth Book of Best New Erotica 8* and *9*, *Best Women's Erotica 09*, *Best Lesbian Erotica 08* and *10*, *Frenzy: 60 Stories of Sudden Sex*, *Please, Ma'am*, and from Circlet Press, *Like a Sacred Desire: Tales of Sex Magick*. She is also in the process of editing the new anthology, *Spank!* due out from Logical Lust early in the fall of 2010. D. L. King is the publisher and editor of the review site Erotica Revealed. Find her at www.dlkingerotica.com

Emerald has been a writer since age seven, though her repertoire did not begin to include erotica until her early twenties. Her erotic fiction has been published in anthologies edited by Jolie du Pré, Rachel Kramer Bussel, Alison Tyler, and Violet Blue as well as online at various erotic websites. Currently, she resides in suburban Maryland where she works as a webcam model and serves as an activist for reproductive freedom and sex workers' rights. She may be found online at her website;
The Green Light District www.thegreenlightdistrict.org.

Heidi Champa has been published in numerous anthologies including *Best Women's Erotica 2010*, *Playing with Fire*, *Frenzy*, and *Ultimate Curves*. She has also steamed up the pages of *BUST Magazine*. If you prefer your erotica in electronic form, she can be found at Clean Sheets, Ravenous Romance, Oysters and Chocolate, and The Erotic Woman.
Find her online at http://heidichampa.blogspot.com.

J. C. Wesner
J. C. is a twenty-nine-year-old who has been writing since she was fifteen to pass the time while her grandfather was in the hospital. She has always been obsessed with what happens after the "Ever After," and often wrote or re-wrote the endings to her favorite books, movies and TV shows. She is an avid reader and often, as a child, was the one caught with her flashlight on reading under the covers at 3 a.m. "*Illicit Desires*" is her very first published work, and she hopes that in the future, J. C. Wesner will become a household name much like Nora Roberts and Nicolas Sparks. She lives in North Carolina with her husband and five-year-old daughter.

Jeremy Edwards is the author of the eroto-comedic novel *Rock My Socks Off*. His libidinous short stories have been widely published online, as well as in over forty anthologies. His work was selected for *The Mammoth Book of Best New Erotica*, vols. 7, 8, and 9; he has read at New York's In the Flesh, Philadelphia's Erotic Literary Salon, and (via telephone) In the Flesh: L.A.; and he has been featured in the literary showcase of the Seattle Erotic Art Festival. Out on the newsstand, he is a frequent contributor to *Scarlet* and *Forum* [UK] magazines.

Jeremy's greatest goal in life is to be sexy and witty at the same moment—ideally in lighting that flatters his profile. Readers can drop in on him unannounced (and thereby catch him in his underwear) at www.jeremyedwardserotica.com

Julia Barrett has lived many lives, but the one central theme of each is her writing. She's written prose and poetry since she was a child. She comes from a long line of men and women who love to read and write, starting with her beloved grandmother, a playwright. Julia has had articles published in medical and nursing magazines and poetry published in various literary journals. Now she writes romance in several genres, including science fiction, futuristic, paranormal, romantic-suspense and she dabbles in contemporary romance.

Julia attended the University of Iowa, where she majored in Creative Writing and the University of Utah, where she majored in nursing. She's been a hospice nurse for ten years. Between the time she graduated from The University of Iowa and found her calling as a hospice nurse, Julia has been a waitress, a bartender, a legal secretary, a caterer, a private chef, a pastry chef, and a restaurant owner.

Julia and the love of her life live on the West Coast with an entire food chain of animals and three children who come and go frequently.

She loves to hear from her readers at Julia@JuliaRachelBarrett.com

Jolene Hui is a writer of literary and erotic fiction and about anything else her fingers feel like typing. She's been known to write a horror column for *The Flesh Farm* and a hockey column for *Inside Hockey*. One of Tonto Books' first authors, her literary fiction has been published in their *Tonto Short Stories*, *Tonto Christmas Stories*, and *More Tonto Short Stories* anthologies. She's also been published by a variety of newspapers, magazines, websites, Cleis Press, Pretty Things Press, Logical-Lust, and Alyson Books. She still holds onto her dream that she will one day be the mother of a Standard Poodle and frequently daydreams about cheesecake. She is based in Los Angeles.

Keeb Knight was born in London. He grew up in the cities of Detroit and Philadelphia. Currently living in Philadelphia, he enjoys writing erotic, multicultural, urban, and romantic suspense stories. His story "Mandatory Overtime" was featured in Zane's New York Times Bestseller *Caramel Flava: The Eroticanoir.com Anthology*.

His most recent story "The Gerswins" was published in *Swing!*, an erotica anthology published by Logical-Lust Publications, edited by Jolie Du Pré. He's currently working on a romantic suspense and an urban erotica novel. www.keebknight.com

Madeline Moore began writing erotica in the twenty-first century. Her short stories have appeared in a number of anthologies including the Black Lace collection, *Lust at First Bite: Sexy Vampire Short Stories*. To date, she has written three Black Lace novels: *Wild Card*, *Amanda's Young Me*, and *Sarah's Education*. In another guise, Madeline's scripts have been produced by the National Film Board of Canada as well as by a number of Independent Television Producers. Madeline lives in sin with Nexus author Felix Baron near Toronto, Ontario, Canada

Rachel Kramer Bussel (rachelkramerbussel.com) is an author, editor, blogger, and reading series host. She has edited over twenty-five anthologies, including *Peep Show, Bottoms Up, Spanked, Dirty Girls, The Mile High Club, Do Not Disturb*, and *Best Sex Writing 2008, 2009* and *2010*, and has contributed to *Cosmopolitan, The Daily Beast, Mediabistro, Newsday, Time Out New York* and other publications. She is senior editor at *Penthouse Variations*, former sex columnist for *The Village Voice*, and host of *In the Flesh Reading Series*.
She blogs at http://lustylady.blogspot.com
and http://cupcakestakethecake.blogspot.com

Randall Lang lives wild and free in southwestern Pennsylvania. He has authored eight books published by Renaissance E-Books (www.renebooks.com), including the five-part *Trailer Park Nights* series, two *Sweet Nothings* books of erotic short stories, and *Pleasure's Choice Older Women, Younger Men*. At Midnight Showcase (www.midnightshowcase.com), Randall was a contributor to the first release of *Midnight Raunch*, a compilation of erotic stories by several authors. His first full-length romance novel, *Magnificent Man*, is scheduled for release in May of 2009. At Logical-Lust Publications, Randall contributed a story to the *Swing!* anthology (www.swinganthology.com) joining twenty-four other hot authors to produce a steaming product.

Shanna Germain's award-winning poems, essays, short stories, and novellas have been widely published in places like *Absinthe Literary Review, Best American Erotica, Eclectica, Harrington*

Lesbian Fiction Quarterly, Juked, Salon and more. She is a Pushcart nominee, as well as the recipient of the Rauxa Prize for Erotic Poetry and the C. Hamilton Bailey Poetry Fellowship.
Visit her at http://yearofthebooks.wordpress.com

Sascha Illyvich started writing nine years ago, first releasing poetry and an occasional short erotica story before focusing on kinky erotic romance. His books have been listed under the Road to Romance's Recommended read list, as well as nominated for the Cupid and Psyche Award (CAPA).
He is also the host of the Unnamed Romance Show on Radio Dentata and continues to write for Renaissance E-books, and Total E-bound. Readers can find his work, plus free reads at http://www.saschaillyvich.com
Sascha is part of the WriteSex Panel, a blog group that's defining erotica for writers in any genre!
Find him at http://writesex.saschaillyvich.com

Tara S. Nichols
Ever since Tara was a little girl, she has had an affinity for romantic adventures. With crushes on the likes of Tarzan and Han Solo, she grew up looking for the perfect gentleman rogue. When she is not writing about romance, erotica, or paranormal fiction, she can be found tending her garden, keeping bees, or reading a spy novel. Tara roams free on the flat prairieland in Manitoba, Canada where she lives with her young son and husband. Currently, she has six published stories with four publishers.
She can also be found at her author website and guest book. www.tarasnichols.com

Trish DeVene's fiction and poetry have appeared in *Rose and Thorn, Not One of Us, Byline, Gold Dust, Sounds of the Night, Wicked Hollow*, and *Karamu*, among other speculative and literary publications, as well as the anthology, *Apparitions*. Her poetry has won the Rhino Reader/Writer contest and her fiction has received honorable mentions in Ellen Datlow's *The Year's Best Fantasy and Horror* (2004 and 2005). She lives in a suburb west of Chicago with her husband and two daughters.

About the Editor

Jolie du Pre (Joliedupre.com) is a full-time freelance writer who writes for a variety of sites, including Associated Content and Seed.

Jolie is also an editor and author of erotica. Her stories have appeared in a variety of Web sites, in eBook, and in print anthologies including, *Cream: The Best of ERWA* edited by Lisabet Sarai, *Best Lesbian Erotica 2007* edited by Tristan Taormino, *Best Erotica 2007* edited by Berbera and Hyde, *Purple Panties*, edited by Zane, and *Making the Hook-Up*, edited by Cole Riley, among others. Jolie is the editor of *Swing! Adventures in Swinging by Today's Top Erotica Writers*, published by Logical-Lust and *Iridescence: Sensuous Shades of Lesbian Erotica*, published by Alyson Books.

Jolie is the founder of GLBT Promo (GlbtPromoBlog.com), a promotional group for GLBT erotica and erotic romance. Her lesbian dating site is MeetHerHere.com.

Acknowledgments

Thanks to Jim and Zetta for providing such a great publishing opportunity. Thanks to Valerie Gibson for offering her support for *The Cougar Book* and for letting us know that older women are sexy and desirable too. Thanks to Robert, my husband and my best friend, for always being there for me. And thanks to all the readers, writers, and publishers across the globe who support and enjoy erotica.

Other books by *Logical-Lust*

Swing!

Adventures in Swinging by Today's Top Erotica Writers

Edited by Jolie du Pré

SWING! is a stunning anthology of swinging adventure stories from some of the world's top erotica writers, compiled and edited by Jolie Du Pré.

Being edited by Jolie Du Pré, you can expect some hot, sizzling sex stories, both well written and highly creative. We don't pull any punches when we say we expect **SWING!** to be one of *the* top erotica releases of 2009!

ABOUT THE EDITOR

Jolie Du Pré is an author of erotica and erotic romance. Her stories have appeared on numerous Web sites, in e-books and in print. Jolie is also the editor of **Iridescence: Sensuous Shades of Lesbian Erotica**, published by Alyson Books, and is the founder of GLBT Promo, a promotional group for GLBT erotica and erotic romance.

SWING! is published in paperback and multiple digital (ebook) formats. Get your copy direct from www.logical-lust.com, or from Amazon (incl. Kindle) and other worldwide online retailers!

Messalina – Devourer of Men

By Zetta Brown

When life imitates art . . .

Eva Cavell is a woman with an embarrassing secret.

She is sexually frustrated and is convinced that her size and race intimidates men.

In an attempt to relieve her sexual tension, every Thursday Eva goes to a local movie theater and allows desperate strangers to fondle her in the dark. She allows no eye contact, no phone numbers—and definitely no names.

During one of her escapades, renowned artist, Jared Delaney, a smooth Southern gentleman with irresistible violet eyes, has Eva breaking her own rules. He has been watching Eva on her weekly visits and sees through her icy defence and straight through to the hot passion burning underneath.

. . . expect to be framed

Messing about in dark theaters isn't a good pastime for Eva. She is a tenure-track instructor at a private Denver college that is currently embroiled in a sex scandal and she is the youngest child of a prominent black family.

To add to her turmoil, Neil Hollister, Eva's classroom aide and former student, is a handsome, barely-legal frat brat whose interest in her is carnal rather than academic—and she's tempted.

Despite desperate attempts to maintain control, Eva's world is spiralling into chaos. As emotional pressures build inside her, an explosion is imminent. Will she ever be able to live her life how she wants and without shame?

The answer may lie with a woman who is bold and unashamed in her sexuality.

Can Eva be more like her? What would happen if she even tried?

Future Perfect
A Collection of Fantastic Erotica
By Helen E. H. Madden

What if you made love to a woman at the end of the universe, only to discover she was devastating black hole? What if the archangel Gabriel fell in love with the Virgin Mary and never delivered the Annunciation? What if a female dominant saw the future . . . every time she had an orgasm? For years, speculative fiction has asked the question "What if . . .?" Now the tales of *Future Perfect* go one step beyond and speculate on the possibilities of the erotic.

From the distant future to a biblical past and everything in between, *Future Perfect* examines the role of sex in a fantastic world. The stories range from hard science fiction to urban fantasy, but through it all runs a thread of explicit sexuality that embraces a wide range of orientations and relationships. Whether presented as the force of cosmic creation or the deceitful lure of Satan, *Future Perfect* takes sex beyond the limits of the everyday to show it as the impetus for change on a universal scale.

So open the cover and leave the mundane behind.
A world of "What if . . ." is waiting for you.

Future Perfect – A Collection of Fantastic Erotica is available worldwide in paperback and digital (ebook) formats, direct from www.logical-lust.com, or from Amazon, Barnes & Noble, and all good retailers!

Bittersweet

Stories of tainted desire
by Amber Hipple

Not all sex is romance or fun. Sometimes there's desperation. Explore the deeper, darker aspects of love and want in "Bittersweet", Amber Hipple's intensely emotive debut collection of tainted erotica. Be moved by the cycle of wanting to be wanted and the pain of wanting too much. "Bittersweet" is a lesson in reality; it's what love and desire can be. Expect no "happy ever after" in these stories, but expect to be left wanting more.

Jim Brown, owner of Logical-Lust, says; *"Amber Hipple has come up with something quite out of the ordinary in 'Bittersweet'. Gone is the sugary-sweet romanticism and the happy-ever-after, to be replaced by the profound emotions and outpourings that are real in love and sex. You'll find your heart being wrenched apart by the yearnings and the despair of the characters, yet still be stirred and aroused by the sheer passion in the erotica she produces."*

BITTERSWEET by Amber Hipple, is released in both digital (ebook) and print formats, and will be available worldwide through www.logical-lust.com, Amazon, Barnes and Noble, and all good online retailers.

Crimson Succubus: The Demon Chronicles

By Carmine

"A few years back, I began receiving emailed submissions to the erotic literary ezine *Sauce*Box* from a writer known to me only as '*Carmine*'. These submissions were short pieces ('flash-fiction', if you will) detailing yet another 'Tale of the Crimson Succubus'. Each was a stand-alone jewel, horrible, cruel, fantastically, outrageously, graphically sexual, but also somehow (dare I say it . . . forgive me, Carmine) charming. I liked them very much and published every one that was sent.

"Now I find that some these short tales along with longer pieces concerning the 'adventures' of the Crimson Succubus, and a third section concerning a mythical nymph Mytoessa who also becomes involved with the succubus have been collected together in one place—a delightfully, tastefully disgusting book, **Tales of the Crimson Succubus, The Demon Chronicles** by Carmine.

"This person, Carmine, is one sick puppy, but one with adorable eyes and floppy ears. The tales involve much blood- and semen-letting, murder, torture, deception and pain, but at the same time, I often want to laugh and wish that the creatures would appear for real, in front of me, so that I could see with my own eyes and even touch (very, very carefully, mind you) these monsters formed from the primordial slime of all of our great cultural myths.

"And of course, like all myths, these tales speak to our deepest fears, and hopes and fantasies . . . perhaps to archetypes from times before even the written word, times long forgotten in consciousness but remembered in the collective genetic code. I don't know. Whatever. They're a great read, an exciting read and one that will tickle your nightmares and daydreams long after you've put this book down."

Guillermo Bosch, Editor: *Sauce*Box*, Ezine of Literary Erotica
Author of **Rain** and **The Passion of Muhammad Shakir**

Crimson Succubus: The Demon Chronicles **is available worldwide in paperback and digital (ebook) formats, direct from <u>www.logical-lust.com</u>, or from Amazon, Barnes & Noble, and all good retailers!**

Logical-Lust Publications

Visit the website to see our other great titles,
including those on ebook only
www.logical-lust.com

For other genres, including sci-fi, horror,
mainstream, etc., and to find out about our
award-winning title PIT-STOP by Ben Larken,
visit our main website
www.ll-publications.com

Get our FREE Newsletter, *Modern Reader*
www.ll-publications.com/newsletter.html